CONTRAPTIONS

PRAISE FOR JEFFREY WEINZWEIG'S
CONTRAPTIONS

"Five stars for this monumental, entertaining, and riveting debut novel."

— ***TRACY STOPLER***,
Award-winning author of *The Ropes That Bind*

"Jeffrey Weinzweig's *Contraptions* offers readers a thrilling journey through a world of espionage, betrayal, and advanced technology. Among the novel's many intriguing elements are the cutting-edge scientific concepts that drive the narrative, blurring the lines between fiction and reality. Weinzweig's use of simulated gravitationless environments in *Contraptions* is a brilliant example of how fiction can push the boundaries of scientific imagination. Weinzweig masterfully intertwines scientific concepts with a gripping narrative, creating a world that feels both futuristic and eerily possible."

— ***USA TODAY***

"Conspiracy is the currency of Weinzweig's techno-medical thriller, *Contraptions*. Weinzweig, who's written several surgical textbooks, keeps the dialogue snappy and the action brisk over the course of his slam-bang fiction debut. Although science and secret codes are the driving forces of the narrative, the author never allows them to overwhelm his novel's themes of how people can be driven by what they can do with technology, even if it's something they shouldn't do. Fans of Michael Crichton and Clive Cussler will feel at home with this fast-paced novel's rogue science."

— ***KIRKUS REVIEWS***

"*Contraptions* is an engaging blend of suspense, mystery, and innovation. The narrative depicts a strong, collaborative partnership between two inventors working together to solve a murder while staying alive. A significant twist involving the depraved world of NEXUS adds a layer of both danger and complexity. *Contraptions* provides a rich foundation for an engrossing and fast-paced thriller that captivates the reader from start to finish."

— ***JOHN WENDELL ADAMS,***
Award-winning author of the Jack Alexander trilogy

"The key element that lifts *Contraptions* above the standard espionage thriller is its collection of ingenious, mind-bending machines: the Triacontagon, the Metallic Immobilizer, and especially the Thermalyzer, a device that captures and converts thermal waves to create images of past events. First-time novelist, Jeffrey Weinzweig, is also an acclaimed surgeon with more than twenty medical patents to his name and he's successfully merged the worlds of science and fiction by creating an impressive cache of inventions that are more than possible—they're probable."

— ***DAVID CHURCH***
Author of *Thomas Edison and the Purgatory Equation*

"A murder and the pursuit of justice employs ingenuity large and small in a fast-paced story. And, always, beneath the machines are the beating and often contrary complexities of the human heart, the most confounding contraption of all. Finely written and packed with a cast of fascinating, driven characters, *Contraptions* is a worthy and entertaining tale."

— ***EDWARD J. DELANEY,***
Award-winning author of *The Acrobat*

CONTRAPLIONS

A NOVEL

JEFFREY WEINZWEIG

NEXUS PRESS

New York   Miami   London

NEXUS PRESS

Contraptions
Copyright © 2025 by Jeffrey Weinzweig
All rights reserved.

Library of Congress Control Number: 2024907218
ISBN 978-1-9172-8179-9
ISBN 978-1-9172-3829-8 (pbk)
ISBN 978-1-9172-8180-5 (ebook)

Published in the United States of America
1st Printing

To Leo, Tyler and Luke,

My three monkeys.

CONTRAPLIONS

CHAPTER ONE

Everything that can be invented has already been invented.

Charles H. Duell

Commissioner, U.S. Patent Office, 1899

The human heart is a fascinating organ. A *beautiful* organ. Muscles, nerves, vessels and valves. All come together to produce a true force of life. Highly specialized nodal cells comprise the pacemaker of the heart and control its rate. The brain controls this activity by regulating membrane receptors of the autonomic nervous system. And the heart just sustains itself. *Until something goes wrong.*

The heart pumps deoxygenated blood to the lungs through the pulmonary arteries which return oxygenated blood to the heart through the pulmonary veins so it can deliver oxygen to the body through the aorta and to itself through the coronary arteries—the ones commonly blocked by dietary indiscretion and genetic predisposition. These are the vessels that frequently require bypass surgery to prevent a myocardial infarction—*a heart attack*—and death.

With the chest cut open in the midline and the sternum divided with a bone saw and spread apart with a sternal retractor, the heart lay lifelessly in plain view. But it was very much alive. By placing the patient on the heart-lung machine—*the pump*—blood was removed from the body, externally oxygenated, and returned to the body while the heart remained motionless to allow delicate surgery to be performed. When the surgery was completed the heart would be restarted with a gentle electric shock, restoring its beating and blood flow. And life would hopefully resume.

With the triple bypass operation almost completed, just a couple more stitches were needed to close the anterior wall of the right coronary artery. Dr. Sanjay DeBakee, the heart surgeon—*no relation to the renowned pioneering cardiac surgeon Dr. Michael DeBakey*—asked for his next stitch.

"Another 8-0 Prolene," he requested and held his hand out to the scrub nurse without even turning his head from the wound. It was as if he was in a staring contest with the heart, unable to take his eyes off his exquisite handiwork. He took the stitch from her then held his other hand out and demanded, '*DeBakeys!*' She was already handing him the elongated forceps before he asked but he always enjoyed asking for DeBakeys. In his mind, he thought they were named after him. Hardly. He was an average surgeon at best. The only thing he shared in common with the world-famous heart surgeon was his last name. And they didn't even spell it the same way. But that didn't matter. It sounded the same and he loved the sound of it.

He put the last stitch in the artery, clumsily tied it with several knots, eyed it proudly for a few seconds, then removed the needle holder from the wound after his assistant cut the stitch. As he was turning to hand the instrument to the scrub nurse, it struck the edge of the sternum and the small curved needle fell from the mouth of the instrument into the opening of the pericardial sac that enclosed the heart, landing on the right atrium. No one noticed.

The heart was restarted and good blood flow filled the coronary vessels. There were no leaks. 'DeBakey does it again!' DeBakee yelled and high-fived with the scrub nurse. "Let's close."

The pericardium was closed while the needle just sat there all alone. The sternal retractor was released, the sternum was wired together, and the skin was sutured. And the needle still sat there in the darkness. All alone.

"Great job," the anesthesiologist told DeBakee as they transferred the patient to the ICU.

"I know."

* * *

The time was 1900 hours. The place, a top secret installation just outside Houston. Several miles from NASA headquarters. Not far from NASA. But definitely *not* NASA. It was NEXUS—*National EXploration of the Unknown and Space*—an independent agency privatizing a narrow sector of the space program in order to monetize and advance certain research endeavors that could not be done within a government-run agency. Certain *highly secretive* research endeavors. NEXUS stood alone on a vast clearing surrounded only by acres of barren desert.

The setting sun threw an eerie glow upon the hot desert ground as it cut through the small diamond-shaped openings in the electrified fence which seemed to rise without end. A honeycomb shadow was cast on the orange sand that overlapped the spiraling shadow produced by the ominous barbed wire coiled around the fence's top. Numerous foreboding 'NO TRESPASSING' and 'PRIVATE PROPERTY' signs hung from different points on the huge fence.

The shadows raced across the ground for fifty or more feet before colliding with a side of the large octagonal structure that rose from within the center of this impenetrable cage. It was a building of some sort. And it was massive. It looked as if it had been chiseled from one tremendous block of granite. There were no windows and just one entrance on the side of the building which stood at the end of a long path that extended from the only entrance in the monstrous fence.

The sides of the building extended at least fifteen feet above its roof. A large satellite receiver that changed position from moment to moment, and two spires, rose from its otherwise flat surface. Two Percy helicopters sat on circular landing pads on the roof. The NEXUS emblem decorated each of the black helicopter's sides and tail rudders. On another clearing about a hundred feet from the helicopters was a large mechanical device bearing several gargantuan finger-like projections. It was a missile launch pad. And not the only one at the installation. Numerous control panels and gears were attached to the intimidating machinery while others were built into the adjoining ground. That such apparatus proudly sat atop this fortress of a building was anything but surprising. It was par for the course.

The sky roared with a thunderous sound as an F-16 jet fell from above the clouds. It flew toward the installation at supersonic speed, spinning numerous times in its flight path till its belly faced the sky. The jet continued along its course until it reached the installation. It spun several more times above the stone building, righting itself before it flew onward, past the installation and out of view as an armored truck appeared on the winding road that led to the formidable fence.

As the truck came within a few feet of the fence, the large entrance gate slowly revolved around its center pole until it was perpendicular to the fence before beginning its descent into the ground. Several moments lapsed before the entire section of the fence had been completely lowered below the surface. When the truck had passed through the entrance and onto the private grounds, the gate rose again and rotated to its original position, sealing the installation off from the outside world.

The truck proceeded on the straightened road that forked as it approached the black fortress, producing two branch roads that led to each of the sides adjacent to the building's entrance. The truck turned onto the left road and continued for about fifty feet before moving onto a large steel grating that lay just in front of the building. Several red lights on the corner of the steel plate flashed as the entire grating, truck and all, slowly descended. As the truck disappeared into the chamber, another grating slid across the gap in the ground.

A handful of men, each wearing a yellow hazmat suit and gas mask, eagerly watched from an observation station as the armored truck was hydraulically lowered into the bowels of the fortress. The hydraulic chamber made a loud hissing sound, then came to a halt as the truck reached the bottom level.

The truck was fed onto a track that directed it past a spacecraft simulator apparatus which hung suspended from several pulleys and toward the area where the men stood waiting. One had already gotten into a transport vehicle and approached the rear of the truck and its precious cargo as the truck's steel doors slowly opened.

Two men, dressed in the same gear as the others, appeared. Beside them were three wooden crates. Three large wooden crates. With some assistance from the other men, they carefully placed each crate on the arms of the carrier which moved them, one at a time, to the transport area. Once there, the crates were loaded onto a hovering bullet-shaped platinum vehicle. A *floatron*. When all three crates had been placed aboard, two of the men joined them. After securing the crates with epoxy cords, one of the men inserted his gloved hand into a transparent compartment at the helm of the floatron. The compartment filled with a bluish gas and a yellow bar flashed on its side.

"Clearance granted," a computerized voice told them as the floatron's doors snapped shut. "Atmosphere controlled," the voice added as the men removed their masks. "Destination?"

"TSI Facility," one of the men answered. And the floatron took off.

* * *

APPROXIMATELY 6 MONTHS LATER

The corridor was dim. It smelled faintly of pipe tobacco and the stale medicinal scent of the hospital. The tunnelish passageway was lined with grey walls and maroon tiles. Right in the middle of it, a door led to a crowded nursing station where five young nurses sat writing their morning reports. Further down the hall, beside the clean utility room, was a square section cluttered with gurneys and a dangerously inaccessible crash cart, and, beyond that, a row of patients' suites. At the end of the hallway, past a block of exam rooms and beyond the Chief of Surgery's office, was a conference room.

Its door was closed. It had been since 8:02 a.m. It was now 8:43 a.m. A small sign on the door indicated that a conference was still in progress. Inside, light from a projector sliced through the room's darkness and lit up the screen that hung in the front of the room. Ten silhouetted figures were seated around a long rectangular table. Their faces were expressionless as they looked at the screen.

Derek Cannon stood next to the screen. He was a tall stocky man with wire-rimmed glasses and a dark mustache. Fine lines at the corners of his eyes deepened when he spoke, highlighting his pale blue eyes. He was thirty-six but the grey at his temples added several years to his appearance. The grey temples reminded Derek of his father whom he had lost in a plane crash almost twenty years ago. His father had been a commercial pilot for over a decade after retiring from the Air Force. Derek never knew his mother. She died during his delivery.

Since childhood Derek had struggled with the guilt of his mother's death. The loneliness of having been an only child had been his personal price. He accepted that. But when his father died Derek changed. He became bitter and cynical. He could not accept the loss of his father. Moreover, questions still remain unanswered so many years after his father's accident. The exact circumstances surrounding his father's death remain unclear.

Derek looked at the screen. A slide of a chest x-ray appeared. The quality of the film was poor but overinflated lungs and an enlarged heart were clearly visible. Also visible was a small curved object within the image of the heart.

"The presence of this *suture needle*," Derek said, laser pointer in hand, "within the pericardium of this fifty-year-old patient, following a triple bypass operation, necessitated his return to the operating room six hours later. Re-exploration led to post-operative complications that resulted in the patient's death and a twenty-two million dollar settlement against this hospital."

"This is pointless!" interrupted one of the surgeons. "That was six or seven months ago. We've been through this over and over!"

"Another DeBakee debacle," an older surgeon near the head of the table muttered under his breath and shook his head.

The surgeon seated next to him heard the remark. "What a fuckup," he added.

DeBakee actually sat a few seats away and probably heard the comments. He said nothing.

Derek ignored the interruption. He continued to speak primarily to Dr. Flint, the white-haired Chief of Surgery. Dr. Flint was an intimidating man. His broad shoulders and pythonic arms pressed at the seams of his lab coat. He had a wide scar on his cheek, the result of an encounter many years earlier with an assailant in the hospital parking lot late one evening. According to legend, that encounter cost the assailant his spleen. Dr. Flint was on-call that cold, winter night when his attacker became his patient after a blow to his abdomen ruptured his spleen.

"Make your point," Dr. Flint said and took a few quick puffs from his pipe.

"One more moment, sir, please," Derek replied. "Next one," he told the projectionist. Several of the surgeons moved about restlessly and spoke among themselves. Two of them had cigarettes lit between their fingers, faintly illuminating the dark room.

The next slide appeared. It was an abdominal flat plate—an x-ray of the belly. The small and large intestinal gas patterns were normal. There was no evidence of obstruction. No evidence of perforation. The positions of the stomach air bubble and the left kidney shadow were unremarkable. The shadow of the right kidney could not be seen. But this was not unusual. The surgeons knew it was often difficult to visualize kidney shadows on flat plates.

"The next one, please," Derek said, and the projector clicked. The following slide was a picture of an aortogram—an angiogram of the aorta. With the use of a contrast dye injected into the arterial system, the blood vessels branching from the aorta were highlighted in white and could easily be followed along their course.

This slide demonstrated the absence of a right kidney based upon the lack of any blood flow from the aorta or other collateral circulation to that kidney. The slide also revealed a completely obstructed artery to the left kidney.

"One more," he said as a CAT scan quickly replaced the angiogram. *"That,"* Derek said, pointing toward the screen, "is the cause of the arterial obstruction." In a cross-section view of the patient's abdomen an object was seen compressing the renal artery against the patient's spine. It was a lap pad— *a gauze sponge*— that had inadvertently been left in the patient's abdomen at the time of her surgery.

"These are the films of a forty-two-year-old woman who had a low-grade, non-invasive carcinoma of her right kidney. Therefore, resection of the right kidney cured the patient of her cancer. With a perfectly normal left kidney the patient should have been able to maintain normal kidney function post-operatively. Wouldn't you agree?" Derek asked, directing his question toward the head of the table as Dr. Flint thumbed the curve of his lower lip and removed the pipe from his mouth.

"That's correct," he replied impatiently. He took a small envelope of tobacco from the breast pocket of his white coat and stuffed a lump into the mouth of his pipe. He tossed the envelope on the table and reached for his lighter.

"Interestingly, seven post-op days had passed before either the angiogram or CAT scan was performed. At that point, the patient had already developed severe intraabdominal infection. After a prolonged hospitalization, the gauze that had carelessly been left in her abdomen finally resulted in her death," Derek stressed. "Not the result of medical *complications*," he said, "but of medical *negligence*."

"Get the lights!" Dr. Flint angrily responded. "And get the hell out of here!"

"Sir, I didn't come here to rub your face in these catastrophes," Derek said. "But to demonstrate how complications like these can be avoided."

"The last thing I need is a lecture from some salesman on safety precautions," Dr. Flint said.

"But that's where you're wrong. I'm an *inventor,* sir, not a *salesman.* My associate, Mr. Jenachukwu," Derek continued as he moved his hand toward the well-dressed man sitting across from him, "and I have the solution." Derek glanced at his associate as a wrestler might invite the assistance of his tag partner. "Ojo."

Ojo nodded back, adjusting his sleeve. He was wearing a navy blue suit and maroon tie. There was no backing out, he thought as he stood and walked toward the front of the room. Ojo was a few inches taller than Derek and about twenty-five pounds lighter. He was almost two years younger than Derek. He had a receding hairline and a neatly trimmed beard.

Ojo glanced around the conference room and flinched for an instant. He had moved to the States from Rhodesia more than twenty years ago, and the combination of dietary change and east coast lifestyle had resulted in a severe ulcer disorder from which he suffered. Most of

Ojo's family still remained in southern Africa. In 1975 the white leadership within Rhodesia had cast his outspoken father aside as a partisan. Exile or political execution were the only options. Ojo, then fourteen years old and the eldest of nine brothers and sisters, traveled to the States with his father. He attended Harvard University where his father taught political science. Six years later, Ojo's father reunited with his family in the independent Republic of Zimbabwe.

Ojo tried not to concentrate on the burning feeling that chewed at his stomach. As he made his way to the small podium beside the screen, he noticed an odd-looking fellow sitting next to Dr. Flint. He was a bald-headed man in his sixties. One of the orthopedic surgeons. His thick-rimmed glasses were set crookedly on his small nose. It was more of a beak than a nose, Ojo thought.

Suddenly it came to him. Professor Wilkins. That's whom he looked like. *Professor Wilkins. M.I.T. 1988. Business G746. Marketing for the Entrepreneur.* Ojo wondered if Derek had noticed him. *He must have*, Ojo thought. He and Derek had both been in the graduate engineering program at M.I.T. In fact, they had met in Professor Wilkins' class.

Marketing lives on the heels of discovery, Professor Wilkins would tell them ad nauseam. But he was right. Marketing is everything. *An ideal product must have an ideal market. Find the demand and fill it.*

"Perhaps, may I have the lights off for a few moments and the next slide on?" Ojo began, only a hint of his southern African origins still in his voice. He spoke with more of a British accent. With a metallic click of the projector, the next slide appeared as the lights dimmed. "There, gentlemen, lies before you the solution." He pointed to the tiny gadget magnified on the screen. "The Jennon QT7. The first thermosensitive surgical misplacement alarm. Next one, please."

"Wait just a second," Dr. Flint interrupted, taking the pipe from his mouth. "Are you *serious*?!"

"Completely, sir," Ojo replied as the slide projector clicked again. "Not larger than the head of a pin," he went on, "the QT7 may be attached to any surgical instrument, or anything that might be inadvertently left within the body during surgery—such as a suture needle or lap pad. When exposed to temperatures in excess of 36.5° Celsius for more than three minutes— as if, perhaps, left in a patient's chest— the QT7 automatically signals a high frequency receiver which can be monitored by the anesthesiologist. Should an instrument be carelessly misplaced, the anesthesiologist would be aware of the problem before the scrub nurse has even begun her counts. Gentlemen, the QT7 will make presentations such as this morning's entirely unnecessary."

Silence filled the conference room. The projector was turned off and the fluorescent lights flickered on. Dr. Flint and the others were not pleased. They were humiliated. And furious. But gradually the silence lifted as the surgeons spoke among themselves, their voices rising and falling. One heavyset man in scrubs crushed the butt of his cigarette in the overflowing ashtray near his elbow. Two others gestured toward the ceiling with raised hands.

Ojo and Derek exchanged a silent glance across the wide table. Ojo rearranged several of the slides in the carousel. Derek ran his fingers over his mustache and wondered if it would always be like this. Science in the real world, that is. *Would technological advances always be met with cynicism and resentment? Would the ego ever step aside in the face of progress?* Derek wasn't sure. But this *was* progress. Like it or not. The snap of a match broke his train of thought and his attention returned to the head of the table.

The comments subsided and silence again filled the room. Dr. Flint took two long puffs from his pipe, exhaling a small white cloud. "We'll take four dozen," he said with a flat expression.

CHAPTER TWO

On the corner of West Broadway and Spring Street was a small shop called *Tick Tock* which contained clocks from all over the world. A short plump man with silver hair and bifocals looked at one of the brass clocks in the window display. He checked the time on the clock's ornate face against that on the timepiece chained to the vest of his suit. It was 5:20 p.m.

The silver-haired man took his wallet from the breast pocket of his overcoat and from it removed a folded piece of paper on which was written an address. *242 E. Spring*

Street. The address of the clock shop was 76 E. He returned the wallet to his coat pocket then adjusted a cylindrical package that had been slipping from beneath his arm. He lifted a small duffle bag onto his shoulder and, with shuffling steps, walked down the street.

The street was too narrow for the busy rush hour traffic. Cars and cabbies crept along the cobblestone street as streams of businessmen spilled over from the sidewalks and walked alongside them. The street was lined with tiny stores. Galleries. Cafés. Clothing boutiques. The silver-haired man adjusted his bifocals and glanced at the storefront of a used bookstore. *148 E.*

A young blonde woman walked ahead of him. The woman was wearing a long blue skirt and tennis shoes. She carried a camel attaché case in one hand and a colorful paper bag in the other. As she crossed at the corner of Spring and Broom an extremely tall, oafish-looking man with a limp brushed against her. The small bag fell from her hand, spilling her pumps into the intersection. She turned for a moment and saw the tall man's badly pock-marked face before he limped away around the corner. As the woman bent to retrieve her shoes, the silver-haired man handed her the colorful bag. He had already gathered the shoes. They exchanged a smile. The woman turned at the next corner and was gone.

The silver-haired man walked along the narrow street for another two blocks until he came to a small shop on the corner of Spring Street and Mercer Street. *242 E.* The shop was called Contraptions. It was sandwiched between a costume jewelry shop and an eclectic art gallery.

Contraptions, the man knew, had been dubbed *'the home of ingenuity'* by the *Wall Street Journal* shortly after the shop opened two years earlier. Although he had never been to the shop, he was quite familiar with its owners. He had read much about their success from articles in *Inc.* and *Business Week*. The rest he already knew.

A black awning hung over the shop's tinted storefront. A crowd was gathered in front of the shop, looking through the window at three-dimensional holographic images of Bud Abbott and Lou Costello. A data card fixed to the window described the invention that created these holograms:

Jennon 5000FX Holografix Generator

Function:	**Holographic Image Design**
Composition:	**Californium-Platinum Alloy**
Inventors:	**D.T. Cannon and O. Jenachukwu**
Completed:	**22 February 1996**
Produced:	**7**
Available:	**4**
Price:	**$3455.95**
Patent:	**US 5,384,493 B2**
Demonstration:	**Level III Holograms**

The silver-haired man gently maneuvered his way through the crowd in order to see the display.

"So, *what's* the name of the player on first base?!" Costello demanded, slapping one hand against the other.

"No, Lou," Abbott proceeded to calmly explain. "*What's* the name of the player on *second* base."

"I don't know!"

"He's on third."

"*Who's* on third?"

"Who's on *first*."

"Who?"

"Right."

"The guy on first base."

"Who."

"The name of the guy playing first base is who?"

"Right, Lou. Who."

"That's what *I* wanna know!" Costello exploded.

The routine continued as members of the crowd stood on tip-toe or moved to the sides of the windowfront to catch the hologram duo from different angles. The silver-haired man kept his ground right in front of the display, carefully holding his package close to his chest. The duffle was on the ground between his feet.

"And *your* pitcher, has *he* got a name?" Costello questioned.

"Tomorrow."

"Why can't you tell me *today?*"

"No, *he's* catching."

"*Who's* catching?!"

"*Who's* on *first.*"

"I don't know!"

"*Third base,*" they said in unison.

The old man laughed loudly as he pulled himself away from the display and entered the shop through a revolving door. Halogen lights hung on suspended tracks from its loft ceiling. The walls were dark grey and decorated with blue geometric designs. The carpeting was black.

Scattered throughout the shop, on black onyx bases or within glass showcases, was an array of gadgets, gizmos, and contraptions. An explanatory data card, similar to the one in the window display, and a demonstrative photograph were beside each display. Blue cellophane strips were attached to the data cards, each imprinted with the item code number. The cellophane strips were used to purchase the products.

The newest invention was exhibited in the center of the room. It stood within a tinted glass showcase on a tall black marble base. An index card was attached to the side of the base:

Jennon ZX3 Image Generator

Function:	3-D Animation of 2-D Images
Composition:	Aluminum
Inventors:	O. Jenachukwu and D.T. Cannon
Completed:	7 July 1997
Produced:	22
Available:	9
Price:	$2449.95
Patent:	US Pending
Demonstration:	Insert Photograph

A small control unit sat beside a color monitor within the showcase. The unit displayed several flashing meters, numerous switches and gauges, a variety of other bells and whistles, and a slot intended for photograph insertion. A three-dimensional screen saver program projected the image of a surfer riding a tube wave on the monitor.

A red arrow on the showcase pointed to a slot in the glass that corresponded with the slot in the main unit. A small sign was affixed to the glass below the arrow:

INSERT PHOTO

PRESS ACTION KEY

WATCH MONITOR FOR THE THRILL OF YOUR LIFE!

(Press ESCAPE key if you wish to Exit)

The silver-haired man with the package stepped back and watched an attractive young woman insert a photo of herself, press the ACTION key, and view the monitor.

The surfer and ocean waves faded. A dark alleyway appeared. Several large cars, circa 1920's, lined the street. A tall man in a yellow hat and overcoat stood with his back turned. A machine gun hung from his hand. Another figure appeared in the darkness of the alleyway. It was a woman. She stood on the other side of the street wearing a red dress and heels. The glow from a streetlamp highlighted her face.

"That's *me*—" the young woman said with excitement, looking at the silver-haired man who stood behind her. He nodded.

The man in yellow turned and looked toward the woman, his face still concealed in silhouette. She ran toward him and they embraced. The silhouette lifted as they kissed.

"—and Warren *Beatty*! I don't believe it!"

The woman stared at the monitor. Beatty ran a hand up and down her back, the machine gun still in his other hand. She looked up for a moment and caught the old man's stare. She blushed and pressed the ESCAPE key.

The woman returned the photo to her purse. Then she took a photo of her boyfriend, inserted it into the Image Generator, and struck the ACTION key. He appeared standing behind a large oak tree within a densely wooded forest. He wore a 13th-century brown suede garb with a steel breastplate. A quiver of arrows hung from his shoulder. He leaned the bow against the tree and a buxomly Maid Marion embraced him. As he bent to kiss her, the young woman immediately hit ESCAPE.

The silver-haired man smiled and pulled one of the cellophane strips from the data card. He lifted the duffle bag onto his shoulder and repositioned the cylindrical package under his arm, and then walked past several crowded displays to a showcase on the other side of the shop. Within that showcase were the disassembled parts of the first Jennon collaboration.

Jennon ARTI-1 Prototype

Function:	**Artificial Intelligence**
Inventors:	**O. Jenachukwu and D.T. Cannon**
Completed:	**12 December 1988**
Produced:	**1**
Available:	**0**
Price:	**Not for sale**
Patent:	**US 4,341,356 B2**
Demonstration:	**Nonfunctional**

Several complex circuitry boards were lined up next to three metallic structures. Two were cylindrical and had oddly-shaped graspers at their ends. The third was pyramidal in shape and turned on its side. A glass dome with peculiar wiring sat propped up on a maroon pillow.

Photographs affixed to the showcase glass beside the data card showed how these parts had once formed a small robot. A blue ribbon adorned the robot's chest and a crown sat atop his dome in one photo. *12th INT'L GADGETRY COMPETITION* was captioned on the bottom of that picture. *Stockholm, 1990,* was printed in smaller type on the next line. In another photo, Ojo and Derek shook hands as an official handed them a trophy bearing a rudimentary helicopter fashioned after da Vinci's famous sketches.

With prideful eyes the silver-haired man recalled the result of Derek and Ojo's first collaborative effort. Both had had project designs accepted for presentation in Stockholm during the winter of their second year at M.I.T. However, a laboratory mishap destroying both of their designs resulted in their combining efforts to create what ultimately became the ARTI-1 Prototype, one of the earliest artificial intelligence robots developed at M.I.T.

Three years later, following numerous software reconfigurations, hardware modifications, mobility adjustments and language recognition refinements, that prototype evolved into the three-and-a-half foot moving, talking, gliding robotitronic that now managed Contraptions. With titanium arms and a pyramidal base, a bulbous glass dome sat atop the cylinder that connected it to its middle section. Dozens of spherical bearings extended from the flat portion of the base and permitted movement in any direction. A number of sparks flew from the colorful metallic rods within the dome, lighting up the name that had been etched in the glass. *Artifintellibot.* Arti for short.

"Who's next?" Arti's human-ish, albeit prepubescent-sounding, male voice asked from the front of the line that had formed by the checkout area. It flowed from a small opening in his dome. As if searching for the next patron checking out, Arti's dome spun around completely, causing the crowd that had gathered to laugh. "C'mon, c'mon, step up."

A young woman placed a couple of cellophane strips on the checkout counter as a blue light shot from the side of Arti's dome to engulf the strips and ring up her purchases.

"That'll be $340 even, ma'am," Arti told her. "I think you're going to enjoy your new contraptions," he said as her items moved along a conveyor belt and into a bag. "Please come back again," he told her. She smiled as she left the store, clearly impressed.

The silver-haired man watched as Arti checked out the next customer, then turned toward the wooden staircase in the rear of the shop that led to the office upstairs. He hesitated for a moment then started to negotiate the narrow steps.

"*Derek!*" Ojo's excited voice called from the workshop upstairs. His accent became more apparent when he raised his voice.

The silver-haired man was startled by Ojo's voice. He lost his footing for a moment as the package slipped from beneath his arm. He steadied it against one of the railings with his hip as he grabbed the other railing with his free hand and regained his step. It was the first time he had heard that raspy voice in almost ten years. He checked the duffle bag on his shoulder and slowly climbed toward the door at the top of the staircase.

"What's the problem?" Derek replied from the office where he sat behind a large black desk. He had a G3 Power Mac computer on one corner of his desk, a copy of *Laser Research* on the other. He was bent over a set of blueprints with a T-square in one hand, pencil in the other, staring at the three-dimensional image rotating on the monitor that hung suspended from the ceiling. "What do you need?" he asked, his eyes still fixed on the screen.

Ojo's desk was on the other side of the cramped office. It was covered with several sets of blueprints, two stacks of articles, and an anthology of Sherlock Holmes stories. A keyboard peeked out from beneath yesterday's edition of the *New York Times Book Review*.

Between the desks was a heavy glass door that led to the workshop. When activated, a lead slab would slide across the glass door, sealing the workshop off from the office and display room. The workshop entryway was flanked on both sides by two filing cabinets. Above the cabinets were shelves that supported the weight of programming and engineering texts and journals, as well as an issue of *Playboy* opened to a pictorial of the mistress of a former presidential candidate.

Ojo called him from inside the workshop. "Just drop

the blues and get over here! I just took a shot with the *Thermalyzer!*"

The Thermalyzer was their newest invention and a major one at that. It resembled a futuristic portable laser cannon of sorts with numerous lenses, gauges and switches, an infrared sensor, a rotating viewer arm that looked like a high-powered rifle scope, and two drive slots for micro discs. It was something to see. They envisioned numerous applications for it and a large potential market which would help the solvency of the shop. The economic downturn was squeezing their business. People just weren't buying gadgets they didn't need these days. The survival of Contraptions could very well depend on clever inventions like the Thermalyzer.

"Why didn't you say so?" Derek said, rushing into the room.

A terminal sat between two monitors on the workbench. Red and orange patterns covered both screens.

"What do you think?" Ojo asked him.

"It's *alive!*" Derek said in his best Frankenstein voice.

Ojo smiled. "All we do now is wait for the program to analyze the absorbed thermal waves. When that is done, we will have a picture of the thermal radiation absorbed by the Thermalyzer—the radiation produced by what I directed the Thermalyzer at."

"Exactly."

Ojo pointed to the left monitor. "The computer's

separating the energy spectra into configurations of high-density and low-density thermal fields," he said, then pointed to the other monitor, "which are then converted to a black and white composite image ..." He paused for a moment. "... right *there!*"

"*Unfuckinbelievable!*" Derek said. "The monitor's beginning to image!" He took a seat in front of the screen as Ojo looked over his shoulder.

An image was slowly forming on the monitor screen. The higher intensity fields appeared first, the lower ones thereafter, adding definition to the evolving image.

Ojo had recently published a paper on the theory of infrared imaging. In that paper, he explained how every object emits thermal radiation—*heat*—in the infrared spectrum. The Thermalyzer absorbs this energy and analytically separates and quantifies its numerous intensities. The data are then stored in a series of computer memories and a composite image is reconstructed.

"What exactly did you shoot?" Derek asked as the black and white image started to come into sharper focus.

"The workbench over there," Ojo replied.

"There it is," Derek said, pointing to the image of the bench on the screen, "with the Thermalyzer sitting on its corner."

Ojo looked puzzled. "Then something is definitely wrong. You see, I was *holding* the Thermalyzer in my hand when I took the shot. The viewer cord would not reach."

"Now *I'm* confused," Derek said. "How can the Thermalyzer be in the image on the screen if it wasn't in the field when you took the shot? It's like you took an image of the past. An image that no longer exists."

Ojo had no answer. "An image back in time," he then said under his breath.

"Why don't you take a shot of me," Derek suggested, "from over there?"

Ojo picked up the device and moved to the other side of the workshop. Derek stored the image and cleared both screens.

"Say 'Makumbi'," Ojo instructed with a playful click in his voice as he held the viewer up, aimed toward Derek, and activated the Thermalyzer unit. The red and orange infrared fields immediately appeared on one monitor as Ojo resumed his position leaning over Derek's shoulder.

"Do you *see* that?!" Derek yelled with excitement as the image took form on the other monitor.

"I see it. But I don't believe it!"

There, on the screen, was the image of Derek sitting in front of the terminal and monitors—and Ojo looking over his shoulder. An image of them as they were *a few minutes ago*. They were both silent for several moments.

"Why not ... *why not?*" Derek finally insisted. "It makes sense!"

"How do you figure?"

"Think about it," Derek explained. "Nuclear radiation

doesn't just disappear after the bomb explodes."

"Of course, not. It decays according to a specific half-life."

"*Exactly*! So why shouldn't *thermal* radiation do the same?"

"It *does* make sense," Ojo agreed. "As long as the infrared energy hasn't decayed beyond the absorption threshold of the Thermalyzer, we should be able to detect it, analyze it and reconstruct an image from it."

"Right again," Derek said.

"Do you realize what we've invented?" Ojo asked, his excitement rising.

"Uh, yeah. A *time* machine! A goddamn *time* machine!" Derek yelled back.

"Yes. But not one that will transport us back in time," Ojo said.

"No. One that will take a picture of the past. A goddamn *photo* time machine!"

"Exactly! A goddamn *photo* time machine!" They high five'd and hugged.

"We're going to be rich as shit!" Derek shot out. "Contraptions is going to fly! *Finally*!" he added. Let's take one more shot," he suggested. "This time let's take a shot of the desk where I was working before you called to me. What do you say?"

Ojo nodded enthusiastically and cleared the screens.

Derek aimed at the desk through the small viewer, hit the activation switch, then raced back to the monitors where Ojo now sat.

"There are the intensity fields ..." Ojo said as Derek looked on, "... and *there*," he continued a moment later, pointing to the screen, "is our answer."

As the image of the desk took form, followed by that of the computer, blues and other papers on its top, a slightly lighter image became visible. It was the image of Derek bent over a set of blueprints with a T-square in one hand, pencil in the other, staring at the image rotating on the suspended monitor.

But there was one additional image.

"Who is *that?*" Ojo asked, pointing to an image of the silver-haired man standing beside the desk with the duffle bag on his shoulder,

A long silence filled the room.

"I don't know," Derek finally replied. "I have no idea who that is."

Then his eyes shifted to the cylindrical package sitting on his desk.

CHAPTER THREE

A new idea must not be judged by its immediate results.

Nikola Tesla

The Village was a twenty-minute drive from Derek's apartment. Ojo parked on the south side of Washington Square Park then walked through the park to his apartment on the opposite end. The park was deserted. He walked past a bronze statue in the center of the park and was approaching the stone arch at its entrance when he noticed the tall shadow of a man. The man stood about halfway between the arch and the statue. His posture was frozen.

"Are you alright, sir?" Ojo called to him. Another

might have said nothing, alone in a deserted park late at night. In spite of the many years he had lived in New York City, it was still difficult for Ojo to ignore someone who looked as though he might need help.

There was no reply.

"Sir, are you alright?"

"A man's been *shot!*" the shadow finally responded with a heavy lisp in his voice.

"*What?*" Ojo said, running toward the unusually tall man as a second shadow came into view.

It was the shadow of another man. He lay sprawled out on the ground between a bench and several shrubs.

"He's been *shot!*" the man insisted.

Ojo paused for a moment. He could not have been more suspicious of the tall stranger than he already was. He was suspicious and he was nervous. Really, frightened more than anything else. Frightened that he might soon be lying next to the body already on the ground. "Did you see this happen?" he quietly asked.

"Thirty seconds sooner and I probably would have," the stranger answered. "I was coming down McDougal when I heard two shots. I ran through the arch and saw him lying right there," he said, pointing to the body at his feet. "I rolled him over to see if he was breathing when I heard a car screech away. He's not ... I mean, he wasn't ... he's dead."

"What's that in your hand?" Ojo asked, pointing to

the small steel tube in the man's gloved hand.

"I found it near the body," he replied, handing it to Ojo. "I'm not sure what it is. What do you think?"

"It's a silencer," Ojo told the stranger, raising it to his nose, "and it's still warm. It could not have been used more than a few minutes ago." The burning feeling returned to his stomach. Now was not the time to reach into his pocket for his ulcer medication. He winced in pain for an instant. Everything inside of him told him to run. But he couldn't. Even if the tearing pain in his abdomen subsided, he wouldn't stand a chance by running. The tall stranger could shoot him in the back as he tried to flee. "Perhaps you also found a gun lying beside the silencer?" Ojo asked.

"No, that's all I found. But it might be on the ground somewhere. Maybe in those shrubs." The tall man glanced over his shoulder and through the arch at the phone on the corner across the street. "You want to look around and I'll call the police?"

"That's a very good idea," Ojo said nervously, looking up at the stranger's pock-marked face as the light from a streetlamp struck it.

The man's face was badly disfigured. An ugly scar ran across his cheek and onto his badly-repaired cleft lip. Another scar traced the angle of his crooked jaw. From the side, he resembled Andy Gump, the cartoon character who had no chin.

Ojo pulled a small black and yellow disc from his

jacket pocket. A row of lights flashed in its center. "Actually, let me see if I can reach them with this," he told the chinless man. "Transmit," he said, and the lights stopped flashing on the voice-activated gadget.

The stranger looked on with some apprehension in his eyes. He glanced over his shoulder another time.

"Nine-one-one."

The line rang twice. "911. What's your emergency?" a woman's voice answered.

The stranger reached deep into his pocket with his gloved hand. Ojo kept a close nervous eye on that hand.

"A man has been shot in Washington Square Park!" Ojo told her.

"911. What's your emergency?" the woman repeated.

"Hello, *hello!*" Ojo yelled.

The line disconnected.

"Transmit," Ojo tried again. "Nine-one-one."

The line rang again. "Police Department, Officer Harris."

"Officer, a man has been shot in—"

"Police Department, Office Harris."

"Zukintii!" Ojo said with a click and stuffed the Teledisc back in his jacket.

Immediately he noticed a relieved look on the tall man's face. When the stranger removed his gloved hand from his pocket, Ojo felt the blood race to his own face. His head began to throb and his stomach burned terribly. His eyes raced to the stranger's hand but found it empty.

"Perhaps you had better try the phone across the street," Ojo anxiously said. "I'll see what I can find here."

"Of course," the man replied. He slowly crossed the park, limping dreadfully as he walked toward the arch. It was only then that Ojo noticed the man's crooked posture. He leaned to the left as he walked, dragging his right leg in a circular, sweeping motion without bending it. When he reached the arch, Ojo saw him lean against it briefly. Then Ojo watched him resume the effort, slowly limping through the arch and across the street toward the phone on the corner.

Ojo stood by the body. He stared for another moment at the stranger and then his eyes fell upon the silencer in his hand. The blue steel was still warm. He wrapped his fingers around it tightly and looked at the dead man.

The dim lighting was enough for Ojo to make out the large puddle of blood in which the man lay. His overcoat had fallen open to reveal his bloodied white shirt and the gunpowder stain over his left breast pocket. The man's face was ghastly pale. Streams of blood trickled from his nostrils and the corner of his mouth. Ojo noticed a splatter of blood on the corner of the bench. *The man must have struck it as he fell to the ground,* Ojo thought. A pair of cracked eyeglasses lay on the ground beside the man's chin. Ojo slowly walked around the body. He carefully examined the surrounding area, including the bench, shrubs, and grassy clearing on the other side of the body. He found no gun.

Ojo turned and looked through the arch. He looked across the street at the phone on the corner. Its receiver dangled back and forth. The stranger was gone.

Ojo remained by the body. He stared at the silencer in his hand—the silencer that had his fingerprints all over it. He thought about the stranger. How could he have *heard* the shots if a *silencer* was used? How could he have *seen* the body lying on the ground with the bench and shrubs completely blocking the view? And how could the practically lame man have *run* from McDougal, two blocks away, to the body *before* the killer's car even pulled away? The answer was obvious—he could not have.

Yet Ojo still stood there, crouching over the body with the silencer in his hand. It was too late to run, he thought. Should he be spotted leaving the scene now, his story wouldn't have a prayer. He glanced at the phone another time. He started to walk toward the arch. If he could just make it to the phone and report the incident, he might have a chance.

But it was too late. The blinding glare of two headlights shot through the arch, trapping Ojo beside the body. The squad car's red and blue roof lights flashed on his face. Ojo held his hands up to block the light from his eyes as the car stopped several feet from where he stood and the doors flew open.

"*Drop it!*" the officer on the driver's side ordered as he went into a shooting stance.

"Don't shoot! *Don't shoot!*" Ojo pleaded.

"Well, what do we have here?" the cop's partner said, a crooked grin distorting his unshaven face as he glanced at the body on the ground. "Looks like homicide to me," he added, pulling Ojo's arms behind his back as he bent him over the hood and cuffed him. "You're under arrest!"

* * *

Derek tossed and turned violently. He was sweating and his face was flushed. He had been struggling with the covers and had kicked them off the bed. Christine sat up in bed next to him. She stared at Derek, silently in thought. Her small nose and thin delicate lips made her deep blue eyes appear even larger than they were. Her long blonde hair fell across her shoulder and disappeared into her lap where her hands nervously folded and unfolded. She glanced at the clock on the glass nightstand beside the bed—it was 3:17 a.m.

Christine Stratton Stryker was a conservative, soft-spoken woman. She was the daughter of Barney Stratton, a wealthy Westchester land developer, and Loretta Blackens, a concert pianist who dabbled as a writer. Christine had been the victim of a brutal custody trial when her parents divorced twenty-three years earlier. She was five years old at the time. Her father had become involved with Scarlet Kellman, a realtor who was twelve years his junior. Scarlet gave him the vigor and excitement that Loretta's world of music and writing had denied him, he would claim. Loretta had neglected him—*and* Christine—for the sake of her own career, Barney told the courtroom during the custody battle. Three years of painful negotiations and instability for Christine resulted in Loretta finally obtaining sole custody. Christine's father had three children with Scarlet before they also divorced.

Christine graduated from the Columbia University School of Journalism in 1990. She worked as a freelance writer for three years, and during that time she completed her first novel, *Suspect*. It was a murder suspense she had begun while in graduate school. The book wasn't a bestseller or anything like that, but it put her name in the bookstores. Her career as a professional writer took off after a piece she had written for *LIFE Magazine* in 1995 received national acclaim. The article explored the societal re-entry phenomenon of post-traumatic stress disorder experienced by Desert Storm veterans and related it to the incidence of a depressive syndrome seen in individuals affected by the fall of the Berlin Wall and the decline of Communism.

Later that year Christine took a job as a staff reporter for *TIME Magazine*. Six months later she married Bill Stryker, a sportswriter for *TIME*. He was very much like her father. He was an ambitious and driven man. He was also an abusive alcoholic who refused to acknowledge the fact that he was destroying himself and those around him. The marriage lasted seven months. Christine resigned from *TIME* after their divorce. She has since resumed her freelance writing and begun work on her second novel.

Derek turned away from Christine. He grabbed the pillow tightly and buried his face in it. He was having the same nightmare he had had almost every night for ten years. He was at an airport, watching planes take off and land. The sun was shining. He was waiting for Flight 758 from Washington. His father was aboard that flight. It had been delayed due to weather conditions but the fog had lifted and the plane was due to land momentarily.

Suddenly that dream disappeared. The shape of a man took form in the distance. The man held out a package and then stepped back into the darkness. The package fell at Derek's feet with a thunderous clap and the darkness turned into blackened clouds.

Rain fell briskly from the sky and made a loud tapping noise as it struck the terminal windows. Derek watched as his father's plane prepared to land. It glided through the air on its way toward the runway. The plane's front wheels struck, then bounced upward as the rear wheels touched down and the engines reversed thrust with a loud roar. The nose of the plane angled toward the ground and the front wheels struck it hard a second time. Suddenly, the right wing dipped and struck the ground and the plane spun off the runway. In moments, flames engulfed the wing and then the plane. A deafening explosion shattered the windows of the terminal. Derek was thrown backward in a puddle of broken glass. In his hand he was holding the torn remains of a child's cloth monkey doll.

The dream became dark again. The airport and fiery explosion were gone. Blurred newspaper headlines flashed in the darkness. Over and over.

Derek's brow tightened as the headlines filled his mind, forcing him to relive the nightmare that relentlessly tortured him.

PILOT ERROR—173 KILLED
PILOT ERROR—173 KILLED
PILOT ERROR—173 KILLED

"Derek," Christine's soft voice called to him. "Derek."

He turned toward her abruptly, still asleep, the dream still alive in his mind. The headlines faded as the fiery explosion occurred again. And again. Derek found himself lying again in a puddle of broken glass. But the doll was gone. In its place was a small cylindrical package.

Christine shook him and he began to stir. He opened his eyes and wrapped his arms around her. "It happened again, didn't it?" she asked him.

He nodded, the terror still in his body as he held her tightly. "But it was different tonight."

"What do you mean?"

"There was something else. I don't know what. But I know it was different."

She rocked him in her arms. Derek took comfort in this. His grip loosened as she pressed her face to his. The ring of his phone cut through the silence. They were both startled. Derek leaned across the nightstand and grabbed it. He pulled it toward him in the darkness, brushing against the cylindrical canister that was on the corner of the nightstand.

A loud ping rang out as the metal canister struck the wooden floor. The top of the canister popped off and rolled toward the desk on the other side of the room, where the package's brown wrapping lay crumpled in the wastebasket. Derek held the phone to his ear but said nothing. He stared at the canister's contents as they spilled on the floor.

"A man was shot in the park tonight," Ojo's nervous voice shot through the phone. "And they think *I* killed him!"

"Ojo, where are you?" Derek asked him. "Are you alright?"

"I've been arrested! I am in jail, Derek. *Jail!* I'm at the 31st Precinct. They're holding me for first-degree *murder!*"

"This can't be happening."

"It's happening," Ojo said. "Help me, Derek!"

"Where's the Precinct?"

"22nd and 3rd or Lexington. Something like that."

"Just sit calm," Derek said. "I'll be there in ten."

"What is it? Is Ojo alright?" Christine asked as Derek was about to put the phone down.

He whipped the phone back to his ear. "Ojo, are you still there? *Ojo?!*"

The line was already dead.

"What were you going to tell him?"

"To keep his mouth shut," Derek told her.

* * *

The precinct station was old and worn. It was on the corner of 23rd Street and 3rd Avenue. It had been a water tower in the 1890s. With renovation, it was converted to a police station fifty years later. The stone block building had barred windows and a large arched wooden door.

Derek parked between two squad cars in the small lot behind the station house. He and Christine sat in the car for a moment and watched as a detective in plainclothes escorted two handcuffed women through a door on the north side of the building.

"I wonder if it's because he's black?" Derek said.

"There's no doubt," Christine agreed.

He and Christine got out of the car and crossed the broken pavement that led to the station house, following the detective and his suspects into the precinct. They turned down a winding corridor and entered the central area of the station. A number of small wooden desks formed a crooked line along the perimeter of the large room. Several police officers stood speaking near the coffee brewer in the rear of the room. They pulled donuts from the large basket beside it as they reviewed the morning's roster assignments. Several others sat at their desks, typing.

The detective escorted the handcuffed women to the large desk at the front of the room. Behind that desk sat

Lieutenant Rutherford, a middle-aged greying officer, bent over some paperwork. The officers exchanged a few words, the women received a few glances from the Lieutenant, and the detective escorted them through another door.

"Excuse me, sir," Derek addressed the Lieutenant as he approached the desk. "I'm looking for a friend of mine, Ojo Jenachukwu."

Rutherford looked up. He said nothing.

"Do you know where I can find him?"

"You his lawyer?"

"No."

"He's gonna need one. Murder weapon was in his possession at the scene."

"There's been some mistake."

"No, it was in his hand alright."

"Do you know where I can find him?"

"Booking, 2nd Floor," Rutherford said. "Stairs over there," he added, pointing to the doorway the detective had just left through.

Derek and Christine walked upstairs and through the door marked BOOKING AND HOLDING. A large holding cell occupied the rear half of the room. A tall hispanic man in his thirties paced back and forth within the cell. He adjusted his blue felt hat and brushed the sleeve of his dark suit with the back of his hand. The man talked to himself as he paced.

"Why do you not understand?!" Derek and Christine heard Ojo say. He was sitting on one side of a desk several feet from the holding cell. A middle-aged cop named Sergeant Brotsky sat across from him. Ojo's hands were cuffed. "I have been *framed! Set up!*"

"Glad to see he kept his mouth shut," Derek whispered to Christine as they approached the desk. Christine put her hand on Ojo's shoulder.

Ojo looked at them, a nervous, defenseless expression on his face.

Derek introduced himself to the Sergeant as Ojo's friend and business partner. "What's going on?" he asked and glanced at the silver shield on Brotsky's chest. *666.* Interesting badge number, he thought.

"We received an anonymous call from an eyewitness tonight," Brotsky began. "We followed a hunch and found Mr. Jena*cujo* in Washington Square Park." He paused and took a swallow from the mug in his hand. "He was crouched over a dead man's body," he said and took another swallow. "The murder weapon was still in his hand. Still warm."

"*What* eyewitness?!" Ojo interrupted. "I keep telling you, that was the man that *I* found standing over the body! Then he—"

"Just a second, Ojo," Derek cut in. He looked at Brotsky. "Has he been Mirandized yet?"

"He was read his rights at the scene," Brotsky told him

flatly. "With the eyewitness' story and your friend, here, standing over the dead man's body, we established *probable cause* and arrested him."

"You don't have to say another word," Derek told Ojo. "Not a single word until Brad Tomkin gets here."

"Who is Brad Tomkin?" Ojo asked him.

"He's Jim Shaw's partner. A criminal defense attorney. I called him from the car on the way over."

Jim Shaw was an old attorney friend of theirs. He had handled their corporate and tax work during the inception and incorporation of Contraptions.

"I don't need a lawyer," Ojo said. "This whole thing is a misunderstanding. It is black and white."

"The only thing black and white here, Jenacujo, are the suspect and the victim," Brotsky said.

"Maybe that's the problem," Derek suggested.

"Jena*chukwu*," Ojo corrected him. "You are dead wrong. I was set up. *Framed!* That *eyewitness* was no witness. He called the station, accused me of what *he* had done, then disappeared! *He* shot the guy!"

"What about the gun in your hand?"

"I was *not* holding—"

"Careful Ojo," Derek warned him.

"I am fine," Ojo said with a quieter voice as he turned toward Derek. "I am just telling him what happened. I came on the scene after the fact. I have not done a single thing wrong! And I have surely not *killed* anyone! Believe me, Derek, I am innocent. I am *completely* innocent."

"I know that, but just realize that you can be completely innocent in our justice system and *still* be royally fucked."

"I do."

"Fine. If you insist on talking, then you may as well start from the beginning. What happened when you left my apartment? It was around 2 a.m., wasn't it?"

"Two, a quarter of two. I walked to my car, which I had left on 73rd and York, a couple blocks from your apartment, and then headed downtown."

Ojo recounted the incident to Derek and Christine.

"I have been set up! *Set up!*" Ojo insisted. He turned from Derek to Sgt. Brotsky, who replaced his mug on the desk after taking a quick swallow.

"Maybe so," Brotsky replied, occasionally eyeing Christine. "But right now *you*, Jenacujo, are our *only* suspect," he went on, tapping Ojo on the chest. "And let me tell you something, it doesn't look good."

"What about the guy in the park?!" Ojo exploded with frustration. "What about *him*?!"

"Look, Jena*cujo*," Brotsky snapped back, "*you* are our suspect—our *only* suspect. And with that silencer in your hand, we've already got one helluva case against you. So until we turn up some concrete evidence that this tall stiff even exists, that's the way it's gonna remain."

"What about the calls?" Christine asked.

"Don't they corroborate Ojo's story?" Derek asked.

"They don't corroborate a thing," Brotsky told them. "Only one call was received from the area between 2 a.m., the estimated time Mr. Jenacujo arrived in Washington Square Park, and 2:24 a.m., the time he was apprehended. The call was from a guy who claimed to have witnessed the shooting. He identified the killer as a medium-built black male. When my men got to the park, guess who they found?" he asked, turning back to Derek. "They found your friend," he went on without waiting for a response, "standing over the body— with *this* in his hand." Brotsky held up a small plastic bag that contained the silencer.

"But what about the 911 calls *Ojo* made?" Christine asked.

"Read my lips, Miss," Brotsky told her. "Only *one* call was received from the area between 2 a.m. and 2:24 a.m."

"Wait a second," Ojo said. "What about those hang ups? Is it not true that *every* 911 call is recorded?"

"You're right," Brotsky responded. "Every 911 call *is* recorded," he said and rolled his eyes. He picked up the phone and dialed the telecommunications office. "Hello, Jeanne ... one question ... how many hang ups between 2 a.m. and 2:24 a.m. this morning ... thanks." He tossed the phone back on its cradle. "Seventeen," he said flatly.

"You still cannot prove I had anything to do with the murder," Ojo said. "This whole thing is a horrible misunderstanding. Don't you see that?!"

"It might be," Brotsky conceded. "It just might be. But then again, maybe you did kill the guy," he added and nonchalantly took another swallow from his mug.

"So what happens now?" Derek asked.

"An investigation into the shooting has already begun."

"What am I to do now?" Ojo nervously asked.

"You'll have to wait for a bond hearing."

"What does that mean exactly?" Ojo asked.

"That means one of several things. You might be released upon payment of a bond or on your own recognizance. Or you might be indicted."

"How soon can the hearing be held?" Derek asked Brotsky.

"Oh, I'd say anytime between now and forty-eight hours from now."

"*Forty-eight hours*?! What happens between now and then?" Ojo questioned.

"*That* happens," Brotsky replied, pointing to the holding cell.

"There *has* to be something we can do," Christine insisted. "There *has* to be."

"I really don't think there's anything you can do, Miss. Or any of you. I think you'd all be better off if you left the police work to us," Brotsky advised.

"That is so easy for you to say!" Ojo yelled. "Zukintii!"

"Look, Jenacujo, if there's something to be found in the park, some piece of evidence that might support your story, we'll find it."

"There *must* be something we're overlooking. But *what?*" Derek wondered.

"Goose and Tucker," Christine suggested.

The mention of those names lightened the air considerably.

"Goose and Tucker," Derek repeated. "That's not a bad idea," he said. "If anyone can help us, *they* can."

Ojo appeared lost in thought. "We *have* overlooked something," he finally said. "I don't know if it will work or not, but I think it is my only chance."

Derek immediately understood. "The *Thermalyzer*," he said.

"Exactly," Ojo quickly replied, his eyes lighting up with hope.

"The *what?*" Brotsky questioned.

"Take the Gemini drive and store the images in separate files," Ojo went on, ignoring the Sergeant's question. There was no time to explain. No reason to. "Shoot up and down McDougal, around the arch, the phone, near the benches, by the—"

"Don't worry," Derek assured him, grabbing his shoulder firmly. "I'm going to shoot every square inch of that goddamn park." He took Christine's hand in his as they crossed the wide room and continued toward the door, anxious to get back to the shop and pick up the equipment.

Christine looked back toward Ojo as Brotsky escorted him toward the holding cell. He unlocked the steel cell gate and welcomed Ojo with an extended arm to its confines.

Derek pulled the door shut behind them. The steel gate made a loud clanking noise as it locked shut. The sound penetrated the wooden door and echoed through the dimly-lit hallway as they turned in to the stairwell. "Tell me more about the *Thermalyzer*," Christine asked Derek as they raced down the steps. "I thought you gave up on that invention six months ago."

"We almost did," Derek told her as they crossed the central area of the station. He caught Lieutenant Rutherford's glance but ignored him. "Till Ojo reprogrammed the infrared sensors."

"Then what?"

Derek reached into the inner pocket of his jacket and pulled a folded piece of paper from it. "Then *this*," he said and handed it to her.

Christine unfolded the paper and stared at it with amazement. She saw Derek's image seated at his desk in the office along with the image of the silver-haired man. She understood its significance.

"It works. It fucking *works!*" he told her.

"Why didn't you tell me?"

"I was too preoccupied with the package I found on my desk," he said and pushed open the large wooden door that led to the street. "The old man must have left it for me."

With a dull clunk, the door struck the head of a thin balding man who was entering the precinct. The man dropped his black attaché case as he leaned back against the wall to regain his balance. Derek bent to retrieve the attaché and noticed the monogram near the lock. *B.N.T.*

"Mr. ... *Tomkin?*"

The man put his hand to his head and nodded.

CHAPTER FOUR

I have not failed. I've just found 10,000 ways that won't work.

Thomas Edison

Goose and Tucker were detectives in the 9th Precinct. Their district included an area of the South Bronx in which drug trafficking, racketeering, and prostitution were rampant. This region was known as *Fort Apache*.

Gus "Goose" Clemens joined the Los Angeles Police Department fifteen years earlier. He transferred to the 21st Precinct in Manhattan in 1989, after his wife left him. That's where he met his current partner, Frank Tucker— then, a rookie from Connecticut. They were introduced during a shootout behind a crack house one cold

December night and eventually became partners.

When Tucker was promoted to Detective two years later, he and Goose transferred to the Special Narcs Unit of the 9th Precinct. Within six months, they had closed down fourteen crack houses and put away five major drug lords. They had more collars than any other unit in the South Bronx and were nicknamed the *Dynamic Duo* by the Police Commissioner.

Christine thought about them as Derek turned onto Fifth Avenue. Washington Square Park was twelve blocks away. She thought about her first meeting with them—an interview for *TIME* two years earlier, just before she resigned. As a writer and reporter she had done countless interviews in the past. But this one was different—and with good reason.

Elriqo Gonzalez and Manny Pimentes, two drug kingpins, had escaped from prison two nights before the interview. Goose and Tucker had busted them five years earlier for possession of more than three hundred kilos of cocaine. Christine had received privileged information concerning Gonzalez and Pimentes from a source of hers shortly after the prison break. The source was a small-time dealer who had worked for them before the bust. He now feared for his life and was considering turning state's evidence in exchange for immunity from prosecution— and protection. Christine was the only outsider whom he trusted. Her source was certain Gonzalez and Pimentes would return to a small two-flat in the hills of Monticello from which they had previously operated. Only two others knew of this hideout. Both were dead.

The *TIME* interview had gone well, she recalled. Goose and Tucker were readily recruited for the stakeout. All that remained was obtaining the right equipment for night surveillance photography. Enter Contraptions.

Derek's Carrera bounced over a pothole before stopping at a light on 14th Street. One of its exhaust injectors cracked in the process. The car made a loud gurgling sound when the engine raced. "Nothing like being inconspicuous, is there?" he asked Christine.

"Did you say something?" she replied after a moment.

"What's on your mind?"

"Just thinking about Goose and Tucker."

"So was I," Derek said. "Quite a pair."

Christine agreed.

"I'm still not sure how you managed to talk us into joining that stakeout," Derek told her. "Four days in that cramped attic. It must have been a hundred and ten degrees in there. And while I was sweating to death in there with Goose and Tucker, you and Ojo sat comfortably in the car outside."

"You volunteered."

"That's right, isn't it? Well, someone had to show you guys how to use the equipment."

"God, you were a sarcastic shit when I met you," Christine said. "I needed a camera that could take shots in the dark. And I still remember what you told me. *'Any camera can do that,'*" she mimicked in a deepened voice.

"*'Ever hear of a flash?'* You jerk."

Derek grinned. "I *was* kind of sarcastic back then, wasn't I?"

"*Back then?*"

"Well, how was I supposed to know you were looking for an infrared sensor with continuous receptor capacity?"

"Well, of course, I was ... or something like that."

The light changed. Derek could see the park up ahead. In his mind was the dilapidated attic. He could see the cluttered boxes and a light bulb that hung from a wire attached to the triangular ceiling. That light bulb hung until Goose smacked it with his head for the third and final time. He then tore it from the ceiling and smashed it against the wall.

Goose was a large man. He was at least fifty pounds overweight and his blond hair was thinning. He had a thick mustache and wore plaid shirts. Tucker was equally large. He wore his dark hair short and usually had a two-day-old beard. He always had a toothpick at the corner of his mouth. A trail of chewed toothpicks usually followed him.

Derek had rotated watch with them through the small circular window in the wall that faced the two-flat across the street. The other windows in the house had been boarded up since the fire that almost leveled it six months earlier. The faint smell of smoke had still lingered in the mildewy air.

"We've got ourselves a real sicko over there, bud,"

Goose had said when he opened the attic door to greet Derek. He pointed toward the other side of the street.

"Looks like we've got a goddamn freak on our hands," Tucker said. "Can't wait to nail his deviant nuts to the wall." Tucker had a way with words.

"As soon as his lover boy returns with the goodies," Goose added.

They both let out a sick laugh. Like this was some kind of game or something.

Goose slapped Derek on the back. "Oh, by the way, welcome aboard."

Even if they could have had a second chance to make a first impression, these two could not have done any better, Derek thought. They belonged in a bowling alley, dripping beer down their chins and pizza sauce on their shirts. The thought that they wore gold badges and carried guns was a scary one.

Guess you never really know someone until you roll up your sleeves and work side by side, Derek thought. He turned left on 10th Street then right on McDougal and stopped on the corner across from O'Neal's Bar.

"Let's do it," he said, returning the Teledisc to its holder on the dashboard.

"No word back yet from Goose or Tucker, huh?" Christine asked.

Derek shook his head and reached for the grey shoulder bag on the back seat. "Seems they're on assignment in D.C. and can't be reached."

He removed three leather-encased units from the bag's central compartment: a small monitor containing a microdisc Gemini drive, a hand-sized keyboard, and the Thermalyzer. He placed the monitor and keyboard on the dashboard and the Thermalyzer on his lap. Derek removed several connector cables and a small plastic case from a side compartment. Within moments, the cables were connected and the Thermalyzer was up and running.

Derek opened the plastic case and emptied the micro discs onto his palm. Each had a tiny label on its surface. HLA IMAGER. PHOTON DISPLACER. GENE SPLICER. ORBIT SCRAMBLER. *THERMALYZER.* When a light below the drive slots flashed he inserted the program micro disc in one slot and a blank micro disc in the other. He struck several keys and the monitor beeped. THERMALYZER ACTIVE flashed on the small screen.

Derek rolled down his window and carefully rested the Thermalyzer on the door frame. He rotated the viewer arm so it faced directly across the street, then struck a switch on the side of the unit to activate the infrared sensor. With a certain gentleness, he kissed the viewer arm and turned toward Christine. "Don't fail me now," he said.

Christine chewed her lip nervously.

Derek directed the viewer toward O'Neal's Bar and pressed the image scanner button. He and Christine stared at the monitor for a few moments in silence. Shades and shadows, bright greys and deeper greys, lines and dots soon appeared and took form on the small screen.

"What do you think?" he asked Christine as a clear image of the bar's entrance appeared.

She smiled. "This is fantastic!" she said, while unfolding the printout Derek had given her earlier. "It's just like—"

"Exactly," Derek told her as his eyes fell upon the image of the silver-haired man standing in his office.

He thought about that for a moment. And about the package left on his desk—the aluminum canister wrapped in brown paper. In his mind he saw the canister lying next to the wastebasket where it had rolled after falling from the nightstand. The canister's top lay beside it, its spilled contents scattered on the cold floor. A black and white photograph of Derek's father lay at the mouth of the canister. He wore a dark uniform in the photo. Two stars adorned his lapels, several medals decorated his chest. Two sets of dog tags lay beside the photo. One of the metal tags had a bullet hole in its center. The others were intact.

Another moment passed and the lighter, blurred images of several people standing outside the bar became visible on the screen.

Derek paid no attention. Thoughts of his father filled his head. Another photograph lay on the floor several feet away, Derek recalled. A man he had never before seen stood beside his father, also in a dark uniform. Next to that photo sat the cut half of a gold medallion that—

"Do you think the killer came this way?"

Christine's question broke into his thoughts.

For a moment, he didn't reply. "Maybe, maybe not," Derek finally said. "Don't know. But if he did, we'll find him ... I hope."

"From the way Ojo described him, it's highly unlikely that he walked from any distance. He probably drove up to the edge of the park then slowly pursued his victim on foot," Christine suggested.

Derek nodded in agreement. He focused the viewer further down the block and activated the Thermalyzer again. Three deserted storefronts appeared on the screen. He moved the car several feet forward then repeated the process. More storefronts and several unremarkable passersby. He moved the car a number of times—finally to the corner of McDougal and Washington Square North. The park was across the street.

Derek rotated the viewer so it faced several vacant parking spaces on the other side of the street, about fifty feet from the park's entrance. He activated the unit another time and gazed at the small screen with tired eyes.

"What do you think?" Christine asked him as the image of a man stepping out of a plain sedan appeared.

"Don't know yet."

Derek refocused the infrared sensor and scanned several feet closer to the entrance. He stared at the screen in silence as the images took form.

"So what do you think?" she asked him again.

Derek turned toward her and flashed a wide grin. "*That's* the son-of-a-bitch!" he exploded as the image of an unusually tall man, slightly hunched to one side with the opposite leg extended sideways and unbent, appeared on the screen. "That's *him*," he went on, feverishly striking the keyboard several times. A white line encircled the man's outline, enlarging his image. "It *has* to be!"

"Well, let's not stop here," Christine said.

"We're not stopping *anywhere*," Derek reassured her. "Not till we trace the killer's last step."

He thermalyzed the entire street from the corner of Washington Square North up to the telephone pole, across the street from the park's entrance. The arch itself was obscured by the brownstone on the corner of McDougal Street. Derek and Christine carefully studied the monitor as multiple images of the killer were produced.

The successive images demonstrated the killer's crippling gait. He leaned toward his right side and dragged his outstretched leg in a sweeping semicircular motion. Several of the thermalyzed scans contained blurred, superimposed images of the killer. The superimposed images were the result of the killer having twice crossed a common path between his car, the park, and the telephone. Other scans were superimposed with images of the numerous police officers, CSI personnel, and investigators who had come and gone in the hours since the shooting had occurred.

Derek turned the corner as the brownstone obscured the killer's path and his thermalyzed images. In an instant, the flashing glare of a squad car's roof lights struck his eyes. The squad car was just beyond the arch. Two unmarked police cars blocked off the park's entrance and a strip of tape connected the limbs of the arch where a small group had gathered.

Derek pulled into a space beside a fire hydrant and thermalyzed the park's entrance. He and Christine watched the monitor as the killer limped through the arch and out of site. Derek then placed the micro disc drive and monitor in the shoulder bag. "Let's go."

"Do you think it's a good idea to park here?"

"A man was killed right over there," he said. "I really don't think the cops are worrying about their parking ticket quotas right now."

"If you say so." Christine stepped out of the car.

Derek unzipped a flap on the side of the bag to reveal the monitor then lifted it onto his shoulder. Together they stepped across the brick street and approached one of the unmarked cars. Christine pulled her PRESS badge from her purse. "I'm Christine Stratton from the *Daily News*," she told the tired-looking officer in the car, offering her pass for his inspection. "This is my photographer."

The officer studied her ID for a moment, then nodded.

Derek and Christine walked behind the arch and into the park. Derek thermalyzed the area just beyond the arch, checking the killer's images on the monitor with each scan. The killer clumsily limped from the arch to the area where the squad car was now parked, its roof lights still flashing. Beyond the car was an area roped off with wooden horses in which the sprawled out shape of a man was outlined in white tape on the red brick ground.

A heavyset Irish officer stood beside the outline. He jotted some notes on a small pad then turned toward his partner who was on his knees, separating a cluster of branches with his nightstick as he ran his flashlight over the bare ground. "Anything?" the Irish officer asked.

"Nothing," his partner replied. He was a small Italian man. "Not a goddamn thing. But the murder weapon has to be around here somewhere. Why don't you check the west side of the park another time?"

The Irish officer nodded and walked away.

Derek and Christine could just barely make out the conversation from where they stood. Derek thermalyzed the outline and the surrounding area. Christine stared at the screen through the bag's clear panel while he activated the Thermalyzer. "They're both right on mark," she said, referring to the killer and his victim.

"Think that's what they're looking for?" he asked, pointing to the gun in the killer's hand. Christine smiled.

"Morning, Officer," Derek called to the cop who was checking the bushes.

With a start, the officer turned. "Do you know this is a restricted area?"

"We're with the *Daily News*," Christine told him, offering her PRESS pass for his inspection. "We just need a few shots and we'll be on our way."

He approved with a nod.

"Just one question, Officer," Christine said. The officer looked up. "Any motive?"

"None yet," he replied and turned back toward the bushes.

"Any ID on the victim?"

"That's two, Miss," the cop called back. "I really don't have the time."

"No murder weapon yet, huh?" Derek asked.

"You don't think I'm on all fours looking for another body, do you?"

"Well, that's interesting," Christine said as the successive images appeared on the screen. She studied the tape outline on the ground for a moment and then turned back toward the screen.

"What is?"

"Take a look." Christine pointed to the image of the dead man lying on the ground. The victim had fallen to the ground and lay on his side. His legs were bent and curled. One arm lay beneath his body and was not seen in the image. The other was folded across his chest.

Derek stared at the image for a moment, then at the sprawled out shape on the ground. "Obviously, he's been moved," he concluded. He thermalyzed the area beyond the bushes where the officer still searched.

"Another image is coming in," Christine told him. "The body's spread out in this one. Just like the outline. The tall guy's bent over it. Going through the dead man's pockets."

"Anything now?" Derek asked after scanning in the opposite direction.

Christine watched the monitor closely as the images took form. "We've got another guy on the screen," she said. "He's coming up the walk."

"Let me guess," Derek said as he scanned the west end of the park where the Irish cop stood beside a large oak tree, searching through some shrubs for the murder weapon. "Could it be Ojo?"

"Lucky guess. He just threw the gun!" Christine excitedly told him.

"*Ojo* threw the gun?!"

"The *killer*, Derek. The *killer* threw the gun!" Christine corrected him. "You can see it in the air. But a part of it is still in his hand."

"The silencer," Derek said, eyeing the monitor. "It's the *silencer*!"

The next image appeared. It was out of sequence but that didn't matter. Ojo stood beside the murderer, taking the silencer from him as both stared at the bloodied victim on the ground.

Derek watched the screen in silence. Christine squeezed his hand as the next series of black and white images came into focus. The rising morning sun cast an orange glow upon the images. The contrast was slightly blurred but the small black object sailing between the trees, knocking several leaves and twigs to the ground as it struck them, was unmistakable. It was, indeed, the murder weapon. The *missing* murder weapon.

With each successive image, the gun sailed further and further across the park, passing the area where the Irish cop now stood and striking the large oak tree behind him. They watched attentively as the final image formed on the small screen. The infinite black, white, and grey dots coalesced once more to create this image as they had each time before. The trees. The bushes. The benches. The gate along the perimeter of the park. All appeared as they had before. All with one important exception.

"What the hell happened to the gun?" Derek whispered nervously.

"It was right there a second ago," Christine said, pointing at the oak tree on the left side of the screen. "In the last image," she added. Suddenly, she became very worried again. An image of Ojo flashed in her mind. She could see him handcuffed in that crowded, windowless holding cell. Without the murder weapon, the evidence— the *silencer*—could weigh heavily against Ojo, she thought. "After it hit the tree it should have just fallen to the ground and—"

"But it didn't," Derek mumbled. He was silent for a

moment. "And I think I know why," he finally said. He took the keyboard from the bag and struck several keys.

"What are you doing?"

He didn't reply. The screen cleared and the previous image reappeared. "What do you see?" Derek asked her.

"The gun striking the tree. Same as before."

"Anything else? Take a real good look at the tree. Study its shape."

"Those two large branches form kind of a Y shape."

"Exactly. Now, look a bit more closely at this one," Derek said, pointing to the branch on the right before he hit the keyboard again.

Christine stared at the screen. She said nothing.

Derek struck the keyboard again, and a white line highlighted the Y-shaped branches. They were magnified until they filled the entire screen. "How about now?"

After a few moments Christine's eyes opened wide and she let out a relieved laugh. She saw the dark image of the gun wedged in the tight angle where the large branches extended from the tree, about ten feet above the ground. "That ought to wrap our shoot," she said.

"I would say so," Derek said. "I think it's time we headed back to the bomb shelter for some additional equipment." That was what he called the shop—the *bomb shelter*. He returned the keyboard, drive and Thermalyzer to the shoulder bag. "And then, back to the precinct."

As they walked through the arch to the car Derek glanced over his shoulder. The Italian cop stood beside the tape outline, still searching the surrounding area. The glare of his partner's flashlight could still be seen in the distance through the gaps between the shrubs where he was crouched.

When they reached the car, Derek opened Christine's door and handed her the shoulder bag. As he walked around to the driver's side, he pulled a folded piece of paper from the space between the door and front fender.

"What's that?" Christine asked.

"Oh, nothing," he answered, stuffing the parking ticket in his pocket as he started the car. The digital display now flashed 7:42 a.m.

"Sure," Christine said.

But the parking ticket didn't matter. A picture of the cops in the park remained in Derek's mind as he drove off. Neither would find the gun, he thought. And that was all that mattered.

CHAPTER FIVE

When you have eliminated the impossible, whatever remains, however improbable, must be the truth.

Sir Arthur Conan Doyle

The hours passed slowly. Ojo nervously paced the length of the crowded holding cell. With each turn he peered between its steel bars. He searched in vain for some hint of compassion from the hostile environment within which he was now imprisoned. He found none.

He stared at the large round clock above the doorway. It was 9:10 a.m. More than two hours had passed since Tomkin left. Derek and Christine had been gone almost four hours. In the time that had lapsed, Ojo had become a part of the microcosm that now occupied the holding cell. An unforeseeable twist of fate had set the wheels of injustice in motion. Just because he had been at the wrong place at the wrong time, Ojo had been assimilated with that segment of society that stood apart from the law. Eight years of engineering training and a successful business career would not distinguish him from those whom the law was designed to protect him against. Not in the crossed eyes of the law. Ojo was now a murder suspect. He was nothing else.

Ojo glanced between the bars at a fading print of Rockwell's *Police Station* which hung above a desk on the wall adjacent to the holding cell. On the opposite wall was pinned a partly torn centerfold of Ashley Britton, a former NYPD cop, above a desk where two officers questioned a handcuffed youth.

Behind a small wooden desk, several feet from the holding cell, sat Sergeant Brotsky. A deaf black girl sat across from him. Her face and arms were badly bruised. Her blouse was bloodied and torn. She was shivering beneath the blanket draped over her shoulders. Brotsky was questioning her at length about her assailant. His questions were met with frightened nods and indiscernible mutterings. At one point Brotsky offered a pad and pencil but the girl was illiterate. Still, it seemed clear that she was trying to describe the man who had raped and beaten her. With the help of another officer who could sign, Brotsky was able to elicit that information. The rapist was her father.

Ojo's attention turned for a moment. His eyes focused on three men in business suits in the rear of the room.

They stood on one side of a long black table. Two officers sat on the other side of the table. Another officer stood beside the businessmen. He watched as each of the men held his cuffed hands out to be fingerprinted. Each of the suspects was then given a booking number and photographed. Ojo moved away from the sliding gate when the officer escorted the businessmen into the holding cell. He immediately noticed the black ink on the men's hands and looked at his own stained fingers.

Ojo pulled an ink-stained handkerchief from his pocket. It was monogrammed in one corner. *B.N.T.* He held the handkerchief inside a loose fist and thought about the man who had given it to him earlier that morning. *Bradley N. Tomkin.*

Tomkin was a third-generation Harvard attorney. He was born and bred in Boston and was the first Tomkin in more than half a century to leave that city. At the age of forty-four he had chosen to depart from the safe environment of Tomkin, Tomkin & Tomkin to build a firm with a former classmate from Cambridge. That was five years earlier. Now he had his own firm—Tomkin, Shaw & Associates, which employed sixteen associate attorneys specializing in criminal and corporate law.

Tomkin was a thin, frail man. He had begun losing his hair while still in college and was almost completely bald now. His face was always pasty white, summer and winter alike. His eyes appeared magnified through his thick, Coke-bottle spectacles. They had become accustomed to the poor lighting of the courthouse, the jail cells he visited at all hours of the night, and his own dreary office. Any more light than that caused him to squint terribly. Ojo recalled Tomkin's words and the reddened lump on his forehead.

"*Hearsay*," Tomkin had told him. "The testimonial of an anonymous witness unsubstantiated by positive identification of a suspect is circumstantial evidence at best. At worst, it's *hearsay*—meaningless in court. However, with or without an actual eyewitness, Mr. Jenachukwu, several facts remain. First, you *were* the only person found at the murder scene, excluding the victim, of course. Second, your fingerprints are all over the silencer."

"While that is true, Mr. Tomkin," Ojo started, "two extremely important things still remain uncovered—"

"— the murder weapon and the motive," Tomkin finished the sentence for him.

"Exactly."

"Assuming you didn't kill the man—"

"I absolutely *did not*."

"That's what I'm assuming. Therefore, no motive exists. If no motive exists, premeditation cannot be proven. Now, if premeditation cannot be proven beyond a reasonable doubt, then *first* degree murder is thrown out."

"What are you saying?"

"Without premeditation, we're talking about *second*

degree murder— *manslaughter.*"

"Please explain to me what is meant by *manslaughter,*" Ojo had nervously said. "In Zimbabwe, we have only the charge of murder. We do not have *manslaughter* or *second degree murder.* Either you killed him or you did not. There is no other alternative. Please explain this to me."

"To convict a person of *first* degree murder, you must prove that the defendant *planned* to kill the victim—we call this *premeditation.* Mr. Jenachukwu," Tomkin had patiently explained, "if you are convicted of first degree murder— the crime with which you have been charged—the sentence in the State of New York is life in prison."

"But since I am innocent, how can there be any evidence of *premeditation?* Would the case not simply be dismissed?"

"Not likely," Tomkin told him. "With your fingerprints all over the silencer, the jury could very easily read that as a planned murder. They *could* find you guilty, Mr. Jenachukwu."

"And what about this *manslaughter* charge?"

"If we were to take a plea of second degree murder, or manslaughter, you would face a sentence of eighteen to twenty years with parole after seven."

"Eighteen to twenty years *in prison?!*" Ojo nervously yelled at the attorney.

"Something like that."

Ojo grabbed Tomkin's shirt. "What the hell are you

talking about, Tomkin? I thought you were here to help me!"

Tomkin was startled. His spectacles fell on the floor.

"I am innocent! What is this *manslaughter* bullshit?!"

An officer had rushed toward the holding cell.

"I'm quite alright," Tomkin had told the officer without taking his eyes off Ojo's. "Now take your hands off me this instant," he said to Ojo, "or I'll walk right through that door and leave you here to consider your options on your own."

Ojo let go of the attorney's shirt. He picked the spectacles up from the ground and returned them to him apologetically.

"Mr. Jenachukwu," Tomkin had said, "I've lost very few cases over the years. *Very* few. I win because I'm realistic. First, I consider the worst possible outcome. Once I've established that, I can decide how I want to approach plea bargaining, should that be necessary."

Ojo listened attentively.

"I believe that you're innocent," Tomkin told him. "All we have to do is convince twelve of your peers of that. If justice were always served, surely you would be acquitted. But we both know the system doesn't work that way. And if it were to rule against you, surely you wouldn't be the first man to pay for a crime he didn't commit. Therefore, we've got to build our defense. Tell me again, now, from the beginning, absolutely *everything* that occurred from the moment you left Mr. Cannon's apartment last night. Every detail. *Everything.* Whether or not you think it's significant, tell me anyway. *I'll* decide."

Ojo recounted the events over and over while Tomkin took notes. For two hours, they reviewed detail after detail until the attorney had no more questions. Finally, Tomkin tucked away a small pile of note sheets in his attaché case and clicked it shut.

"What now?" Ojo asked.

"I'll be back in the morning for your arraignment."

"What about bail?"

"We'll take care of it once it's set," Tomkin said.

Ojo grabbed Tomkin's hand. He stared at the goose egg on his forehead. "You better put some ice on that," Ojo had told him.

They shook hands again and Tomkin left.

A loud crashing sound broke into Ojo's thoughts. On the other side of the cell, a skinny black kid lay on the cold floor surrounded by the broken pieces of a wooden chair. Blood trickled from his nose and the corner of his mouth. He gathered himself and looked up at the imposing form of another black youth who angrily waved a leg of that chair in the air. He had broken it off before throwing the chair at the boy.

A heavyset officer opened the cell gate and threw the boy up against the wall. He handcuffed the youth and pushed him down onto the wooden plank, which hung suspended from the ceiling by four chains. With a quick turn, he eyed the others in the cell, including Ojo, then stepped past the boy on the ground and slammed the steel gate shut behind him. Ojo watched the officer walk to the back of the room where he had left his clipboard and coffee mug.

Ojo looked at the handcuffed youth who now lay on the suspended plank, shouting profanities. Ojo turned toward the corner of the cell where a thin man was hunched over the small seatless toilet, vomiting violently. A loud angry voice startled Ojo. He turned back toward the kid on the plank. But the boy had stopped shouting. He leaned on his side and laughed while the man with the blue felt hat angrily yelled at the walls in response to an imaginary adversary. The boy on the ground slowly stood and leaned against the cell's bars. His nose was bent to the side and still bleeding. The boy pinched it with his fingers but the blood continued to drip onto the ground. Ojo walked over to the boy and offered him the handkerchief in his hand.

Ojo took another look at the large round clock. It was 9:22 a.m. The heavyset officer slowly crossed the room, sipping from the mug he held in one hand while he glanced at the notes on the clipboard in the other. As he approached the door, stopping briefly to compare the time on his watch with that on the large clock, it flew open.

The officer caught the door before it could knock the coffee mug from his hand, securing the clipboard against his side with his elbow. Derek and Christine entered the room. The grey carrying case hung from Derek's shoulder.

In his hand was a small manilla envelope.

"Excuse me, Officer," Derek said as his eyes darted toward the cell, catching Ojo's anxious stare from the other end.

"No problem," the officer mumbled, brushing by Derek on his way out. The door closed behind him. A moment later, the sound of a cup crashing against the ground was heard and a thin stream of coffee appeared flowing beneath the door.

The door slowly opened. Tomkin stood in the doorway. The front of his shirt and overcoat were splattered with coffee. His tie was badly wrinkled and the end of it had been torn off. He entered the room holding his spectacles in his hand.

"What the hell happened to you?" Brotsky asked as he stood and walked toward the attorney.

"I was about ten feet behind them," Tomkin replied, nodding toward Derek and Christine, "when they stepped onto the elevator. I ran for the door but it closed on my tie." He held up the end of the tie for Brotsky's inspection. "Damn thing would've strangled me if I hadn't been able to tear it free."

"That's too bad," Brotsky said. "Guess you're here to see Jenacujo?" He took a pair of handcuffs from a ringlet on his belt and opened the cell gate. Ojo held his hands out for the Sergeant.

"I really don't think that's necessary," Tomkin protested.

Brotsky nodded. "Fine. Do all of you know each other?"

Derek glanced at the lump on Tomkin's forehead. It was still red but a bit less impressive than it had been. "We've met," he said.

Ojo stepped out of the cell and looked at Tomkin. "I'm sorry about what happened earlier," he told the attorney.

"It's forgotten," Tomkin said and adjusted his spectacles.

Christine took a long look at Ojo. The last six hours had taken their toll on him, she thought. His white shirt was badly wrinkled and stained in a few areas. Beads of sweat had accumulated on his tired brow, there were large bags beneath his bloodshot eyes, and he needed a shave. He looked exhausted. Christine turned and glanced at Tomkin. He appeared even more frazzled and worn than Ojo, she thought.

"What's the good word?" Ojo asked.

"Arraignment is set for ten-thirty," Tomkin told him. "We've still got some ground to cover before then."

"So have we," Derek said.

"I was told Judge Perkins wouldn't be available for bond hearings until tomorrow morning," Brotsky commented.

"That may very well be," Tomkin said, "but I just came from the D.A.'s office. Kent Selby, the Assistant

D.A., made a few calls. It seems Judge Edgerton will be sitting in for his colleague. The arraignment proceedings *will* take place this morning."

"If that's even necessary," Derek said. "Which I highly doubt."

"What are you saying?" Ojo anxiously asked. "What have you found?"

"What are you getting at, Cannon?" Brotsky asked.

"Exactly what we were looking for," Derek told Ojo.

"Are you saying you've uncovered something?" Brotsky asked Derek. "Something on that other guy in the park? The *real* murderer?" he mocked.

"That's exactly right."

"Well, what is it? What have you found?"

"I've got it all right here, Sergeant," Derek told him, holding up the manilla envelope.

"Let's have ourselves a look," Brotsky said. He reached for the envelope but Derek pulled it away.

"In a moment," he said. "Wouldn't want to present the evidence prematurely then have it deemed inadmissible afterwards."

Derek took the attorney aside and explained to him the nature of his findings in the park. Tomkin's main concern was that of establishing evidential creedibility. Derek assured him that would not be a problem and Tomkin agreed to proceed with the demonstration.

"What's the verdict gonna be, counselor?" Brotsky asked Tomkin impatiently.

"Let's go ahead with this," Tomkin said. "In fact, why not give Judge Edgerton the opportunity to sit in on this demonstration? If the evidence meets with his satisfaction he could go ahead and dismiss charges without any further delay."

Brotsky agreed and stepped away to call the Judge.

Tomkin turned to Derek. "You realize this is most unconventional, don't you?"

"This whole situation is *most unconventional*," Ojo commented. "Wouldn't you agree?"

"I would," Tomkin said flatly. "But I see it all the time."

Brotsky returned from his desk. "Judge Edgerton asked that I inspect the evidence. If it meets *my* satisfaction, I can dismiss or modify the charges as I see fit. Otherwise, you'll be arraigned at 10:30 a.m.," he told Ojo.

"Fair enough," Derek said. "All we need is a screening room."

"There's a conference room at the end of the hall," Brotsky told him.

He led the others out of the room and down the hall toward an unmarked door at the corridor's end. He opened it with a key that hung with several others from the pull-chain clipped to his belt.

"Well, here's your *'screening'* room," Brotsky said, pushing the door open and hitting the small switch on the wall inside.

The small windowless room lit up with a dull kind of lighting. A decrepit wooden table was in the center of the room, flanked by folding chairs. A rolled-up projection screen hung over a greenish blackboard on the front wall.

"All yours," Brotsky offered, pointing toward the screen as he motioned Ojo toward the table. He and Ojo sat on one side of the table. Tomkin and Christine sat on the other side.

Derek pulled the screen down, then set the carrying case on the table, the manilla envelope beside it, and withdrew a pyramidal, black onyx device from the bag's central compartment. He positioned it in the center of the table and then reached back into the bag for the small remote before placing the case on a chair.

The small pyramid glistened in the dimness like a black diamond, its narrowing points pin-like, its sleek edges razor-sharp. Several raised words emerged from the stone's smooth surface. *JENNON LASER IMAGER.*

Derek unfastened and gently shook the manilla envelope. A cartridge disc slid into his palm. He struck a switch on the back of the device. The top of the pyramid slid back and sloped upward, revealing a slot from which an icy blue glow emanated. He placed the cartridge in the slot. The top of the pyramid slid back in place and the device hummed for several moments. Two small panels on the front face rotated inward as a thin beam of fiery red light shot from each and exploded on the screen.

"All set, Sergeant," Derek said as Brotsky sat up in his seat.

"Well, go on then. I haven't got all morning."

With the remote in hand, Derek moved to the side of the screen. He pressed a button on the small box and the device hummed again as the first thermalyzed image appeared on the screen. Brotsky's eyes opened wide. Tomkin sat on the edge of his chair.

From the innumerous black and grey lines and dots that added shape and definition to the picture, and from beneath the reddish hue that coated the screen, the figure of a man, stretched out on the ground, could easily be seen.

"Your *first* victim, Sergeant," Derek said and pressed the remote again without turning from the screen.

"Your *second* victim," he went on as the image of Ojo appeared bent over the dead man's body while the bright beams of a squad car trapped him.

"Your *killer*," Derek said. He activated the device again and the tall crooked figure of a man standing beneath the arch appeared.

"*And* your *murder weapon*," he continued, turning to Brotsky as the Y-shaped branches appeared and the missing gun came into view. Successive images of higher magnification revealed the gun's wedged-in position.

Ojo's face lit up. Tomkin shook his head with

enthusiasm.

"Alright, you've got my attention," Brotsky said. "But you're gonna need more than *that* to convince me. I don't even know if those pictures, or whatever they are, are legit."

Tomkin and Derek exchanged a brief glance.

"Relax, Sergeant," Derek said, "there *is* more. You've just seen the highlighted images. What follow are about a thousand more images arranged in sequence and time-delayed to produce the effect of motion and recreate the scene just as it occurred. Watch," Derek told him and pressed another button on the remote.

The projector produced a high-pitched tone as the tip of the pyramid pivoted on an oblique axis, revealing a miniscule aperture from which a thin, sheet-like, blue laser burst forth. It grew wider as it approached the reddened screen and engulfed it, coating it with a violet hue. Like dancers on a stage, the lasers played on the screen. A brilliant range of reds, blues, and violets appeared in a seemingly random fashion.

Yet there was nothing random about the thermalyzed grey forms that took shape on the screen or the colorful beams that added definition and animation to the previously lifeless images. A strobe-light effect was produced as the images sequentially appeared.

Derek took a seat by the table as he and the others attentively watched the series of events unfold.

They watched as the killer slowly limped through the

deserted, darkened street, stalking his victim into the park. As the victim turned in fear, his attacker upon him. As one man drew a concealed gun and the other fell dead. As the killer searched the dead man's pockets then smashed the man's eyeglasses on the ground. As Ojo entered the park, offering assistance to the tall stranger who quickly threw the gun across the park, locking it between two large branches of a huge oak tree, the silencer still in his hand. As Ojo came upon the body, the silencer offered by its owner. As the killer slowly limped out of sight, leaving both victims for the cops who were soon upon them.

"There you have it, Sergeant Brotsky," Derek said as the images faded and the projector turned itself off. "One man *murdered*. Another man *framed*. Both by the *same* son-of-a-bitch. The evidence on this disc," he went on as he removed the cartridge from the projector, "is proof *positive* that Ojo had absolutely *nothing* to do with the murder."

"You've uncovered some startling evidence," Brotsky said. "If I could just be sure this laser show of yours wasn't produced by Nintendo," he continued, pulling the phone to the table. "Operator, Sergeant Brotsky," he started after hitting a couple keys on the phone. "Can you patch me through to Cobra 44?" he asked after a brief pause. "Please ring me back when you get 'em," he finished, returning the receiver. "I'm gonna have to double-check your story."

"That shouldn't be a problem," Derek said.

"Just have your officers in the park retrieve the gun from the tree," Ojo suggested as the phone rang.

"That's *exactly* what I'm gonna do," the Sergeant said as he lifted the receiver. "Brotsky."

"O'Connor, sir," a loud Irish voice sounded through the phone and into the quiet room.

"Have you found the murder weapon yet?" Brotsky asked.

"Haven't retrieved it yet, sir," the cop replied.

"Well, just listen to me, O'Connor. Can you see a huge oak tree on the east end of the park?"

"There are *two*, sir."

"Do *both* have a pair of large branches that look like arms?"

"Only one does, sir."

"*That's* the one, O'Connor."

"Salavari's standing right by it."

"Fine. I want you to get up there and tell me what you find between those branches."

"*Between* the *branches*, sir?"

"*Yes*, O'Connor! *Between* the *branches!*"

"Okay, sir. Okay. I'll be right back," he said.

Brotsky rested the receiver on his leg. "No *gun*, no *case*," he said as he turned from Derek to Ojo.

Tomkin jotted several notes on a small pad but remained silent.

"And what if it *is* there?" Ojo asked, his knee

nervously bouncing up and down.

"If it *is*? Then your story's got a chance. But there's still one thing that needs to be proven—that your buddy didn't plant the gun in that tree and then concoct this whole—"

"We've *got* it, sir!" the cop's voice shot through the phone. "The *gun*! We've got it! Are you still there, sir?"

"Right here," Brotsky answered.

"We've got the gun! Right where you said it would be!"

"Good work, O'Connor."

Derek smiled.

"But how did you know it would be there?" O'Connor asked.

"Just a hunch," Brotsky said.

"*Right*," Derek mumbled.

"I guess that's why you're the Sergeant, sir."

"Yeah. Guess so. Anyway, just tag it, bag it and be careful for prints."

"Already done, sir," O'Connor said.

Brotsky placed the phone on the floor. "Well, we've recovered our murder weapon," he said. "But there's *one* thing I still need."

Derek exchanged another glance with Tomkin then removed the Thermalyzer from the carrying case.

"What the hell is *that?*" Brotsky asked.

"Your answer," Derek said as he ran a cord from the Thermalyzer to the back of the projector, activating the onyx device. "What you still don't know is whether or not the images are fakes. Am I right, Sergeant?"

"You're damn right."

"Then I'll show you how I obtained them—using *this*," Derek said as he lifted the viewer and scanned the small room. "The images are produced by absorbing the heat given off by the scanned objects, whether the objects are there *now* or were there *recently* enough so the heat hasn't completely dissipated. You follow? It's a *photo time machine*," he said and winked at Ojo.

Ojo nodded.

"Uh ... yeah, sure," Brotsky replied.

Derek activated the projector and the images appeared on the screen, one at a time. Brotsky was amazed as the first picture appeared. He saw his own darkened image standing by the door. Images of the others stood behind him.

The projector hummed as the next image appeared. Then the next. And the one after that. Derek was seen with remote in hand, standing to the side of the screen. Brotsky with phone receiver to ear. Christine seated beside Tomkin. Ojo pensively viewing the projector.

Like clockwork, the images appeared. Brotsky seemed delighted. Until the images focused on the front of the table.

A naked man, visible from the neck down, was slightly hunched over the table's edge with a pair of smooth, toned legs thrown over his shoulders. The rest of a slim, well-contoured body lay spread across the table. The man's hands barely covered the large breasts they held as he pressed them together, the large, firm nipples rising between his spread fingers. A young woman's face, partially obscured by the superimposed image of the projector and the shadow produced by the rim of the policeman's cap she wore, could be made out. Her eyes were almost completely closed, her mouth partly open as she bit her lower lip. Her arms were thrown back, partly covered by her long hair as her lover pressed into her.

Brotsky's jaw dropped and Christine blushed. Tomkin's spectacles fell from his nose and cracked on the hard table.

The next image appeared. A more direct angle provided a full view of the woman's face and the tilted cap on her head. Its shield shone out in the dim lighting and the three numbers on it could easily be read.

666.

Familiar numbers, indeed.

"Want to see it in motion, Sergeant?" Derek asked.

Ojo started to laugh.

Brotsky turned furiously red. "That won't be necessary, smart ass!" he snapped.

"I'd say we've established evidential credibility, wouldn't you, Mr. Tomkin," Derek asked the attorney.

Tomkin nodded with a smile.

"You've made your point," Brotsky conceded.

"Then am I free to leave?" Ojo anxiously asked.

"Yeah. You're outta here," Brotsky replied as Derek returned the projector and Thermalyzer to the case. "But don't disappear on me. You're my only witness."

"What do you think of that?" Ojo asked. "A few hours ago, I was a murder suspect. And now, I am a witness," he said as Christine threw her arms around him.

"Only in America," Derek said, grabbing Ojo's hand.

"Just one more thing," Brotsky interrupted. "I'll need those discs."

"Of course," Derek said, pulling the cartridge from his pocket and offering it to Brotsky.

"*And* your little *demo* cartridge," he said with a flat expression.

"Oh, that *too*, huh?" Derek said with a narrow smile as he reached into the case and withdrew the disc from the drive. He dropped both in Brotsky's open hand.

"As much as I hate to admit it, you did some fine detective work here," Brotsky said as Derek and Christine walked around the table toward the door. "If there's *anything* I can ever help you with—"

"As a matter of fact," Derek interrupted, a wide smile on his face as he pulled the folded parking ticket from his pocket, "there is."

Another piece of paper fell from Derek's pocket. Tomkin bent to retrieve it and noticed the image of the silver-haired man on the paper. He stared at the image for a long moment.

"Van Husted," Tomkin finally said.

Derek and Ojo exchanged a silent glance.

"That's Elmer van Husted."

CHAPTER SIX

The definition of insanity is doing the same thing
over and over again but expecting different results.

Albert Einstein

Christine sat by the small desk several feet from the bed. Her eyes glided from the picture of Derek and herself that sat in a glass frame beside the turquoise lava lamp on the nightstand, to the large bed where Derek lay asleep, to the array of papers on the desktop.

She would kill him in his sleep, she thought. She would kill him tonight. It was already planned. Nothing could go wrong. Nothing. When the Boston shuttle passed overhead at precisely 12:10 a.m., as it did every night, she would pull the trigger. No one would hear. He would be dead. Finally.

She eyed the clock. Already midnight. Just a few minutes longer. And it would be done. Her eyes dropped to the pistol in her hand. The trigger was already cocked. She ran her fingers over the barrel almost affectionately. With both hands she lifted the heavy weapon and carefully aimed.

As she awaited the deafening cry of the jet's engines she lowered the gun and moved to the window at the other side of the room. She parted the blinds and peered toward the sky. The moon was full. A thick fog partially obscured it.

She turned again. Streams of moonlight burst into the room through the gap in the blinds and shot across her lover's face. She stared at his tense brow. At the troubled look on his face. At his tightly drawn lips. If he had suffered just half the pain he had caused her. Just half, she thought. But he would pay. For all the pain. All the suffering. For everything. He would pay. And he would pay tonight. With his life.

A distant sound could be heard in the still sky. She raised the gun again as the sound grew louder. The jet passed overhead with a thunderous noise as the blinds fell shut and the room darkened again. She fired. It would soon be over, she thought. She kept shooting, almost without looking. She loaded shot after shot into the motionless body that lay there in the darkness. Until the pistol clicked. She had emptied the gun's contents. It was done. Finally.

She dropped the gun at her feet and moved toward the window again. She parted the blinds and watched the plane disappear in the distance. Light from the moon made its way into the room another time. She would turn and look at him one last time. She didn't want to. She had to. With a quick gesture she faced her dead lover. She was horrified. There was no blood. No bullet holes. Nothing.

"Should've used these," a voice called from behind her as several small objects struck her back lightly, then fell to the ground.

She turned quickly. In the dim light of the room she could make out the figure of a tall woman standing in the doorway. She hadn't even heard the door open. The woman stood there loading one bullet after another into the gun she held.

"Guess I didn't have a chance to tell you," said the dead man who now sat up in bed as she nervously turned to face him. "I switched the bullets with blanks last night," he explained with a crooked smile.

"That's right," the woman with the gun said. "But you can have them back. All of them."

She fired several times. The room echoed. The woman fell dead.

Christine was pleased. She leaned back in her cushiony seat, lightly tapping her pen against the edge of an open drawer as she eyed the rows of hardcovers in the glass bookcase that sat to the side of her desk.

Her eyes passed from *Dune* to *Scruples* to *Blood Simple* to *Suspect,* her first novel, to the tall stack of papers that sat in a neat pile atop the desk, to the page attached to the clipboard she was holding. *The woman fell dead.* She reread the line several times, then turned to the pile of papers.

"We're almost there," she proudly said as Derek moved about, his legs tangled in a ball of sheets, his head buried beneath a pillow. "C'mon, you lazy bum. Wake up," Christine told him.

"Huh?" a dull tired voice came from beneath the pillow.

"C'mon, it's already noon!" she said, pulling the pillow off his head as he turned on his side, covering his eyes to block out the light. "A little of this," she teased, sticking her tongue out playfully as he squinted between his fingers," and you're out for the count!"

"Do that again."

"I think I'm gonna have to cut down."

"*Go* down?"

"*Cut* down!"

"Oh."

"What about the museum?"

"Museum?"

"Museum. You promised."

"I did?"

"You did."

"You sure?"

"Sure, I'm sure."

"Museum."

"Yes. Museum."

"Okay. But first," he said, sitting up and leaning forward as he grabbed Christine's arm, pulling her into the bed as they both fell backwards laughing, "do that again."

A mischievous grin rounded her lips.

* * *

The museum was crowded. Small groups of people flocked around the various exhibits. Around the Engels. The Hegels. The Picassos. The Monets. The largest group stood admiringly before the tremendous Miró which hung from the wall above the parallel escalators. The ordered randomness of the colorful images carefully placed on the black background intrigued Derek. This was one of his favorites. One of Christine's too. They stood apart from the crowd and off to the side where they mused over several of Dali's works. *Persistence of Memory*, the work that epitomized the surrealistic expression, was another piece that fascinated Derek.

He stared intensely at the center of the painting, an area in the foreground where a horse-like caricature lay on its side near a small pit, saddled by a willowing timepiece with a spade at its feet. *What could it mean*, Derek asked himself this time as he had each of the other dozen or more times he had studied this piece.

Images of the Spanish Civil War came to mind as Derek placed the work within that period and envisioned the caricature to represent a Spanish soldier and the pit his grave. The soft melting timepieces draped across the central figure and other objects in the painting, each bearing a face displaying a different time, seemed to represent more than just the passage of time but the passing of a historic era. Another image filled Derek's mind as he stared at the gold timepiece in the corner of the painting—the gold medallion in the canister. *What did it mean? Why had the silver-haired man left it for him with the dog tags and photos? And why was it cut in half? What did it mean?*

What did it all mean?

As Derek lost himself in these images and thoughts, his eyes aimlessly danced around the large gallery and settled upon a bronze bench several feet away where a rather distinguished-looking, middle-aged woman sat.

"Jesus Christ!" he muttered under his breath.

On the bench beside the woman was the morning paper which he hadn't yet seen. Closed and folded in half, the headline could easily be read.

"What's the matter," Christine asked.

He just nodded in the direction of the bench.

'SURGEON SHOT DEAD IN PARK,' the headline read.

Derek moved toward the woman.

"'Scuse me, ma'am. Mind if I—" he began, pointing to the paper when the woman interrupted.

"Done with it, dear. All yours," she said with a smile.

Derek returned the smile, then grabbed the paper and quickly unfolded it. He read to himself, letting a word or phrase slip through his lips now and then as Christine looked on.

"*Washington Square ... successful surgeon ... University Hospital ... found shot ...* holy shit ..." Derek said as he looked up for a brief second. He nervously turned several pages and read on. "*Calvin Barnes ... Chief of Orthopedics ... this* is our poor schlub ... *thought not to be a robbery ... eyewitness questioned ... real* smart ... *suspect with limp described ... gun found by police ...* yeah, *right!*" He looked up again and ran a couple fingers over his unshaven chin. "I know this guy," Derek said.

"Huh?"

"The dead guy. I know him from somewhere," he insisted as his eyes casually returned to the Dali. He stared for a moment at a number of bugs that crawled on the gold timepiece. "That's *it!*" he suddenly said.

"What do you mean?"

"Just find a phone."

"How do you know him?"

"I don't."

"But you just said—"

"I *met* him. I meant I *met* him!"

"When?"

"Yesterday."

"Yesterday?"

"Yeah, yesterday. Why do you always repeat everything I say?"

"I *don't* always repeat everything you say. Where'd you meet him?"

"*There's* one," he said, lightly jogging across the marble floor.

Just as he reached the phone, a shriveled old lady with

blue-streaked platinum hair from out of nowhere grabbed the receiver and dropped a coin in the box with one hand as she leaned her hand-whittled cane against the wall with the other.

"Damn!"

"So where did you meet him?" Christine asked again when she caught up with him.

"He was one of the surgeons Ojo and I met with at the hospital yesterday. We were pitching the QT7."

"Why would anyone want to kill a surgeon?"

"You don't know some of these surgeons."

"*What?*"

"I'm joking. Keep it down," Derek said as he motioned with his hand. "I really don't know. The tall stiff had to be a hired gun."

"How do you know that?"

"Can't be sure. But the silencer. The gloves. The half-brain he used to set Ojo up. Couldn't have been his first hit."

"You're probably right."

"I know I'm right," he insisted as he turned and watched the woman dig deep into the large pocketbook hanging from her shoulder and pull a fistful of change from it.

As she dropped several coins into the box, she intentionally turned to catch Derek's eye. A satisfied grin rounded the corners of her mouth and added additional wrinkles to her shriveled face.

"Old bitch," Derek mumbled as he pulled his wallet from his pocket and a thin metallic card from one of its flaps. "Last time I leave my damn Teledisc in the car," he added. When the woman turned her back, he pressed a small button on the card's face.

"Hello, hello ... *hello!*" the woman yelled into the phone.

There was no answer. The line had gone dead.

"*Hello! Hello!*" she yelled again before dropping another coin into the box and redialing. Derek pressed the button again as he tried to restrain his laughter.

Again, the line went dead. She pressed the hook down but nothing was returned. "Damn thing!" she mumbled. "Must be busted!" she went on under her breath as she slammed the receiver down, picked up her cane and hobbled away.

"Now, that wasn't very nice," Christine said with a devilish smile as Derek lifted the receiver and pressed another button on the card. The phone clicked and a handful of change dropped into the phone's receptacle. He scooped it out and quickly placed his call.

"Guess it's not busted after all," he said with a chuckle. "But the line's busy."

He held the card to the receiver and slid a tiny bar from one side of the card to the other then back again, before returning the receiver to its hook. He winked at

Christine and she smiled back.

"Three, two, one," Derek counted down, then shot the phone with his finger just as it rang. He answered it. "Phone busters."

"Hey, Derek," Ojo's tired voice crawled through the receiver.

"Seen the paper?"

"You kidding? I've been in a coma all afternoon. Since I got back from the police station. You just woke me."

"Sorry. But get this. Our buddy in the park turned out to be one of the surgeons from yesterday."

"The killer is a *surgeon?!*"

"No. The *dead* guy, Ojo. The *dead* guy!"

"Holy shit!"

"Exactly. There's more. Those idiots at the station told the reporters about a *witness!*"

"Anyone we know?" Ojo asked.

"Three guesses."

"I was afraid you'd say that."

"Probably nothing to worry about but stay there. We'll be over in fifteen."

"Oooooh, shit!" Ojo said before the line disconnected.

"Well, you can't say I didn't take you to the museum," Derek said as he replaced the receiver and turned toward

Christine.

"A big twenty minutes with Dali and Miró. How can I complain?" she said half-seriously with a slight snicker.

They raced down the narrow escalator, across the large lobby and out the main entrance onto 53rd Street. As they walked down the block toward the parking lot on 6th Avenue, they passed a disheveled, dirty-looking vagrant who offered a cup with one hand and an open palm with the other. They walked several steps past him when Derek stopped suddenly and stuck his hand deep into the pocket of his overcoat. From it, he pulled several coins. They probably belonged to the woman with the cane but it didn't matter. As if this small effort of his might make some difference in some way, he backed up a few steps and tossed the change into the man's cup. It didn't. The coins dropped into the half-filled coffee cup with a soft plop and a small splash. The man looked down into the cup with saddened eyes, then up at Derek's apologetically-raised brows and the pathetic look on his face. The two stared at each other for a moment. Nothing was said.

* * *

"I am *screwed!*" Ojo said as he stood over the paper spread across the coffee table and carelessly tucked in his wrinkled shirt. "Those *idiots!*" he said, referring to the *Post*, as he read pieces of the story out loud. "'*Witness said to live in area of park ... returning home ... discovered body in park ... saw suspect standing over victim ... provided description for police.*' I'm a *dead* man! That's *it!* I'm *dead!*"

"Ojo, there's something else," Derek carefully interrupted as he caught Christine biting her lip through the corner of his eye.

"What now?! I'm *already* dead! Something else? What is it? Another paternity suit? Or maybe Arti sold the shop while we were out? Oh, no, I've got it. The stiff from the park's waiting for me downstairs with a box of chocolates. After all, *life is like a box of*—that's it, isn't it?"

"Not exactly."

"Well, *what* then? Huh? *What?!*"

"We passed your Corvette on the other side of the park."

"A real beaut, isn't she?"

"Sure is."

"Oh, no. Damn! Not another boot!"

"No, nothing like that."

"Oh, good. Did you check out the Pirelli tires? All 'round. Cost a small fortune. Worth every penny. Almost a shame to ride on them."

Ojo was proud of his car. He wasn't a materialistic man but he had a weakness for fast cars. And his new ride was his favorite yet.

"I don't think you'll have to worry about that."

"Guess you're right. But what am I going to do about this?!" Ojo said as he angrily grabbed the paper off the table and crumpled it in his hand. "Huh? What about *this?!"*

"We're gonna have to keep our eyes open. Even when we sleep. We have to get this guy before ..."

"Go ahead. Say it. Before *he* gets *me*!"

"You're damn right. Before he gets you or anyone else."

"Why don't you hand me some of that paper," Christine interrupted. "Your tank's still leaking," she said as she watched the tiny droplets of saltwater slide from one of the corners of the hundred-gallon aquarium that sat against the wall opposite the couch onto its black marble base then down one of the granite column supports onto the already-soaked pages of newspaper that lay at the foot of the structure.

"Yeah, I know. The only thing the epoxy glue sealed were two of my fingers," he said as he handed her several more pages of the newspaper. "Had to use a razor to separate them," he added as he turned a small dial on the wall by the couch. The narrow vertical blinds rotated more and more as the dial turned, allowing hazy rays of sunlight to fall inside the room.

"This is really interesting," Christine said, flattening a wrinkled page with her hand while she quickly read through a short article.

"What is?" Derek asked.

"This," she answered as she folded the page in half twice and pointed to an article on the bottom of it. "Take a look."

Derek took the folded page from her as Ojo moved alongside to look on.

She continued to pack the dry pages around the column, scooped the wet ones into a ball and tossed it several feet toward a waste basket in the corner that resembled a miniature mailbox. Before the ball of paper hit the box, a red light flashed on its side and the mail chute automatically opened to catch its midair delivery.

'ANOTHER CHILD HAS BEEN BORN WITH GROTESQUE DEFORMITIES,' the headline read.

'3rd MONSTROSITY BORN IN PAST THREE WEEKS,' the byline added.

Derek and Ojo looked at each other for a moment and then returned to the article as Christine squeezed between them.

"Is that the strangest thing or what?" she asked. "I read about it last week in the *Post,*" she went on as they continued reading. "The first two were born in Houston a couple weeks ago. Doctors say they've never seen anything like it. They thought the two women had been exposed to some toxic waste or something in Texas but the third kid was born in New York with the same deformities and the mother has never even been to Texas. Isn't that crazy?"

"That's an understatement. Listen to this," Derek said as he read from the article. "'*Child's limbs severely shortened ... long bones of both legs fused together ... ribs attached to form sheets of solid bone.'* Do you believe this?"

"The kid's wearing a suit of bony armor," Ojo said.

"Sounds like it," Derek said as he read on. "'*Fingers fused into a single bony mass ... brain severely malformed due to the extent of bony overgrowth of skull ... child has neither eye sockets, auditory canals, nor any remnant of a mouth!*' What in hell could've caused this nightmare?"

"The doctors are baffled," Christine said.

"Kinda makes you put things in perspective, doesn't it?" Derek suggested.

"Yeah," she answered, "and think about what's really important. Like asking ourselves if our little problems are really problems at all. What d'ya think?" she asked Ojo.

"Guess so. And having asked myself that, I realize mine are!" Ojo said, turning to face Derek. "What do we do now? What do *I* do now?"

"*We* find the killer," Derek flatly responded.

"How do you suggest we do that? He could be anywhere by now," Ojo said.

"Could be. But he's gotta be *somewhere*."

"Would you check those drawers over there, please," Ojo asked Christine facetiously as he pointed to a bureau to the side of the tank.

"Look. We're gonna find this son-of-a-bitch. And I think I know how."

"Oh, yeah? *How?*"

"We're gonna hunt him down. Get him on the run.

Set *him* up! It is *his* turn, isn't it?" Derek asked with a calculating grin.

"You bet your ass it is! But where does the hunt begin?" Ojo asked.

Derek avoided the question. "Well, what're we waiting for? Grab your coats, guys. We're outta here," he said. "First stop, the bomb shelter."

"Now you're talking. We can take my car," Ojo offered.

Derek and Christine exchanged a silent glance.

From the steps of the brownstone, they could see the gathering around the roped-off area where the body was found on the other side of the park. It didn't surprise them. It would probably continue for days.

"You guys think I may have overreacted?" Ojo asked as they walked across the street and onto the park grounds. "I mean, the paper didn't give enough details for anyone to really know *I'm* the witness. Did it? I don't think so. Besides," he went on, "why would anyone come after *me*? It's not like I *know* anything. What do you say?"

There was no response. They passed a group of men playing chess in the shade of several huge trees, a number of children who flew by on the back wheels of their skateboards, and several gymnasts who performed various stunts for the large group that had gathered around them, as they crossed to the other side of the park.

"Well, what do you guys think?"

"I'd sure like to think so," Derek began, "but I'm really not so sure it's gonna be that easy."

"What do you mean?" Ojo asked as they crossed under the Arch.

"There's something else."

"Something *else?*"

"Afraid so."

"That's right. You started to say something upstairs but didn't finish. Well, what is it? What?!" Ojo nervously asked as they turned the corner and walked past a row of cars.

Derek exchanged another glance with Christine before he responded. "Over there," he said and pointed across the street toward Ojo's car.

Ojo had forgotten all about it even as they approached it from down the street. But there it was. Nothing was said for a few moments. Ojo just stood there. Numb. The blood drained from his dark face. Derek and Christine looked on silently.

"My baby," he finally said in a cracked whispery voice.

The glistening black convertible pathetically sat flat on the ground. All four tires had been slashed, the canvas top ripped apart, and both sides keyed all the way across.

"This was taped to the windshield," Derek said as he handed Ojo a folded sheet of paper.

He opened it. Several words were smeared on the

paper in blood.

'DEAD NIGGER WALKING!'

Ojo was silent. He crumpled the paper in his hand and let it fall to the ground. "So where does the hunt begin?"

Nothing was said for a long moment. Then Derek bent to retrieve the paper. "Right *here.*"

CHAPTER SEVEN

Eureka! [I have found it!]

Archimedes

And a hunt it would be. *But who would be hunting whom? After all, what do we know about tracking down a killer,* Derek asked himself. *And how close would we come to getting ourselves killed in the process? But it wasn't something we'd gone looking for,* he kept telling himself. Ojo had walked right into it. And the killer was not going to let him walk right out. Not without more blood on his hands. Ojo's. *But there has to be a way out. And we will find it,* Derek convinced himself. *We have to. But how? How?!*

Derek sat by one of the terminals in the far corner of

the workshop while Ojo and Christine worked on the computer in the adjacent office. As they plugged away, trying to break into the medical databank at Bellevue where the dead surgeon was taken, Derek stared at the frozen image on the monitor. Bits and pieces of unfinished thoughts raced through his head.

This wouldn't be the first time we had played Dick Tracy, he thought. *And it wouldn't be the first time someone's neck was on the cutting block. But it would be the first time it was one of ours! Sure, we had come close. A number of times,* Derek recalled. *A good number. But the circumstances had never centered around murder. A case or two of bigamy here, some embezzlement there. But never a murder. More than that, never had either of us been among the principal players. Just a couple of outsiders looking in, trying to help out. Surveillance equipment, perhaps. Maybe an occasional high-tech laser for one purpose or another. But nothing this dangerous. But then,* he remembered, *there was the bank heist. That's right. And the stakeout.*

He thought about that for a few moments. The image on the screen became hazy as his mind wandered. Back almost two years. *Some stakeout,* he thought. *Lasted four days. Cramped in a stuffy attic during a blistering summer week with two huge side-of-beef, dumb-as-shit detectives while Ojo sat in an unmarked sedan with the blonde. It was a miracle that they realized the statuesque brunette who returned to the brownstone under scrutiny each night was the same as the tall guy who left in a business suit each morning. A goddamn freak! That's what he was. With all the trimmings. Then it got weird.*

But how exactly did he get involved with the whole thing anyway, Derek's mind wandered. And why? He thought for a moment as a soft smile rounded his lips. He recalled it well. An image of himself in a black trench coat and crooked hat, with a cigarette dangling from the corner of his mouth, flashed in his mind.

Of all the invention joints in all the towns in all the world, she walked into mine. Mounds of blonde hair and curves in all the right places. She was gorgeous. An absolute doll. And she needed my help. This was better than a Bogie flick, he thought. *This was real.*

She was a reporter. And a damn good one I learned later on. Not the sort that sat on her rump waiting for a story to fall into her lap. No, not this one. She would follow a lead and produce a story. That's why she came to the bomb shelter. Another lead. And there was something she needed. From me.

"I'm looking for a camera."

"Can you give me a little more to work with?"

"One that can take shots in the dark."

"Any camera can do that, honey. Ever hear of a flash?" *Yeah, I was a sarcastic shit even then. But she was serious.*

"I mean without a flash. Without any light! Look, if you can't help me, I'll just be on my way," she said, then turned and started to walk out.

"Okay, okay. Just relax. No need to get all steamed." Derek tried to back-peddle. "I may have just what you need."

A relieved smile rounded her pretty face.

"What was it you said you needed it for, anyway?"

"I didn't."

"That's right. You didn't. Why don't I show you the camera?"

"Why don't you?"

I took it from the shelf and handed it to her.

"It's gorgeous. How does it work?"

"Very simple. Has infrared and sonic sensors. They serve the same purpose as a light sensor in any other camera. A microchip cartridge analyzes the info from these sensors and produces a picture."

"This is exactly what I need—I think."

"You still haven't told me what you need it for."

"Is that so important?"

"Guess not. But if you only need it for a short while, maybe I could let you borrow it. Otherwise, it'll cost nineteen hundred."

"Nineteen hundred *dollars?*" she asked as her eyes opened wide. "So, did I tell you I write for the *Times?*"

"Yeah, yeah. I think you were just mentioning that."

"Well, the bottom line is I'm trying to crack a story."

"I'm listening, Miss Lane. Or can I call you Lois?"

She grinned but ignored him. "You heard about the guys that knocked over First National last year?"

"Can't say that I did."

"Well, they made away with seven million—"

"Not too shabby."

"And killed two bystanders. The point is, they slipped up and were caught three days later."

"Sounds like the story's already been written."

"Except for this—they escaped from prison two nights ago and I received a tip as to where they may be heading."

"Let me guess. How about back to where they stashed the loot?"

"Well, that didn't take a brain surgeon. But only I know where that is. Not even the cops know."

"And the camera?"

"I want to stake them out. Get the exclusive story and shots."

"Would that be shots of them or by them?"

The woman said nothing.

"I'll let you use the camera on one condition, Miss—"

"Stratton. Christine Stratton. On what condition?"

"That you let me help you," Derek offered. "Don't spend too much time thinking, now."

"Hmmm," she pouted.

"Your pretty lips are saying one thing but your sexy eyes are saying another."

"My eyes didn't even open their mouth," she answered with a grin. "But I guess I'm out of luck without your help, huh?"

"Completely."

"Then help all you want," she said with a shrewd smile.

"Don't you even want to know my name?"

"Already do. You see, Mr. Cannon, I take my reporting very seriously and I always do my homework. I knew you had the camera before I walked into your shop and I was counting on your insisting on helping. That's why I came to you."

"Clever. Very clever," Derek said and laughed. "Well, that was the best move you could've made. But for starters, why don't you call me Derek?"

"Okay, Derek."

"Why don't we meet tonight and set things in motion—I mean, get started."

Christine laughed. "That would be great."

"I'll probably bring my partner."

"Ojo?"

"Yeah, Ojo. Know him too, do you?"

"Kinda. I already spoke with him. This morning. Before you arrived. He was pretty sure you'd be interested."

"He was, was he?" Derek mumbled. "You do do your

homework, don't you?"

She just smiled warmly.

"I like that."

Derek crossed his feet on the bench and took a swallow from the cup he had been holding. His focus returned to the frozen image on the monitor. The killer stood above his fallen victim. Derek struck several buttons on the keyboard on his lap and the image thawed.

The tall stiff kneeled beside the curled up dead man. He turned him flat on his back and searched his pockets. He removed several small objects from the man's pants pockets, although it was difficult to tell what they were. He quickly put them back in, so neither did it matter. He pulled the man's wallet from his overcoat pocket and spent a moment going through its contents tossing it back into the man's pocket a moment later without taking anything. The killer looked up at the sky for an instant and then looked back at the body that lay at his feet. There was something he wanted. Something important, it seemed. Something worth killing for. He removed the man's watch and examined it carefully. He did the same with a bracelet the dead man had been wearing. But he took neither.

While replacing the watch on the man's wrist, the killer's gaze fell upon the cracked eyeglasses that lay on the ground. He lifted them from the ground and studied them for a few moments. A smile broad enough to detect on the monitor distorted his ugly face. He carefully broke one of the arms off the frame and replaced the eyeglasses beside the man's head. As he stood, stuffing what he had killed for in his pocket, he turned quickly as if someone had called to him from behind.

Derek pressed another key and the image froze. He knew the rest of that story. No need to run through it again. But the eyeglass frame. He hadn't noticed that before. There was something special about that frame, Derek thought. Something worth killing for. But what? He hit several keys and the scene moved in reverse one frame at a time. When the killer appeared holding up the broken arm of the frame, Derek locked on the image and sent it to the printer.

His thoughts wandered while he waited. He tried to take another swallow from his empty cup, then unfolded its rolled up edge as an image of the dilapidated attic became fresh in his mind. *He could see the cluttered boxes and the light bulb that hung freely from a wire attached to the shallow triangular ceiling. The same bulb that either one or the other detective would bang his head against every few minutes. That is, till the fatter of the two tore it from the ceiling and slammed it against the wall, smashing the bulb and almost blowing their cover.*

They made some twosome, Derek thought. *One looked like a redheaded version of Dom DeLuise and the other could have been John Candy's double. But they needed them. If Christine was going to get her story, they had to make the bust. Simple as that. No cops, no bust. No bust, no story.*

So there we were. Larry, Moe and Curly. Stuck in a tiny attic rotating watch through the small circular window in the wall that faced across the street. The other windows in the house had been boarded up since the fire that almost levelled the place six months earlier. It wouldn't have been a good idea to start changing things around. The windows and all. Would've drawn suspicion.

From time to time Tucker, the redheaded detective, would radio the car where Ojo sat with Christine. Goose, as the other liked to be called, checked their location with binoculars, exchanging spots with either of them every couple of hours.

Aside from the fact that the guy in the house was a transvestite, nothing else seemed to be going on. Certainly nothing that was front page news. The stakeout looked like it was running dry. Christine's lead seemed to have been a diversion. And the effort, a waste. Until the fourth night.

It was around midnight. A black sedan with two men in it pulled into the driveway across the street. A short guy in a grey vest got out of the car. *That's our man,* Derek thought. Tucker pegged him in a second. The stakeout had not been entirely useless. The wait had paid off. He pulled a duffel bag from the back seat onto his shoulder and headed for the front door. With the door already open as he reached the top step, his significant other appeared, in full garb. They embraced passionately.

"This is disgusting!" Tucker yelled as he watched through binoculars while Goose tipped back to finish off another root beer. "Next thing they'll be ..." he started, then paused. "Jesus Christ! He's got his tongue down that pervert's throat!" he said as Goose sprayed his entire mouthful, soaking Tucker's face.

They entered the house and the door closed behind

them. Several moments later, they appeared in an upstairs bedroom. The windows had no curtains. The view was clear. The tall guy in the dress and heels began packing a suitcase that had been spread open on the bed while his short partner searched through the bureau drawers and then the closet, angrily throwing things all over the room. He turned to the tall guy who pointed toward a small nightstand beside the bed. He pulled the drawer free and dumped its contents on the bed. From among the numerous papers, pill bottles, coins and other things that fell on the bed and floor as he sorted through them almost frantically, he found what he had been looking for. A key.

Perhaps the arm of the eyeglass frame was a key of some sort, Derek thought. He thought the same of the gold medallion he held in a closed hand. He nervously fingered its cut edge as the printer beeped. A photo slid onto the printer tray. He lifted it into the light and studied it closely. He could barely make out what appeared to be a scratch that ran almost the entire length of the arm. Derek placed the photo back in the tray and with the tip of a fiber optic pen, outlined the broken frame on the surface of the screen, pressing a red button on the keyboard.

The image on the screen disappeared. Except for the area Derek had outlined. He turned a dial on the side of the monitor and grinned slyly as the scratch on the side of the frame enlarged. The scratch was no longer a scratch but an engraving. The engraving—a code. INHHSOOXOO22619435. *A key, indeed,* Derek thought while he stared at the medallion in his hand.

Maybe as important as the one the short guy found in

that drawer. His mind raced back to that eventful night. As they left the room and fell out of view, Derek watched through the small window while Christine stepped out of the car that was parked down the block.

"What the hell is she doing?!" he yelled, grabbing Goose's walkie. "Ojo! Get her ass back in the damn car! Before she gets it blown off!"

But it was too late. She had already begun walking toward the house. Ojo went after her. But there was no turning back. Together they walked past the driveway where the sedan was parked then turned at the corner and walked toward the back of the house.

The odd couple appeared at the front door with the suitcase. And a large attaché case. They walked toward the car.

"They've got it!" Derek said with excitement. "What're we waiting for?"

"Hold on there, young fella," Tucker said. "This is where experience comes into play." He spoke into the walkie. "Cobra 4 and Cobra 7. You read me?" They responded. They were ready.

The tall guy tossed the suitcase on the back seat. But neither got in the car. They started walking toward the abandoned house with the attaché.

"They're coming here," Derek nervously said. "We're trapped!"

"Think it's more like *they're* trapped, buddy," Goose said.

"But we're stuck up here in this shithole of an attic!"

"Yeah. Just you, me, Tucker and a coupl'a sidekicks," Goose said as he patted the gun that hung at his waist. "Ya gotta figure like this," he went on. "In the four days we've been in this hole, we've searched every goddamn square inch and found nothing. The bucks ain't up here. But should those clods come up here anyway, we blow 'em away before they even open the door. My hunch is they're on their way down to the basement. They probably hid the green stuff there after the fire," he said as the creaky sound of the backdoor turning on its rotting hinges echoed through the silent house.

"Showtime, fellas," Tucker said as he checked the barrel of his gun. "You keep an eye on the guy in the car," he told Derek, "and you stand by the door," he told his partner. "I'm gonna have me a look around."

"You don't have a gun, do you?" Goose asked.

"Only this," Derek said with a hint of pride as he opened his palm to reveal a triangular object that glistened in the darkness like a prism. It had two red buttons on the top and a small hole on the front edge.

"You gonna beam our asses up or somethin'?" Goose kidded.

"I'll be fine with this," Derek responded.

"Just watch your asses," Tucker told them as he quietly opened the door and slid out.

Derek peered out the window at the black car while Goose stood by the door with his gun cocked and ready for business. He watched as Christine crawled up the driveway to within a few feet of the rear of the car, snapping several shots as she went. Ojo had gone around to the other side of the house and was now about ten feet in front of the car.

Derek's attention was distracted for a moment as the sound of a crowbar working its way through the latch on the basement door was suddenly heard. A sharp noise followed as the latch snapped and the basement door was thrown open.

He turned again to look through the window and found Christine lying beside the open car door with a gun pointed right at her head. The guy behind the wheel got out of the car. He pulled her to her feet wrapping his arm around her neck and rested the side of the barrel on her temple.

"Fuck," Derek muttered under his breath.

Ojo appeared a few seconds later with his hands in the air. He looked toward the attic window for a moment and nodded subtly. He knew Derek had been watching.

In an instant, Derek grabbed the walkie that Goose had left sitting on a box and smashed the window with it. He knocked out the remaining pieces of glass with the side of his fist and extended his arm through the hole. Derek had realized that there wasn't a clear shot through the dense branches otherwise. Aiming the triangular object across the street, he pressed one of the buttons with his thumb. The device produced a reddish glow.

"What the fuck are you—" Goose started to say as he came up from behind Derek.

"Just watch," Derek said. As the glow became brighter and brighter, he pressed the other button. A fiery red beam of light shot out of the small aperture like a bullet.

Almost immediately, Christine's captor fell to the ground. She pulled the gun from his limp hand as Ojo looked toward the window and nodded.

"You just can't be too safe these days," Derek said with a grin.

"I'm tellin' you," Goose said. "Better see what's goin' on downstairs."

They left the attic and carefully climbed down the two flights of decrepit stairs that led to the first floor of the house. Behind the stairway was the door that led to the basement. The broken latch and several large splinters of wood sat at Tucker's feet as they stood in the doorway, his gun held at eye level with both hands.

Goose nodded as Tucker passed through the door and slowly descended into the basement.

"Cover him," he told Derek. "I'm goin' around the side," he said, leaving through the backdoor.

Tucker moved further into the basement as Derek followed several feet behind. They could see the culprits standing by the far wall with their backs to them as they worked hard at removing several planks from the wooden floor with the crowbar. Tucker and Derek moved still closer and watched.

"You sure you didn't hear that a minute ago? Like broken glass or somethin'?" the short guy asked as he pulled another plank free and tossed it several feet onto a pile of broken wood.

The tall guy shook his head. "I don't think I did."

"There she is," the short one said as the small steel door that had been hidden beneath the planks of wood was uncovered. In its center was a dead bolt safe lock. He pulled the key from his pocket and turned the lock. "And there they are," he added as he opened the heavy door. "Seven big ones."

A soft rustling sound was heard. Derek turned to find Christine standing in the doorway. He waved for her to stand back. There was nothing else he could do.

"You hear that?" the short guy asked.

His partner nodded as he pulled one stack of money after another from the safe on the floor and piled them neatly in the attaché case.

A broken step creaked beneath Derek's foot as Tucker turned and caught his eye. All hell would soon break loose and they knew it.

"Freeze!" Tucker yelled as he jumped over the banister and landed in a shooting stance on the basement floor.

The short guy turned quickly, wildly firing off several shots as Tucker pulled the trigger of his .357 Magnum just once.

Derek tumbled down the stairs and landed on his back alongside a huge box as the triangular weapon slid across the basement floor. His shirt was bloodied. He'd been shot.

The short guy was thrown back several feet and slammed hard into the wall as blood spurted from his chest and pieces of flesh flew in all directions. His legs collapsed from under him and he fell to the floor as the bloody mess on the wall behind him was revealed. He was dead.

Tucker turned for a moment to see what had happened to Derek as the other guy quickly lifted his dress up to his waist and pulled a knife from under the garter belt on his thigh.

"Look out!" Derek yelled as the man's arm was thrown back and the knife was about to fly from his hand.

Another shot was heard and the knife dropped to the ground. The guy in the dress grabbed his wrist and fell to his knees as the blood dripped from his hand onto the floor.

A loud banging noise was then heard. Derek looked toward the far end of the windowless basement at a vent grill that protruded several inches from the low ceiling falling onto the floor. From the vent space, Goose jumped to the ground while Tucker handcuffed the fugitive.

"Glad you could make the show, buddy," Tucker said with a relieved smile as he stuffed the remaining money from the safe into the attaché. "Ball game's over," he said as he pulled the hood to his feet.

"How's Capt'n Kirk, over there?" Goose asked.

Christine was already by his side.

"Just a grazed shoulder," Derek answered. "I'll live."

"I'm so proud of you," Christine said as she brushed the hair away from his eyes. "I've got it all on film."

"You mean while we almost got killed in here, you were up there shooting photos?" He didn't wait for a response. "Never mind."

They left the house and walked across the street. They found Ojo sitting on the fender of the sedan in the driveway. Two men sat tied back to back on the ground several feet in front of him. Both were unconscious.

Before they could ask, Ojo told them. "Found the other guy in the house. Zapped him like the first one. They'll both be out for hours."

"Quite a toy you've got there," Goose said.

Ojo opened his palm to reveal a triangular device like the one Derek had used earlier. "Never leave home without it."

That brought a wide smile to Derek's face. He stared at the monitor and the code in the center of the screen, still fingering the gold medallion in his hand. INHHSOOXOO22619435. *What could it mean*, he asked himself. *And how did it connect to the dead surgeon?*

The detectives and those hoods were still on his mind. *Maybe they didn't look as swift or sharp as one would've expected. They were. Maybe they looked like they belonged in a bowling alley. They didn't. Maybe first impressions just don't matter sometimes,* Derek thought.

But the code. That mattered. Derek's eyes wandered to the photo he had found in the canister. It was propped against the monitor. The silver-haired man had left it for him. *Another piece of some puzzle,* he thought. He stared at the photo and squeezed the medallion. Suddenly he recognized the man standing beside his father. He was at least ten years younger and his bald head was covered with an officer's cap. But Derek recognized him. The Coke-bottle spectacles. The narrow eyes and small chin. The man in the photo was Tomkin. *Bradley N. Tomkin.*

CHAPTER EIGHT

*If we worked on the assumption that what is
accepted as true really is true, then there would be
little hope for advance.*

Orville and Wilbur Wright

"I-N-H-H-S-O-O-X-O-O ..."

Christine and Ojo exchanged a silent glance as they overheard Derek calling out a series of letters. Then a string of numbers.

"... 2-2-6-1-9-4-3-5."

It made no sense.

He repeated the strange message as he walked into the office, reading the numbers and letters on the computer-generated photo in his hand.

They exchanged another glance then stared at Derek for a moment with puzzled faces.

"*What?*" they both asked.

"A code," Derek answered.

"What code?" Ojo questioned.

"*This* code," he said as he held out the enlarged print. "Take a look," he offered. "*This* is what the killer was after."

"Where did he find it?" Christine asked. "Where'd *you* find it?"

"Right here," he replied and showed the two the earlier photo of the eyeglass frame and grinned proudly. "Who would've known?"

"*Unfuckinbelievable!*" Ojo said as he and Derek grabbed each other's hand.

"And you didn't think it was a professional hit, did you?" Derek asked Christine. "I don't know about you, but I don't think I ever would've thought of searching a man's *eyeglasses*. Not two minutes after shootin' out his lights. I guess you would have."

"I didn't say it wasn't a professional hit. I couldn't be sure. None of us could."

"Well, what do you think now, *Lois?*" Derek asked her with a teasing smile. He liked to call her 'Lois' when they disagreed. She didn't mind.

"Look, wise ass, it doesn't matter if the hit was professional or not. It doesn't even matter *why* the surgeon was killed. Or what that code has to do with anything. *If* it does," Christine responded, a bit put off.

"You don't think it does?" Derek asked her as Ojo took a seat by the door.

"Not right now, it doesn't. What matters now is making sure this nut doesn't make Ojo roomies with the doc in the icebox."

"So what would you do now?"

"Well, if it was a 'professional hit' like you said, then we'd better get hold of the slime that hired that killer. 'Cause you can be sure they're gonna try to get rid of any loose ends."

"You're damn right. Except for one thing. If we knew why the surgeon was killed that might lead us to his killer or, more importantly, the guys that wanted him dead. Wouldn't you agree, *Lois?*"

"Absolutely, *Clark,*" she responded, playing along.

"So, where do we stand with the Bellevue morgue?" Derek asked.

"Why don't I just show you," Ojo volunteered as he took a seat by the computer.

He struck the keyboard a few times. "The code is *history,*" he proudly announced as **STIFFdata** flashed on the screen. The three of them broke into laughter.

"I'm gonna have to get you started on *this* code,"

Derek said, waving the photo.

Ojo typed in the surgeon's name. *Barnes, C.* The computer spit out the entire file. *Medical history. Autopsy report. Organ damage. Histology reports. Cause of death. Bullet ballistics.* Everything.

Derek leaned over Ojo's shoulder and ran his finger down the screen. He stopped about halfway down.

"That's what we want. *Blood type AB positive. Hemoglobin HbA.* Not sure how it's gonna help us but let's compare it to the blood on that note for kicks. Nothing to lose."

"Arti's still working on it," Ojo told him.

"He's been at it forever, hasn't he?" Derek questioned as he looked through the glass door and past the spiral staircase down into the main area of the display room.

A number of people waited in line at the self-serve purchase area in the rear of the shop. As each stepped to the front of the line, they were greeted by a rather unusual computer that sat on an onyx counter. With a synthesized voice, the computer instructed the shopper to insert the cellophane strip containing the item code into a slot on the side of the small machine. After producing a number of tones, the computer displayed the item's price on its liquid crystal screen. The customer was then asked to insert either cash or credit into the appropriate slot below the readout and proceed to the pickup area several feet away. Once there, only moments would pass before the packaged item appeared on the counter, delivered by a conveyer belt system from the shop's inventory room in the basement.

Derek was pleased as his eyes passed from the lengthening purchase line to a group of young people that had gathered around the novelty section several feet away. They mused over the mixed drink gag for those who wanted to remain sober yet appear social. Once set down, the glass appeared empty. Once lifted, the glass would fill or empty depending on the position of the person's fingers. The more you choked up, the fuller it became. A xenon gas chamber within the glass reacted with the person's body temperature to create the illusion.

They also laughed over Contraptions' solution to Rubik's puzzles. In the center of a glass cube constructed from interlocking jigsaw-shaped pieces that did not disassemble sat a caricature of Ernst Rubik on a small stone in a position inspired by Rodin. Hanging from the ceiling of the cube just above the inventor's head was a sign that read 'Let *Him* Figure *This* One Out!'

The customers sorted through dozens of novelties as Derek panned the rest of the room. No sign of Arti.

"Where the hell is that little guy?" he asked. A moment later, he heard Arti's unmistakable voice coming from within the workshop.

He and Ojo turned as Arti walked through the door between the office and the workshop. Christine put her arm around him.

"*Little*' guy?!" angrily responded the three-and-a-half foot tall robot, with a cowboy hat on his head and gun belt strapped crookedly below waist level. "I'd watch my words if I were you, pardner," he squeaked. He had a definite John Wayne complex going on.

"First off, you pile of shrapnel, don't you remember your manners in mixed company?" Derek teased him.

"Hmmm," Arti buzzed, "what *do* I do when there's a black guy in the room?" he asked himself aloud. "Only kiddin', Ojo," he went on. "Can you ever forgive me, Miss Christine?" he pleaded as the top of one of his two side cylinders rotated inward. A latch from his central cylinder opened and a metal arm lifted the black ten-gallon hat. With a quick jerking motion Arti flung the hat way across the room toward a small hook that caught it.

"Nothin' to forgive, cutie," she told him as she stroked his glass dome.

"She does give good—" Arti started.

"Watch it, Arti," Derek warned. "So what's the deal with the blood on the note, big guy?"

"Oh, sure, pardner. *Now* you suck up. Now that you want something," Arti told him as numerous infrared sensors moved up and down the side cylinders and a digital blue spatial sensor revolved around the upper portion of the central cylinder.

"What's this *'pardner'* stuff?" Ojo asked him.

"And what's with the hat and guns?" Derek added, pointing to the gun belt that sported a pair of .38 Specials and hung loosely from Arti's central cylinder just above the point where the cylinder widened slightly then flared into a conical section.

"I tuned in to one of the Duke's films last night. Besides, the ladies seem to like it."

"Don't you think he's adorable?" Christine asked, again stroking his dome.

"See? So what's it to you?"

"Are they loaded?" Derek asked.

"Are you feelin' lucky?" Arti responded. "Well, *are you* punk?!"

"That's not the Duke. Never mind. Have you even looked at the note yet?"

"Maybe yes. Maybe no."

"*Arti!*" Derek yelled, frustrated but relishing every second with his unique creation.

"Okay, okay. Yes."

"Aaaaand?"

"And what?"

"And what did you come up with?"

"With what?"

"The note, Arti, the *note*!"

"I feel like Spencer Tracy in *Inherit the Wind*," Arti told him. "But you don't look *anything* like Katherine Hepburn," he beeped and turned toward Christine, his dome spinning around several times and his lighted sensors flashing wildly. "Miss Christine's a much closer match. Brighter, too."

She laughed.

"Do you know what happens if I remove your artificial intellichip?"

"I become a boring *robot*," Arti responded on a more serious note. "I think I see where you're going with this."

Derek laughed. "Good."

"Can we get back to the note, Arti?" Ojo asked.

"Okay. Just when I'm having a little, having a little, having a little fun," he joked. "Sorry about that. Now, what were we talking about?"

Derek reached for the control panel on Arti's central cylinder.

"Oh, yes, the note," he quickly added. "Type O positive."

"Type *O* positive? So it couldn't have been the surgeon's blood on that note. How does that *help* us?" Derek asked Ojo.

"Fetal," Arti added.

"Excuse me?" Christine asked.

"The blood on the note was type O positive. The hemoglobin *in* the blood was HbF. *Fetal*," Arti told them.

"*Fetal?* Are you sure?" Ojo asked.

"Sure I'm sure!" Arti snapped. He didn't handle

criticism particularly well. "I removed several nanograms of blood from different areas of the note and dissolved each sample in buffer. Then I fed them through my structural analyzer circuit and wham!"

"*Wham?*" Derek asked.

"Wham!" Arti repeated. "After typing each sample I sequenced the amino acid structure of each and compared them. I came up with the same answer each time. Take a look," he said as a panel on his central cylinder slid down, revealing a tiny monitor below the revolving digital sensor.

Several three-dimensional protein structures appeared on the small screen. "The structure on the left is adult hemoglobin. The structure on the right is fetal hemoglobin. The one in the middle is from the blood on the note. *Also,* fetal hemoglobin. All three human. Why do you doubt me?"

"Nothin' personal, kemosabe," Derek told him. "Just keepin' you on your bearings."

"I could be wrong, but the dead butcher looked a little too large to be a fetus," Ojo said. "So where'd the fetal blood come from?"

"Hmmm. How about a fetus?" Christine suggested sarcastically.

"It's a tough room," Ojo said.

"To the head of the class with you, at once," Derek told her.

"Where *did* this blood come from?" Ojo asked again.

"How could the killer have had access to fetal blood? And why?"

"Think for a second," Derek said. "First we stumble upon a murdered surgeon. Then we find a love letter written in blood on your windshield. Next, a code of some kind turns up on the dead guy's eyeglass frame. Probably the reason for the killing. Finally, the blood on that note turns out to be fetal blood. Who would have access to that?"

"Another doctor," Christine suggested.

"Another doctor," Derek repeated. "Exactly. Either the killer or the guys that hired him. The 'why' part's going to be a little tougher."

"Could have something to do with this," Ojo said, taking the photo with the code on it from Derek's hand. "Maybe everything."

"There's more," Derek said. "And this may be totally unrelated. Apples and oranges," he went on. "But we may as well assume everything crazy going on *is* related till proven otherwise. Might keep us from getting burned."

"I agree. You're referring to—" Ojo started.

"*This*," Derek said, holding up the picture he found in the canister. "Interesting how Tomkin easily recognized the thermalyzed image of the old man—*'Elmer van Husted'* I believe—who left it for me along with these." He opened his hand to reveal the cut half of the gold medallion and the dog tags. "Coincidence? Take a closer look at this photo of my father. Recognize anyone else?"

Ojo and Christine scrutinized the photo in silence.

"It's *Tomkin*," Ojo finally said.

"Your *lawyer*?" Christine asked.

Ojo nodded with a concerned look in his eyes. "What does it mean? Or those?" He pointed to the dog tags in Derek's hand. "What does it all mean?"

"*Jonathan Cannon*'—my father—and *Michael Branton*,'" Derek read the tags. "Don't know what all this means. Not yet. But I will. In the meantime, why don't you get started on the eyeglass code," Derek suggested. "There are a few other things I want to check out."

"Like?"

"Like Tomkin, for one. He didn't happen to give you his card back at the precinct, did he?"

"As a matter of fact," Ojo began, sorting through his wallet until he found the card, "he did."

Derek took it from him. "I think it's time we had a little talk, don't you?"

Ojo agreed. "Be careful. We don't know where he fits into all of this—if at all. And he is Shaw's partner. So tread lightly," he advised.

"Don't I always?"

Ojo shook his head and they shared a laugh. If there was one thing Derek never did, it was tread lightly. He just wasn't the light-treading type.

"Weren't the two of you heading somewhere

tonight?" Ojo asked, checking his watch. It was 7:30 p.m.

"To the Comedy Dungeon," Christine told him. "Why don't you join us? I think we could all use a few laughs."

"Thanks, but I think I'm going to work on this code for a while longer. Maybe I'll come by later on," Ojo said as the phone rang. "So go on, get outta here," he insisted. "Have a good time."

Ojo answered the phone as they left the office and stepped down the spiral staircase. "Contraptions."

"Well, hello," a woman's whispery voice flowed through the receiver as Arti beeped on his way back to the workshop.

"'*Well, hello,*' yourself," Ojo said, steadying the receiver against his shoulder with his chin as he copied the code from the photo onto the computer. "How can I help you?"

"I think you know."

"Something in particular you have in mind?" he asked, watching the screen as the computer scrambled the code.

INHHSOOXOO22619435

//eRTyoo/33/x35jf7>wr3c ... 99nbW[TY/4/55mna//

99nbW[TY/4/55mna// ... //5eeHa300xxiq33-ssl-f35

//5eeHa300xxiq33-ssl-f35 ... xv3sl7-656-awqs//01tz

WORKING!

"Only you," the mysterious voice replied.

"Well, what is it? Your dime, lady," he told her.

"I've got it," she said.

"Excuse me?" Ojo said, striking several keys as the decoding process began.

xv3sl7-656-awqs//01tz
::::: [xv3] [sl7] [656] [awqs] [01tz] :::::
::::: x [v3s] [176] [56a] [wqso] [1tz] :::::
::::: xv [3sl] [765] [6aw] [qs01] [tz] :::::
::::: [zt] [10sq] [wa6] [567] [1s3] vx :::::

"I didn't catch you."

"I said I've got it," she repeated.

"*It?*"

"It."

"You've got '*it*'."

"*It.* Got it."

"Exactly what is '*it*'?" Ojo asked.

"Exactly what you're looking for. What you *need*."

"Really now? And what is it you think I'm looking for? Or '*need*'?"

"Oh, why play games, Mr. Jenachukwu?" she said with an almost breathless voice. "We both know that answer."

"How do you know me?" Ojo asked. He was intrigued. "Have we met?"

"Only in your wildest dreams."

"And your name?"

"I'm called Nastasia."

"I know no Nastasia."

"Oooh, but you do," she cooed.

"What is it *you* want?"

"Only you."

"In what way?"

"In time, Mr. Jenachukwu," the woman whispered. "In time."

The screen flashed as the computer tapped into a classified data bank.

CLASSIFIED INFORMATION!
CLASSIFIED INFORMATION!

UNAUTHORIZED ENTRY FORBIDDEN!
UNAUTHORIZED ENTRY FORBIDDEN!

He paid no attention to the monitor.

"You're doing nothing for me long distance, honey."

"Ooh," she moaned softly. "Is that right?"

"Well, sorta," Ojo mumbled.

A dialing sound was heard and the screen flashed again.

WELCOME!

INNHHSOOXOO22619435

xv3sl7-656-awqs//01tz

::::: [zt] [10sq] [wa6] [567] [1s3] vx :::::

WORKING!

Ojo remained silent for a moment. His eyes returned to the screen and the hint of a smile curved his lips. He thumbed his nose pensively and responded to the sensuality flowing through the receiver.

"Still there?" the woman asked.

"Oh, I'm here alright. You were saying?"

"I can tell you how I long to touch you. To feel you. To taste you. How I long to run my wet tongue slowly up your thigh until—"

"Don't tell me," Ojo told her. "Just show me."

"We must meet."

"I would think."

"The Sunken Treasure. Midnight."

"How will I know you?"

"Ooh," she moaned again. "You'll know me."

The line went dead.

Ojo stared at the receiver for a moment, then returned it to its hook. He glanced down into the display room and watched as Arti escorted the last of the customers out the door. Then he sat back, crossing his arms behind his head as thoughts of Nastasia ran through his mind.

She fascinated him. Her mysterious voice. Her words. Everything about her. He eyed his watch. In less than four hours it would be midnight. He was sure this would be one memorable night. Unless it was a setup. He thought about that for a moment and grew nervous. The burning returned to his stomach.

The computer produced a few tones, interrupting Ojo's thoughts.

AMER//MED//ASSOC//DATABANK
AMER//MED//ASSOC//DATABANK

INHSOOXOO22619435
XV3SL7-656-awqs//01tz
::::: [zt] [10sq] [wa6] [567] [1s3] vx :::::

NOT FOUND!
NOT FOUND!

"Damn!" he said. "Let's try this," he went on, quickly typing several codes onto the screen. If it was important enough to someone to have a surgeon *killed*, Ojo thought, it might just be important to a few others.

//4867395//::///::/PentagonBANK//NEXUSdata//
//5734259//::///::/PentagonBANK//NEXUSdata//

The computer responded:

CONNECTION IN PROGRESS ...

ERROR! ERROR! ERROR!
ERROR! ERROR! ERROR!

"Don't do this to me!" he told the computer and tried another code.

CONNECTION IN PROGRESS ...

CLASSIFIED INFORMATION!
CLASSIFIED INFORMATION!

UNAUTHORIZED ENTRY FORBIDDEN!
UNAUTHORIZED ENTRY FORBIDDEN!

A few moments passed as Ojo eagerly watched the screen.

PNTGNBANK ENTRY ACHIEVED!

PNTGNBANK ENTRY ACHIEVED!

INHHSOOXOO22619435

xvsl7-656-awqs//01tz

:::: [zt] [10sq] [wa6] [567] [1s3] vx ::::

SEARCHING ... SEARCHING ...

"Hmm," Ojo said as he relaxed in his seat and eyed his watch another time. "This is good." The burning feeling subsided.

CHAPTER NINE

"Science is a *wonderful* thing," the comedian on stage began. "Until something goes wrong, of course. Remember the Three Mile Island meltdown? Or the Challenger explosion? *Makes you wonder.* Remember the film *'Capricorn One'* where NASA faked the first mission to Mars? Some say they did the same with the moon landing. True or just a conspiracy theory? *Makes you wonder.* They recently cloned Dolly the sheep from a single cell. Cool stuff! But do we really need to clone sheep? Can't they just fuck like the rest of us?"

Laughter filled the packed room. The Comedy Dungeon was a small downstairs club on 60th Street. It was one of those elusive hole-in-the-wall night spots that was worth the search. A narrow hallway lined with signed headshots led to the brick wall backdrop and a mic stand on stage. About twenty deuces and a half dozen high tops filled the club. Each set usually included five or six comics before the headliner. Joey D'Angelo, a clever comedian from Boston with a loyal following, was the headliner this week. He killed it every show. The audience loved him.

"All this recent talk about healthcare reform reminds me of a true story," D'Angelo continued as the laughter subsided. "I recently visited a psych ward—just to find some new material, you understand." He looked over his shoulder, then jumped back in Krameresque fashion. "In the first patient's room I noticed a man in bed, flat on his back masturbating. Asked the doctor what his problem was. 'That man's schizophrenic,' the doctor said. 'Believes he must climax every hour on the hour or he'll explode.' Fair enough, I thought. A common disorder. Then I looked into the next patient's room. Another man, also naked and flat on his back. But this one had two young nurses going down on him. I looked at the doctor puzzled. 'Same problem,' the doctor told me. 'Better health insurance.'"

Christine bellowed. But she could barely be heard over the louder laughter of the audience. A couple of the other comics laughed the loudest. D'Angelo was on his game. He made you laugh but he also made you think.

"Lot of talk these days about setting up space colonies to control the population and developing '*designer genes*' so we can select our kids' traits in advance. This whole genetic engineering thing concerns me. Like those monstrosities that were recently born. Have you heard about them? *Crazy* shit! Missing ears. Fused fingers. What the fuck? Did some sadistic parent actually select *those* traits?" He paused for a moment and eyed the audience as if waiting for a response. Silence. "Coincidence or experiment gone awry? Any thoughts?" he asked. "Any of you hear about this?" A few hands went up. "Well, sounds like a fuckin' medical disaster if you ask me. Makes you wonder what secret research is really going on, doesn't it? One of these days they'll be sending pregnant monkeys into space to populate those colonies!"

"Anyway, all this talk about science and medicine reminds me of this black guy with a stuttering problem. He went to his doctor and asked him, 'Is th-th-there anyth-th-thing you can d-d-do for m-m-me, doc?' After examining the man, the doctor told him, 'The problem is you have a ten-inch penis. It's just too long. It's causing your stuttering.' 'Really?' the man asked. 'Wh-wh-what can you d-d-do for th-th-that?' 'A penis transplant,' the doctor told him. The man agreed and the doctor removed his penis and replaced it with one that was six inches long."

"Two weeks later the man returned to the doctor's office complaining. 'Doctor, I'm very depressed. I'm not stuttering anymore, but I'm not happy at all with this baby dick you gave me,' he said, pointing to his crotch. 'Can I have my old one back?' The doctor looked him in the eye and told him, 'I d-d-don't th-th-think that's g-g-going to be p-p-possible.'" The crowd roared.

Derek checked his pager and leaned over to tell Christine that Tomkin had finally returned his message. His mind wandered for a moment. It was ten o'clock. He wondered if Ojo had come up with anything on that code. And he wondered about Tomkin. He motioned to Christine, then stood and walked to the rear of the room toward the exit as the comedian spewed several mocking comments after him.

In the lobby of the comedy club, Derek removed a Teledisc from his pocket. "Tomkin," he said quietly and the device dialed the man's number.

Tomkin answered with a meek whispery tone. They spoke for a few minutes when Derek asked directly, "Then what *is* your real name, Tomkin?" After a moment of silence, he asked, "Is it *Michael Branton?*"

"You're getting ahead of yourself, Derek," Tomkin told him. "As I've already said, your father and I served together in Vietnam—*many* years ago. You were just a child. At that time my name *was* 'Branton'—as you see it on the dog tags. But it hasn't been for decades."

"Why the change?"

Tomkin hesitated for a moment. "I entered the witness protection program in 1986," he then explained.

"My father was killed that year."

"I know that, Derek. I know that all too well. And I've been running ever since."

"What are you running from?"

"Not 'what', Derek, *whom*," Tomkin corrected him. "I was your father's friend, Derek. From our days together in Nam to the day he was killed. I tried to save him. I tried to decode a top-secret communication that might have prevented his plane crash. But I couldn't do it in time. I just couldn't do it in time. And they've been after me ever since."

"Who, Tomkin? *Who*?!"

The line was silent.

"Tomkin? *Tomkin*?!"

"I'm here."

"Where does Elmer van Husted fit into this? And what do you know about the cut half of the gold medallion he left for me?"

"Do you have the *medallion*?" Tomkin anxiously asked in a quiet, nervous voice.

"What do you know about it?"

"Nothing. Nothing at all. I meant *a* medallion. You said you have some type of medallion, didn't you? Interesting."

Tomkin tried to play it off. It was a lame attempt. It was obvious he knew more than he was willing to spill. Much more.

"What about Elmer van Husted?"

The line was silent again.

"Tomkin?"

"I have much to tell you. But it is too dangerous like this. We must meet. And talk. I'll be at Columbus Circle in two hours. Meet me there."

Derek agreed.

"And bring the medallion."

* * *

The floatron produced a humming sound before it shot into a transparent chute. On a cushion of air it soared freely through the winding and interconnecting tunnels that provided a continuous conduit of access throughout the vast premises of the installation. The lights within the floatron dimmed as it filled with a purplish mist. A small porthole window on each of its sides provided a view of the transparent tunnel system and the many levels within the installation for the two passengers who sat strapped to the large reclining seats.

They eyed the crates now and then and each other but didn't utter so much as a word, as they watched through the windows. They could see several men working in one of the labs on the Weapons & Antigravity Testing & Experimental Research level. The WATER Facility, it was called. As were all the levels within the underground complex, the WATER Facility was enclosed by an impenetrable laser field. Entry without clearance authorization was impossible.

Just moments before the floatron entered a vertical pressurized chamber, its passengers caught a glance of what seemed to be some sort of demonstration in progress. A small glass-encased object hovered several feet above the floor of the lab before it exploded, producing a brilliant reddish glow that caused the goggled men to cover their eyes for an instant although the case remained unshattered and its position unchanged. Yet the enclosed object was gone.

Once in the large chamber, several gauges affixed to the roof of the floatron flashed as it rapidly descended seventy or eighty feet, then suddenly halted. The gauges stopped flashing and the mist cleared.

"TSI Facility," the computerized voice echoed as the doors slid open. "Atmosphere controlled."

The men carefully removed the cords and loaded the crates onto the unmanned carrier vehicle that waited on the ramp just outside the floatron. They boarded the carrier as the floatron shot into the tunnel that branched off the chamber's side, disappearing from view within seconds.

As they approached the Facility's glass entrance, one of the men held his hand high in the air. A flash of blue light burst from a small panel atop the double doors, colliding with the man's hand before it vanished.

"Entry granted," another computerized voice sounded as the doors swung open.

The carrier proceeded into the main area of the Facility. It followed the curve of the wide corridor, gliding past numerous laboratories, cold rooms and test areas that lined the octagonal level before coming upon a sign that read 'TSI CRYOGENIC STORAGE' and an arrow that pointed toward an open entryway. Open but not unguarded. Several red lights in the chrome that trimmed the triangular entrance indicated the invisible laser field was active. As the carrier approached the entryway, a viewer above the entrance flashed several times. The lights turned blue and the vehicle moved into the room.

The men pulled the crates from the carrier and slowly moved them to an area where several steel drums were stacked. Behind the drums were three cryogenic chambers. They were attached to a computer which sat against the back wall. With crowbars the men carefully lifted the tops off the large wooden boxes. From each, packaged within a bulky Kevlar cooling blanket, they removed a shiny black canister.

Each stood about three feet tall. Two of the canisters produced a beeping tone that coincided with the beating of a red light. The light flashed below several words that had been engraved in the black steel. 'NEXUS LIFE SUPPORT SYSTEM,' they read. One of the lights flashed more rapidly than the other but both produced that same rhythmic tone. A small antenna extended from the top of the third canister. A continuous buzzing sound was produced as two yellow lights quickly revolved around its circumference.

Together the men placed a canister into each of the chamber chutes. One of the men pressed a switch on the computer's control panel and they watched as the chambers filled with liquid nitrogen and the frozen mist it produced. The computer monitored the temperature of the canisters. Within seconds it had dropped to 180° Celsius below zero. Several moments passed and the liquid nitrogen was drained. A bluish gas was piped in that coated the canisters and filled the chambers. The temperature fell to 273° Celsius below zero.

The men covered the crates and loaded them onto the carrier. The entrance lights turned red again as they left the room and continued down the corridor, moving past several more labs, the TSI Terminal Center, and the Glenn Amphitheatre. They stopped beside the entryway that led to the top secret conference hall.

Into a small intercom on the side of a chrome panel one of the men spoke. "Phase Three accomplished," he said in a deep dry voice.

The words echoed from the speaker high on the front wall like a wave through the conference hall. The ten or twelve people who sat scattered throughout the arched rows of seats stirred. A tall white-haired man in a long lab coat with oval wire-rimmed eyeglasses stood by the large podium around which the rows of seats curved.

Nothing was said for a few moments.

"Proceed to the OZONE Platform," he finally responded with a heavy accent after removing the pipe from his mouth and bending to speak into the intercom on the podium.

The carrier moved onward through the corridor.

"Sector 13," he added after a brief pause but the men

had already turned and were on their way back to the floatron tunnels.

The speaker lifted his head from the intercom and stood upright as his eyes passed over each of the doctors and scientists who sat before him. He carefully set his pipe on the podium shelf and addressed his audience.

"Well, then," Dr. Flint cleared his throat and told his colleagues, "the project is now more important than ever. Our only obstacle thus far has been our failure to accurately insert the Omega gene we synthesized more than a year ago into the single strand of DNA that comprises the lambda plasmid within the *Escherichia coli* bacterium. This is crucial if we are to successfully clone the gene. As a result of inaccurate or incomplete DNA insertion, the gene has functioned improperly, producing a number of undesirable effects as we have already witnessed. Genetic mishaps are bound to occur. It is part of the process. It cannot be prevented. The key is in preventing their exposure to the public. That must *never* happen again," he calmly told the group and shook his head.

"But that is all behind us now. I stand before you with news of a breakthrough. The answer was right under our noses all this time. We are quite fortunate that Dr. Takagawa picked up on it," he went on, extending a gratified smile in the direction of the small Japanese scientist who sat in the second row. "Using a modified EcoR1 restriction endonuclease enzyme that she developed, we have accurately manipulated only those nucleotide bases of the *E. coli* plasmid DNA at the appropriate incorporation site, thus producing a sequence of receptor nucleotides or, if you will, 'sticky ends', onto which we have interspliced our gene. Lady and gentlemen," he proudly told his colleagues, turning slightly and affectionately nodding at Dr. Takagawa, the only woman in the group, as his voice cracked with emotion, "the Omega gene has finally been cloned!"

The group applauded loudly.

"It is with godspeed and unparalleled anticipation, then," Dr. Flint continued as the applause subsided, "that we proceed to Phase Four of our project."

They applauded again as several of the men reached over to shake Dr. Takagawa's hand. This was a great moment for NEXUS.

* * *

PNTGNBNK ENTRY || || NEXUSdata
PNTGNBNK ENTRY || || NEXUSdata

CONFIRMING PASSWORD
CONFIRMING PASSWORD

ACCESS GRANTED
ACCESS GRANTED

::: **[llzt] [45f2] [3ff] [uqq] [1a5]** :::
::: **[cq3] [7hg] [2e65] [je57] [54]** :::

ψωασ ••• χξαθ ••• φλππ ••• ϖβμχ
ΣΦΨΛ ••• ΔΦΩΧ ••• ΠΛςΞ ••• ΦϑΠΩ

PROJECT INHHSOOXOO22619435
PROJECT INHHSOOXOO22619435

SEARCHING ...
SEARCHING ...
SEARCHING ...
SEARCHING ...

PROJECT INHHSOOXOO22619435
PROJECT INHHSOOXOO22619435

TSI DATA FOUND!
TSI DATA FOUND!

PROJECT OMEGA GENE
PROJECT OMEGA GENE

UNSCRAMBLING TSI DATA ...
UNSCRAMBLING TSI DATA ...

* * *

"There *is* an additional issue that needs to be addressed," Dr. Flint went on, adjusting his eyeglasses with a smooth gesture as a sharp chirping tone sounded from the pager attached to his belt.

A digital readout flashed 'TERM*CTR'.

"Yes, what is it?" he spoke into the intercom.

"You'd better come right over, Hans," a nervous voice shot through the podium speaker as Dr. Flint held a hand up to silence the audience. "We've got a problem, sir. A *real* problem."

"Be right there," Dr. Flint responded. "Koshi, would you elaborate on the cloning process while I tend to this matter?" he asked Dr. Takagawa as he left the podium and walked toward the amphitheatre's exit.

Dr. Flint left the hall and briskly walked through the corridor. His shoes made a clicking noise against the stone floor. He quickly came to the Terminal Center entryway. The laser field guarding the computer systems that kept the TSI Facility running smoothly inactivated itself as Dr. Flint stood before it. When the entryway lights turned blue he entered the room.

The Center was at least twenty degrees cooler than any other room in the Facility, he noticed. He squinted for a second or two as his eyes adjusted to the bright lighting before they darted past the rows of terminals and toward the glass-enclosed room at the rear of the Center.

Within the room sat three men. Two worked busily at the long control panel that extended from one side of the room to the other. They carefully monitored the hundreds of switches, gauges, buttons, meters and flashing lights on the complex panel. The third sat by a terminal on the opposite side, just in front of the large plate of glass that separated the room from the rest of the Center.

Dr. Flint quickly walked toward the room, brushing past a young woman who stood by one of the printers. The coffee she had been holding spilled onto the pile of documents that sat in the printout bin. Dr. Flint mumbled several apologetic words under his breath but kept walking till he reached the glass door that led to the backroom.

"Damn!" yelled the man seated by the terminal. He brought his fist down hard on the keyboard in a rage as Dr. Flint opened the door and stepped into the room. The men by the control panel glanced over for a moment then returned to their work.

"Hawkins, what in *hell* is going on?!" Dr. Flint asked him.

"We have an intruder!" the man angrily said, pointing at the circuit map on the monitor. "Someone has penetrated the TSI System!"

"But that's *impossible!*" Dr. Flint responded. "The code has been retrieved."

"I'm telling you, Hans, *someone* has gotten their hands on it," Hawkins insisted.

"But *how?!* How can that be?!"

"Don't know."

"That damn *Barnes.* Probably leaked it before we got to him. Should've killed him sooner," Dr. Flint thought aloud. "Well, what are you going to do about it?"

"We've already jammed the signal and rescrambled the code," one of the men sitting by the control panel answered.

"Can you trace the break-in signal?" Dr. Flint asked.

"We're working on it now, Dr. Flint," the other man responded.

"So far, we've localized an overlapping signal to the east coast," Hawkins said. "It's coming from either Boston or New York," he added.

"Keep working on it if you have to go through the night. Get Tomkin on it, too. I *want* the bastards!"

"We'll find them, sir," Hawkins assured him.

"And when you do," Dr. Flint started, pausing for only a brief moment, "bring them to me. I want to know what they know. And if you can't, then have them *killed!*"

CHAPTER TEN

Men of lofty genius sometimes accomplish the most
when they work least, for their minds are occupied
with their ideas and the perfection of their
conceptions, to which they afterwards give form.

Leonardo da Vinci

Midnight was but minutes away.

The full moon punched a hole in the clear black sky. Ojo gazed at it and the countless lights that flickered in the heavens as he turned onto 18th Street. Pieces of unfinished thoughts occupied his fatigued mind as he walked along the block.

STIFF data.

Hacking into the database at Bellevue had proved vital, he thought. A plethora of information had been retrieved. *Histories. Lab reports. Statistics.* Ojo wondered what role that information would play in shaping the events that would soon follow.

He pulled a sheet of paper from his pocket and unfolded it. He reviewed his notes while he walked.

Calvin Barnes—the victim of the shooting—was an orthopedic surgeon on staff at University Hospital and Bellevue. The *Chairman* of the Department of Orthopedic Surgery, in fact. In addition to his blood type and ballistics report, Ojo was able to retrieve Barnes' *Curriculum Vitae* which was stored in the Bellevue database. Barnes had been on staff since 1982, after completing a fellowship in sports medicine at the Hospital for Special Surgery in Manhattan. A Professor of Surgery at the University since 1992.

His area of special expertise had been joint reconstruction of the lower extremity in professional athletes. And he was the best in the field. A number of experimental breakthroughs of Barnes' had attracted such players as Namath, Marino and Rodman for treatment. His research endeavors had focused on the prevention of bony demineralization, atrophy and, ultimately, destruction under unloaded conditions of weightlessness—simulated *microgravity and zero gravity* environments. Barnes had published a number of classic articles in the *Journal of Bone and Joint Surgery, Space Medicine,* and *Bone,* using nonhuman primate models and computer-generated simulations of frictionless and weightless environments. He had essentially created a *space* environment.

Barnes was an innovator. A brilliant surgeon and scientist. A man who had made significant contributions to the world of medicine. And now he was dead. One question kept running through Ojo's mind. Over and over. *Why?*

Ojo took another look at the paper. He had printed out the titles and references of a number of articles on the page in his hand. Several names appeared frequently as co-authors of Barnes—Hans Flint, Benjamin Hawkins and Koshi Takagawa.

Ojo stuffed the paper back in his pocket and kept walking.

* * *

Derek thought about Tomkin. Or whatever his real name was. *Michael Branton*, perhaps. And Elmer van Husted. *Why did he leave that canister at the bomb shelter?* Derek held the medallion half in a clenched hand and wondered how they were connected. And, even more importantly, he wondered how his father was connected to them.

Derek parked on 62nd Street across from Lincoln Center, several blocks from Columbus Circle. He had many questions for Tomkin. He checked his watch and stepped out of the car. It was 11:57 p.m., Tomkin would be along momentarily, he thought. And he would get his answers. There was no doubt Tomkin knew his father. The picture seemed real enough. Derek had already run it through an image analyzer. It was real, alright. But *how?*

How did he know him? Only Tomkin could answer these questions.

Derek walked along the narrow street then turned onto Broadway and continued toward Columbus Circle on 59th Street. Tomkin had not given a specific meeting place. He simply said 'Columbus Circle', Derek recalled. Shouldn't be a problem, he thought. The streets were not terribly crowded at this hour. In fact, they were relatively quiet. Lincoln Center and the Met had already let out. A small crowd ushered out of the Rose Theater just up ahead. Tomkin would likely be in the vicinity, Derek reasoned. He walked past the theater and then crossed 61st Street and continued toward the Circle. A gentle breeze brushed against his face as he walked along the broad street.

In the distance Derek could see the frail shadow of a man two blocks away. He walked briskly toward him in the cool midnight air. The glow of the full moon struck the man's face as Derek crossed 60th Street. From a block away Derek could appreciate the ghastly pallor of Tomkin's face. He hadn't taken much of a careful look at the attorney at the police station but in this lighting he could now see how the thin skin of his face was pulled tightly over his high cheekbones, giving him an emaciated, almost cachectic appearance. In his mind Derek could see the pale image of Tomkin standing beside his father in the photo. As he approached the attorney, he noticed a badly torn hat in the man's hand. Light from the moon struck Tomkin's bald head, creating a shadow that highlighted the lump on his forehead.

He and Derek shook hands.

Nothing was said for a moment.

Derek squeezed the medallion half which he held in his overcoat pocket.

"Do you have it?" Tomkin directly asked.

Derek eyed the lump on Tomkin's forehead and caught his piercing stare.

"The *medallion*. Do you have it?"

* * *

Flint's name was familiar to Ojo. Flint was the Chief of Surgery at both University Hospital and Bellevue. Ojo and Derek had met with him—*and* Barnes—the morning before the orthopedic surgeon's murder. The Bellevue database confirmed Flint's academic standing at the two hospitals but provided no information on Hawkins or Takagawa.

As Ojo neared the corner of 18th Street and West Broadway, the banging sound of a drum together with the gust of a cool breeze hit him hard in the face. A bass and at least two guitars joined in as the blaring sound overflowed into the silent street.

He turned on West Broadway and continued walking toward 17th Street and the flag that convulsed almost violently in the wind. A white skull and crossbones were painted on the black fabric. A long pole held the flag high above the entrance of the unusual dance club on the corner of 17th Street. The freestanding building was shaped like the hull of a ship. Its wooden plank sides curved as they moved forward and came to a point about fifteen feet from the ground. It was from that point, the bow of the hull, that the flag hung from its pole. Several feet below the flag was mounted a cracked wooden sign on which an open chest with overflowing jewels had been painted and into which two words had been burned. SUNKEN TREASURE, they read. The sign hung above the club's saloon-style entrance.

A seven-foot bouncer in pirate attire guarded the entrance. He was quite believable in his sea-faring garb. The black eye patch, telescope, and saber sword added to the outfit. But the wooden peg leg clinched it. It was the proud memento of his encounter with the great white that took his eye. In a rage, he tore his own leg off to beat the shark with it. Or so he claimed. More likely the result of a motorcycle mishap. In either case, he was a colorful man, indeed. He was called *Ishmael.*

Ojo nodded at him on his way through the entrance. Ishmael did the same after a slight hesitation. Ojo pushed through the wooden doors and stepped into the club.

A flash of yellow light caught Ojo's eyes as he walked toward one of the bars in the crowded club. His eyes followed the bright beam as it shot from one end of the overstretched S-shaped bar that curved along the left wall and exploded on the ceiling above the other end. From the center of the yellow burst of light shot three orange rays. They soared above the crowd that danced in the middle of the sunken floor and splashed on the far right wall.

Ojo walked toward the long bar. He leaned against an empty stool with his back to the neon designs that decorated the wall behind the bar and watched the band for a while. The Flesh Tonz was an all-female alternative band. They played from atop a slanted platform that rocked from side to side, suspended above the dance area. They were responsible for the loud metallic sound that poured into the street. Electronic percussion boards and synthesizer keyboards. No guitars. No drums. Each of the band's four members wore above-knee boots and leather corsets. Lyrics spewed forth, evoking images of relationships gone sour and dreams of bitter retribution.

Ojo took a swallow from the drink he had ordered as a carousel laser rotated above the bar. Blue and red lights flashed in his eyes. In an instant, he was back in the park, entrapped by the squad car. It was an image that would likely recur frequently, he thought. He took another swallow of his drink as a soft whispery voice called from behind him. The image of the squad car faded.

"Well, hello."

He recognized the voice and turned slowly. The woman's green eyes sparkled as the light caught them. They contrasted marvelously against her olive complexion and waist-length jet black hair. She stood facing him and with a long finger twirled the ice in her drained glass.

Ojo grinned but said nothing.

A subtle smile softened the woman's face as their eyes met. For a few moments they just shared a silent stare.

Then Ojo's eyes fell upon her moist red lips before dropping to her creamy bare shoulders and low-cut genie outfit. He eyed the black silk that hung loosely over her full breasts and the string of pearls that lay between them. The shiny material flared into ballooning sleeves with slits that raced from above her wrists to just below her shoulders. It tightened at her narrow waist and continued to her muscular calves where it tied off with exaggerated knots. Two generous slits ran the length of the silk, providing a glimpse of her long legs. She was certainly dressed appropriately for this club, Ojo thought.

"*Well, hello*', yourself," he finally responded.

"I think we've had this conversation."

"Another White Russian, please," Ojo told the bartender. "How 'bout you?"

"Same."

Ojo held up two fingers for the bartender. "Great minds drink alike," he told his stunning admirer.

She winked.

"So tell me, Nastasia. It *is* Nastasia?"

"All that you see."

The loose silk pressed against the woman's large breasts. Her hardening nipples produced very distinct creases in the clinging material. Ojo casually took it all in as the bartender handed him the drinks.

"To *mystery*," he toasted with a mischievous smile.

"And *fantasy*," Nastasia added with a raised brow as they tapped glasses. "C'mon," she said and took his hand.

They maneuvered through the crowd to a small gap on the tight dance floor. Nastasia threw her arms in the air and let out a soft howl as she swayed her hips from side to side. They danced around for a while in the small space that had opened around them. Nastasia spun around several times as Ojo moved behind her. He wrapped his arms around her waist and they swayed back and forth in unison.

Ojo enjoyed the subtle scent of her perfume and the sight of her streaming black hair. It flowed past her shoulders down to the soft contour of her behind. He brushed her silky hair from the side of her face and ran a couple of fingers over the curve of her small ear. He held her hair back for a moment and slowly ran his lips over the edge of her ear.

Nastasia turned her head and glanced over her shoulder at Ojo as she leaned back into him. "Let's get out of here," she told him with a devilish grin.

He let the question go.

"Well? I only ask once."

"Do you really think I'm *that* easy?" he asked her with a flat expression after another brief pause.

She turned quickly and faced him, throwing her arms over his shoulders and her hands behind his head, pulling him toward her as she pressed her lips to his. Ojo wrapped one arm tightly around her tiny waist and the other around her bare back as they kissed. It was a deep lingering kiss that would have gone on without end had Nastasia not loosened her grip and eased back.

With a fiery stare she looked into his eyes. "You were saying?"

"I think the exit's over there."

* * *

"Nice hat," Derek told Tomkin, eyeing the torn fabric in his hand that reminded him of the amputated tie that had almost strangled the attorney when he caught it in the elevator door the day before.

"An odd story, really, Mr. Cannon," Tomkin told him.

"No doubt." This was one clumsy, accident-prone man, Derek thought.

"I'll save it for another time."

"What do you know about my father?" Derek wasted no time in getting to the point. "About his death?"

"Your father completed fifty-six missions in Nam."

"I know that."

"I flew with him on every mission but two. He was the best fighter pilot in the squadron. A genuine American hero."

Derek nodded. "What's your point?"

"Point is he was a flawless pilot. He never made an error. Not one." Tomkin stared intently at Derek. "*Not one.*"

"I'm listening," Derek replied.

"Your father was *not* responsible for the crash of Flight 758."

"I never believed he was," Derek quickly said.

"The plane did not crash due to a *pilot error*," Tomkin said with a slight hesitation. "The landing gear had been *sabotaged*."

"*Sabotaged?* What are you saying?"

"The plane was returning from D.C., Derek. A decent number of government diplomats were on that flight. *International* diplomats with political immunity. Men who were above the law in our country. Men who were guilty of war crimes *against* our country. *Monsters*. But, still, above the law. *Untouchable*. And our government wanted them dead."

"How do you know this?"

"I was teamed with your father in Nam because I was the best flight strategist in the Force. They put the best with the best. I could tap into *any* enemy communication. Decode *any* signal. Unscramble *any* message. I tried to decode a top-secret communication but I was too late. If I just had a little more time," he said and shook his head, the anguish of the loss still evident on his drawn face. "When your father's plane crashed, I personally investigated the black box data. I knew first-hand that there had been absolutely no pilot error. I did some additional research. Tapped into some classified information and uncovered the coverup. Before I could expose it, the black box disappeared. The evidence was destroyed. Then the CIA came after me. So I became 'Bradley Tomkin'. And now I work for NEXUS."

"Why are you telling me all this?" Derek asked. "And why *now?*"

A part of Derek was furious to learn this now. After all these years. A part was relieved. Finally, his father's memory was absolved. But why had it taken so long? And why would Tomkin entrust him with this information? Derek wondered.

"I've been loyal to your father for many years. Since the day I met him. But I'm also loyal to NEXUS. And they're dangerous. *Very* dangerous. I'm trying to *warn* you, Derek. I owe that to your father," Tomkin told him.

"Warn me about what? What are you trying to say?" Derek asked him.

"Just be careful. NEXUS isn't playing games. They have a lot at stake and won't let anyone get in their way," he said. "*Just be careful.*"

Derek didn't understand Tomkin's tie to NEXUS or the ramifications but he nodded. Then he thought for a moment. "But aren't you a *lawyer?*"

"I am," Tomkin answered.

"This makes no sense. You're tied to NEXUS but running from the CIA? And you're a *lawyer?* This makes no fucking sense."

"Sometimes the best place to hide from the law is to

be in a position of defending it. It's the perfect cover," Tomkin explained.

"Suppose that does make some sense," Derek acknowledged with a skeptical tone.

"Do you have the medallion half?" Tomkin cut to the chase.

Derek took it from his pocket. "Why does this interest you so?" he asked. "You seemed to know nothing about it on the phone."

"I couldn't speak on the phone," Tomkin told him and eagerly grabbed the medallion. He held it close to his thick spectacles, examining it feverishly.

"What does it mean?"

Tomkin reached beneath his collar with a finger and pulled the chain that hung around his neck. "Your father and I became fast friends. We cut the original medallion in half before our first mission," he said and showed Derek the other medallion half that hung on the chain. "We vowed that if one of us was ever killed, the other would keep both medallion halves together. Forever. Your father was like a brother to me."

"Be that as it may," Derek said, "I can't let you have it."

"I understand," Tomkin replied and reluctantly returned the medallion half to Derek.

"I don't have your dog tags with me but I'll get them to you."

"*Don't,*" Tomkin told him. "Just destroy them! 'Michael Branton' no longer exists. If my original identity is revealed it could jeopardize *everything!*"

"Jeopardize *what?*" Derek asked.

Tomkin ignored the question. "I *never* need to see them again. Just *destroy* them!" He insisted. "Promise me you will do that for me, Derek. Promise me!" Tomkin pleaded in a nervous tone as his voice cracked.

"I will, I *will,*" Derek assured him. "But where does that old man—*Elmer van Husted*—come into play? *He* came into our shop and left the canister for me. Right on my desk! The photos, the medallion half, the dog tags were all in it. *Why* did he do that? And how do you know him?"

"The CIA, Derek. He's from the CIA. I urge you to stay away from him," Tomkin warned. "He's dangerous. *Very* dangerous!" the attorney nervously added.

"Was he involved in the coverup?"

"*Directly* involved."

"Doesn't make sense. What would he want with *me?* What would *anyone* from the CIA want with *me?*"

"A tie to *me.* I'm the only one who can finger him."

"Finger him for *what?*"

After a long pause Tomkin looked Derek in the eye and told him. "For sabotaging your father's plane."

"*What?!*"

"It was a top-secret CIA operation. He was one of their best operatives. He was protecting our country. This had nothing to do with your father. Van Husted killed the monsters on that flight. It had to be done. Unfortunately, he also killed your father. He didn't mean to but your father was collateral damage," Tomkin told him with sadness in his eyes. "Just collateral damage." He paused again. "*Horrible.*"

Derek was silent for a moment. Numb. "But what about—" he started.

Tomkin's pager interrupted Derek's question. He checked the readout. 'TERM*CTR'.

"I must go now. But we will meet again. Be careful," he cautioned Derek. "Be *very* careful," he warned him again and turned to leave.

"Tomkin, you can't just drop this bombshell on me and take off!" Derek called to him. But that was exactly what he did. "Tomkin!" The next moment he turned the corner and was gone.

* * *

The checkered cab turned onto 14th Street then turned again onto 6th Avenue and weaved a path around the countless potholes as it crossed to Houston Street on its way to Soho. The driver mumbled several slurred curses as a double-parked van cut into his lane at the Prince Street intersection. He maneuvered to avoid the small truck and just made it through the changing light.

Nastasia leaned against Ojo. He watched her as the

moonlight made its way through the window and reflected off the glare in her gorgeous eyes. He admired the long black leather coat she wore draped over her shoulders and tied at her waist. He noticed a small piece of silk sticking out from a pocket. He recognized the black material and slowly pulled it from the pocket as Nastasia watched. They both smiled as he removed her silk outfit and held it in his hand.

His eyes fell on the leather belt that tied the coat at her waist. He undid the knot in the belt with a couple of fingers and moved the straps apart. The coat fell open just slightly. Nastasia's stockinged leg was now exposed. Ojo ran his hand over her knee and up her thigh as the sides of the coat separated. He caressed her inner thigh as his fingers reached the lace trimming of her stocking. The straps of a garter belt were attached to it. He reached under one of the straps and touched her soft skin. She threw her head back and her coat parted further to reveal a hint of the cutoff lace bra that struggled to hold her full breasts. She spotted the driver's surprised eyes in the rearview mirror but ignored him. She seemed to enjoy the watchful eyes of a voyeur.

Ojo's eyes moved over her voluptuous body. They passed from her smooth thighs to the neatly trimmed triangle of hair between them to her deeply tanned belly to her firm dark nipples which now extended over the edges of the black lace. They contrasted sharply with the much lighter skin surrounding them and the pearls that rested between them. Ojo's eyes lifted to catch the pleased look on Nastasia's face.

"A girl can catch a draft like that," he told her, letting his hand drop between her thighs as his tongue traced the outline of her hardened nipples. After a few moments he lifted his head to catch her warm stare. He grabbed the edges of her coat and pulled it closed, retying the knot in her belt as she sat up in the seat.

"269 Broome," the driver told them as he turned and hungrily eyed Nastasia.

"What do I owe you, chief?" Ojo asked him.

"This one's on the house, buddy. *I should be payin' you*," he said with an elated smile. "Go have a great night."

They stepped from the taxi and walked arm in arm toward the building on the corner. They greeted the doorman who stood beneath its awning as they quickly passed under its cover. He swiftly walked to the tinted glass door beside the revolving chamber and held it open as they entered the building.

"Lovely evening, isn't it?" the middle-aged doorman politely asked.

Nastasia and Ojo exchanged a mischievous glance.

"Can't complain," she told him.

They walked through the impressive lobby at a hurried pace, passing beneath the tremendous crystal chandelier that hung from the high ceiling and between the two marble waterfalls that lined the sides of the mirrored entranceway as they stepped into a waiting elevator. Nastasia quickly pressed the button for the 44th floor and the door promptly closed.

She turned and gently pushed Ojo against the back of the elevator, then untied the belt at her waist, letting her coat open wide. The dim lighting threw an interesting silhouette over her face and breasts. She pressed herself against Ojo, throwing an arm around his neck and kissing him deeply as her free hand moved under his jacket and across his chest. He held her tightly, kissing her as her hand moved downward along the side of his thigh. Her fingers gently traced the edge of the denim material over his zipper.

The elevator came to a quiet stop and the display over the door flashed '44'. Neither paid any attention. As the door clicked and was about to open, Nastasia reached over and struck the STOP switch on the panel beside it. The elevator jumped slightly but the door remained closed.

Her fingers moved back and forth along the edge of the black denim a number of times before settling on the tightly-fastened brass button. She skillfully maneuvered the button through the small hole in the material then unzipped the sturdy zipper under the flap of denim.

Ojo steadied himself against the railing and played with Nastasia's dark hair as she knelt before him.

Nastasia undid the zipper and pulled the black jeans down off Ojo's waist until they hung bunched up above his knees. She ran her fingernails up and down his boxers from the outside before lowering them and gently kissing his warm skin. She watched his eyes as she took him in her mouth. Her tongue danced playfully on his skin as she took him deeper and deeper. She could feel him in the back of her throat and taste him at the same time. She moved back and forth as he stood there. Her lips touched his belly each time and she squeezed his hand. She closed her eyes and greedily inhaled his scent.

Ojo pulled her hand to his lips and kissed it. The coat fell from her shoulders as she stood. He kissed her neck softly and motioned her toward the railing. She leaned forward, holding the railing as Ojo moved behind her. His lips slowly ran down her back and across her tan lines onto the curve of her firm behind. Ojo held her at her waist as he knelt to kiss her soft skin. She moved her feet apart as he kissed the back of her thighs. Ojo then ran his tongue up and down along her moist skin as Nastasia threw her head back in delight.

He stood, holding her behind with both hands as he leaned into her. They moved back and forth in synchrony, shaking the railing that had become loose as Nastasia gripped it tightly. Ojo grabbed her waist and pushed deeply into her. She let out a muffled gasp and tossed her head from side to side as her body shook. Ojo folded his arms around her and remained deep within her. She turned to kiss him just as the elevator jumped.

"I think we're there," Ojo said with a broad smile.

"Oh, we're there alright," she said with a satisfied grin.

Nastasia pulled her coat on while Ojo tucked himself away. She struck the START switch and the elevator door slid open.

They walked through the hallway to the door at its far end. She pressed several buttons on the keypad adjacent to the door. Ojo lifted the large brass ring that hung from the center of the door and tapped it against the hard wood several times as a green light flashed on the keypad.

"That's just for show, you know," she told him.

"I know, but I have a thing for—"

"Yeah, I know," she interrupted. "Big knockers," she told him with a playful smile and pushed the door open.

They stepped into the roomy duplex as a soft light brightened the dark foyer area.

"So tell me, *'Nastasia'*, how was your trip to L.A.? Things going well on the set?"

"We're just about done shooting. Two more scenes and we'll be ready to start editing. I'm pleased. I think the director is, too. And Spielberg is *not* an easy man to please," she replied. "*Perfection is everything*'," she imitated the renowned director.

"Not too shabby. Not shabby at all, Sasha," Ojo told his girlfriend of two years. So, how'd you come up with 'Nastasia'?"

"Oh, I thought you might just get a rise out of her," she said with a smile as they climbed the stairs to the loft.

"Oh, I'd say you were definitely right about that."

Sasha smiled.

Ojo tossed his keys and wallet on the night table as he

and Sasha undressed for bed. From his pocket he pulled the paper with his notes from the Bellevue database. He unfolded the paper and wondered how Derek's meeting with Tomkin had gone.

CHAPTER ELEVEN

I believe you have to be willing to be
misunderstood if you're going to innovate.

Jeff Bezos

Soft waves rippled through the calm turquoise waters.

The setting sun hung low on the horizon, its rosy fingers spreading across and embracing the water which glistened in its warmth. The picturesque sky, tainted by not a single cloud, reflected the tranquility of the Bermuda setting. In the remote distance, where the ocean and sky seemed to converge, the white sands of the archipelago island shores appeared as tiny fingers of land in the vast Atlantic.

Several miles off the southern coast cruised the USS Nimitz. From the distance, the thousand-foot aircraft carrier appeared as nothing more than a mere speck challenging the unruly ocean currents that dominated the offshore waters.

At thirty-one knots steady, and undaunted by the formidable display of nature's supremacy, the carrier sliced through the rough white waters that crashed loudly against her steel sides. Several large waves smacked against the ship's starboard side while the ship maintained her course, cutting more deeply into the vast ocean. The coast soon grew smaller and smaller until it appeared as several grains of sand in the distance. The white waters gradually gave way and the ocean's surface laid down smooth as glass.

Suddenly all was still. The massive ship, with her twelve hundred passengers and seventy-two crew members, had suddenly come to a complete halt as if two gargantuan anchors had fallen from her sides and bitten into the crust of the ocean's floor. She floated motionlessly. Silently. So silently that the silence had become deafening and the tranquility uncanny. For a moment.

The clear blue heavens darkened. They were no longer clear. No longer blue. A dark nebulous mist filled the sky above the formidable USS Nimitz. The mist reddened then began to spin. It spun and spun, faster and faster. A frighteningly fierce howling filled the sky as the tip of the fiery red tornado reached far into the heavens. Its broad funnel end, in diameter easily twice the length of the massive aircraft carrier, hovered directly over the ship.

A huge bolt of lightning flew from the open end of the tornado and struck the ship's bridge deck. A tremendous clap of thunder followed a moment later. The ship's compass spun wildly yet the ship remained motionless. The lightning had caused no damage. The ship remained completely intact. The gentle surface of the ocean again rose with a fury. It crashed violently against the ship's unyielding hull. Yet the USS Nimitz maintained her position. She remained unshaken. Somehow protected. Destruction seemed not the objective of this annihilative manifestation.

The tornado hovered a few moments longer before its whirling motion slowed then stopped completely. The monstrous upside-down conical firestorm, frozen in midair yet still floating above the ship, slowly collapsed onto itself, folding inwardly from its apex like an accordion until only a thin disc of red mist remained.

A small aperture in its center began to widen. It grew wider and wider until an opening at least two hundred feet wide was created. From along the innermost edge of the disc emerged five metallic sheetlike structures that glistened blindingly. Each was twenty or thirty feet wide and at least a hundred feet long. They were equally spaced along the inner perimeter of the disc but were not connected to the disc itself. They hovered within it. The panels extended downward, imprisoning the USS Nimitz in a pentagonal cage of some sort before smoothly cutting into the depths of the ocean without disturbing its calm surface.

The howling suddenly stopped. A high-pitched echo raced through the heavens for a moment then all became silent. The heavens. The waters. The USS Nimitz. All were consumed in the silence. Then it happened.

The aircraft carrier, all hundred thousand tons of it, stirred in the passive water, surrounded by the shiny panels which began to vibrate gently. Then it moved. Finally. But not forward. Nor backward. Straight up! The ship rose from the silky blue water as if hoisted by some humungous pulley system. But there was no pulley system. It lifted into the air then hovered several feet over the mouth of water it had been drawn from, still imprisoned by the glistening panels.

In an instant, the razor-like sheets lifted from the depths of the ocean and flew toward the thin disc. The ship moved with them as they approached the disc, then hovered motionlessly for a moment.

A blinding flash of amethyst light suddenly consumed the warship. Not another moment passed before the entire ship burst into a thousand pieces. Yet not one piece fell from the sky. In an instant, each piece dematerialized into millions of gleaming light particles. They remained motionless for a moment. Then they shot into the mouth of the disc and disappeared.

The rim of the disc quickly narrowed. In a brief moment, the entry was completely sealed. In another, the fiery red disc darted into the heavens and was gone.

The sky lightened and the crystal blue waters were again overrun with soft ripples. All was calm again. All was tranquil. But the ship was gone.

"Aaand cut!" a raspy voice yelled as a thunder of applause filled the large studio. "Not bad," the voice added. "Not perfect, but not bad."

Those encouraging words sounded from a small blowhorn. It was held by the disheveled fellow in the director's seat that was lifted about fifteen feet off the ground and suspended over the twenty-thousand gallon hexagonal tank which sat in the center of the tremendous warehouse set. The man ran a couple of fingers over his unevenly trimmed dark beard, then adjusted the wireframed glasses on the bridge of his nose as the mechanical seat backed away from the tank and lowered him onto the set.

"Set it up again," he said as fifteen or twenty grips and stagehands scurried across the set. "Once more and we oughta be wrapped."

The thin man, dressed in loosely fitted black jeans and a baggy black T-shirt, walked across the massive set, the blowhorn dangling from his hand, to a large pentagonal table atop which sat several colorful monitors and numerous control panels, one piled on the other. Ojo and Sasha sat behind it.

He caught Ojo's hand and kissed Sasha on the cheek as they stood to congratulate him.

"So, Steven, was I right?" Sasha asked him teasingly, pointing at Ojo. "Is this man a genius or what?" she added.

"Might just be," the famous filmmaker mumbled through the corner of his mouth, rounded by the hint of a content grin as he squeezed Ojo's shoulder.

"I'm glad you're pleased with the Fractionater," Ojo responded while several grips repositioned each of the eight Ikegami lasers at different levels along the perimeter of the huge tank. "It's working well. But I've been studying the monitors closely and I think we can come up just a bit on the image resolution."

"I agree," Steven told him with a subtle smile. "You see, Sasha, this is the attitude that separates the giants from the mere mortals."

Sasha and Ojo exchanged a proud smile.

"Thanks," Ojo responded, "but Derek's the genius in this case. He upgraded the Fractionator system so now, by kicking in the additional two-megawatt amp," he went on, pointing to the complex apparatus on the table, "you can disengage an image into 10^{12} particles. A thousandfold increase over any other state-of-the-art technology. And by employing the laser filter system the particle resolution is increased a hundredfold!"

"Well, what're we waiting for?" Steven asked as he grabbed Ojo's hand. Sasha had already made her way across the set and was directing a number of grips as they waded through the tank, repositioning and adjusting the four submerged laser prisms while a large pulley lowered the thirty-two-foot USS Nimitz model back into the water.

Ojo made the necessary adjustments on the Fractionator apparatus and continued fine-tuning as Steven walked back across the set and stepped onto the seat which lifted him high above the tank.

"Ready on one and three," a cameraman called from off-set.

"We have speed on four and six," another cameraman sounded.

"Fractionator ready and activated," Ojo called to the crew.

The light above the tank became dim for a moment then suddenly brilliantly blue as the soft ripples appeared.

"Ready … aaaand … action!" Steven announced.

The scene was shot again and again. And again. But finally, flawlessly. Separating the giants from the mere mortals. Spielberg was pleased.

As he and Ojo sat in a couple directors' chairs alongside the tank discussing the details of the next scene, one to involve the crash landing of a UFO within the mouth of an erupting volcano along the coast of Bora Bora, a subdued chirping tone rang out. The sound came from Ojo's watch. He eyed the face of the knockoff Rolex that he had reconfigured with a digital microprocessor and refaced with a liquid crystal mini display output. The digital readout lit up. WTF911. It was the emergency code. The signal flashed quickly. Another replaced it. SOS*9477. It was Arti's disabled relay code. There was trouble.

* * *

Derek pressed a small button on the side of his matching watch and the chirping tone ceased. The readout was replaced by the time. 2:40 p.m.

The large checker cab turned on the corner of Broome Street and West Broadway. It came to a halt about halfway down the block in front of a large driveway.

Derek slipped several bills into the hungry palm the elderly driver eagerly extended. It was only when the driver turned to face him that Derek noticed the terrible scar that ran from just below the man's right eye down past the side of his mouth and narrowed off about half an inch below his jawline. He didn't have much of a neck.

"Thank ya much, sonny," he said with an appreciative smile, displaying his three or four badly corroded teeth.

"You have a good one, now," Derek told the man, returning a smile as he opened the door and stepped out of the cab.

"You too, sonny, you too," he heard the man calling to him as the door clicked shut and he walked up the driveway.

It led to a large glass showcase. Etched in the center of the tinted glass were the words 'Corvette City.' Behind them, on a cylindrical block that slowly rotated, sat a '65 yellow convertible Stingray.

Derek pushed through the glass door on the side of the large showcase front. It led to a huge driveway in the service area where several Vettes rested, one a deep red convertible, another a turquoise twin turbo Calloway, and a third an orange-and-white striped '68 racer. Behind the Calloway, a black convertible ZR1 Stingray glistened. *Ojo's Stingray. With four new Pirellis. Awesome.*

Derek quickly maneuvered through the poised Vettes to the one he had come for. In one swift move, he seated himself behind the wheel and reached for the Teledisc which sat on the dashboard.

He anxiously dialed the shop as a heavyset sales manager approached the car. The number rang several times but there was no answer. It was rare for Arti not to answer the phone, Derek thought as the fellow jotted some notes on the clipboard he was holding. He quickly dialed another number—*9477*9477*—the direct interface code that linked with Arti's modular receiver. Again, no response. This had never happened before. Something was wrong. Dead wrong.

"That'll come to a flat sixteen hundred," the man told Derek as he looked up from his notes. "Best tires made, ya know," he added with a deserving smile.

Derek pulled a folded paper from his shirt pocket. He scribbled in the sum on the blank check Ojo had given him earlier as a chirping tone again sounded from his watch. *969-9010.* He quickly dialed the number.

"Derek," Ojo's voice shot through the phone.

"Right here."

"We've got a problem."

"I know. I already tried interfacing with Arti."

"So did I. No luck, right?"

"That's right."

"What about my Vette?"

"I'm sitting in it. Where are you?"

"Studio B. 23rd and 9th."

"I'll be there in ten."

Derek returned the phone to its seat on the dashboard and reached for the empty ignition.

"That'll be sixteen hundred, sir." The sales manager reminded him, dangling the keys with a loose wrist.

"Sorry 'bout that," Derek replied, handing the man the check in exchange for the keys.

He quickly started the engine and was off. In a second he maneuvered between the other Vettes and through the entranceway as a huge pane of glass lifted up and slid out of the way on some track.

A thunderous screech was heard as Derek pulled onto West Broadway. He flew down the wide street, weaving around the numerous cabbies that cluttered it. Prince Street … Houston Street. The lights were with him but it wouldn't have mattered. 4th Street … 8th Street … 14th Street. He was brought to a stop at 18th Street and turned down the narrow road. He raced along 18th Street, avoiding as many potholes as he possibly could, then turned on 9th Avenue. In another moment he was on the corner of 23rd Street where Ojo stood waiting.

He got in on the passenger side.

"Let's roll," he told Derek as the door clicked shut. "What's the damage?" Ojo asked as the car sped off.

"Sixteen hundred."

"Bastards."

"What d'ya think's going on with Arti?"

"No idea," Ojo responded. "How'd your meeting with Sony go?"

"They want to market our TV-Holography Converter," he answered. "After they combine it with the technology of their top-of-the-line big screen set," he added, exchanging high fives with Ojo.

"They do know we're gonna maintain all rights to the patent, right?" Ojo cautiously asked. "They'll get a 2-year renewable license."

Derek turned toward him and a widening grin squeezed through his lips. No need for an answer. It went without saying.

"How'd the shoot with Spielberg go?" Derek asked.

"Like clockwork. Twenty-three takes but we wrapped the Nimitz scene."

"Any problem with the Fractionator?"

"None. Worked like a charm."

"Great. And what about last night with Sasha?"

Ojo just looked Derek in the eye and smiled. That too

went without saying.

"Thought so," Derek said. "So how far did you actually get with that code on the eyeglass frame?" he asked as the car cut the corner on 7th Avenue as they flew through Greenwich Village on their way back to the bomb shelter.

"I broke into the databank. After about an hour of further decoding I left the search on autopilot. Far as I know, it's still going," Ojo told him.

"I'll bet that message of Arti's has something to do with that code."

"I don't doubt it. But I want to know why he didn't respond when we interfaced."

"So do I," Derek agreed as he pulled into a space right in front of the shop.

"Where the hell did *that* come from?!" Ojo asked as he pointed a finger toward the sign that hung taped to the door of the shop. In large unfamiliar handwriting was written one word. 'CLOSED'.

He and Derek ran from the car toward the door. Ojo tore the sign from the glass, crumpling the paper in his hand as he slowly pushed the door open. In the silence that filled the empty shop, the door hit something that rustled across the carpeting.

Derek bent to pick up a small piece of broken glass. He and Ojo examined it and then eyed each other. One word was etched on the glass. *ARTIFINTELLIBOT.* Nothing was said for a moment.

"Jesus *Christ!*" Derek muttered through clenched teeth, pulling a diamond-shaped laser stunner from the pocket of his jacket.

"C'mon," Ojo urged him, doing the same as they cautiously moved between the displays and toward the spiral staircase.

As best they could tell from a panning glance, none of the displays had been damaged or stolen. Nothing seemed even touched. Almost nothing. As they climbed the sharply angling stairs which led to the office, they noticed the gun holes in the ceiling. There were four of them. Two in the ceiling several feet from the staircase. Another two in the ceiling several feet from the front door. The gunman had cleverly found the two hidden cameras and destroyed them. This was no amateur. But what did he want? What did he find? And where was Arti?

Derek and Ojo passed through the glass door at the top of the staircase and entered the office. It had been ransacked. The drawers of both desks had been pulled open and papers had been thrown everywhere. Books and journals had been tossed from the shelves onto the floor. Several gunshot holes marked the sites where locks had kept the steel drawers of the large filing cabinet on the side wall secured and the confidential files within it. Like the desks, the cabinet's drawers had been ripped open and their files strewn about. Numerous papers and photos had haphazardly been tossed atop the cabinet. Others had been left on the floor at its base. One or two disarrayed folders lay on the bottom of each of the otherwise emptied drawers.

Ojo's eyes quickly passed from the mess that lay at his feet to the door that led to the workshop. The lead slab had been moved aside. It was open.

Derek ran a nervous finger along the smooth edge of the laser weapon. He held it tightly in his palm. He signaled with a quick nod and Ojo moved to the right side of the doorway as he moved to the left.

The room was dark. They stood by the doorway in silence for a moment. Then Ojo spoke.

"Cover me," he whispered.

In an instant, Ojo swung around the jam and was in the workshop. As his eyes adjusted to the darkness, he could make out the shapes of several objects which lay on a pile of papers on the floor beside a workbench on the right side of the room. One was a keyboard. Another a parachute release timer. And another the Thermalyzer.

Derek stood several feet behind him. Both anxiously searched for anything that moved. Or breathed. They could find neither. Until their eyes focused on the far left corner of the large room. There, bent against the leg of a workbench, lay the silhouetted image of their beloved friend.

"Arti!" Derek called to him with a cracked voice.

He darted across the room. Ojo flipped the light switch and followed. Derek stood a few feet from the workbench. His eyes welled as he took in the pitiful sight that lay before him.

Arti had been shot. In a puddle of glass fragments,

there he stood, the leg of the workbench his only support. The broken glass was all that remained of Arti's revolving dome. Two steel rods and several badly charred wires dangled defenselessly. A piece of paper had been slapped onto one of the metal rods. Written on it in blood were two words. 'YOU'RE NEXT!'

Ojo and Derek eyed each other for a moment, then turned back toward Arti. Derek furiously tore the note from the rod and crumpled it in a tight fist.

"Guess again, you son-of-a-bitch!" he said with unparted teeth.

In some random, uncontrolled fashion, Arti's right cylinder shook back and forth ever so slowly. From time to time, it violently jerked up and down once or twice, then resumed its previous oscillatory activity. A blue light pulsed the length of his left cylinder while a red light flashed repeatedly on the upper rim of his central cylinder. Both remained motionless. And without sound.

Derek pressed a small button on the side of the central cylinder. Arti's power system was now deactivated. With a screwdriver that lay on the benchtop, he freshened the ends of the exposed wires. After several minutes of rewiring, adjusting and fine-tuning, he pressed the button a second time.

At first nothing happened. Then several sparks of yellow light began to bubble on top of one of the steel rods. The same thing happened on the other rod. The sparks of light played back and forth between the rods until a steady stream of hazy yellow light glowed between them. The light turned bright orange and the rods slowly began to spin. Blue lights pulsed up and down the side cylinders while glaring red lights revolved around the central one.

"That oughta do it," Derek said as he adjusted one last dial on the side of the central cylinder, watching with Ojo as Arti slowly came back to life. "Should be good as new," he added in a relieved voice.

"All he needs now is—" Ojo started.

"Some head," Arti interrupted with a squeaky voice as several bursts of blue and orange light danced between the coiled wires and rods. His glass dome was gone. Shattered.

Derek and Ojo eyed each other for a silent moment, then laughed loudly.

"I was going to say 'some charging,' but okay," Ojo finished.

"Welcome back, 'pardner'," Derek said.

"Good to be back."

"So what the hell happened?" Ojo asked.

"Oh. Did I forget to mention? I got *shot!*"

"C'mon, Arti. This is important."

"Okay, okay. Do you mind? My head is spinning," Arti said as his metal rods whirled around, "and already it's back to work. No massage. Not even a coffee break. Nothing," he rambled.

"You don't drink coffee," Derek told him.

"How do you know? Have you ever offered me a cup of Joe?" Arti quickly responded. "No, you haven't. Never. Not once!"

"You don't have a mouth, Arti. You're a *robot!*" Ojo told him.

"A mere detail. Maybe one you should consider when you replace my dome," Arti suggested. "No need to be rude."

"Sure, we'll get you a dome with a mouth so you can drink coffee. And maybe have a donut with your coffee," Ojo offered.

"That would be great," Arti replied. "Thank you."

"Then we'll also need to build you an *asshole* so you can take a robot dump," Derek jumped in.

"No need," Arti flatly told him as his rods rotated from Derek to Ojo and then back. "I already have two."

Derek and Ojo shared a glance for a silent moment, astonished and amused by their own AI creation. Then they all laughed loudly. Arti's shrill staccato inflection made them laugh even louder. They were certainly relieved to have their friend back.

"Touché," Derek conceded. "Now tell us what happened already."

"Okay, okay. I was standing over there," Arti started, rotating on his bearings and pointing to the printer that sat on the bench against the right wall. "Ojo's search started printing out," he went on. "While I was waiting I sensed someone's presence by the doorway. Then, suddenly, everything went black … Then I saw this tunnel … And this bright light … I was looking down at myself … Then I started to float toward—"

"Spare us the out-of-body routine, would you?" Derek interrupted him and laughed.

"Can you tell us what the shooter looked like?" Ojo asked.

"Well, I only saw him for a split second before it was lights out, you know. This probably won't help any but he was six-foot-three and a half, dark hair, weighed a hundred and eighty-seven pounds, and wore a flattened gray hat, silver-rimmed bifocals, a long black trench coat over a pair of gray pants and a white shirt, and clunky orthopedic shoes. Ugly scar on the right side of his face. And his left foot stood two and a quarter inches higher than his right. Wish I could give you more."

Arti paused for a moment. Derek and Ojo shared another amused glance.

"Must've had one helluva limp," he added.

CHAPTER TWELVE

If I have a thousand ideas and only one turns out to
be good, I am satisfied.

Alfred Nobel

"He's dead!" Ojo furiously said. "When I get my hands on
that son-of-a-bitch, he's dead!"

He and Derek stood by the printer on the right side
of the workshop, horrified and infuriated by their
discovery. Derek leaned against the workbench, looking
down at the Thermalyzer in his hands. Both pieces of the
Thermalyzer. The viewer had been ripped clean from its
delicate connection with the main unit and its lenses
smashed. The main unit, whose function depended upon
the thermal vacuum within its chromium shell, was

cracked wide open. The priceless invention was now useless. Worthless. Six months of research and development. The device that brilliantly proved Ojo's innocence. The *photo time machine*. Gone. Destroyed.

"Better get online," Derek told him in an icy tone, lifting his eyes to meet Ojo's burning stare.

Derek put the pieces of the Thermalyzer beside the printer as Ojo placed the parachute timer and keyboard on the bench near the terminal. It was then that Derek noticed a sheet of paper in the printout bin.

"Look at this," he told Ojo, pulling the paper from the bin.

Together they started at it in silence for some time.

PNTGNBNK ENTRY NEXUSdata
PNTGNBNK ENTRY NEXUSdata

Xv3??s17-656-awqs//01tz
::: [llzt] [10sq] [wa6] [567] [1s3]vx:::

*ƒ*ŒŸ¯??"»'¯–??*ƒ*¯÷'
Œ»–÷???'''÷'»???"ÿŸÀ
„ÊË_???Û¯_÷Ê??ÓÊ¯Ë

PROJECT INHHSOOOO22619435
PROJECT INHHSOOOO22619435

INHHSOOOO22619435 DATA CONTINUES 0026

INHHSOOOO22619435 DATA CONTINUES 0026

Insertion of the Omega gene into the double-stranded lambda plasmid DNA of the *Escherichia coli* bacterium has been accomplished. Subsequent cloning of the Omega gene has yielded sufficient genetic copies to complete in vitro analysis of timed embryonic gestation within genetically dissimilar environments. The Trans-Species Implantation Facility will proceed with surrogate embryo implantation as designed and put forth in the protocol. Organogenesis and osteogenesis will be monitored and evaluated throughout the gestational period up until delivery in the described zero gravity environment.

INHHSOOOO2261945 DATA TERMINATES

INHHSOOOO2261945 DATA TERMINATES

"What does this mean?" Derek asked with a puzzled look on his face.

"I haven't a fuck of an idea."

"Think it looks like something worth killing for?"

"Doesn't matter what I think. We already know the answer to that. *Someone* thinks it's worth killing for. We've got a dead surgeon for a witness."

"Hey, what about me?" Arti interrupted. "What am I? Three cans of stinkin' sardines?"

"He's just making a point, Arti," Derek told him.

"I know, I know. But let me tell you," Arti went on, "From my experience—"

"Experience?" Ojo questioned sarcastically.

"That's right, dumbass!" Arti snapped. "Now where was I?"

"Experience, Arti, experience," Derek helped him along.

"Oh, yeah, experience. I'll have you know I've read every Clancy novel and seen every Bond flick and let me tell you something—"

"Please do," Ojo interrupted.

"Do what?"

"Tell us!"

"Okay, okay. Let me tell you," Arti continued, "this guy means business."

"Thanks for pointing that out," Derek told him, glancing at the broken Thermalyzer.

"No problem fellas. Just earning my oil."

"Anyway," Derek went on, "this can't be all of it. We're missing something huge. I know we are."

"I think you're right," Ojo agreed, tapping his finger on the center of the page. "What d'ya think this here means?"

0026.

Derek smiled. There *was* more. Twenty-five pages if Ojo's hunch was right. And it usually was.

Derek turned the terminal on and began the retrieval process. He had no way of knowing what damage the killer had done to his data system. If any. Maybe none. Could this guy have been careless enough to have left behind the last sheet of the top secret document he himself had killed to obtain? Or could the last page have simply been printed out after he grabbed the pile of papers already sitting in the bin? Then again, no one has accused this guy of being a rocket scientist. Seemed more like some windup zombie marching to some other psychopath's beat.

These thoughts raced through Ojo's mind as he quickly logged in and accessed the VAX computer system. Neither scenario mattered, he thought. All that mattered was retrieving the rest of that file. He was convinced that the key to understanding the motive for the surgeon's murder was somewhere in that file. It had to be.

The screen cleared and the terminal beeped. It awaited his search commands. Ojo pressed several keys and the screen readied itself. The code had already been broken, the work already done. Assuming no changes had been made, it all came down to three lines of what may as well have been Greek coding. He entered them as they appeared on the page that was printed out earlier.

ƒŒŸÿ???"»'ÿ–???ƒÿ÷'
Œ»–÷??'"÷'»??"ÿŸÀ
„ÊË_??Û‾_÷Ê•••ÓÊ‾Ë

The terminal beeped again. Several times.

"Hard to believe the code hasn't been changed," Derek said. "Even as a routine process, you'd think their security algorithm would scramble it every night," he added.

SEARCHING … SEARCHING …

"Probably has," Ojo responded, "but with any luck at all," he went on, "the SEARCH program will automatically accommodate the revised code changes."

"So as the code is changed the program locks onto it and immediately begins the decoding process, right?"

SEARCHING … SEARCHING …

"The tertiary code. Right. So even if it took the program a hundred or more decoding generations to finally break the code, we should never be more than two generations behind the rescrambled code," Ojo explained.

"Child's play for the VAX," Derek said.

"Exactly. But only if that scumbag hasn't screwed up our database."

"This might be our lucky day," Derek started as the screen flashed. "It looks like he hasn't," Derek said. "We might be good."

PNTGNBNK ENTRY || GENEdata

PNTGNBNK ENTRY || GENEdata

xv3||s17-656-awqs//01tz

::: [llzt] [10sq] [wa6] [567] [1s3]vx :::

"I think you're right," Ojo said. "But the code has definitely been changed," he added. His eyes remained fixed on the monitor.

Û„_¯Ë_ËÊ••Ó¯Û••¯ÓÊ_„Ê‰Á

„_·¯ËÁÊÛ••·_Î••ÂÊ_Â_Ë‰¯

ÂÏÎÓ‰·,Ë••¯„,••ÏÊ„Â¯_‰Ë

"*And* ..." he went on. The screen cleared then flashed again.

PROJECT INHHSOOOO22619435

PROJECT INHHSOOOO22619435

INHHSOOOO22619435 DATA BEGINS 0001

INHHSOOOO22619435 DATA BEGINS 0001

"…we are *in*!"

Ojo keyed in several additional commands and the printer began humming. Several seconds later the first page of the document glided into the printout bin.

"This is good," Derek said with a gleaming smile.

"Real good," Ojo agreed as they viewed what appeared to be the document's header page.

PHASE ONE

ON TRANS-SPECIES IMPLANTATION

Focus on the Omega Gene

Derek and Ojo eyed each other for a silent moment.

"We're onto somethin' here," Derek said. "Don't know what it is, but I know we're onto it."

"I hear ya, guy," Ojo responded. "What d'ya think of this?" he said as he pulled the second page from the bin.

They looked at it for some time as the next several pages slowly made their way into the bin.

INHHSOOOO2261945 DATA CONTINUES 0002

INHHSOOOO2261945 DATA CONTINUES 0002

The successful implantation of an embryo from one animal species into a surrogate host of another species has, until now, only been theorized. The greatest hindrance to the successful 'take' of a trans-species embryo by a heterologous species has been humoral- and cellular-based immunologic rejection with consistent embryo loss. The discovery of a 22-kilobase mutated segment of viral DNA called XZ35yp245 has recently been made. This segment of DNA has, following bacterial plasmid DNA intersplicing, provided evidence that transplant-specific rejection can be completely prevented without inducing an adverse host immunosuppression response. XZ35yp245 is the Omega gene.

Derek slowly read the paragraphs then looked up from the page.

"How does some genetics experiment connect with the Chief of Orthopedics?" he asked as he took the next few pages from the bin. "Where does he tie into all this?"

"And why was he murdered?" Ojo asked. "What d'ya have there?"

They skimmed the next several pages. More of the same. A discussion of transplantation immunology which neither understood nor cared about. A nucleotide map of the Omega gene. And a brand new protocol for DNA gene splicing. Nothing too unusual here, they thought. New cutting-edge research, maybe. To some people, perhaps. But nothing worth killing for.

The seventh page of the document somehow slid over the bin and drifted onto the floor. Derek bent to retrieve it. Another header page.

PHASE TWO

ON SURROGATE GESTATION

Focus on Stimulated Fetal Osteogenesis and Organogenesis

"Think we might be chasing our tails," Derek said.

"How d'ya figure?"

"You're the computer whiz but I think the code may have been rescrambled and the output fed into another file."

"You mean a dead file."

"Exactly."

"Let's first see what we've got before we write it off," Ojo suggested, scooping the next few pages from the bin.

INHHSO0002261945 DATA CONTINUES 0008

INHHSO0002261945 DATA CONTINUES 0008

In a protected environment without concern for immunologic disturbances, in vitro embryonic gestational development will be monitored with specific emphasis placed on cerebral, internal organ and bony development. Following successful in vitro development and term or near-term live delivery of the fetuses, similar trials will be performed in immunologically hostile environments with fetuses in which the Omega gene has been genomically interspliced within chromosome 14 of the maternal complement. Once it is established that the Omega gene can yield live births from embryos implanted within a surrogate, immunologically and genetically adverse environment, implantation will be performed in vivo first between homologous species and afterwards between similar yet heterologous species.

"Worth killing for yet?" Derek asked in a disappointed tone.

"Not yet," Ojo answered. "Let's keep going," he said and grabbed the seven or eight pages that patiently sat in the bin as the printer continued humming.

They eyeballed the first few. More genetics and

immunology discussion. Some postulated theory. More protocols. Again, nothing extraordinarily out of the ordinary.

"Wait a second," Derek said as Ojo quickly flipped through the pages. "Look at this," he added, putting his hand between two of the sheets and his index finger on the next header page.

PHASE THREE

ON FETAL DEVELOPMENT IN ZERO GRAVITY

Focus on Fetal Morphogenesis and Adaptation in Space

"Hmmm," Ojo muttered, tracing the curve of his chin with a few fingers. "Still think we're chasing our tails?"

"I think we may have just caught them," Derek answered with a curious grin.

Their enthusiasm was renewed. Even if for no other reason than simply the mention of 'space', their enthusiasm was renewed.

"Worth killing for?" Ojo asked.

"Don't know."

They read the next few pages very quickly. They knew not what to expect nor where this was all leading, but they knew, by this time, that it was leading somewhere. They had stumbled upon something. *Something big.*

INHHSOOOO2261945 DATA CONTINUES 0012

INHHSOOOO2261945 DATA CONTINUES 0012

The study of fetal development in a specialized zero gravity or microgravity environment has, since man first accomplished departure from the gravitational reigns of this world more than two decades ago, been attempted in only unsuccessful models utilizing simple life forms. With the breakthrough discovery and successful intersplicing of the complete Omega gene into chromosome 14 of the ovum, zero gravity and microgravity gestation may now feasibly be explored using higher species. Fetal adaptation in these challenging environments is essential if the development of surrogate-derived space colonies is to succeed.

"Fuckin' *space colonies*!" Derek blurted with childlike excitement.

"Worth killing for?" Ojo asked with a restrained grin.

"Could be," Derek mumbled. "Look at this," he said, turning a couple pages.

INHHSOOOO2261945 DATA CONTINUES 0016

INHHSOOOO2261945 DATA CONTINUES 0016

Once surrogate fetal adaptation and development have been consistently accomplished without adverse consequences, trans-species embryonic implantation will be performed routinely within the protected zero gravity environment of Starbase 7, the first satellite space colony. Three subsequent satellite colonies will be established, each with its own unique orbit. From this unified space colony system will emerge the New State.

Ojo and Derek stared at each other for a long silent moment.

"*New State?* Worth killing for?" Ojo asked.

"Uh, yeah. I definitely think this has some killing potential."

"So do I, guy. But from whom are they going to build the 'New State'?" Ojo sarcastically asked. "White mice?"

The printer hummed once more then made a beeping sound. There were no more pages in the bin. Ojo looked at the monitor and closed his eyes tightly for a second.

"Those bastards!" he screamed. "They fucked us!"

Derek looked on as Ojo furiously worked at the keyboard.

"There's not a damned thing I can do," he said with a defeated tone in his voice as he struggled to maintain the connection to the NEXUS research data portal.

But it was lost. The portal was closing and there was nothing they could do about it at this point.

$$\sigma\upsilon\psi\theta\omega\theta\zeta\cdots\xi\psi\sigma\cdots\psi\xi\zeta\upsilon\gamma\zeta\delta\eta$$
$$\beta\pi\alpha\psi\theta\eta\zeta\sigma\cdots\alpha\omega\lambda\cdots\epsilon\zeta\upsilon\epsilon\omega\theta\delta\psi$$
$$\epsilon\mu\lambda\xi\delta\alpha\beta\theta\cdots\psi\beta\gamma\cdots\mu\zeta\gamma\epsilon\psi\pi\delta\theta$$

PROJECT UNAUTHORIZED
PROJECT UNAUTHORIZED

PROJECT NONEXISTENT
PROJECT NONEXISTENT

SEARCH TERMINATED
SEARCH TERMINATED

"Well, you were absolutely right," he told Derek. "The code has been rescrambled. We're locked out."

He paused for a moment and seemed to nervously chew on his upper lip.

"Guess we're lucky we got what we got," Ojo added. "Damn!" he exploded, bringing his fist down hard on the printer.

A quiet moment passed.

"Maybe a bit luckier than you think," Derek said as one more header page slid from the printer onto the bin. "Now, what were you saying of mice… and men?" he asked Ojo with a raised eyebrow.

"Unfuckinbelievable!" Ojo mumbled in a low voice.

They were silent for some time as they stared at that page. It just sat in the bin as they stared at it. Neither picked it up. It just sat there. And they just stared at it.

PHASE FOUR

ON HUMAN-RHESUS MONKEY TRANS-SPECIES IMPLANTATION

Focus on Rhesus Monkey Surrogate for Human Fetus

CHAPTER THIRTEEN

The advance of technology is based on making it fit
in so that you don't really even notice it, so it's part
of everyday life. If you can't make it good, at least
make it look good.

Bill Gates

The setting sun cast an unusual glow upon the still water. Several small clouds slowly moved through the reddening sky. Rays of hazy sunlight made their way through the fluffy white forms, falling on the dark water that filled the diamond-shaped swimming pool. Its floor and sidewalls had been coated with a black enamel which gave a silverish sheen to the water's surface as the lines of fading sunlight cut across it. A trim of turquoise stone defined the sharp angles of the diamond. Several slabs of turquoise formed steps at two of the diamond's points. One where Christine sat at the edge of the pool on a bright yellow tanning chair, her long legs extending the length of a couple of steps before disappearing into the dark water. The other at the opposite end of the pool.

On her lap lay a blue aluminum clipboard. A number of papers were fixed beneath its rubber clip. Several paragraphs covered the page that sat on top. Christine eyed the page carefully. With a pen in hand, she slowly reviewed the work. She crossed out a word here, replaced another there. The order of two phrases was reversed with a double-headed arrow. With another arrow she moved a sentence from the second paragraph to the fourth, then crossed out the third paragraph entirely. One comment was changed to a question and the sentence's structure reversed.

Again, she reviewed the entire page. All of it. The crossed-out words, others inserted with carets, arrows which bounced within sentences and between paragraphs. She reread the paragraphs several times then, with a quick snap of her wrist, she tore the page from under the clip and crumpled it into a tight ball with a frustrated fist. She held the crumpled paper in her hand and closed her eyes as she leaned back and rested her head against the bright yellow fabric that stretched across the chair's black metal frame.

After a long moment, Christine's head tilted slightly toward the side as her hand slid from its position on her belly and dangled over the edge of the chair. Her fingers loosened their grip on the wad of paper and it rolled onto the ground. Its path was shortened by the twenty or thirty similarly crumpled papers that formed a scattered pile on the travertine deck that surrounded the pool. The crumpled ball rolled into the side of the printer paper box that peaked out from under the pile. Its cover was partially off and cast a sharp shadow on the tall stack of papers within the box.

A rush of cool air passed through the large oak trees that enclosed the backyard, sending a steady ripple through the dark water of the pool as several small leaves floated onto its surface, and brushing the strawberry strands from Christine's face as her long blonde hair flowed over the chair's back and freely in the breeze though she lay motionlessly and silently. Several of the crumpled paper balls moved about as the breeze caught them, scattering them in several directions and brushing them from atop the printer paper box to reveal a sheet of light grey paper that was fixed to its cover. On it was printed just one word. *Deadlock.*

One of the paper balls lifted from the ground as the wind carried it across the turquoise trim and slammed it into the stone and glass house that sat about fifty feet from the pool. From just the right angle with the sun at just the right position in the sky, the way it was now, a beautifully distorted reflection of the large white house shimmered in the dark water.

It was a special house. Designed by Augustave Clemens. A student of Frank Lloyd Wright's. White stone and jade glass. Nothing else. Two large stone cylinders, one taller than the other, rose from a wedge-shaped stone foundation. Two layers of windows encircled the taller of the two cylinders, one encircled the other. Connecting the cylinders were two massive panes of glass. The front and rear entrances to the house had been cut from the glass panes and automatically pivoted on some mechanism within the center of each to allow entry. A roof of wavy solar panels—*Jennon SolarFlares*—hung between the glass panes. Derek had proudly installed them several months ago. The wavy panel concept produced a supercharging effect so only a few panels were needed to power the entire house and pool. The solar panels and jade glass together brilliantly reflected the reddened sun onto the glistening surface of the swimming pool's black water.

The house stood proudly on its generous lot, distantly neighboring several other unique homes in this exclusive Westchester community. Just twenty minutes from Manhattan, and a far greater distance from the headaches of city living, this area had become home to many celebrities, physicians, corporate execs and others who could afford it and preferred to commute to the city daily but live elsewhere. It was a pleasant community. Very tranquil. Very peaceful. *Bronxville*, it was called.

A number of leaves and flower petals whirled past the house as the gentle breeze gradually grew into a tempered wind. A soft whistling sound filled the air as the leaves rustled. A tiny blue jay sat in its nest on a delicate branch high above the pool. Another sharp gust of wind violently shook the thin branch. The small bird fled from its home as the branch snapped and the nest and its three eggs tumbled helplessly through the sky, landing in the pool several feet from where Christine sat. The small splash just barely struck her thighs. She stirred for a moment and her eyes opened. The water was calm again. The small branch floated where the nest had landed and sunk.

Christine stared at the branch. Beside it floated a broken piece of eggshell. She watched as the shell slowly filled with water and sank. Shortly afterwards, the branch rose from the pool, spun around several times, then fell back into the water and disappeared beneath its surface. That was odd, she thought.

She watched and watched, waiting for the branch to float back to the surface. It never did. That made no sense, she told herself. A moment later, she noticed something else that made no sense. The level of water in the pool slowly lowered as the pool began to overflow. The water rose along the sides of the turquoise and flowed over the edge of the pool and onto the stone deck.

The water level within the pool continued to diminish as the water continued to flow onto the stone. Within seconds the crumpled papers and printer paper box were submerged. The pool was soon half empty as the level of water outside the pool began to rise. Christine's legs were completely submerged as the level approached her waist. She seemed frozen with fear for a moment, then tried to lift herself from the chair. She could not.

The pool was now almost empty. The level of water outside the pool was now way above Christine's waist. The harder she tried to stand, the more tightly she was restrained. Her effort was useless. She was trapped. There was no way out. She would surely drown.

As the last few feet of water emptied from the pool, it became clear that two objects lay on its floor. Two objects in a puddle of blood. Christine struggled to make them out as the water rose above her shoulders. She moved about as much as she could on her imprisoning chair, trying to figure out what they were. Finally, just before the water covered her mouth, she let out a loud gasp. She could recognize the objects. They were not objects at all. The figures of two men, stretched out on the floor of the pool, suddenly became crystal clear. One lay on his back, his arms extended and knees curled. The other lay beside him, face down with his head cocked to the side in quite an unnatural position. Christine knew the men. She knew them well. Both of them. One was Derek. The other Ojo.

She jerked from side to side in the chair, mumbling several garbled words as the clipboard fell from her lap, making a cracking sound as it landed on the crumpled pieces of paper. The noise caused her to stir as she groggily opened her eyes. The sky was now a deep orange tone with overthrown reddish hues. The pool was still filled with water. A small branch floated on its surface.

Christine smiled. She brushed the hair from her face and lifted the clipboard from the ground. Her pen was still in her hand. She looked at it and smiled again.

Then she looked at the ground. She picked up several of the crumpled papers and quickly unfolded them. In a few seconds she had eyed each of them and recrumpled them. She tossed them to the side and picked up several others. Again Christine quickly unfolded and eyed each of the papers then recrumpled them and reached for several more. As she unfolded the first of this lot, she realized she had found the paper she sought and tossed the others back on the pile.

Christine laid the paper on the clipboard and smoothed out some of its wrinkles with the side of her hand.

"Now, let's see what we have here," she said out loud with a hint of renewed enthusiasm in her voice, taking another look at the page she had painfully edited several times before falling asleep.

She made several additional changes to the wrinkled paper and then quickly copied the work onto a fresh page. When she was done, she crumpled the wrinkled page, tossed it back on the pile and continued her work. After some time Christine stopped writing for a moment and lifted her eyes from the clipboard. She stared at the small branch as it floated in the center of the pool, then shifted her focus back to the paragraphs she had just completed. She read them over a couple of times as she had before. Then she just sat there for a content moment.

"It works," she mumbled with a relieved smile, gently removing the page from under the clip and placing it beneath the other papers. *The scene finally works,* she told herself and laughed as the chirping tone of her phone rang out.

A small black and yellow disc, just barely larger than a makeup compact case, sat on the turquoise stone a few feet away from Christine's leg. The disc had a row of lights in its center. A blue one now flashed as a high-pitched tone sounded. It was one of Christine's private lines. Only Derek had the number to this one.

"Could it be handsome Derek?" she asked by calling into the air.

The blue light stopped flashing as the voice-activated phone automatically received the call.

"Could be and it is," Derek's voice flowed from the small gadget and filled the air. "What're you up to, gorgeous?" he asked her.

"Just sittin' by the pool, tryin' to finish this novel."

"How's it comin'?"

"It's comin'," Christine replied. "Fell asleep in the middle of my own sentence, but it's comin'."

Derek laughed.

"What're you up to?" she asked.

"A lot, actually," he told her. "We're onto something."

"Do tell. I'm all ears," Christine said.

"We're onto something big."

"What are you talking about? The murder in the park?"

"You got it."

"Well, what have ya come up with? C'mon, c'mon. What is it?"

"We don't have all the pieces yet," Derek started, "but it's got something to do with genetic engineering and the space program."

"You sure it's safe to talk about on the phone?"

"Yeah, yeah. Don't worry. We're on the DriftNet circuit. I designed it to bypass AT&T and all the rest. Forget already? It's impossible to tap into this line because I created the frequency. No one else knows it exists. Not even the FCC. But good thinking."

"So, c'mon, c'mon," Christine urged him.

"Okay, okay. You know that code Ojo was working on last night?"

"Uh, huh."

"Well, bingo!"

"Bingo?"

"Bingo! Jackpot!"

"Jackpot?"

"Jackpot!"

"Well, are you goin' to tell me about it or just tease the crap outta me?!"

"Okay, okay. We still don't know why Dr. Barnes, the orthopod, was killed."

"Buuuut?"

"But get this. What do you think when I mention the word 'surrogate mother'? Okay, two words."

"Well, I think—"

"Don't think yet," Derek interrupted. "What about *monkey* surrogates?" he added and paused.

"Go on, go on."

"…for *human* fetuses!"

"What?!"

"That's right! These guys are growing human embryos in test tubes. Then they're implanting them in monkeys and watching them grow. Get this," he went on, "if I'm not mistaken, or having some sick nightmare, they want the fetuses to hatch in space."

"In space?!"

"In space! Some colony their building."

"Is this Kosher?"

"If it is, what d'ya think the dead surgeon had to say about it?"

"Don't know."

"But wait. There's more."

"More?"

"That's right. There's more. If you order now, at no extra cost, you'll also get this sixty-nine-piece set of Ginzu marital aids. They vibrate, they probe, they—"

"C'mon, wacko. Tell me!"

"Okay, okay," Derek said with a loud chuckle. "We're not really sure about this part, but what comes to mind when you hear the term 'New State'?"

"'New State'?"

"'*New State*.'"

"Hmmm…" she said again and paused. "I think neo-Nazis," she finally responded in a quiet, worried voice.

"Yeah. Neo-Nazis."

"This is better than the stuff I'm writing," she said. "Almost."

"Speaking of writing," Derek said.

"Yeees," Christine anxiously said, smelling an opportunity.

"This could be another *LIFE* cover story for you… or *TIME*," he went on then paused for a moment, "…if you want it."

She didn't respond for some time. A broad smile curved her smooth lips.

No response was necessary. Derek smiled. The thought of working with Christine again pleased him very much.

"Should I take this deafening silence as a '*yes*'?" he asked her.

"Yes, yes, yes!" she enthusiastically answered.

"But only under one condition," he told her.

"Anything."

"Anything?"

"Anything."

"Hmmm, that kinda puts a snap in my trunks. Anyway, you are not involved in the fact-finding process. Only the writing. Everything else is strictly off limits. You hear that?"

"Yeah, yeah. Only the writing. No facts. Just the writing. Got it."

"I'm serious. These guys are killers. They almost nailed us today. I don't think—"

"What?!" Christine interrupted. "Are you guys alright?"

"Look, I'll tell you about it later. We're fine. But I don't want you anywhere near this mess until it all blows over. Then you have your story. Got that?"

"Uh, huh. Got it."

"Promise?"

Christine was silent for a moment. On a piece of paper she quickly jotted a list of key ideas that would shape her story. *Barnes. NEXUS. Surrogate. Implantation. Monkeys. New State. Space colonies. Neo-Nazis.* She wasted no time.

"Promise?" Derek repeated.

"Uh, huh. Sure hon, promise," she said and dotted her i's while she wondered if there was any connection between the deformed babies that have recently been in the news and this crazy monkey-space research. She could smell a story. And this one was starting to stink, she thought.

CHAPTER FOURTEEN

Necessity is not the mother of invention. Invention,
in my opinion, arises directly from idleness, possibly
also from laziness, to save oneself trouble.

Agatha Christie

"Dammit, Morgan, would you get that bleeder already?!" Dr. Atkin yelled, lifting his eyes from the field for a brief instant to catch his assistant's before they fell again upon the small vessel which pumped a steady stream of bright red blood into the wound. "Never mind, let me have a hemostat," he told the scrub nurse who stood beside him. "C'mon, *c'mon!"*

She snapped the instrument into his waiting gloved hand.

"Like working with rookies," Dr. Atkin mumbled.

With a sponge in one hand and hemostat in the other, he reached into the wound with both, gently dabbing the uterine incision where the bleeding was coming from, then grabbed the small vessel with the clamp. The bleeding stopped.

"3-0 silk tie on a passer and a forceps for my partner."

Dr. Atkin held the clamped end of the vessel up as his assistant maneuvered the tie around the instrument's tip, then carefully set a square knot in place.

"Okay," Morgan said. Dr. Atkin released the hemostat and tossed it on the scrub nurse's instrument stand.

Morgan laid two additional knots down and then held the stitch up by its end. The resident beside him eagerly cut the suture. And the knot. The tie fell off and a thin stream of blood squirted from the vessel, spraying Dr. Atkin's mask.

"This woman ever fuck you over, boy?!" Dr. Atkin loudly asked the resident.

"Uh, no, sir. I don't even know her," the resident responded with a certain quiver in his voice.

"Then why are you trying to kill her?!" Dr. Atkin stammered, and looked the startled resident square in the eye. "C'mon, let's go, let's go!" he urged as he adjusted one of the overhead operating lights. "There!" he said, swinging the large dome into a better position and throwing some additional light on the field. "Let's give this woman a fighting chance, shall we?!"

He grabbed another hemostat from the scrub nurse's hand and quickly reclamped the vessel. Morgan swiftly wrapped another tie around the vessel and laid three knots in place as Dr. Atkin removed the clamp.

"On the goddamn knot this time, boy," Dr. Atkin instructed the resident who carefully cut the suture as Morgan held it up. "Good," he told the resident with a subtle wink.

The resident's eyes gleamed with pride. One word was all it took. Just one. But one word was often rare. And always short-lived.

"Bovie," Morgan said and the scrub nurse handed him an instrument that resembled a pen with a long flat metal tip on one end and a long cord connected to the other. It was the electrocautery.

With it, he continued to cut through the muscular wall of the uterus. The instrument buzzed as he slowly moved the tip back and forth along the separating tissue.

The process took longer than Dr. Atkin's patience would tolerate. "What's the Bovie on?!" he snapped.

"Thirty-five," the circulating nurse told him.

"Then turn the coag up to fifty, please, would you?"

"Will do," she replied.

The Bovie buzzed again and a small stream of smoke rose from the wound as Morgan moved through the layers of the uterine wall like a knife through butter. The smell of burning flesh overflowed in the field.

"Nothin' like down-home cookin', huh, boy?" Dr. Atkin asked the resident.

He called all the residents 'boy'. All the male residents, that is. The female residents were hardly acknowledged in the OR. He never really believed there was a place for women in surgery. Even OB/GYN surgery. He resented women. And blacks. And Jews. A real open-minded man. But at forty-eight, he was *the* unquestioned authority on ovarian disorders and had written the classic texts on human fertility. Not a well-liked man, but one whose reputation was internationally renowned and no one could take that away from him.

Morgan Reeves, the OB/GYN Chief Resident, had had his differences with Dr. Atkin over the last four years and learned there were times when it was best to just simply keep your mouth shut. A low profile, he had learned, was a successful profile. Especially when the politics of obtaining fellowships lingered in the near future.

The resident didn't respond.

"Got a name, boy?"

"Scott Rubinstein," he replied in a low voice.

"A Jewboy, ain't that right?"

The resident nodded.

"Well, let me tell you something, Dr. Rubinstein," Dr. Atkin went on, "If you don't start using that sucker to clear this smoke real soon I'm gonna shove it up your Jewboy ass!"

"Uh, yes, sir," the resident promptly responded and conscientiously held the suction instrument near the field where Morgan was working.

"We're in," Morgan told his attending.

"Fine. You want a coffee break now?" Dr. Atkin sarcastically asked him.

Morgan lifted his eyes for a moment but didn't respond.

"Gonna need a handful of mosquito clamps right on the field," Dr. Atkin told the scrub nurse.

"And two clamps for the umbilical cord," Morgan added. "Take one," he told Scott. "When I clamp, you clamp an inch above."

"How's the little guy doing?" Dr. Atkin asked the anesthesiologist.

"Still getting long runs of deceleration with little variation on the monitor," a voice replied from behind the drape at the head of the operating table.

"Those units of blood in yet?"

"Fifth unit's almost in," the anesthesiologist responded.

"C'mon, *move!*" Dr. Atkin told Morgan. "Two small Richardsons!" he yelled at the scrub nurse. "You see what we're doing, don't you?!"

He pulled them from her hands as she held them out. "Grab this one, I've got the other," he told Scott after he positioned the retractors in the uterus. "Now, pull!"

Scott pulled as hard as he could on the retractor. Dr. Atkin did the same. Morgan slid both hands into the uterus and lifted the baby out. He rested the slippery infant in the wound for a moment as he clamped the umbilical cord. Scott did the same.

It was only then that the horrifying appearance of the baby was seen in Morgan's eyes. He was astonished. Scott knew not what to think. Dr. Atkin seemed more disappointed than surprised.

"Dear God," the scrub nurse whispered in a low voice.

Morgan had no idea what to expect. He hadn't seen the woman once during her prenatal course. She came in through the Emergency Room. Hysterical. Vaginally hemorrhaging. Turned out she had what's called *placenta previa*. The placenta had grown right over and completely occluded the cervical os, or uterine outlet. The delivery passage through the uterus was blocked. The fetus, therefore, had to be delivered by Caesarian section and the hemorrhage controlled immediately or the woman would bleed to death.

Everyone in the OR had clustered as closely as possible around the operating table to catch a glimpse of this medical monstrosity. The circulating nurse. She stood behind Scott on a small step stool. The anesthesiologists. One peered down at the grotesque infant from behind the sterile drape at the head of the table. The other stood behind Morgan. And the pediatricians. Both stood a few feet from the OR table. One had walked around to Dr. Atkin's side. The other stood beside the anesthesiologist.

The baby's head was grossly deformed. Its forehead protruded markedly beyond the level of its face. The posterior aspect of the baby's skull was severely depressed. Looked caved-in. The baby had no eyes. Or ears. A small mouth was barely discernible behind the incredibly disproportionate mandible which protruded terribly. The baby's tiny hands and feet did not contain individual fingers and toes. Each hand and foot was but a fused mass of flesh and bone. The baby was truly grotesque.

"Jesus Christ!" Morgan said. "What the hell happened here?!"

"Just keep going, boy," Dr. Atkin told him. "We've still got a patient on this table."

"Mayo scissors," Morgan said as the scrub nurse slapped them into his palm.

He cut the cord and handed the baby to the pediatricians who nervously took it from him, staring at it in amazement. Their eyes were filled with disappointment. With shock.

"Pair of Metzenbaums," he said.

He took the fine scissors from the scrub nurse and carefully dissected the placenta off the wall of the uterus. There was still some bleeding which Dr. Atkin controlled with the Bovie.

"What are the Apgar scores?" Morgan asked the

pediatricians as he removed the placenta from the uterus and put it in the specimen bowl that the scrub nurse held out.

The Apgar score is a quick assessment scale to evaluate the health of a newborn. Dr. Virginia Apgar, an anesthesiologist at Columbia University, developed the Apgar score in 1952. Scores are calculated one and five minutes after birth based on five criteria—appearance, pulse, grimace, activity and respiration.

"Two after one minute, one after five," one of the pediatricians responded. "He's not gonna make it," she added. "Poor thing didn't have a chance."

"Damn!" Dr. Atkin muttered in a barely audible voice. "Why don't the two of you close," he told Morgan as he stepped away from the table and pulled his gloves off. "I'll be in my office."

"I'll send the specimens to the path lab," the circulating nurse told him.

"No!" Dr. Atkin quickly responded in a loud voice. "The fetus goes to my lab!" he said, stuffing his gown in the bin and glancing at the lifeless form that lay in the incubator as he left the OR. "Straight to my lab!"

Scott and Morgan watched as the door to the OR slowly swung shut. They looked at each other for a long silent moment. Neither said a word. There was nothing to say.

* * *

"*Brotsky?*" Ojo asked with a raised brow and tightly drawn lips as his eyes darted around their trashed office.

"Okay, maybe not Brotsky," Derek responded. "But we're onto something here, Ojo. Something big. Probably even bigger than we think."

"I agree. And at some point we probably will need to call in a few extra hands. The FBI. Maybe the CIA. I don't know. But do us both a favor for now and get Brotsky and his Keystone cops out of your mind," Ojo told him.

"Fine. But I'm just trying to think of every move. Every possibility. So we don't get fucked. And Brotsky came to mind," Derek told him.

"Well, so am I. But what if that schmuck does have some lead on our friendly-neighborhood killer? Remember? The one that makes house calls?" Ojo reminded his partner as he bent to pick up a small piece of broken glass that had somehow made its way from the workshop onto the bottom shelf of the bookcase in their outer office.

Ojo leaned back in his chair as his eyes fell upon Arti who busily continued reorganizing the endless stacks of folders and papers that lay scattered on the floor of the office beside his desk. He picked each folder up, carefully gathered and organized its contents, then returned it to its appropriate place within the filing cabinet. As Arti continued working, streams of blue and red and yellow and orange sparks flowed between the rods and across the coiled wires which now safely sat within the shiny new glass dome that Derek had replaced. Ojo smiled as he watched Arti. Then he lifted his eyes and caught Derek's stare.

"Fine!" Ojo said and quickly swung his legs off the top of his desk as his chair straightened. "Dial Brotsky."

A yellow light flashed on the small circular phone that sat on the corner of the desk. The sound of the line ringing was heard a moment later.

"Go ahead," he told Derek. "But only if you really think Brotsky knows any more than we do about the killer."

Nothing was said for a moment. The line continued ringing. Derek glanced at his watch for a second. 8:23 p.m.

"Cancel Brotsky," Derek said and the yellow light stopped flashing. The line disconnected.

"Why'd you do that?" Ojo asked.

"Cause you're absolutely right," Derek told him. "I figured if we kept Brotsky busy working on this," he said, holding up the piece of glass with one hand, "that would give us more time to work on this," he went on, holding up the small pile of pages that had printed out with the other.

"That does make some sense," Ojo conceded.

"Maybe. But he's not gonna show us what he's got—"

"Unless we show him what we've got," Ojo interrupted.

"Right. Of course, we could just tell Brotsky about the

break-in and then play dumb."

"Maybe, but what would that accomplish? He'd end up bringing his *'finest'* losers in blue to our shop to scout around for clues. There are none. Except for these," he told Derek, pointing to the papers in his hand.

"And for the time being, no one sees these," Derek said.

"Not till we know exactly what we're dealing with."

"Agreed. So we scratch Brotsky for now."

"Good man."

"Question. The note on your car and this one," Derek said, holding up the note they had found on Arti. "Are they related?"

"'Course they are," Ojo quickly responded. "Are you strokin' out on me? Arti has already matched the blood on those notes. Both type O positive. Both fetal."

"No, no, no. Of course, it's the same blood on those notes. Of course, they're related. That's not what I'm asking," Derek continued. "Somehow the killer knew your car. I'm not sure how. Maybe he saw it that night at the park. I don't know. It doesn't really matter. But did he also know you work here? Or..." Derek paused for a second, "...and this is a big 'or'—"

"*Or* did our friends at NEXUS trace our signal right back here after they discovered we had broken their code?" Ojo interrupted. "Right? And then send the big ugly goon after us. Or is it purely coincidental?"

"Exactly," Derek agreed.

"Derek, nothing is coincidental," Ojo told him. "You know that. Plus, take a good look at the two notes," he went on, taking the note from Derek's hand and placing it beside the wrinkled one that lay on the desk. Ojo read the notes aloud. "'Dead nigger walking,' and 'You're next.' What d'ya notice?"

Derek thought for a moment in silence.

"You're right," he finally responded. "If the killer thought the shop was yours and was coming after you specifically because you're the only witness who saw him at the park the night he killed the surgeon, he would have called you…" he started, then paused.

"A nigger, Derek, a *nigger*," Ojo went on. "It's okay to say it. It doesn't bother me. He would've written 'You're next, *nigger*.'"

"But he didn't," Derek said. "He simply wrote 'You're next.' Know what that means, don't you?"

"Yes, I do," Ojo answered. "Means someone wants us dead."

"And there's not a damned thing Brotsky can do about that."

"Now you see my point?"

"I do," Derek said and rubbed a couple of fingers across his brow. "It's all us."

"Us…," Ojo said and nodded his head at the pages in Derek's hand, "…and them."

"And we're gonna have to nail them before they nail us."

"You're damn right, we are," Ojo said.

"So to avoid getting *our* heads blown off, too," Derek went on, looking at Arti for a moment, "we, my friend, are officially on vacation and the shop," he continued, glancing through the glass walls of the office and across the display room before he turned to face Ojo, "is officially closed. For now."

"No argument from me," Ojo agreed.

"We can keep the cars at Christine's place and stay there till we come up with a plan."

"I already have," Ojo said with a shrewd smile.

"Why am I not surprised?"

"You didn't think I'd let those space fuckers cut into my program without tracing *their* signal, did you?" Ojo said as he took the printed pages from Derek's hand.

"So where do we start?" Derek asked him.

"Right here," Ojo responded, writing three words across the first header page of the secret document.

"Willow Valley, *Texas*?" Derek asked, a bit surprised as he read it.

"Willow Valley, Texas," Ojo confirmed. "That's the place. About five miles outside Houston. Just a few miles from NASA. Right at NEXUS headquarters. That is where our signal was traced from. That is where those space fuckers are. Willow Valley, *Texas*."

"Looks like we're headin' to *NEXUS* in *Texas*," Derek said. "Got a nice ring to it, don't you think? *NEXUS* in *Texas*."

"Maybe an evil ring," Ojo said. "Better start packin' our toys,"

"For sure. We're definitely gonna need them."

"Yeah. Before someone else is killed."

* * *

With a steady crash, the rain fell from the darkened sky. A huge flash of lightning cut through its darkness every few minutes, brightening the sky with a glorious jolt of white light. In the brief moment it took for the tremendous clap of thunder to follow, the darkness would reform. Thirteen stories above the ground, the droplets of rain incessantly tapped against the windows of Dr. Atkin's laboratory. Through a window that had been left just a crack open, the rain quickly marched, creating a path several feet along the length of the granite sill and across a number of papers that sat on it.

"I keep telling you, I just don't know how this happened!" the balding surgeon frantically yelled into the phone receiver he nervously held with an unsteady hand. He took his eyeglasses off and rubbed the beads of perspiration from his forehead with the back of his hand as he closed his eyes tightly for a moment, then opened them. "I just don't know!"

Dr. Atkin tossed his eyeglasses onto the disarrayed pile of papers that covered the top of his desk, then reached for the curved handle behind a small centrifuge and quickly pulled the window shut. He twisted the handle and the window locked.

"Atkin, you son-of-a-bitch, you were responsible!" a furious voice shot through the receiver. "You were *responsible!*" the voice repeated.

"I had no control, Hans," he answered. "None! Why do you refuse to understand this?!"

"I refuse to understand nothing! *This* I refuse to *accept!*" Dr. Flint hammered him. "You're no better than Barnes!" he added.

"*Barnes?* Why would you compare me to *Barnes?!*"

"He betrayed me by stealing the code," Dr. Flint told him. "But you have betrayed me with your recklessness! With your arrogance!"

"We have known all along how the fetus was progressing," he told Dr. Flint as his eyes ran the length of the sill and fell upon a green plastic bag which sat within a small plastic bin at its end. "The woman should not have been allowed to leave the Facility! That was not my decision!" Dr. Atkin yelled. "It was not my decision!"

A sharp burst of lightning filled the sky. As the light passed through the end window and into the corner of the lab where the bin sat, an outline of the dead baby that lay within the plastic bag could be seen.

"No, but you were responsible for returning her to the

Facility one month before she went into labor."

"How could I know she would rupture her membranes six weeks early? How could I know?!"

"Perhaps you couldn't," Dr. Flint answered. "But this is not the first time you have jeopardized the secrecy of this project. And its success. This is not the first time!" he yelled. "But it *will* be the last!"

"It will not happen again. I assure you," Dr. Atkin said and the line went dead. "Hans? *Hans*?!" Dr. Atkin nervously called into the receiver. "Damn!" he screamed and slammed the receiver down. "Damn!"

Dr. Atkin sat in the wooden chair by his desk. He closed his eyes and rubbed them for a moment, then looked at the mess that lay scattered before him. Flint's comment sounded like a threat and Atkin didn't like being threatened. The more he thought about it the angrier he became. Angry but still a bit nervous and worried. Flint had that effect on him. In an instant, he brushed his hand across the top of the desk, sending the papers flying in all directions. Then he sat back in the chair. He was exhausted. He lay there quietly for some time as one hand fell by his side and dangled from the edge of the chair. The other rested in his lap as he dozed off.

Almost two hours passed. And he lay there quietly. Until a loud explosion startled him. His eyes opened wide and raced around the small lab as he quickly sat up in the chair. They passed from the workbench on the opposite side of the lab, where a large round clock that had been fixed to the wall above flashed 10:54, to the sink beside it, atop which hung dozens of beakers, flasks and other glassware, to the large glass cabinet against the other wall in which dozens of bottles, some containing formaldehyde-fixed specimens, others containing various chemicals and drugs, filled the shelves, to a shorter cabinet that housed a number of texts and journals, to the various balances and surgical instruments which sat atop a metal cart in one corner to the computer terminal and printer which sat atop another cart in another corner, then, finally, to the window that had somehow become unlatched again and blown open at the end of the granite sill where the dead baby in the green plastic bag had been sitting in the plastic bin. It was no longer there. The bin was gone.

Dr. Atkin grew nervous for a moment. He anxiously searched for the dead baby. Then his eyes fell upon the floor. The rush of wind that burst into the lab as the window flew open must have swept the bin off the top of the workbench on which it sat, just below the sill, and onto the floor where it now lay. The bin had tumbled over and the plastic bag was thrown from its hold. The baby's deformed head protruded from the open end of the bag.

Dr. Atkin quickly stepped to that corner of the lab. He grabbed the handle of the open window and slammed it shut, twisting the handle as he bent to retrieve the fetus. He lifted it from the floor, its grotesque head still protruding from the bag. He stared at the horrible site for a moment then quickly pushed it into the bag and twisted the plastic end into a bulky knot. He returned the bag to the bin and the bin to the workbench. Then took his seat behind his desk.

With a key that he pulled from his pants pocket, he unlocked the top drawer of his desk. He pulled the drawer open with a quick tug and stared into it. A bunch of papers and folders filled the shallow drawer. He pushed the papers aside, reached below the folders, and found what he was looking for—a large manilla envelope with a fastener on the back flap. He quickly undid the fastener of the envelope and from it he removed a thick manuscript. Its cover had a header page similar to the ones Ojo and Derek had retrieved from the NEXUS research data portal. Similar. But different.

Dr. Atkin eyed the cover of the manuscript for some time.

PROJECT KYINNXSS5983345
PROJECT KYINNXSS5983345

On the Prevention of the Zero Gravity Induction of
Fetal Osteoporosis and Bony Deformities
Focus on the Use of Calcitronase

His eyes moved from the manuscript cover to the green plastic bag at the far end of the workbench, then back to the cover. He sat there silently with the manuscript in his hand. He didn't open it. He just held it. And closed his eyes. He dozed off again with the manuscript still in his hand.

After some time had passed, he was awakened by the

edge of a cold metal object pressed hard against his temple. Then he heard a loud click. Right in his ear. He quickly turned his head and found himself staring into the barrel of a gun. He gasped loudly but said nothing. All he saw was the gun. And one long finger curled around its trigger. Nothing else. His eyes had frozen on that. The barrel. The trigger. And the finger. Nothing else.

The finger pulled back and the trigger released. Again, the gun clicked. But nothing happened. The finger jammed the trigger furiously but the gun only clicked.

Dr. Atkin quickly reached for the gun. He could feel the barrel in his hand. His fingers wrapped around the cold metal. He tried to twist it from his killer's hand but it was pulled from his grasp.

Immediately, he felt the whipping blow of the gun's butt against the back of his head. That was all he would feel. He slumped over in the chair and the manuscript slid from his lap onto the floor. With an arm around his shoulders and another beneath his knees, his killer clumsily lifted him from the chair and placed him on the sill. He opened one of the windows and a rush of wind shot into the room, forcing the bin and its contents back onto the floor. The killer lifted the unconscious surgeon from the sill, struggling a bit as he forced his portly body through the small window. His head and shoulders easily passed through the rectangular metal frame but the frame grew tight around his waist. The killer pushed and pushed until the man tumbled through the window and over the narrow ledge. Then he watched with satisfaction as the surgeon plummeted thirteen stories to his death.

He left the window open and bent to retrieve the fetus. The knot had somehow become undone and the fetus slid from the bag. It lay there completely uncovered on the cold floor of the lab.

The killer eyed the distorted, ashen-looking fetus for an instant then turned his head. He let out a loud gurgling sound then emptied the contents of his stomach onto the top of the workbench.

After a moment, he bent down again and quickly tossed the fetus into the plastic bag, tying two knots in its end. He grabbed the manuscript from the sink where the wind had blown it and slowly walked toward the door, dragging his right leg in a sweeping fashion as he went. He looked back for a second. The open window flew back and forth on its creaking hinges as the wind and rain rushed through it. With the green plastic bag under his arm and the manuscript in his hand, the killer opened the door and was gone.

CHAPTER FIFTEEN

Talent hits a target no one else can hit. Genius
hits a target no one else can see.

Arthur Schopenhauer

The rain kept falling. Lighter than it had been. But still falling. The sky remained darkened. The lightning less frequent. The storm seemed to be lifting but the flooded streets remained a testimony to its wrath. Twenty-seventh Street, in particular, stood out from the countless other streets on this gloomy night. Where it ran between the FDR Drive and 1st Avenue, its marred surface, with too many potholes, cracks and crevices to count, was evened out only by the deep puddles which formed as the drains overflowed. It was a street driven on for the sole purpose of entering the hospital's side entrance where parking was often negotiable.

But on this evening, with three minutes till midnight, there would be no additional vehicles passing the length of this narrow street. A crossing block stood at both entries to the street. One where it transected the FDR Drive service road. The other where it transected 1st Avenue. Two uniformed officers stood beside each block to ensure that.

In the middle of the street, about ten or fifteen feet from the entrance, was a roped-off area. A number of men in trench coats stood by this area. Several of them wore golden badges on the breast pocket of their coats. One held a camera and moved back and forth numerous times as he shot one photo after another. The others talked among themselves. One gazed into the sky at the open window on the side of the research building, then back at the sight on the street before him. He did this several times, with his hands trying to simulate the trajectory of the fall as a shorter man whom he stood beside quickly jotted some notes onto a small pad.

Several physicians also stood at the scene. In their dampened white coats, they formed a small group a few feet from where the others stood. One said several words to the others, then shook her head in disgust and walked back toward the hospital's entrance. Two stood speaking under a black umbrella that one held. Another two stood beside them.

One of the physicians glanced at the darkened streaks of blood that stained the curb within the roped-off area. The rain beat upon the concrete pavers but the streaks remained. Small puddles of blood and fragments of glass encircled the police squad car which sat within this area. The car's roof had been crushed by Dr. Atkin's body. The rear portion of the roof had collapsed on its corner supports and the rear windshield had been completely shattered.

A large hole in the front windshield accommodated the dead surgeon's head. The impact had forced his neck backward and driven his head right through the glass, shearing off a large portion of his face below his eyes. The pale flesh shone out with a ghastly tone as the dim light from one of the entrance night beams struck it where it lay spread across the shattered windshield. Through the bloodstained glass of the squad car, the surgeon's eyes were visible. They were open. One eye dangled from the socket on a thin string of blood vessels and its optic nerve. The eyelid of the other had been torn off by a long spear-like fragment of glass which now lay embedded in the eye. A large area of the man's scalp had been avulsed and now hung freely. In a puddle of blood, the edge of the scalp rested on the dashboard.

The surgeon's body lay sprawled across the crushed roof of the squad car, facing the dark sky. Portions of it had spread onto the street around it. His body had virtually exploded on impact. Fragments of torn flesh, bits of fractured bones and pieces of ripped clothing all lay raveled in the bloody mess that covered the roof of the car and the ground around it. Segments of naked bone jutted through the lifeless flesh that had once covered the man's ribs and shoulders. The long bones of his legs shot through the skin where his knees had once been as his legs lay twisted on the car's trunk. This was not a pretty sight.

"Right on the roof of a goddamn squad car! Do you believe that?!" a husky man with an unlit cigar dangling from the corner of his mouth and a gold badge pinned to his overcoat told the two men who stood beside him. "Poor son-of-a-bitch."

"Suicide's illegal, ya know," one of the other men said.

"No kiddin', O'Connor," another answered him.

"Poor schmuck takes a thirteen-story nosedive and lands on a cop car," the first man added, taking the cigar from his mouth for a moment. "You gonna book'm, Salavari, or am I?" he asked with a straight face then all three laughed loudly.

"Couldn't help overhearing," one of the physicians interrupted and the laughter quickly subsided, "but what makes you so sure this was a suicide?" he asked.

"Never said it was. Just a possibility that's gotta be considered," the man with the cigar said as he returned it to the corner of his mouth. "What makes you so sure it wasn't suicide?"

"I didn't say I was sure," the doctor answered. "Especially after tonight."

"How's that now?"

"We were in the OR a few hours ago. Dr. Atkin and myself."

"And what did you say your name was?"

"I didn't. I'm Dr. Reeves. Morgan Reeves."

"Glad to know ya, doc," the man replied with an extended hand. "Sergeant Brotsky. And you were saying? About tonight in the OR?"

"Well, there was something about Atkin. I mean, he wasn't himself."

"How d'ya mean, lad?" O'Connor asked him.

"Something was eating at him. Hard to describe 'cause something was always eating at him. No one could stand to scrub with him. But I could tell when we started the case that something was different tonight," Morgan told them. "And then…," he went on, then stopped for a second.

"And then what?" Salavari questioned.

"Well, then he flipped out. After we delivered it."

"*It?*" Brotsky asked.

"The baby."

"No, you said 'it'. Why?" Brotsky pressed him.

"'Cause it was an '*it*.' A grotesquely deformed fetus. A monstrosity."

"How'd that happen?"

"Don't know. But Atkin didn't seem very surprised

when everyone else's eyes were poppin' out of their heads."

"Looks like he's havin' a delayed reaction," Salavari said with a chuckle and pointed at the windshield.

O'Connor howled with laughter for a brief moment that was cut short by a glance from Brotsky.

"What d'ya mean, not surprised? Like he expected it?"

Brotsky turned toward a couple of cops on the other side of the car. "That's enough shots," he told them. "Get rid of the reporter and cover'm up."

"He claimed he had never seen the woman before she came into the Emergency Room tonight bleeding. She was from outta town, supposedly. Why would he have lied?" Morgan asked.

"Don't know," Brotsky responded. "But sure as hell would like to find out."

"So would I," Morgan said with a pensive look on his face.

"What happened to the fetus?" Brotsky asked.

"Yeah, that's another thing."

"What d'ya mean?" Salavari asked.

"The nurse was going to send it to our pathology lab. That's where all OR specimens go."

"So," Brotsky remarked.

"So, Atkin flipped when she told him she was going to send it there."

"What do you mean when you say he 'flipped'?" Brotsky asked Morgan.

"I mean he flipped. Absolutely refused to have the fetus sent to the path lab."

"So where'd it go?" O'Connor questioned.

"Where else? Atkin's lab, of course," Morgan told him.

"Hmmm," Brotsky muttered in a quiet voice as he rubbed the dark stubble on his cheek with a few fingers. "Flaherty, Thompson," he called to the two officers on the other side of the squad car as they struggled to unroll the black plastic sheet over the car.

They didn't respond. They were too preoccupied with covering the body.

"Flaherty! Thomson!" he called to them another time.

"Uh, yeah, Sarge," Thompson replied.

"Find anything unusual in Atkin's lab?"

"We sure did, Sarge," Flaherty answered. "A whole mess of puke right on the bench by the window."

"Anything else?"

"Uh, yeah," Thompson added. "Bunch of papers all over the floor, Sarge."

"That it?"

"That's it," Flaherty said as the plastic sheet slid off the car.

Brotsky turned toward Salavari and Morgan with a smirk on his face. "Ya know something," he told them, "those two are almost as productive as two goddamn lepers arm wrestling."

Morgan laughed quietly. Salavari and O'Connor remained silent for a few moments then joined in.

"Not much more to be done down here," Brotsky said. "How about joinin' us for a look in Atkin's lab?" he asked Morgan.

"I'd be glad to."

Morgan accompanied the three officers as they walked around the car and toward the research building while Thompson and Flaherty secured the plastic sheet over the car. The four men followed the broken cement path that led to the gray and white brick building. The path curved alongside the parking lot, then veered off and led to several cracked steps at the building's main entrance. Brotsky opened the glass door and the others walked through. The elevator was waiting at the main level. They quickly rode it up to the thirteenth floor.

"Over there," Morgan said as he pointed to a closed door about thirty feet down the narrow corridor.

Several small boxes cluttered the corridor and two large freezers, one atop the other, sat outside the door to the lab. On the door was a small metal plate. DR. AVERY ATKIN, it read. A young-looking officer stood near the door. "Anyone in or out, Hopkins?" Brotsky asked.

"Only Thompson and Flaherty, Sarge. No one else," he answered.

"Good," Brotsky told the officer and pushed the door open as a sharp gust of foul-smelling air hit them hard in the face.

"Holy shit, it stinks in here!" Salavari said.

"Pick those up and hold onto them," Brotsky told O'Connor, eyeing the scattered papers on the floor.

"Will do, Sarge," he replied.

Brotsky looked past the floor and toward the open window on the other side of the lab.

"Kinda narrow for a hefty guy like Atkin to dive through without a little help, wouldn't you say, Sergeant Brotsky?" Morgan asked.

"You've got a good eye there, doc. Yes. I would say."

Brotsky's eyes fell upon the mess that decorated the top of the workbench.

"How common would you say it is for a jumper to barf his brains up and then take a dive?" he asked Morgan.

"I have no idea."

"Me neither. I was just wondering," Brotsky said, then turned to Salavari. "Save some of that, would you?"

"Uh, yeah, Sarge."

"Now, what were you saying about that fetus?" Brotsky asked Morgan as his eyes quickly panned the lab. "I think Thompson and Flaherty may've been right. Do you see it anywhere? Any of you?"

No one answered.

"Well, doc? You sure it was brought here?" Brotsky asked.

"Positive."

"Why 'positive'?"

"'Cause I brought it to Atkin myself right after surgery. The scrub nurse was too flustered."

"Well, it be gone now," Brotsky told him as he stopped in front of the specimen cabinet.

"Anything there?" Morgan asked him.

"You tell me, doc."

Brotsky forced the handle on the door and pulled it open. He slowly passed his hand among the many jars that sat on the top and middle shelves. Most of them were labeled. Some were not. A number of jars contained dissected rabbit and monkey organs. Brains. Hearts. Bones. Skulls. Nothing too unusual. Others contained various drugs and chemicals. Calcitonin. Beta-endorphin. Calcitronase. Calcio-phosphonase. Again, nothing too unusual. On the bottom shelf, behind a number of similar jars were two boxes. Brotsky pulled them from the back of the shelf and handed them to Morgan who sat them on the bench beside the cabinet.

Brotsky closed the cabinet doors and stood beside Morgan. Morgan watched as Brotsky took one of the boxes from the bench. He wrapped an arm around the box as he tried to remove the large jar it contained. O'Connor reached over to steady the box as Brostky used both hands to lift the jar free. O'Connor gasped loudly as he eyed the jar's contents and jerked the box. The jar slid from Brotsky's hands and crashed on the hard floor. The odor of formaldehyde immediately filled the lab. On the floor, in a puddle of the foul-smelling liquid, lay a small human fetus. Grossly deformed. Not unlike the one Morgan had delivered several hours earlier.

Salavari quickly walked toward the door. A loud retching noise was heard as he ran down the corridor.

Morgan quickly opened the other box. In it was another jar. Another human fetus. Another monstrosity.

"This what you were talking about before?" Brotsky asked him as O'Connor gently placed the fetus in a black plastic bag and gathered up the broken pieces of glass.

With a sullen look in his eyes, Morgan nodded.

CHAPTER SIXTEEN

And now the announcement of Watson and Crick
about DNA. This is for me the real proof of the
existence of God.

Salvador Dali

A conical beam of crisp blue light slowly spiraled from a thin slot on the edge of the small black and turquoise disk. The light made its way across the room and struck the lithograph which hung within a black lacquer frame centered on the rich fuchsia wall. The double-stranded helixes of DNA, the crystal blue streams, the numerous arthropods, the small blond-haired blue-eyed boy in the foreground, and all else that made this wonderful creation of Dali's the unique masterpiece it was remained within the beam of light for a brief moment. Then it was gone. Only the fuchsia wall remained. And the wall safe which had previously been hidden by the lithograph.

"Where the hell did it go?!" Christine nervously asked.

"Just watch," Ojo told her as Derek lifted the top of the disc. A small round screen appeared. It was coated with a reddish hue. On it was the image of the lithograph.

"Keep watching," Derek said.

He adjusted a dial on the side of the disc and the spiral beam of light whirled faster and faster. "This controls the intensity of the beam," he told Christine. "And the depth of penetration," he added, looking her in the eye as he raised an eyebrow several times.

Christine smirked skeptically.

As he turned the dial, the speed of the beam increased until the steel door of the wall safe vanished. A number of black velvet jewelry boxes, several long narrow canisters, and quite a few stacks of manilla envelopes and papers could be seen. In another moment, they too were gone.

"This is amazing!" Christine yelled with excitement. "I can't believe you really got that thing to work!"

"You bet we did," Ojo said.

"After we got all the bugs out," Derek commented. "Now take a look at this," he told her.

He pressed a yellow button on the face of the disc and the image of the safe's contents appeared on the tiny screen as the Dali reappeared on the wall.

"It's all stored in here now," Derek said, tapping a finger on the disc as he rotated the screen so it faced in the opposite direction. "But this is the fun part," he went on, pointing the disc toward another wall in the large living room.

He pressed several controls on the small gadget and the image of the safe's contents faded. An image of the fuchsia wall, coated with a hue of blue, replaced it as a spiral beam of red light shot from the disc and landed on the bare wall. An instant later, the image of the safe, its door wide open and contents in clear view, covered the wall. All just a brilliant illusion.

Christine smiled gleefully.

"I've got a feeling we're gonna get some good use outta this baby," Ojo said.

"So do I," Derek said with a slight smile as he placed the invention in a small pocket inside the shoulder bag which rested on an elliptical glass table beside the black leather couch where Ojo sat sifting through the contents of his steel attaché case.

"I'd say we're just about set," Ojo said, his eyes moving from the Laser Stunner which sat in a soft rubber case, to the Hologram Generator unit and miniature keyboard beside it, to the Image Scrambler that lay encased within its protective lead box, to the two plane tickets that were held inside the attaché cover by an elastic band. He took the tickets from the case and slipped them into a pocket in the lining of his leather jacket.

"I absotively, posilutely agree," Derek said, adjusting the shoulder strap on his bag. "I think we've got everything we're gonna need," he added, carefully setting the bulky miniature Image Fractionator on the floor of the bag and the Metallic Immobilizer on top of it.

"We sure as hell better," Ojo said.

"What's that for?" Christine asked, pointing to the Immobilizer as Derek began zipping the bag shut.

"Who knows?" he said as the opened the bag and removed it. "But watch."

"C'mon," Ojo said, eyeing his watch. It was 6:42 a.m. "We've gotta get a move," he went on. "Plane leaves in less than two hours."

"This'll just take a minute," Derek told him and pulled an L-shaped brass case from the large bag. "This," he told Christine as he turned a small dial on the side of the case clockwise, then counterclockwise, then back again until the tumblers fell into position and the case sprung open to reveal a small lucite rod, "is the Metallic Immobilizer."

Like the case, the rod was bent in the shape of an L. On the shorter end of the rod were several grooves. Two triangular buttons, one red, the other black, sat on the other end of the rod. A turquoise filament coursed the length of the rod from one end to the other.

"*Immobilizer?*" Christine quizzically asked.

"Immobilizer," Derek replied.

"What does it do?"

"Watch," he said and positioned the device in his hand like a pistol. He pointed the rod at the brass grandfather clock in the corner of the room.

Christine looked at the clock. She watched as its long pendulum rhythmically swung back and forth.

"So?"

Ojo smiled. Derek waited a moment for the pendulum to reach its peak height, then pressed the red button. A needle-thin jet of turquoise light shot from the end of the rod. In an instant, it struck the clock and vanished. The pendulum immediately froze.

"Very nice," Christine said in a sarcastic tone. "You needed a fancy laser gadget to break my five-thousand dollar clock."

Ojo started laughing.

"What's so funny?!" Christine snapped with pouting lips.

"It's not broken," he told her in the voice of the Monty Python legend John Cleese. "It's frozen. *Immobilized.*"

"Keep watchin'," Derek said as he pointed the rod at the clock another time and pressed the red button again.

Another thin beam of turquoise light shot from the end and struck the clock. The pendulum fell from its suspended position and swung through its curved path. Once at its end, it hovered for a brief moment, then swung back in the opposite direction. It did this incessantly. Back and forth. Back and forth. Without fail.

"How'd you do that? Get it working again?"

Ojo smiled. "Good demo, guy," he told Derek and lifted a large black duffle bag onto his shoulder as he grabbed the steel attaché case from the couch.

"In a nutshell," Derek began, "the turquoise beam of neutrino particles freezes every metallic atom in its path by reversing the polarity of its electron cloud."

"Got it," Christine responded with a confused smile.

"I'm gonna start loadin' up," Ojo broke in with an extended hand.

Christine tossed him the car keys.

"And that second beam reverses the effect and thaws those little atoms, right?" she asked Derek teasingly.

"Yeah, actually. Something like that," he responded with a grin as he returned the lucite rod to its brass case. He placed the Immobilizer back in the large bag and zipped it closed as Ojo walked through the door, stepping over the morning newspaper on his way to the garage on the side of the house where Christine's BMW was parked, duffle on his shoulder, attaché in his hand.

"What're you gonna use it for?" she asked.

"Who knows," Derek replied. "When the time comes, the need will be obvious," he added.

"You really think so?"

"Sure hope so. Same goes for all our toys."

"Well, look you," Christine said as Derek stood and lifted the strap of the bag onto his shoulder. She grabbed his shirt and pulled him toward her. "You just be careful," she told him and threw her arms around him, embracing him as she pressed her lips to his.

Derek let the bag slide from his shoulder onto the floor as he wrapped his arms around her small waist and held her tightly. He held her for a long silent moment.

"I will," he whispered in her ear in a quiet voice. "Don't you worry. You hear me?"

"I love you so much," Christine told him as her eyes welled.

"I love you, too," Derek said, looking into her big blue Scandinavian eyes. They sparkled. He brushed away a tear as it fell on her cheek. "I'm gonna be fine. Ojo and I will both be just fine," he reassured her.

"I know you will," Christine said and smiled as she wiped her eyes with a couple of fingers.

She grabbed him again and they kissed for some time.

Ojo returned with the newspaper in his hand. He stood by the door and eyed that morning's headline.

'SURGEON PLUNGES 13 STORIES TO HIS DEATH'

He folded the paper in half and stared at the small photo at the bottom of the page. The form of a body, covered with a black sheet, lay atop a squad car. A brief caption and several paragraphs accompanied the photo.

Ojo quickly read the few lines and then flipped through the pages to find the rest of the story.

Derek and Christine turned toward the door as they heard the rustling of the newspaper. They hadn't noticed Ojo had returned to the house. They watched as he stood by the door reading. Completely oblivious to their stare. Completely engulfed in what he read. Derek lifted the strap of the bag back onto his shoulder and grabbed the handle of his black aluminum attaché, which sat beside the leather beanbag in the corner of the room.

"Think we're all set. Let's roll," he told Ojo as he carried the bags over to the door.

Ojo continued reading.

"What've you got there that's so interesting?" Derek asked him as he eyed his watch. "C'mon, we better move if we're gonna catch this flight."

"Listen to this," Ojo replied. "'…*and despite the absence of any witnesses or evidence of a struggle, Sergeant Brotsky suspects the cause of Dr. Atkin's death was not suicide.*'"

Christine stepped beside Derek and rested a hand on his shoulder. They listened as Ojo read out loud.

"*He believes the surgeon was thrown from the window of his thirteenth floor lab to his death. When questioned about the recent slaying of another Bellevue surgeon, Sergeant Brotsky told reporters, 'A connection between last night's incident and the murder of Dr. Barnes remains undetermined at this time.'*"

Ojo closed the newspaper and folded it in half. "Nice landing, huh?" he said, pointing to the photo on the front page as his eyes passed from Derek's to Christine's.

"Brotsky's car?" Derek asked with a slight grin.

"No such luck," Ojo told him. "Two rookies were taking a coffee break when the good doctor dropped in for a donut."

Derek took the paper from him. He and Christine quickly read the few paragraphs on the front page. Derek opened the paper and they read the rest of the story.

"What d'ya think?" Ojo asked.

Derek lowered his bag and attaché case onto the floor. "I think we're catching a later flight."

Ojo agreed.

* * *

An unlit cigar butt dangled from the corner of Brotsky's mouth as he leaned back in his wooden chair and rested his feet on the pile of papers that lay on his desk. He chewed on one end of the cigar as the other end bounced up and down. He ran a couple of fingers across his unshaven chin then pulled the cigar from his mouth as he took a quick swallow of the stale black coffee from the mug in his hand. Brotsky balanced the mug on the police report that sat on his lap, then grabbed a matchstick from an open drawer and struck it against the side of the desk. With an unsteady hand, he lit the cigar. He took a few puffs and then dumped the butt in the mug, making a quick hissing sound. Brotsky smiled and put the mug on the corner of the desk as his tired eyes returned to the report on his lap.

It was an account of Dr. Atkin's untimely death. Thompson and Flaherty, the two rookie cops on the scene at the time it occurred, had prepared it earlier that morning. Brotsky skimmed through the report another time as he searched for some clue, some piece of evidence, anything that could connect it with Dr. Barnes' murder. His gut told him they were connected but he could not figure out how. Or why.

His eyes drifted from the typewritten report. They fell upon the wooden tiles that interlocked to form the badly worn floor and followed a darkened coffee stain which led to the desk across from his where Detective Riggs, a young British fellow who had just joined the force, sat questioning a handcuffed black youth. The boy, a fifteen- or sixteen-year-old whom Brotsky recalled having busted about two years ago for dealing crack, sat on the backless wooden chair beside the detective's desk, staring at the thirty or forty small brown vials that formed a large pile in the middle of the desk. A blank look covered the boy's face. Surely the crack had been planted on him, he insisted. Surely.

Brotsky reached into a side drawer of his desk where several cigars sat in a flattened box. Beside them was a pack of Camels. He took one from the package and nonchalantly tucked it in the corner of his mouth. His eyes drifted from the vials of crack on the detective's desk to the other side of the busy room where an unusually pretty redhead sat sobbing in front of Salavari's desk. Brotsky overheard a portion of the questioning.

"I just don't know how he could do that!" the woman

said in a hysterical voice. She looked past Salavari and caught Brotsky's curious stare. Only then did he notice the large bruise on the side of the woman's face and the tears that kept pouring down her cheeks. She tried to wipe them away with a crumpled piece of tissue. "I just don't know how!" she yelled, looking back at Salavari.

"Can you tell me a little more about the gerbil, ma'am?" Salavari asked the woman with a confused look on his face. "And this Riko fellow."

"Well, like I was starting to say, I got out of work early last night and thought I'd surprise my boyfriend, Riko. His name is Riko. Yesterday made six months that we're going out, you know."

Salavari nodded.

"I was about to knock on the door but I noticed it wasn't locked so I just walked right in," she went on. "I couldn't believe my eyes!"

"What did you see, ma'am?"

"Riko…and one of his friends. I met this one once. His name is Tony. Tony something or other. I don't remember. And there he was. On the floor of the living room."

"Riko?"

"Tony! On his hands and knees. Naked! Right there in the middle of the goddamn living room floor. Right where Riko made love to me the night before!" she yelled and began sobbing louder.

"What about Riko? Where was he?"

The woman took a few moments to catch her breath. "Where do you think?! Right behind Tony! With a goddamn animal in his hand. It looked like a gerbil. It wasn't moving or anything, you know. Like it was dead. Or frozen. He had his hand on Tony's ass! He held the gerbil in his other hand and kept pushing it and pushing it! It was the sickest think I've ever seen!" she screamed and burst into tears again. "How could he do that to me?! How?!"

"What happened then?" Salavari asked in a quiet soothing voice.

"Well, then they saw me. Riko stood up and grabbed me! He threw me onto the rug next to Tony. He tore my blouse open and kept slapping my face as I tried to get away! Then Tony pushed my skirt up and got on top of me so I couldn't move!" she said and became even more hysterical.

"Take your time, ma'am."

After a long pause, the woman continued. "Then Riko got on top of Tony! Oh, my God!" she yelled and covered her face with her hands.

"Sick bastards," Brotsky mumbled under his breath as his eyes moved to the holding cell where only the vagrant remained, dressed in torn rags and still asleep on the plank which hung suspended from the ceiling by chains. He stared at the man for a moment as he lay silently on the wooden boards. Then his eyes returned to the report. He thought about the two murdered men again. Barnes and Atkin. Both surgeons. Both from Bellevue. He wondered how they were related. Or were they? *Could Atkin's death have really been a suicide?* Brotsky asked himself as the phone rang.

Brotsky took the report from his lap and slapped it onto his desk with some frustration then grabbed the receiver from its hook. "Sergeant Brotsky," he spoke into the phone.

"Morning, Sergeant," a vaguely familiar voice sounded through the receiver. "Just read about the murder at Bellevue."

"So. What about it? Who is this?!" Brotsky demanded.

"Cannon, Sarge. Derek Cannon. 'Member me from the other day?"

Brotsky rolled his eyes and leaned back in his chair. "Yeah. What can I do for you, Cannon, Derek Cannon?"

"It's more like what *we* can do for *you*," Derek offered.

"*We?*"

"Yeah. Ojo Jenna*cugo* and I. 'Member him?"

"Uh, yeah. How's that now?" Brotsky asked.

"According to the papers, it seems you're not convinced the two killings are connected," Derek told him.

"Go on. I'm listening."

"Trust me," Derek said and paused. "They are."

"Still playin' detectives, are you?" Brotsky asked mockingly.

"Yeah. You're damn right!" Derek snapped. "After Ojo was framed, his tires were slashed and our workshop was broken into. I think that gives us the right to get involved. To start lookin' for some answers. What d'you think, Sarge? Come up with any yourself lately?" he sarcastically asked.

"You didn't tell me about those incidents," Brotsky said.

"Why bother. What would you've done about 'em? Besides, I'm telling you now," Derek told him without a care whatsoever.

"Is that what you called for?" Brotsky asked.

"No. I called to put you back on the right track. The two murders are definitely connected," Derek said in a definitive tone.

"Is that so, now?"

"You bet your fat ass it is, Sarge. And we can prove it," Derek said.

"Oh, yeah? How's that?"

"Just meet us in front of the research building in twenty minutes," Derek told him.

Brotsky slammed the receiver down. "Damn!" he yelled. "How do they do that?!"

He grabbed his windbreaker from the hook on the wall behind his desk and walked toward the door. He eyed the large round clock on the wall above the door on his way out and noticed how the minute hand shook as the long second hand brushed against it. It was about 7:25 a.m.

CHAPTER SEVENTEEN

Vision is the art of seeing the invisible.

Jonathan Swift

Atkin's body was gone. Removed from the roof of the police car. Its many pieces collected into a large plastic bag and stored in a chilled drawer at the morgue. A drawer not unlike the one in which Barnes lay toe-tagged.

The blood-splattered squad car, with fragments of its smashed blue and red roof lights scattered across its hood, its front tires blown out from the impact, its badly dented roof collapsed onto the seatbacks, its rear windshield completely shattered, and its front windshield bearing the large ovoid hole created by the victim's head, was slowly hoisted up a couple of steel track ramps and onto the flatbed surface of a blue and white police tow truck by chains fastened around its front wheel axles while Christine clicked off one shot after another with her Nikon.

"Where is that son-of-a-bitch?" Derek asked, eyeing his watch impatiently as he and Ojo waited by the steps outside the research building. It was 7:51 a.m.

A small group of curious passersby, several of them nurses and physicians, others residents who lived in the area, gathered around the barricaded area and watched with mortified expressions as the mangled squad car was lifted onto the tow truck and carried away on this quiet Sunday morning.

One of the nurses, a thin black woman who had had the displeasurable experience of having worked with Dr. Atkin in the neonatal ICU on numerous occasions, gazed up at the side of the research building. With a long narrow finger she pointed at the window from which the surgeon had plunged. The nurse exchanged a word or two with the two physicians whom she stood next to. All three turned to catch a final glimpse of the wrecked police car as the tow truck turned the corner.

"Just the header page," Ojo replied, referring to their upcoming meeting with Brotsky. "He gets nothing else," he went on. "No mention of the code. No details of the fetal research. Or NEXUS' involvement. And absolutely no mention of our trip to Willow Valley."

Derek nodded in agreement.

"Here he comes," Ojo said as Brotsky's unmarked Chevy Caprice crept along the narrow broken street.

Brotsky pulled right into the barricaded area from which the squad car had been towed. He grabbed the flashing red bubble light from the roof and sat it on the dashboard as he got out of the car.

Christine snapped her lens cap in place and adjusted the shoulder strap on her camera as she walked along the winding cement pavement that formed a path from the street to the research building.

"Hey, blondie," a raspy voice called from behind.

Christine turned to find Brotsky jogging up the path to where she stood.

"Don't I know you from somewhere?" he asked her with a smooth smile.

"Sergeant Brotsky, isn't it?"

"It is. And may I ask, what's a nice girl like you doing in a mess like this?" he questioned her, quickly passing his eyes over her once or twice. "Doesn't look like you're just along for the ride," he added, eyeing the camera that hung from Christine's shoulder.

"How observant of you," Christine told him with a quaint smile. She turned away from him for a moment and rolled her eyes. "Actually," she added, turning to face him, "I'm researching a story."

"Guess that makes you a writer. Or a reporter?"

"Both. Sort of. I do freelance writing between novels,"

she replied and continued walking toward the building.

"Veeeery impressive," Brotsky commented.

Christine rolled her eyes again.

"Say, you wouldn't happen to know what information your friends have up their sleeves, would you?" he slyly asked her.

"Actually, I would. But you'll have to ask them if you want to find out. It is kinda hush-hush, you know," she told him flatly and put a finger to her lips.

"Oh. Of course," Brotsky mumbled as they came to the end of the walkway.

Derek and Ojo stood at the foot of the steps which led to the building's entrance. Derek lifted the attaché from the stone block it was sitting on with one hand and greeted the Sergeant with the other. Ojo caught Brotsky's eye and nodded.

"Now what was all that babbling over the phone about? Some proof that the murders are connected?" Brotsky asked Derek.

"It was about this," Derek responded, pulling a folded piece of paper from the pocket of his jacket. He handed the paper to Brotsky.

Brotsky unfolded the sheet of paper and studied it for some time.

PHASE TWO

ON SURROGATE GESTATION

Focus on Stimulated Fetal Osteogenesis and Organogenesis

"You call this proof? Of what?! What *is* this?!"

Derek exchanged a glance with Ojo then proceeded to explain.

"The killer retrieved that page from Barnes. He took it from his inner coat pocket the night he murdered him. There were probably other pages attached to it but we could only produce a clear picture of the page on top. The one in your hand."

"How does this piece of paper connect the two murders?" Brotsky asked without a clue of insight.

"C'mon," Ojo said as he walked up the stairs and led the others into the building.

"Where d'you think you're goin'?" Brotsky asked him as they stood by the elevator.

"To Atkin's lab, of course. The scene of the crime."

"Guess again," he told Ojo. "You're not getting anywhere near that lab until you explain yourselves."

"Gee, Sarge, it's really as plain as the nose on your face," Derek said, putting his hand on Brotsky's shoulder.

Brotsky shrugged his hand off.

"Don't you see?" Ojo explained. "Both Atkin and

Barnes were involved in some type of fetal research. And now both are in the icebox. Sounds like a connection to me."

"How did you get a hold of this?" Brotsky asked, holding up the page.

"Same way we got hold of all those other wonderful pictures. With the Thermalyzer device we demonstrated at the precinct the other day," Derek answered.

"And speaking of wonderful pictures, Sarge," Ojo said, "how is what's her name? You know, the one who looks so good in a Sergeant's cap?"

Christine blushed. Derek tried to restrain his laughter.

"Don't you worry about 'what's her name,'" Brotsky told Ojo with tightly drawn lips. "Let's just get back to this," he went on, taking another look at the page in his hand. "So both Atkin and Barnes were into similar research. So what? I'm sure lots of doctors dabble in that sort of research."

"Maybe, but how many of them end up dead?" Derek asked him. "And in both cases, the killer was after something. *That*, in Barnes' case," he said, pointing to the page that Brotsky held.

"And what about Atkin's case? Huh? What was the killer after in Atkin's case?" Brotsky said with excitement in his voice, certain that he had found the flaw in their logic.

"I'm sure you questioned that resident, what's his name?" Ojo began. "The one that scrubbed with Atkin the night of his murder."

"Reeves," Christine jumped in. "Morgan Reeves."

"That's it, Reeves," Ojo continued. "His name was all over the papers. According to him, he personally delivered the dead fetus to Atkin's lab right after surgery.

"That's right. He told me that himself," Brotsky said.

"Well then, Sergeant, where is it?" Christine asked him with a coy smile.

"Surely, you've retrieved it?" Derek asked Brotsky. "Or have you?"

"Uh, no. Actually, we never did. It wasn't in the lab," Brostky replied.

"And now, the sixty-four dollar question, Sarge. Who could've taken it?" Ojo sarcastically asked him.

There was no response for a few seconds.

"I think we better have ourselves another look," Brotsky finally suggested in an uncertain tone as the elevator doors opened.

They stepped onto the elevator and rode it up to the thirteenth floor. No one said a word during the silent ride. Brotsky pulled a wrinkled white handkerchief from his pocket and wiped the beads of perspiration from his brow. He carelessly stuffed the handkerchief back in his pocket and anxiously pressed the elevator button several times. A tense look suddenly distorted his face. A hard crease formed between his eyebrows as he nervously chewed on the corner of his lip. Derek wasn't quite sure what it meant. He looked at Ojo for a moment, then looked back at Brotsky. Ojo did the same, then turned toward his partner. In the subtlest way possible, they both smiled.

The elevator jerked slightly as it came to a stop. Christine carefully stepped across the uneven landing as Brotsky held the door open with his hand. Derek and Ojo followed her into the cluttered corridor.

"This way," Brotsky said, stepping past Christine as he led them toward Atkin's lab, about halfway down the corridor, between two other labs. One belonged to Dr. Koshi Takagawa, the molecular geneticist who had actually been one of Watson and Crick's research assistants at the time of their discovery of DNA almost four decades earlier. The other, occupying the corner of the corridor, belonged to Dr. Flint. Dr. *Hans* Flint, the Chief of Surgery.

A greying black officer sat on an overturned waste can outside the open door that led to Atkin's lab. A half-filled coffee cup rested on one knee. On the other, the officer tapped a few fingers.

"Morning, Baker," Brotsky greeted the officer.

"Morning, Sarge," the man replied. "Back for another check?"

Brotsky nodded. "Anyone come by?"

"No one, Sarge."

"Good. You airing out the lab?" he asked Baker, pointing to the open door.

"Sure am."

"Good."

Brotsky walked into the lab and turned the light on. Christine followed him as Derek noticed an unusual red and white sign on the door of Dr. Flint's lab. He nudged Ojo who eyed the sign with raised eyebrows. 'ABSOLUTELY NO ENTRY,' it read. They looked at each other for a silent moment then followed Brotsky into the lab. The first thing they noticed was the fading stench that still lingered.

"Jesus Christ, Baker!" Brotsky yelled.

Baker came running into the lab.

"How on God's green earth d'you expect to air this place out without opening one goddamn window?!"

Without responding, the startled officer ran across the lab and quickly opened each of the windows.

"Sorry, Sarge," he said on his way out.

Brotsky just shook his head. "Yeah."

Derek carefully inspected the lab. He walked from the door to Atkin's desk. He stood there a moment as his eyes passed over an issue of *Surgery, Gynecology & Obstetrics* which sat atop a number of disorganized papers on the desk's far corner. Beside it was another journal. The *British Journal of Fetal Surgery*. Ojo walked over to the granite window sill. His eyes fell upon the vomitus that still remained.

"Atkin's?" he turned and asked Brotsky who stood

several feet away near the sink.

"Don't know," he answered.

"I doubt it," Ojo told him. "I'll give you ten to one it was the killer who upchucked his lunch. Now, what do you think made him do that?"

Brotsky didn't answer.

"What about the sight of the dead fetus, all mangled and distorted, wrapped up in a plastic bag? Think that could've done it?"

"Could've," Brotsky replied in a quiet voice.

Ojo gazed out of one of the windows to the ground thirteen stories below. "Helluva first step," he mumbled.

Christine stood near the door, adjusting the flash on her camera as her eyes moved from one cabinet to the next, examining the contents of each from a distance. "Is that where you found the fetuses?" she asked Brotsky, pointing to the glass cabinet on the side of the room which contained an assortment of bottled specimens.

Brotsky nodded.

"You don't mind, do you?" she asked him as she focused.

"Knock yourself out," he told her.

She clicked off a number of shots and then moved to the corner of the lab opposite the windows. She made a couple of adjustments to the lens and continued shooting.

"Take a look at this," Derek said.

He pointed to a tiny drop of blood on the back of the wooden chair that sat behind Atkin's desk.

"Did you see this when you were here last night?" he asked Brotsky.

"Uhh…no. But I had one of my men scoop up a sample of the puke over there."

"I'm sure that'll prove real useful," Derek said in a sarcastic tone. "So I guess you didn't type it," he added, staring at the small spot of blood.

Christine quickly walked over and took a shot of the chair.

Brotsky didn't say anything.

"No need to," Derek said. "It's Atkin's."

Nothing was said for a moment.

"How can you be so sure?" Brotsky asked him.

"'Cause Atkin was probably sitting at his desk working when the killer struck him from behind. Boom, he knocked him out, then carried him over to the window and waved bye-bye," Derek cockily proposed. "Type it if you really want to prove me right."

"Baker," Brotsky called to the officer in the corridor.

"Yes, Sarge," he replied as he stepped into the lab.

Brotsky showed him the mark on the chair. "Would you scrape that off and send it to Forensics?"

"Absolutely, Sarge."

Derek and Ojo exchanged a glance. They smiled.

"Anything else you think I missed?" Brotsky asked in a bitter tone.

"Not sure yet," Derek answered.

He sat the attaché on the desk and opened it. From a pocket inside the cover he removed a black and turquoise Delta Ray Viewer. He tossed it over to Ojo, then removed the other Viewer disc from the pocket and closed the case.

"But we'll let you know in a minute or two," Ojo told Brotsky with an ear to ear grin.

Derek and Ojo let loose on the lab. Conical beams of blue light were everywhere.

"What the hell—" Brotsky started then remained silent and just watched in amazement.

Christine also watched. But she watched with delight.

Ojo aimed the disc at the cabinets against the wall on the side of the lab. The spiral beam of light shot from the disc, stripping away layer after layer of the numerous rows of bottles and jars in the cabinets to reveal the bare wall behind them. Nothing there.

"Check the bottom drawers," Derek told Christine. "See what those papers are," he said as the turquoise light which engulfed the desk faded. There was nothing behind the desk.

Brotsky made himself useful by flipping through the numerous texts and journals which lay stacked in piles on the shelves of the small cabinet that sat beside the taller glass one. Surely he wasn't attempting to read any of them. Only to see if anything had been tucked away between their pages. Perhaps a note. Or a letter. Or anything.

Christine sifted through the piles of papers that filled the bottom drawers of the desk while Ojo examined the printer which rested on a cart beside the computer terminal in the corner of the lab.

As the blue light bounced off the printer, he carefully studied the small screen on the disc in his hand. With the body of the printer stripped away, he could see a sheet of paper jammed between its rollers. Ojo closed the disc and placed it in the terminal as he touched a lever on the side of the printer. The front panel swung open. He reached in to pull out the toner cartridge which revealed the jammed paper stuck behind it. He gently pulled if from the rollers, taking care not to tear it.

"Well, what d'ya know," Ojo said as he smoothed out the sheet of paper with the side of his hand and held it up. "Would you take a look at this?"

Brotsky eagerly jumped ahead of Derek and Christine. He had no idea what he was looking at but thumbed his chin a couple times as if he was trying to figure it out.

PROJECT KYINNXSS59833445

PROJECT KYINNXSS59833445

On the Prevention of the Zero Gravity Induction of Fetal Osteoporosis and Bony Deformities
Focus on the Use of Calcitronase

It was the header page of the manuscript that Dr. Atkin had been reading at the moment his killer was upon him.

"Let's have another look at that other paper," Ojo told Brotsky.

He pulled the sheet from his pocket and handed it to Ojo. Ojo unfolded the paper and placed it beside the one he removed from the printer. It was obvious they were somehow connected. Both had to be part of a larger project. The same larger project.

"Still not sure the murders are connected, huh, Sarge?" Ojo asked.

Brotsky mumbled a few inaudible words under his breath.

"How're you doing over there, Christine?" Derek asked as she returned to the papers in the desk drawers.

"There's nothing here," she told him.

"Fine. Why don't you help Brotsky," he suggested as he focused the beam of light on the large refrigerator, which sat a few feet from the door against the wall that Atkin's lab shared with Flint's. A padlock prevented the refrigerator's door from opening.

The blue light penetrated the door to reveal a number of small specimen bottles and several packages of unopened film. Otherwise, the refrigerator was empty. Derek adjusted a dial on the side of the disc and the beam of light cut through the wide body of the refrigerator to reveal the wall behind it. And the small door within that wall.

Derek pushed on the side of the refrigerator. He noticed how it slid rather easily.

"What're you doin' over there?" Brotsky asked him.

"Why don't you have yourself a look," Derek told him as he revealed the door behind the refrigerator.

A large padlock secured the door handle to a steel latch on the wall. Ojo tapped Brotsky's shoulder as he moved past him, removing the Immobilizer from its brass case. He pressed the red triangular button and a turquoise jet of light struck the lock. Nothing happened. Ojo looked at Derek and nodded with a confident grin. He struck the button again and another burst of light hit the lock. Then there was a clicking noise and the lock fell open.

Ojo kissed the end of the Immobilizer and returned it to its case. Derek quickly removed the lock from the latch and pulled the door open. The back of another refrigerator was what he found. He gently pushed it aside and stepped through the door. And into Flint's lab.

"Do you realize this is breaking and entering?" Brotsky asked him.

"Call a cop," Derek responded with a sharp smile.

"C'mon," he told the others. "Let's do it."

They followed him into Flint's lab. It was slightly larger than Atkin's but otherwise more or less the same. Against one wall was a bulky wooden desk, a comfortable-looking swivel chair beside it. Against another were a number of glass bookcases and a large metal filing cabinet. In one corner, two dome-shaped operating lights and a dissecting microscope hung from the ceiling. In another, seated on a wide rectangular stand, were a computer terminal and printer. A small centrifuge sat on the floor beside the stand. All in all the two labs were not dissimilar.

Ojo and Derek quickly went to work with the Delta Viewers while Christine and Brotsky sorted through the numerous papers and journals in the cabinets and desk drawers. The refrigerator. The printer. The filing cabinet. But there was nothing to be found. The bookcase. The centrifuge. The operating lights. Nothing.

"Can someone give me a hand with this?" Christine asked as she pulled on the top drawer of the desk. It was locked.

"One sec," Ojo told her as he pulled the Immobilizer from its case.

The drawer unlocked and was found to contain just one small stack of papers. About twenty or so pages. Stapled together.

"I think we've got something here, fellas," she said.

The others rushed over to see what Christine had found. She took the stapled papers from the drawer and placed them on the desk. The first page was identical to the one Ojo had found jammed in Atkin's printer.

Nothing was said for a few moments. They just stared at the manuscript. Then Derek took a thin metal rod from the breast pocket of his shirt. It looked like a pen. But it wasn't. He pressed a button on one end and a glow of dull light flowed from the tiny holes that formed a line and ran the length of the rod. He placed the rod horizontally across the top of the first page and moved it over the printed paper. Then he turned the manuscript to the second page and did the same. The light became bright as the rod passed over the printed lines on each page then dull again when it was removed from the paper. Derek repeated this process with each of the twenty-two pages, closed the manuscript and returned it to the drawer. He pressed the button again and the light faded as he returned the rod to his shirt pocket.

With a raised eyebrow and peculiar pitch to his voice, he finally spoke.

"The plot thickens."

CHAPTER EIGHTEEN

The greatest invention of the nineteenth century
was the invention of the method of invention.

Alfred North Whitehead

A cool rush of air poured from the overhead nozzles as the cabin's pressure-controlled environment was prepared for departure. The powerful hum of the jet's engines penetrated its steel and platinum shell as the Boeing aircraft was carefully pushed out of the gate by a small truck attached to the front end of its landing gear. The plane smoothly swung away from the terminal and then slowly taxied along the winding service path that led to the main runway, where a number of other aircraft were lined up as they awaited clearance for takeoff.

"God, I hate flying," a very attractive young woman remarked. She sat staring out of the small oval window at her seat as she twirled a lock of her long dark curly hair with a nervous finger.

"I know exactly how you feel," a sympathetic voice from over her shoulder told her.

The woman turned around and caught Ojo's warm smile. She hadn't even noticed that he and Derek had sat down beside her.

"You do?" she asked him.

"Absolutely," Ojo told her. "Seems a lot of beautiful women have a fear of flying," he went on, staring directly into her deep green eyes with a playful grin on his face.

"I didn't say I have a *fear of flying*," she corrected Ojo, "only that I *hate* flying. There's a difference, you know," she said flatly.

Ojo nodded with a handsome smile.

After a slight pause, the woman let out the most adorably soft giggling sound. "Hi, I'm Selena Hawkins," she introduced herself with an extended hand.

"Ojo Jenachukwu," he replied, taking her soft hand in his. "And this here is…uhh…" Ojo hesitated as he turned to his left.

"Derek," his partner helped him out, slapping his shoulder. "Derek Cannon," he said with a friendly smile.

"Very nice meeting you," she told him.

"The pleasure's all yours," Derek said. "I mean *mine*," he quickly corrected himself and smiled.

Selena laughed. "You guys are nuts."

"We may be crazy," Derek said in his best Jack Nicholson imitation. "Crazy as a one-eyed bat flying upside down in a bottomless pit. We may just be as crazy as that. But we're not nuts," he told her with his teeth clenched and eyes bulging. "Don't ever call us nuts!"

Ojo and Selena laughed some more.

"Where are you heading?" Ojo asked her.

"Isn't this plane going to Houston?" she responded.

"It better be."

"Then I guess I'm headin' to Houston," Selena replied with a teasing grin.

"Wiseass," Ojo snickered at her, then winked. "Are you from Houston?"

"Sort of," she answered.

She watched through the window and wrapped several long strands of hair around a couple of fingers as the plane came to a stop at the foot of the runway. A loud humming noise filled the cabin as the engines reached full thrust. The jet raced along the runway a moment later until it lifted off the ground and was airborne. The plane veered away from the airport and leveled as it soared through the overcast sky. Selena watched as the ground turned into countless rows and columns of neatly arranged squares.

"*Sort of?*" Derek asked her. "I bet you're great with fill-ins."

"Well, I was born in Houston but we moved to D.C. when I was a year old. We lived there for about three years then we moved to Tucson. Four or five years later we moved to Jacksonville. From there we moved back to Houston. Then to San Diego. Then to Nova Scotia. No, I mean Salt Lake City. Then to Nova Scotia. And finally back to Houston. That's where I finished design school last year and that's where I'm stayin'. Got it?"

"Anything you say, lady," Derek said with his hands in the air.

"Let me guess," Ojo said. "You're either in the witness protection program or you're an Army brat."

"Bingo," Selena answered. "But it's the Air Force, not the Army. Whenever they need a laser expert to set up a tracking system, they call on good ol' Daddy," she said sarcastically. "And away we go."

"Sounds pretty tough," Derek commented. "How did you deal with constantly movin' around like that? How did you develop any roots?"

"I guess you just get used to it. It's your life. You don't know any other way," she told him.

"Now why did you say you hate flying?" Ojo asked. "'Cause of the psychos you're always stuck sitting next to?" he added and opened his eyes wide.

"That and the fact that the planes are always two hours late, your luggage is power-tested by eight gorillas, and all they give you is a stupid pack of roasted nuts! Like that's everyone's idea of a snack," she explained with a cute pout.

Derek and Ojo laughed.

"You don't have to tell me. I know you two are from New York," she said.

"Aay, you, does it really show?" Ojo said.

"Naaaah," Selena answered.

"An what'sa madda wid bein' from Noo Yawk, lady?" Derek asked, exaggerating his native accent just a bit.

"Oh, nothing," she said and giggled. "Nothing at all. What's in Houston?"

"Well, there's NASA, the Johnson Space Center, NEXUS, shitloads of oil, not too many trees—" Derek rambled.

"No, no, no," Selena interrupted. "I mean why are you headin' to Houston?"

"Oh. I didn't understand the question. You know us Noo Yawkas."

"Okay, okay. Forget I ever said that."

"Said what?" Derek asked.

"We're into uhh…consulting. Yeah, consulting. That's the ticket," Ojo said.

"Consulting?" Selena asked.

"Consulting. You know. *Consulting*," Ojo teased her.

"Okay, okay. Actually we do a lot of space navigational simulation software programming for NEXUS. So all our satellites and space probes don't crash in Red Square," he explained then turned to face Derek. He bent his head and crossed his eyes for a quick instant then turned back to Selena. "But we've also developed programs to cover our asses if they do."

"Very impressive. Small world. My father works for NEXUS too. Maybe you know him. Lieutenant Hawkins?"

Ojo turned toward Derek for a brief instant, long enough to catch his burning stare.

"Doesn't ring a bell," Derek interjected. "Most of our projects are actually with NASA but they're classified so we can't divulge too many details," he added and put a finger to his lips.

"Exactly," Ojo said, turning toward Derek again, this time with an apologetic expression for the slip.

"You guys are intense. I bet my father would love to discuss that stuff with you sometime."

"Yeah, maybe sometime," Ojo said then turned back toward Derek and crossed his eyes another time. Derek shook his head and laughed quietly.

"How long will the two of you be in town?" she asked.

"Probably two or three days," Derek told her.

Selena took a business card from her purse. Several words were printed in the center of the glossy black card.

DESIGNS by SELENA, the raised pink words read. An address and a couple of phone numbers were printed in the lower corners.

"If you have some time, call me. I'll introduce you to Daddy."

"That might be nice," Ojo said as he took the card from her. "Will do."

"Great," Selena said and turned to look out the window. She watched as an ocean of white clouds obscured any view of the ground thirty-six thousand feet below. Every so often a gap in the fluffy nebulous forms would provide a blurred glimpse of land.

Seated in the fifth row behind the lavatories which separated the first class section from the main cabin, not much could be seen up ahead. Especially with the red curtain drawn between the sections. Derek glanced from his aisle seat at several passengers on the plane's opposite side. A middle-aged woman sat sleeping in an aisle seat. Her head rested against a slightly younger man's shoulder who held her hand in his. Two rows behind them were seated three solemn-looking men, each in a navy blue suit and red power tie. One of them scribbled some notes on a legal pad while another sat punching a number of keys on his laptop. The third lay soundly asleep in his reclined chair with his head bent against the window.

Derek's roaming eyes were suddenly caught by a pair of firm calves which could be seen below the curtain. He recognized them and the black pumps in which they stood. They belonged to the attractive flight attendant who warmly greeted him as he boarded the plane. Moments later, they vanished into the lavatory.

Derek continued to survey the passengers. Behind the row of business clones sat a most unusual man. Derek eyed him for some time, then looked away. There was something about this man, he thought. Something familiar. Something that worried him. Yet he was sure he had never seen the man before. He looked back another time.

The man wore a flattened gray hat which sat unevenly on his head. His expressionless face was badly scarred. Numerous pockmarks covered his cheeks and continued onto his neck. He wore a pair of silver-rimmed bifocals which sat unevenly on the bridge of his crooked nose and nervously glanced at his watch from time to time. Beneath the man's long black trench coat was a badly wrinkled white shirt.

Derek's attention was again drawn toward the red curtain. Beneath it, he could see the navy pants and freshly polished black shoes which he recognized as the pilot's. The man stood by the lavatory for a moment. He seemed to be waiting for the flight attendant to finish but before she came out, he opened the door and walked in.

Derek turned toward Ojo. He wondered if he had seen that.

"So that's what they do when the autopilot kicks in," Ojo said with a raised brow and playful grin. "I always wondered."

"That must be where the extra thrust comes into play," Derek added.

Selena had also seen the pilot walk into the lavatory. She blushed at Derek's comment.

Derek reached into his hip pocket for his wallet. He opened it and removed a dime-sized silver disc from a small fold. He pulled a slightly larger black disc from another then looked up to catch Ojo's wide-eyed stare.

"Why don't you give 'em a minute or two to heat up?" he told Derek with a devilish chuckle.

"What are you two doing?" Selena asked.

"You'll see," Ojo answered. "Actually, you'll hear. We don't want to be too invasive, now, do we?"

Derek waited for a brief moment as he positioned the silver disc between two fingers. With a quick snap of his wrist, the disc rolled off his fingers and flew across the cabin and beneath the curtain. It struck the door of the lavatory and remained stuck to it.

Selena watched with curious eyes.

"And now," Derek said with a mischievous grin as he ran a finger over a small groove on the side of the black disc, "for a blow-by-blow account."

Nothing was heard at first. Then the whispery sound of a woman's voice became clear. It flowed from the tiny receiver in Derek's hand. The voice was the flight attendant's.

"Ohh, yes..." she said and then paused.

"Umm…ohh, baby…yes, yes."

Derek and Ojo exchanged a mischievous smile. They turned toward Selena and watched as she blushed.

"You want more, don't you?" the pilot asked her. "You want all of it."

"Ooh, more…yes…gimme more, more…umm, oh, oooh," the flight attendant purred as the sound of several objects falling to the floor was heard.

Ojo started to laugh until tears rolled down his cheeks. Derek unsuccessfully tried to restrain himself. He let out a loud howling laugh as several passengers turned around. Selena tried to hide her beet-red face by looking out the window but she was unable to hide her giggling.

"Tell me," he insisted.

"Ohh, please…gimme all of it…yes…yes, yes, oooh," her pace quickened. "Ooh, yes…ooh, ummm, yes, yes, yes, yes…oooh."

Then she was silent. A few moments later, the lavatory door opened slightly and the pilot stepped out. He walked toward the cockpit. Subsequently, the door opened again and the flight attendant exited the lavatory. Derek could see a long run in her dark stockings from beneath the curtain as she bent to fix her shoe with a finger. He smiled again and returned the black disc to his wallet.

"What typical New Yorkers," Selena teased them.

"Oh, right," Ojo said. "That's why you had your ears covered, huh?"

Derek laughed.

Selena blushed but didn't answer. She turned back toward the window and watched as the plane flew over the glistening dark water of Lake Superior.

Derek's attention returned to the unusual man across the aisle. He casually glanced over his shoulder. The man was still there. Nothing about him had changed in the last five minutes.

There was something about this man that worried Derek. He stared at the red curtain for a moment as a voice came alive inside his head. "…*gray hat, silver-rimmed bifocals, long black trench coat…gray pants, white shirt…*" Arti's words repeated in his mind. They faded as several comments of Ojo's returned to him. "…*the tall stiff in the park…that's the guy that framed me! …leaned to the left as he walked…dragging his right leg in a sweeping motion…limping and dragging…*" The Thermalyzer images suddenly filled his head. Images of that dark night in the park. Of the dead surgeon. And of the killer. A couple more comments of Arti's shot into Derek's mind. "…*clunky orthopedic shoes. His left foot stood two and a quarter inches higher than his right.*"

Derek pulled the thin metal rod from his pocket. His eyes focused on the red curtain another time as it was drawn to the side by the flight attendant. She pushed a small cart through the cabin's aisle and offered a pack of nuts and a drink to the elderly couple in the first row.

"What did I tell you?" Selena asked Ojo as the flight attendant's voice awakened her.

They exchanged a pleasant smile. Then Selena leaned her head back against the small pillow she had propped up against the window and returned to her nap.

Derek turned toward Ojo. "It really is a small fuckin' world," he told him with a serious expression on his face.

"What're you talking about?"

"Don't turn around. I might be wrong. I've never even actually seen him. But I think he's on the plane."

"Who?" Ojo asked with a touch of concern in his voice.

"The killer."

"*What*?! Are you serious?"

"Do I look like I'm joking?"

Ojo reached for the attaché case beneath his seat. He opened it and removed a small glass object from one of the compartments. It looked like a huge diamond. About the size of a golf ball. But it wasn't. Though it did have just as many facets. Both on the surface and in its center. Some convex. Others concave. They reflected the light like a thousand mirrors. It was their *Triacontagon*. Ojo turned the object in his hand as images of the passengers reflected off the glass surfaces. He could see the gargantuan woman who sat smothering her puny husband on one of the convex facets and the teenage girl who avidly turned the pages of some novel on one of the concave surfaces in the object's center. Ojo rotated the object at an angle and several new images appeared. One of the elderly pair of twins who sat knitting ends of the same scarf. Another of the back of a man's head as he looked out the window. The man turned around and his ugly pock-marked face was reflected on one of the convex surfaces. Ojo stared at it in silence.

"You're right," he said in a muffled whisper with clenched teeth. "That's him! *That's* the motherfucker!" Ojo confirmed. "I'll never forget his ugly fuckin' face."

Both sat without saying a word for some time.

"What d'we do? He knows what I look like," Ojo nervously said as the flight attendant offered them a drink. He nodded and she moved past their row.

Derek thought for a long moment. "Well, for one thing, we certainly can't let'm see you," he said and took the black disc from his wallet. "For another, I've got an idea."

He ran a finger along a flat dial on the disc's smooth surface, then held it against the side of his leg in the aisle. The small silver disc flew back from the lavatory door and landed on the one in his hand. As he returned the black disc to his wallet, he let the silver one fall to the floor. When the flight attendant stepped just past the killer's row, Derek grabbed the disc from the floor and quickly flicked it backwards with a couple of fingers. It struck the sole of the killer's bulky orthopedic shoe and remained stuck to it.

"All we have to do now," Derek said, "is get out of here without getting killed. And we've got our own personal homing pigeon."

"This is not bad," Ojo commented. "As long as we know where he is, we know he's not where we are."

"Exactly."

"But this world really is too fuckin' small," Ojo said as he pulled a thin stack of white paper from the attaché case and set it on the tray in front of him. "Why don't we have ourselves a look at the good doctor's notes," he went on, holding out a hand as Derek handed him the metal rod.

Ojo glanced at Selena and found her leaning against the window fast asleep. He pressed the button on the end of the rod and a dull light filled the line of holes. He passed it over the top sheet of blank paper and the light brightened as the rod printed the first page of the manuscript they had found in Dr. Flint's lab. Ojo quickly passed the rod over twenty-one more blank sheets of paper and printed the entire manuscript. He pressed the button again and returned the rod to Derek's pocket as the light faded.

They stared at the closed manuscript for some time. Then Ojo turned the header page over and they carefully read its contents. The first section discussed the problem of bony atrophy and demineralization which occurred in zero gravity and microgravity environments. Something astronauts have been concerned with since man first walked on the moon. It cited this problem as the main obstacle to developing permanent space colonies. If fully developed healthy adults are susceptible to bony atrophy, the manuscript proposed, surely the fetus cannot be expected to achieve normal bony development in a zero gravity environment.

"Makes sense," Derek said.

Ojo nodded and turned the page. The next section of the manuscript discussed the properties of a complex synthetic enzyme, *calcitronase*, which had been engineered by a team of geneticists headed by Dr. Koshi Takagawa. Several animal models detailed in the manuscript demonstrated the utility of calcitronase in preventing bony atrophy and demineralization. By working backwards, a specific messenger RNA strand had been created to code for this protein enzyme. Subsequently, a double-stranded DNA gene was produced to specifically code for the messenger RNA—*Zq-253-634-Gfy* was the gene's mapping label. It was called the *Osteonic gene*.

"Pretty impressive," Ojo said as he looked up.

"Yeah," Derek said with an agreeing nod and turned the page as the pilot announced they would soon be landing.

The final section began on the thirteenth page. In excruciating detail, it described an experimental protocol whereby the Osteonic gene would be genetically interspliced within the DNA of one of the maternal X chromosomes. The egg would afterwards be artificially fertilized and the bony development of the fetus would then be studied.

"This is *amazing!*" Derek said as they read the last paragraph on the twentieth page. "Do you realize the significance of this?"

Ojo looked at him with a smirk.

"I meant that rhetorically," Derek quickly added.

"First they splice the Osteonic gene into the egg which supposedly prevents abnormal bone formation—" Ojo began.

"And then they splice in the Omega gene," Derek interrupted, "so they can implant the human fetus into a goddamn monkey without it being rejected. How the fuck did they come up with this?!"

"It's ingenious," Ojo commented.

"On paper, anyway," Derek commented, "but it's good for shit in practice," he added, his mind recounting the vivid descriptions of the grotesquely malformed fetuses he had gotten from Brotsky and Dr. Reeves earlier that morning.

"And now NEXUS wants to sweep it under the rug."

"With a few extra bodies," Derek suggested.

"Yeah," Ojo said with a flat expression. "Ours among them," he added, eyeing the reflector in his hand. He could still see the ugly face of the killer on one of its concave surfaces.

"But what I'd really like to know is where they've been getting the eggs," Derek said.

"Or rather, from *whom*," Ojo said as Derek turned the page.

Ojo froze as his eyes fell upon the next page. They

widened as his jaw dropped open. The glass object slid from his hand and rolled over the banister between the seats, settling on Selena's lap. He quickly retrieved it as she stirred in her seat.

"Unfuckinbelievable!" Derek said. He quickly turned to the next and last page, then back again. Both were covered with names. *Women's* names. And addresses. Most of them just outside Houston. In Willow Valley. A few of them in New York. One in Chicago. "This is absolutely *unfuckinbelievable!*"

Selena stared out the window as the plane flew over the freeway that ran perpendicular to the Houston International Airport and touched down on the narrow runway. It was a rough landing at best, another thing she hated about flying. After reversing its engines' thrust, the plane slowly taxied along the runway until a loud tone indicated it had come to a stop by the terminal.

The tall man a few rows behind them was the first to stand. He was obviously in a bit of a hurry to deplane. He carried an old brown leather attaché case which he held close to his side as he slowly moved through the aisle, bending slightly to avoid hitting his head on the ceiling and dragging his right leg as he walked. Ojo and Derek remained seated until the man had moved a couple of rows past them. They quickly gathered their things from below their seats and the compartments above, exchanged a few words and a warm smile with Selena and, from a safe distance, followed the killer as he moved through the concourse. They watched as he gradually made his way across the huge terminal and into the street. Limping and dragging, limping and dragging. Finally, he stepped into a checkered cab and was gone.

Ojo and Derek stood watching from the curb as the cab disappeared into the airport traffic.

"Mark my word," Ojo told Derek with a determined look in his eyes. "I'm not sure how and I'm not sure when, but before it's all over and the fat lady sings, I'm gonna nail that motherfucker's nuts to the wall."

CHAPTER NINETEEN

Where the telescope ends, the microscope begins.
Which of the two has the grander view?

Victor Hugo

A small Japanese woman sat uncomfortably hunched on her relatively tall three-legged stool as she bent with crooked posture over the ocular lens attached to the similarly-bent arm of the microscope which sat on the bench before her. The woman's feet curled around one of the wooden stool's crosspieces. She carefully removed her eyeglasses and held them by the frame with one hand for a moment as she adjusted the microscope's magnification by swinging a more powerful objective lens into place with the other. She gently dabbed her forehead with the sleeve of her white coat. She sighed deeply and then returned her eyeglasses to their proper position. Her attention returned to the contents of the petri dish, which was held in place by a small spring attached to the stage of the microscope.

The woman angrily adjusted her eyeglasses on the bridge of her nose and then looked through the ocular lens another time. Sighing deeply again, she looked away from the microscope.

"Okami," the woman called to her assistant on the other side of the laboratory. "Would you come here, please?" she asked in a tired voice.

"Yes," the man replied, walking around the island covered with various apparatus in the center of the lab, "what is it, Dr. Takagawa? What is the matter?"

Dr. Takagawa stepped from the stool and motioned for her assistant to look through the lens. He did so, positioning himself on the stool and making several fine adjustments with the microscope's numerous levers and dials before he stepped off the stool. As he did, a nervous twitch subtly shook the corner of his lip.

"I do not know what to say, Dr. Takagawa," the man said apologetically.

"But I do. This is the third fertilized egg," she said and paused briefly, "the third *human* fertilized egg that has had both the Kryptonic gene and the Omega gene successfully spliced into its chromosomes. And it is the third that you have allowed to die in the twelve-day period between gene splicing and implantation," Dr. Takagawa continued in a quiet, collected voice. "Why are you not more careful, Okami?" she asked her assistant, raising her voice ever so slightly. "Why?"

Dr. Okami Nekura, a rather large Japanese man in his late thirties who had been one of Dr. Takagawa's assistants for some six years, bent his head, acknowledging his failure. No additional words were exchanged over this matter.

"We will begin again," Dr. Takagawa told Okami.

Okami nodded.

"But later," Dr. Takagawa told him. "First we must examine the embryos in which we have spliced the Osteonic gene. That they have developed without complication and are ready for implantation is vital. Do you understand that?" she asked Okami, bending her neck back to look him in the eye.

"I do. There will be no further slip-up," Okami assured her.

"Very well. But keep in mind, next time I may not be there to step between you and Dr. Flint," Dr. Takagawa warned him, referring to an earlier incident.

Okami nodded but did not reply.

Together they stepped through the triangular entrance and onto the automatic hoverway several feet from the laboratory. The blue lights in the entryway's chrome trim flashed for a moment then turned red, indicating the invisible laser field had self-activated. Dr. Takagawa and Okami stood on the stationary hoverway for a moment.

"Please identify," a computerized voice told them.

Dr. Takagawa had forgotten for an instant.

"I've got it," Okami told her as he placed his palm on the glowing blue surface of the sensor pad. It was attached to the germanium pole that stood beside the hoverway. The pad beeped several times as a steel rod with several small black handles rose from one of the rectangular plates on the floor of the hoverway. Dr. Takagawa and Okami each grabbed onto one of the handles as the hoverway began to move forward.

"Destination?" the voice asked.

"Floatron tunnels," Dr. Takagawa answered.

The hoverway began to move faster. Much faster. Within little more than a few seconds it soared past the twelve laboratories which occupied the Alpha-1 Station of the Octagon 3 level, turning effortlessly on its air-cushioned track as it flew beyond the Alpha-2 Station and the WATER Facility, stopping instantly as it came to the main area in front of the Beta-1 Station where forty-four species of animals were maintained and bred. Three men in long white coats stepped onto the hoverway several feet ahead of its two other passengers. One of the men placed his hand on the sensor pad and the hoverway slowly moved away from the station.

"Destination?" the same voice asked him.

"Space-3 Heliport," he responded, turning to greet Dr. Takagawa with a subtle nod and hint of a smile as the hoverway took off.

It sped past the Beta-1 Station, angling around the curvature of the level. As it approached a passage adjoining the Beta-2 Station, the section of the hoverway carrying the three new passengers immediately split off and disappeared into the narrow chute while the section on which Dr. Takagawa and Okami stood continued on its way until it came to a quick halt on the opposite end of the Octagon 3 level. Right by the floatron tunnels.

They stepped from the hoverway and walked several feet into the tunnel where a floatron awaited their entry. They boarded the bullet-shaped vehicle as several others left. Okami inserted his hand into the transparent compartment at the helm of the floatron. It immediately filled with a bluish gas as a yellow bar flashed on its side.

"Clearance granted," a computerized voice told them as the doors slid shut. "Atmosphere controlled," the voice added as its passengers strapped themselves into the large seats. "Destination?"

"TSI Facility," Dr. Takagawa replied. "Sector 13."

The floatron produced a humming tone before it shot into the transparent tunnel system, instantaneously achieving maximal velocity within its frictionless chute. Its lights dimmed as it filled with a purplish mist. Soaring freely and without resistance on a cushion of air, the floatron glided from one tunnel into the next, moving between levels and across stations as it flew from one end of the massive installation to the other. Once there the floatron entered a pressurized chute. After a brief delay it quickly descended seventy or eighty feet straight down into the bowels of the installation.

"TSI Facility," the computerized voice told them. "Transporting to Sector 13."

The floatron soared from the pressurized chute into a winding chamber, which it followed beyond a series of parallel levels until it reached its destination. "Sector 13," the voice said as the purplish mist cleared and the doors slid open. "Atmosphere controlled."

Dr. Takagawa and Okami stepped off the floatron and onto another hoverway. It carried them directly to the Sector 13 entryway. As they approached the glass entrance Okami held his hand high in the air. A flash of blue light burst from a small panel atop the double doors, colliding with his hand before the light vanished.

"Entry permitted," another computerized voice told them as the doors slid open.

They passed through the glass doors and walked across the wide corridor to the operating facility at its end. Several words flashed above it—IMPLANTATION IN PROGRESS: NO ENTRY. Dr. Takagawa stood before the triangular entryway and the invisible laser field deactivated. She and Okami entered the room.

* * *

"No one ever told me I was part of an experiment!" the woman yelled, struggling to get the words out as she tried to catch her breath. Tears raced down the sides of her face.

Ojo and Derek looked at each other and then back at the woman who sat hunched over and sobbing. She sat between them on a small couch in her living room.

Her name was Mary Jo Parker. She was an attractive woman. About twenty-four. She was born and raised in Willow Valley. Married her high school sweetheart right after graduation. A fellow named Jon Parker. He became a test pilot for NASA. After unsuccessfully attempting to become pregnant for over three years, she and Jon approached Dr. Atkin. That was over a year ago. Artificial in vitro fertilization was the answer, he told them. Three months later, Mary Jo was pregnant. Six months after that, Jon was killed during a test flight mishap. Really a freak accident, as she explained it, but nonetheless, Jon was gone. Forever. All that remained to keep a part of him alive was their baby. Three months later, Mary Jo gave birth.

"I held him to my breast," she told them, "and rocked him back and forth." With folded arms, she moved back and forth on the couch. "His little face was all…all…," she tried to get the words out then covered her face in her hands as she sobbed heavily, "all bunched up," she mumbled through her fingers, "and his little b-body was all…all dis-distorted!"

Derek put his hand on the woman's shoulder. "I wish there was something I could say," he told her in a gentle voice, "to make it all better. But there isn't."

"I still would've l-loved little Jonny, but then…then the nurse took him away from me! She said he was d-d-dead!" Mary Jo yelled and buried her face in her hands again.

"Were you ever told that any of this might happen?" Ojo asked her and handed her a few tissues from a box on the coffee table.

Mary Jo wiped her eyes and took a deep breath. "Never. *Never!* Those bastards didn't tell me one damn thing! Only that there was no guarantee I would become pregnant. Once I was pregnant, Dr. Atkin assured me everything was coming along just fine. That's what he told me every time I saw him. 'Just fine.' Everything is 'just fine'! Then," she went on, "then, after he delivered my baby dead he told me, 'These things just happen. No one can explain it.' That's what the bastard told me! No one can explain it?! *You* just did!" she said and looked from Ojo to Derek. "I was a guinea pig. A goddamn guinea pig! In some sick experiment!"

Nothing was said for a few moments. Ojo and Derek exchanged another glance.

"You can't give me back little Jonny," Mary Jo said, crumpling the tissue in a closed hand, "but don't let them do this to anyone else. Please. Don't let them."

"We're gonna do our best," Ojo told her. "I'm really sorry we've upset you so."

"I'll be alright," she said. "Don't worry about me. Just don't let them do this to anyone else," Mary Jo pleaded. "It hurts too much."

Ojo and Derek left the woman's house. They got back into their rental and drove off as a soft clap of thunder was heard. A light rain began to fall.

"Well, that finishes the list," Ojo said, eyeing the last two pages of the manuscript and the numerous notes he had written beside each woman's name while Derek drove. "Mary Jo makes seven that we've seen. Stevenson, McMurphy and Westcott aren't around. Taylor's in Chicago. And the others are in New York."

"Christine's probably already tracked 'em down," Derek said, looking from the road to catch Ojo's eye for a second. "Probably the one in Chicago too," he added with a slight smile, "if I know her."

"All of them have the same story. Couldn't get pregnant so they went to Atkin or Erikson, some other groinecologist. And *sha-zam*! After a little medical hocus-pocus at this research facility they're all pregnant within six months."

"Yeah. But no one told 'em that their eggs were scrambled," Derek said.

"Or that a bunch of 'em were poached for the other implantation protocol," Ojo added.

"Which way?" Derek asked as he came to a fork in the road.

Ojo pointed to the Route 41 sign and Derek took the road that veered to the right as he carefully studied the small map which he had fixed to the dashboard with a velcro strip. It was a computerized map which detailed a specific region based on the latitudes and longitudes that were programmed into it. And it tracked the yellow light which flashed in its center. That light corresponded to the signal produced by the transmitter attached to the sole of the killer's shoe.

The map now displayed every highway, road and street that ran through one small town just outside Houston. *Willow Valley.* And every road led to Rome. Or at least to the killer's shoe.

"It's about two miles past the junction of Route 41 and Banner Creek," Ojo said. "Right where that other woman, what's her name…" he paused and glanced at the list another time, "…Bessie Simpson, said it would be."

"There's nothing like consistency," Derek said as the car sped along the narrow highway. "Especially when you're already in way over your head."

* * *

A sharp clicking sound was heard. It alternated with a scratchy dragging noise. First the sharp clicking sound. Then the scratchy dragging noise. Then the clicking sound. Then the scratchy dragging noise. The clicking sound. The dragging noise. Clicking sound. Dragging noise. This went on for some time. Then neither was heard. For a brief moment there was silence.

"Atkin's dead," a deep Lurch-like faceless voice finally said very matter-of-factly.

"Good," another faceless voice replied, "and the fetus?" the voice asked with a rather distinct German accent. A familiar German accent.

Nothing was said. In his mind Derek saw the killer point to the old beat up attaché case they had seen him carry off the plane.

He and Ojo listened without distraction to the voices which finally flowed from the small black disc which now sat on the dashboard. After hours of clicking and dragging noises alternating with dead silence since the killer had disappeared from the airport in a cab, finally the oaf had made it to the research facility. Finally, he spoke.

After surveying the vast clearing on which the massive octagonal structure stood, Derek parked the car atop a high cliff about a quarter of a mile from the wall of electrified fence that surrounded it. It was one of several cliffs which overlooked the installation. The computerized map had directed him and Ojo about two miles past the junction of Route 41 and Banner Creek and onto a dangerously narrow and winding unpaved road which led them to this spot.

"What about the intruders?" the accented voice questioned.

Ojo and Derek exchanged a glance.

"Any idea whom he's referring to?" Derek asked with a crooked grin.

"None at all," Ojo replied with a raised brow.

"Are they taken care of?"

There was no response for a moment. "They won't be interfering again," the killer finally replied.

"Guess again, you motherfucker," Ojo said with clenched teeth.

"You have done well," the man praised him. "Do not miss the demonstration on Sector 13 at 1900 hours. Erikson and Hawkins want everyone there."

"I'll be there, Dr. Flint."

The sound of brisk footsteps was heard for several moments until they faded. And the clicking sound and dragging noise returned. Clicking and dragging. Clicking and dragging.

"Flint," Ojo said in a quiet voice as Derek checked his watch. It was 6:43 p.m. "Hmm… *Flint*," he repeated in a mocking German tone and they both laughed loudly.

They sat in the car and stared at the formidable black structure as their laughter subsided. The setting sun hung remarkably low in the sky. Its rays cast a most unusual shadow as it struck the electrified fence. A honeycomb pattern raced along the ground and collided with one of the building's eight walls as the shadow created by a departing helicopter's propeller blades cut through its interlocking diamond-shaped links and became entangled with the ribbon-like shadows of the fence's barbed wire. Ojo and Derek just stared in silence for some time.

Derek finally spoke. "How the fuck are we going to penetrate *that*?" he asked.

There was no response.

"That's not going to be easy," Ojo finally said as he pulled a small pile of cards from his wallet.

"I wonder if Christine's come up with anything," Derek said, reaching into the large bag which sat on the back seat for the black and turquoise disc. He placed the phone on the console. "Dial Stratton."

A yellow light flashed on the small circular phone. The line rang three times. There was no answer.

"Forward call," Derek said.

A blue light flashed and the line rang again. The light stopped flashing as the line connected.

"Hello," Christine's soft voice filled the car.

"Well, 'hello' yourself," Derek said.

"Where are you?" she asked him.

"Where are *you*?"

"I think we have a bad connection, hon," she said.

"Bad connection my ass. Where are you?" Derek asked her with concern in his voice.

"At the airport."

"*Which* airport?"

She didn't answer.

"*Which* airport?"

"O'Hare," she finally mumbled.

"In Chicago?" he asked and looked at Ojo.

"Yes, Derek, the Windy City," Christine responded. "Thought I could get some answers with my reporter's cap on so I hopped on a plane. We really need to know what the hell is going on with these poor women and these horrible birth deformities. And we need to know *now*, before anyone else is hurt."

Derek didn't say anything. He just sat there and shook his head from side to side. Then a smile rounded the corners of his lips and he started to laugh.

"You're too much," he told her. "I can't disagree. So, what've you come up with?"

"The three women in New York," she started, "each had the same story as the woman you told me about. All three artificially fertilized. Six to nine months later each gave birth to some monstrosity. Most recent was Melanie Thomas, the one Reeves delivered with Atkin last night."

"Any of them know anything about this experiment?"

"Of course, not."

"Anything different with the woman in Chicago?"

"Don't know. I just got here."

"Couldn't you get her on the phone?"

"I tried. But she's in labor even as we speak. I want to be there when she delivers."

"Great. Why don't you get some 8 x 10 glossies while you're there," Ojo teased her.

"You can count on that," she told him.

"You know," he said and smiled, "I think we can."

"Anything going on in Willow Valley?" Christine asked.

"We're right outside the factory," Derek told her.

"Just getting an earful."

"You just be careful," Christine warned.

"And you be in touch."

"Ciao," she said and the loud sound of a kiss was heard before the line disconnected.

"She really is too much," Ojo said.

"Yeah," Derek agreed, a wide smile on his face. "We're lucky guys. You know that? But it's too bad Sasha had to head back to the set so early this morning. Then again," he went on, "you did need *some* sleep."

A distant gaze coated Ojo's eyes. "Yeah," he said with a mischievous smile. His eyes returned to the cards in his hand. "You were saying, about…*penetrating?*" he continued, quickly shuffling through them. Then he handed one to Derek. "How 'bout this?"

Derek took the card from him and stared at it for a moment. 'DESIGNS by SELENA,' the card read. "That'll work," he said with a scheming smile.

* * *

The smell of alcohol filled the room. Ivory tiles lined its walls and plates of ebony covered its floor. Three large overhead surgical dome lights hung from the ceiling. Beneath the lights was an operating table. On the table lay a patient, her face covered by the blue drape which hung between two IV poles, an anesthesiologist behind it, her arms tucked in at her sides and a blue sheet neatly placed over her body, her legs spread wide apart, supported by stirrups and similarly covered.

A short stocky man wearing a surgical gown and mask, with magnification loupes secured by a pair of croakies, stood between the patient's legs. With a Betadine-soaked sponge, he prepped her.

"The most important step in artificial implantation," he explained, tossing the used sponge into the pan beside him as he took another and soaked it in the Betadine solution, "is securing the embryo entirely beneath the endometrial layer of the uterine lining as it would occur naturally."

Using the sponge he cleaned the patient's genitalia with several circular motions then discarded it in the pan. He repeated the process once more then held his hands out toward the scrub nurse who pulled his gloves off and replaced them as the sound of one heel clicking and another dragging was heard.

From behind the triangular turquoise stone which blocked the similarly-shaped entrance to the operating facility emerged the unusually tall man, his ugly face hidden behind a surgical mask.

"Sorry, Dr. Erikson," he said with an unconcerned tone.

The surgeon mumbled several indiscernible words as he clipped his towels in place and finished preparing his operative field. "We can begin," he said.

From a barrel-sized steel drum on the side of the room, two men carefully removed a shiny black canister.

The liquid nitrogen which filled the drum bubbled over its rim as they pulled the canister out. They set it on a stand near the table as two other men replaced the drum's steel cover. Two yellow lights revolved around the top of the canister as a red light steadily flashed. Several letters were engraved beneath the red light. 'LSS', they read.

"Hawkins, open the life support system and start doing what you do best," Dr. Erikson told the Lieutenant who was now wearing scrubs.

Hawkins pressed several buttons on the back of the canister. The yellow lights stopped revolving and then turned off. The red light kept flashing. With steady motions, he unscrewed the top of the canister. A bluish gas was released as he removed the top and handed it to one of the others. He held his hands out and the scrub nurse placed a second pair of gloves over the pair he already wore then handed him a curved clamp.

Hawkins placed the clamp into the mouth of the canister and from within it withdrew a metal disc. He handed the disc to the scrub nurse who carefully set it on her Mayo stand. His attention then shifted to the apparatus that sat on a tray beside the operating table.

A small silver instrument resembling a dentist's drill sat on that tray. A cord ran from one end of the instrument to the keyboard beside it. From the keyboard extended several cords which connected with two monitors. Hawkins struck several keys and the screens came alive with color. He hit a switch on the side of the instrument and a blue light pulsed up and down its length.

It was the CO_2 laser he would use to cut and elevate the endometrial flap.

"Whenever you're ready, Dr. Erikson," he said.

The surgeon held a hand out and the scrub nurse instantly handed him a cylindrical dilator. With the use of a large speculum, he gently maneuvered the dilator through the patient's cervix and into the body of her uterus.

"Laser, gamma setting," Dr. Erikson said, turning the dial on the speculum to tighten and maintain its position then adjusting the large overhead lights.

Hawkins removed a cap from the instrument's tip to reveal a clear filament then handed it to Dr. Erikson.

"Ready," Hawkins said.

Dr. Erikson positioned the laser within the uterus then glanced at the monitors which Hawkins had positioned beside him. He could see the uterine wall. He adjusted the instrument then pressed a button on its handle. A beam of invisible light shot from the laser's tip and cut into the superficial lining of the uterus.

"Lamda setting," he said and Hawkins struck several pads on the keyboard.

"Ready," Hawkins said.

Everyone watched the monitors as one displayed the entire uterine cavity and the other the path of the beam of light. With the laser Dr. Erikson carefully created a small flap of endometrial tissue.

"Hand me the disc," he told the scrub nurse.

He took the disc from her and carefully removed its cover. Within it, swimming in a tiny pool of fluid, was a human embryo. With a pair of long microsurgical forceps he delicately grabbed the amnion and lifted the embryo from the disc. He steadied the retractor and inserted the embryo through the dilator into the patient's uterus. With a pair of Castroviejo micro-dissecting scissors he raised the flap of tissue and carefully positioned the embryo beneath it.

"8-0 Chromic," Dr. Erikson said and the nurse handed him a suture. "After suturing the amnion to the deepest portion of the furrow I have created in the uterine wall," he explained while he worked, tying several knots as the nurse cut the stitch, "I will suture the flap of endometrial tissue over the embryo. And that is all there is to it," he modestly said.

A few minutes later, he was done. The group applauded loudly.

"Pretty wild shit," Derek said as he and Ojo heard all of it through the transmitter on the killer's shoe.

"Yeah," Ojo agreed. "Looks like Selena's Daddy does a little extra work on the side," he said with some sarcasm. "Wonder if she does too."

"Well, we'll find out tomorrow. The meeting with her and Daddy is all set," Derek said.

"Too bad I won't be there," Ojo said as the phone rang.

"Too risky," Derek said. "Scarface can put the finger on you."

Ojo nodded.

"Hola, señorita," Derek answered with a Mexican accent. "How may I be of service?"

An unmistakable giggle filled the car. It was Christine.

"Guess what?" she asked.

"I don't know. What?" Derek asked.

"Taylor gave birth," she told them.

"Aaaaand?"

"The kid's adorable."

"Just like the others, huh?"

"No, well, except—"

"Except he's got three heads," Ojo interrupted.

"No, he's completely fine except for two fingers on his right hand. They're sort of fused together. But nothing else."

"Hmm," Ojo said and ran a finger along the smooth edge of the phone.

"'Hmm', what?" Christine asked.

"Just hmm. That's really interesting."

"Yeah, I thought so too. I've got a couple ideas I want to bounce off you guys," she said.

"Start bouncin'," Derek said.

"I thought we'd discuss them over dinner."

"But we're gonna be here for a couple more days," Ojo told her.

"I know that."

"Christine, my dear," Derek said, "I really hope you're not thinking what I think you're thinking."

"Then it's settled, my dear," she said.

"No fuckin' way, Christine," Derek firmly told her. "I don't want you anywhere near this place, you got that?!" he insisted.

"You worry too much," she told him. "I'm a big girl, remember? See you at midnight," she said and the sound of another loud kiss filled the air before the line disconnected.

"God, she pisses me off," he told Ojo.

"Hope she doesn't have trouble finding us," Ojo said.

"Well, aside from the fact that she's a smart-ass photojournalist, and that Willow Valley's got but one fuckin' motel which is run by Norman Bates, Christine also happened to have made our reservation. I don't think she's gonna have much trouble finding us. God, she pisses me off," Derek said then paused for a few moments. "But I do love that girl."

He and Ojo exchanged a quiet smile and continued to listen to the transmission from the OR within the installation.

Hawkins and one of the other men in scrubs, one with a dreadful limp, transferred the patient from the operating table to the gurney beside it. As they maneuvered the gurney through the triangular exit which led to the Sector 13 recovery room, Hawkins' assistant clumsily ran the head of the stretcher into the side of the sloped wall. With a quick motion the patient's hand slid from under the blue sheet and dangled loosely over the edge of the gurney. It was a large hand. One covered with dark brown fur. One displaying long curved claws. It was the hand of a monkey.

"*Idiot!*" Hawkins mumbled, tucking the hand back under the sheet as he pushed the stretcher into the recovery room.

CHAPTER TWENTY

We all have our time machines, don't we. Those
that take us back are memories. And those that
carry us forward are dreams.

H. G. Wells

A thin crescent of hazy light was all the moon had to offer on this clear night. Lightning and thunder rose from the light rain that fell earlier in the evening, creating a storm that left the lower part of Willow Valley flooded. But the storm subsided. And the puddles gradually dispersed. With its passing a quiet stillness lingered in the cleansed air. The sky which had been overcast and filled with dark clouds just a couple hours earlier was now crystal clear. And the air country fresh. Countless stars flickered brightly in the heavens. So a thin crescent of hazy light was all the moon needed to offer on this clear night.

Streams of light crossed the unpaved road that passed in front of the Valley Inn. The light struck several of its numerous doors, the others provided with only the dimmest lighting that shone from the small bulbs attached to the wooden beams, which connected to form a row in front of the Inn. On the other side of that road stood a dense forest of oaks and pines. A number of blackberry bushes adorned the banks of the small pond, which lay thirty or forty feet beyond the rows of tall trees. It was called Willow Pond.

It was said that the owner of the Inn, a man of middle age by the name of Herman Tate, would plant another blackberry bush along the pond's bank with each new victim that he drowned. About twenty bushes lined that bank. Men of Tate's year, after terrifying their wives with this yarn, would usually confess that it had evolved from the similarity between Herman Tate's name and that of the famed *Psycho* killer, Norman Bates. Men of Ojo and Derek's year would usually ignore that part of the tale.

A slovenly dressed man could be seen through the glass door of the Inn's office. It was Tate. He stood behind a long desk as a young couple negotiated the fee for a short stay. Tate handed them a key and they hastily emerged from the office without any luggage, brushing past Ojo and Derek who stood near one of the wooden beams outside the door on which a wooden plaque marked 'ONE' hung, and quickly disappearing into one of the rooms. A plaque marked 'SEVEN' rattled on its hook as the door smacked shut.

Ojo and Derek looked at the door and laughed quietly.

"I'm gonna start heading to the airport," Derek said, eyeing his watch as he pulled the car keys from the pocket of his windbreaker.

It was 11:12 p.m.

As he walked toward the rented Bronco that sat parked right outside the room, a green Chevy with a sign that said 'TAXI' on its roof, pulled into the next space. A moment later, the backdoor swung open and Christine stepped out of the car. A camera hung from one shoulder, a Gucci overnight bag from the other.

She stood there for a silent moment while they looked at each other.

"You wouldn't happen to be pickin' up some chick at the airport?" she asked him with a bright smile.

"Actually, I would be," Derek answered with a straight face, opening the door and climbing into the Bronco. "Catch you later."

Christine watched as he sat behind the wheel and closed the door. Then he started the car and after a long moment, slowly turned to her with a mischievous smile on his face. Ojo laughed. Christine pouted adorably as she set her shoulder bag and camera on the hood of the car. Then she threw her arms through the open window and around his neck.

"One of these days," she said, kissing his mouth and

cheek and ear, "I'm really gonna surprise you."

"You surprise me every day, Christine," Derek said then pulled her through the window as he fell back onto the passenger seat with her on top of him. Her feet dangled out the window as they laughed loudly.

After a few moments, Ojo opened the passenger door. With an extended hand he helped Christine crawl over Derek. She gave him a hug and peck on the cheek as Derek made it out of the car.

"You know I didn't want you anywhere near this place, Christine," Derek told her in a disciplining tone.

"I know, I know, but just wait till you see these," she said, reaching across the hood for her shoulder bag. She quickly unzipped a side pocket and removed several photos.

Derek took them from her. The first photo was a shot of the newborn infant. Looked totally normal. The next a closeup shot of the baby's right hand. His index and middle fingers were fused together. Otherwise normal. The next several photos were more of the same but from different angles.

"It's really interesting that this kid's almost completely unaffected. Unlike those other kids," Ojo said.

"Yeah," Derek agreed. "Whatever the Frankenstein club has been up to, it looks like they've modified their methods."

Ojo nodded.

"I know you've got something more for us," Derek said. "What is it?" he asked Christine. "You didn't fly in just to show us these photos, did you?"

"Well, actually …" she hesitated.

"'Well, actually' *what?*" he asked her.

"Sort of."

"'Sort of' *yes*, you mean?" Derek asked her.

"Actually, sort of, no."

"'No' *what?*"

"No, that's not why I flew in," Christine replied.

"Then *why?* What were those ideas you wanted to 'bounce' off us?"

"Well, I thought I could help—"

"Help? *How?!* By getting yourself or us killed?!" Derek asked her.

"No!" Christine snapped back at him. "I just thought maybe we could work together the way we did that time when we staked out those bank robbers. I thought it might be nice."

"Nice? *Nice?!*" Derek yelled in a quiet voice. "We're not dealing with a couple transvestites here, Christine. We're dealing with some depraved fuckers at NEXUS. *NEXUS!* And they've already put two surgeons in the icebox."

"And hurt a lot of others along the way," Ojo added.

"Our mission," he said and turned to Ojo, "which we've chosen to subject ourselves to for God-only-knows what reason, is to put an end to this nightmarish research. One way or another, we've gotta expose these fuckers. And shut them down."

Christine didn't respond. All three remained silent for some time. They stood by the car as Derek took her camera and shoulder bag from the hood.

"Maybe there is a way you can help us," Ojo said.

"Careful, Ojo," Derek said. "This doesn't involve her. Christine can fly home in the morning."

She looked at Ojo with defenseless eyes.

"Okay," Ojo said with some reluctance in his voice. "I'll take her to the airport when you leave to meet Hawkins," he added, then looked at Christine and winked when Derek was turned the other way.

A wide smile was building inside of her. She knew Ojo had an idea. He wasn't planning to take her to the airport at all.

"Okay, you win," she told Derek. "Can we at least take a walk in the moonlight?"

"I think that can be arranged," he replied. "You mind?" he asked Ojo, handing him Christine's things.

"'Course, I mind," Ojo answered. "Go on, you two," he said and smiled. "Get outta here."

They walked arm in arm across the dirt road and between the trees on the other side. Ojo watched for a moment as they disappeared into the forest and grinned. He turned and walked into the room, closing the door behind him.

They passed among the trees in complete silence, taking in the sound of the dry leaves rustling beneath their feet, the shadow of an occasional squirrel scurrying after an acorn, the smell of the cool fresh air filling their welcoming lungs.

They walked for some time until they reached a clearing. In its center was Willow Pond.

Derek took Christine's hands in his and held them to his lips.

"I wasn't expecting you till midnight," he told her.

"Well, you lucked out," Christine replied with a cute wink. "I caught an earlier flight."

"A part of me wants to kill you."

"And the rest of you?" she coyly asked in a whispery voice.

Derek pulled her toward him. He gently touched his lips to hers as they stood embraced a few feet from the dark water of the pond. A featherlike breeze sent ripples through the water as the moonlight magically danced across its surface and engulfed them.

Christine stepped back for a second. She stared into Derek's adoring eyes in silence, running her fingers slowly through his thick black hair and along the sides of his neck, locking them behind it as she stood tip-toed, pulling him toward her.

He kissed her softly on the lips. His tongue met hers and they touched for a teasingly brief moment. Then he kissed her again. And again their tongues met for but a teasing instant. Barely long enough for him to taste her. Or her him. But long enough.

With all his senses Derek could feel the desire she had for him as he looked into her deep blue eyes. The moonlight reflected the pond within them and they sparkled. He felt not differently. Not in the least.

He wanted her. And he would have her. Here, beside the small pond and within this private enclave of theirs, he would have her. The trees and water—their only boundaries. The moon and stars—their only witnesses. Here, he would have her. And she, him. Here, they would have each other.

Derek kissed her again lightly as she closed her eyes and fell into his arms. Their tongues danced unseen. Christine cooed as his tongue coiled and uncoiled around hers. First they danced slowly. Softly. Then more rapidly. More passionately. Then more slowly. More softly.

Christine ran a long finger over the strong angle of Derek's chin as he held her. One of his hands gently cushioned the small of her back, the other pressed against her side. The back of several fingers softly outlined the swell of her breast as they slowly traced the lines of her blouse.

With her other hand, she freed the tucked edge of Derek's shirt. Her long nails admiringly moved up and down his strong back as he pulled her toward him. She could feel his warm tongue move from hers. It passed along the sculpted lines of her jaw and onto the delicate curves of her neck. Barely touching her at all. Barely. But touching her. Touching her so lightly that she quivered inside.

Her fingers desperately traced the edge of his pants, fumbling with the brass button. Derek's eyes met hers and they smiled. He greedily inhaled the delicate scent of her neck, kissing its length as she pulled the button open. The softest moan passed through Christine's lips as her fingers undid his zipper and slid beneath the cotton material that lay against his skin for a brief moment.

In the few seconds it took for his hands to play along the front of Christine's silk blouse, her buttons were undone. With a feathery touch, his hand passed over the white lace that she wore underneath. She cooed as he undid the latch on the front of her bra, its material falling to the side and exposing her full breasts as the moonlight fell upon them. A shadow soon obscured that light as Derek's tongue passed over them.

Christine excitedly undid the buttons of his shirt, one of them falling on the ground as they caught eyes and laughed softly. She pushed the shirt over his shoulders and it fell to the ground. Her eyes passed over his muscular chest and her lips followed.

Derek unzipped her skirt with a single stroke and it fell to her ankles, revealing the white garter belt that secured her lace stockings. She wore nothing else.

Christine stepped out of the skirt. She held her arms out and let her blouse and bra fall to the ground between her and Derek. He admired her beauty with loving and desiring eyes as she stood before him.

He took her soft hand in his, pressing it to his lips as he knelt before her. He kissed the inside of her thighs and she moaned ever so softly, squeezing his hand as his lips moved between them. He could taste her excitement in the sweet moisture he found there.

Christine stepped out of her heels. She gently pushed Derek onto his back, easing his pants down below his knees as he kicked off his shoes. Her lips slowly passed over the strong contours of his chest and the hard lines of his abdomen. They teasingly drifted onto the thin material that barely contained him. She playfully pulled the briefs with her teeth to his ankles where his pants lay bunched up. She smiled and freed his legs, tossing his clothes onto the small pile that hers had formed.

With soft kisses, her lips passed the length of his muscular legs and then settled between them. She held him with both hands, her tongue eagerly flickering to and fro. With every beat of his heart, she could feel his excitement.

Derek traced the smooth curve of her back as he pulled her on top of him. His hands moved onto her tight round behind as she arched her back and gazed into his eyes. After a long moment, they fell upon her breasts. He stared at them for some time, admiring their perfect proportion, the way they swelled and curved upward as she bent backward, and the way their firm nipples rose from their smooth surface. He gently kissed them, passing his tongue over each as Christine reached back and touched him. She moaned softly as his teeth pressed into her nipples.

Derek pulled her toward him and wrapped his arms around her back. He kissed her with excitement as his tongue moved in and out of her mouth. The next instant, they rolled over and Christine lay beneath him. They laughed playfully.

Their eyes locked and their lips met. Derek slowly moved back and forth over her and she moaned softly. His pace quickened as she gently moved her fingernails over his back. Their lips parted for a second as Christine reached down and led him inside her. She gasped as he moved within her.

Her hips moved up and down and her breathing quickened. Derek moaned softly in her ear as his tongue traced its edge and slowly moved up and down her neck. The faster he moved inside of her, the slower his tongue passed over her delicate neck. Christine held him tightly to her, digging her fingers hard into his back as his teeth closed over her neck. He pressed hard into her and in one lingering moment, she could feel the passion within his entire body release all at once. Her hips bucked and her back arched as her hands flew over her head and grabbed fistfuls of the damp grass. She let out a loud cry and then dropped back onto the ground. Derek collapsed on top of her.

They lay there silently for some time, smiling and kissing each other tenderly as they bathed in the moonlight. They watched the tiny ripples glide across the distance of the pond and casually studied the irregular shapes that reflected on the silvery surface of the water along its edges. Derek took particular interest in several of the unusual reflections as his eyes passed from the water to the surrounding foliage to Christine's beautiful face.

"See those blackberry bushes over there …" he began with a teasing smile.

CHAPTER TWENTY-ONE

The greatest inventions are those inquiries which
tend to increase the power of man over matter.

Benjamin Franklin

The annoying sound of a car horn pierced the wooden
door and rushed into the small motel room. Two beds
with badly worn mattresses, a dilapidated night stand
between them, a bureau that stretched the length of the
wall opposite the beds with one drawer that had been
nailed shut and another without a handle, and two vinyl-
upholstered chairs finished it. A sketch of some has-been
gunslinger hung crookedly above the bureau. On the far
side of the room, on the bed that required a number of
matchbook covers to even out its warped legs, lay

Christine. She stirred beneath the thin blanket while Derek sat on the corner of the bed. One of the aluminum attaché cases lay open on the blanket beside him.

Ojo sat across from him on the other bed. Together they reviewed its contents, carefully double-checking that everything was in its proper place and nothing was forgotten. It was crucial that absolutely nothing be forgotten on this important day. For on this day, their strategy would evolve. They would penetrate the black fortress. Derek would, anyway. And in broad daylight. And once penetrated, it would just be a short matter of time before the rest of their game plan unfolded. They hoped.

Derek glanced at his watch. It was 7:42 a.m.

He closed the case and touched a small thermosensitive panel on its side. Then he held the case up and turned it in several directions. Ojo watched the room spin on the small wireless screen in the palm of his hand. The wide-angle lens that lay hidden behind a pinhead-sized aperture beneath the thermosensitive panel was attached to an image-forwarding microcam transmitter within the case. Derek touched the panel again and the transmission ceased.

"I think you're all set," Ojo said as the horn sounded another time.

"I'd better run before the cab splits on me," Derek commented as Christine moved about.

His eyes fell upon her adorable face as it peaked out from beneath the covers. "Make sure you get her on that plane," he whispered and gently brushed away several strands of her long hair, then bent to kiss her on the cheek as she lay sleeping. He stood and watched her for another moment, then turned toward Ojo.

Ojo grabbed his hand and their eyes met. They stood there and exchanged a quiet smile. Neither spoke for a few seconds.

"I know," Derek finally said in a sincere voice and they embraced.

"Now get outta here," Ojo told him as the impatient sound of the cab's horn was heard another time.

Derek grabbed the attaché case and quickly walked across the room and out the door, quietly closing it behind him.

Ojo's attention returned to the black disc which sat on the bureau. He adjusted a dial on the credit card-sized digital analyzer to which it was now attached. The clicking sound and dragging noise he had become so familiar with were no longer audible. He had programmed the analyzer to filter them out along with a number of other annoying interference transmissions. Everything else was digitally recorded.

Christine moved about as the screech of the taxi awakened her. She sat up in bed, covering herself with the blanket, and looked at Ojo with scheming eyes.

"Is he gone?" she asked him.

Ojo turned around to face her as he sat on the bureau. "Sure is. He's on his way to meet Hawkins."

"Hawkins?"

"Derek didn't tell you about Hawkins when you were out in the woods last night?"

Christine shook her head.

"I was sure you guys were out there talking 'bout this stuff," Ojo said with a mischievous smile while Christine blushed. "Well, Hawkins is one of Flint's cronies."

"Flint's the surgeon whose lab we found the manuscript in, right?" Christine asked.

"Exactly. And Hawkins is our ticket into their show."

"How's that?"

"Well, actually it's Hawkins' daughter. We met her on the plane. She's our backstage pass," Ojo told her.

"So she's gonna introduce Derek to her father?"

"You got it."

"I like that."

"Well, I'm glad you approve," Ojo teased her.

"What if you hadn't met her on the plane?"

Ojo ran a finger over the stubble on his chin. "C'mon," he said with a confident smile, "we've always got a plan B."

"Which is …?"

"Why waste time thinking about it now if we're already groovin' with plan A?"

"Right," Christine said with a teasing grin.

"Now, about you, young lady," Ojo said and she started to pout, "you can cut the adorable act. I mentioned last night that I thought you could be of some help."

"Aaaand?"

"And I still think so. But if you think you're gonna pull a number like the one you pulled two years ago when you almost got yourself killed during that stakeout, *I'm* gonna kill you *first*. You got that?"

"Yes, sir," Christine replied with a salute.

"Christine, I'm serious," he said with a straight face. "Do you understand me?"

"Yeah."

"I'm taking a real big chance here. Derek's gonna have my ass if anything goes wrong. He's probably gonna have it either way."

"Nothing will go wrong," Christine assured him. "Nothing."

"Okay."

"So, what's your plan?"

"First we scratch your 9:00 a.m. flight. Derek's expecting me on the cliff by 9:30 so that—"

"What cliff?"

"This cliff about a quarter of a mile from the research facility. Anyway, while he's inside schmoozing with Hawkins, we're gonna be outside monitoring him. *And* the killer."

Christine stared at him with a blank look on her face. "The killer?"

Ojo eyed the black disc another time and grinned. "Yeah," he replied. "The killer."

* * *

"333 Hogshead Drive," the cab driver said in a hurried voice, cocking his head to the side and extending a dirty-looking bony hand over the seat.

And not a moment too soon. The smell of the driver was overwhelming. He was an extremely thin foreign fellow. Probably Iranian. His eyeballs seemed to drown in their sockets, while his cheekbones seemed to burst through the sheer layer of skin covering them. He was about thirty. It was hard to tell. He may have been older. He may have even been an Arab. They smelled about the same, Derek thought. And the ride back to Houston was more than he could stand.

"Forty-four even," the driver said with a thick accent.

Derek looked the impish man square in the eye. "Bullshit," he told him flatly. "That wasn't more than a fifteen-dollar ride," he added and slapped a twenty in the man's greedy palm. He took the attaché case from the seat and slammed the door as he stepped out of the cab.

"Scoombahg!" Derek heard the driver call to him as he raced off in a rage.

The gall of the cabbie to try to rip him off, he thought as he walked up the curved path that led to a modestly-sized red brick house. He glanced at his watch as he stepped under the large concrete awning that extended from the main entrance of the house over the walkway and across the driveway. It was 8:27 a.m.

Derek lifted the brass knocker and gently tapped it on the door a couple of times. While he waited, his eyes casually glided from the white 911 Targa that sat in the driveway to the large freshly-cut lawn in front of the house and the white hydrangeas that formed a chain along its perimeter, then back to the closed door. As he lifted the knocker another time the door opened.

In a yellow sundress that pressed tightly against her full breasts and a matching sun hat that could barely contain her dark curls stood Selena. She greeted Derek with a very welcoming smile.

"Well, hello there, Mr. Noo Yawka," she said and giggled.

Derek smiled. "Well, hello there to you, Miss Texas."

"All set to meet Daddy?"

"All set."

"Then let's get a movin', as we Texans say."

Selena pulled the door shut and led Derek to the car.

"Now, how d'you feel about the feminist movement?"

she asked him as she opened his door then walked around to the driver side.

"To tell you the truth, I've always been right behind women's movements," he answered with a devilish grin.

"You know, I kinda figured that about you."

Selena started the car and in an instant they were out of the driveway, beyond the curved path, and soaring along Route 41.

"Ever drive one of these?" she asked Derek.

He hesitated for a moment and smiled. "Oh, once or twice," he responded nonchalantly.

"Quite a thrill, isn't it?" she said as her fingers curled around the knob of the stick shift. She lifted her eyes from the road for a second to catch Derek's stare.

"It sure is," he told her as his eyes lifted from the stick shift.

Selena blushed. She scrolled her tuner to the Information Society channel and adjusted several levers on the equalizer as the sound of synthesized drums burst from eight speakers and filled the car. It was the richest sound Derek had heard since the last time he had been in his Carrera about a day ago, he thought and smiled.

She drove along the congested interstate highway without commenting for some time, weaving in and out of the morning's rush hour traffic. At 8:30 a.m. on Monday morning, Route 41 into Willow Valley was almost as congested and frustrating as the East River Drive into

Manhattan, Derek thought. Almost. But not quite. No, not quite.

"So, what happened—" Selena started to ask when a tractor-trailer pulled alongside and the loud noise of his horn interrupted her. She ignored the friendly trucker and sped through an opening between a couple of cars up ahead.

"You were saying?" Derek asked her.

"Yeah, what happened to your friend? Wasn't he joining us?"

"He was going to but he ran into a client of ours from West Point. Some four star General named Bradley. Know who he is?"

"Sounds familiar, but not really."

"He's the guy who first developed war game technology in the sixties."

"Really?"

"Sure is," Derek said. "General Bradley. That's the guy." He turned toward the window and his eyes followed the gentle slopes of the green mountains off in the distance as they approached Willow Valley. "General Milton Bradley," he mumbled under his breath.

"You say something?" Selena asked, turning to face him for a second.

"Oh, uh, no. Nothing. Just talking to myself. Don't mind me."

"I won't," she replied and laughed.

"You know something?" Derek asked.

"What's that?"

"Well, I recently learned something about myself. And it came as a real surprise," Derek told her.

"Oh, really?"

"Yeah. I noticed I'm really not much of a conversationalist when I'm alone. I've kinda suspected it for some time now but it wasn't until recently when I was forced to leave my car stereo in the shop for a few days that it really hit me."

Selena looked at him and then returned her gaze to the road.

"I think that's good," she said and laughed again. "But what do I know?"

Derek looked at her and smiled.

"Anyway, you were saying about this General?" she asked him.

"Oh, yeah. He was having some problems with the blueprints for a laser weaponry simulator we designed. Ojo's meeting with him this morning to iron all the wrinkles out."

"Hope it goes alright."

"It will. So tell me about your father," Derek asked. "All you've told me is that he sets up laser tracking systems."

"That's pretty much all I know," she told him as she cut across two lanes and glided along the curved exit marked Banner Creek. "Daddy doesn't ask me very much about fashion design and I don't ask him very much about lasers."

"Sounds fair to me."

"It works for us. We respect what the other does but don't really have too much interest in the details. Sometimes I think Daddy wishes I had been a boy."

"Maybe. I guess it's easier for a man to accept a son who's into designing clothes than a daughter," Derek teased her.

"Noooo," she said and slapped his shoulder playfully. "You know what I mean."

Derek laughed. "I know."

The car slowed down as it moved over an unpaved road that ran alongside a narrow stream of water. *Banner Creek.* The clear fresh water glistened as it raced over the shallow bed of the creek, smacking into the algae-covered rocks that jutted through its surface and gliding over the innumerable pebbles, branches and trout that lay beneath. The narrow road soon curved away from the creek and merged with a larger road that ran between two dense forests. One on each side. Selena followed the road for about a mile. Then it ended. Derek anxiously chewed on his lip as the road gave way to a vast clearing. Within its carefully guarded center sat the octagonal structure.

"Besides, you can ask Daddy yourself."

* * *

"… so I think everyone would be better off if you both just hung up your Dick Tracy caps and left the detective work to the pros until the investigation is over. But call me at the station as soon as you can."

The line disconnected and a dial tone was heard.

"Hmm," Ojo mumbled with a pensive look on his face as he turned toward Christine and scratched the back of his head. "Repeat," he said and a red bar flashed on the side of the round phone.

"Fellas, this is Sergeant Brotsky. I never did see those papers we found in Flint's lab yesterday morning. And now they're gone. Someone else took 'em. Probably Flint. I don't know what they're about but I have a good feelin' they've got something to do with the homicides. And I wanna know what it is. I wanna know what you guys found. You owe me. I got reamed by one of the other surgeons for letting you into that lab to play detective. A guy named Haywood. The Commissioner got wind and my ass is in a sling so I think everyone would be better off—"

"Trash it," Ojo said and the red bar stopped flashing. "Brotsky really pisses me off," he said to Christine as he sped along the winding country road on their way to the cliff. "First off, Dick Tracy doesn't wear a cap. Sherlock Holmes does. And secondly," he continued, "on the one hand Brotsky tells us to stay out of his way, on the other he wants to know what we've found." Ojo sighed loudly and shook his head. "What an asshole!"

Christine laughed.

"Dial 'Arti'," Ojo said.

A small yellow light flashed and the line rang. And rang. And rang.

"Contraptions," a squeaky voice finally responded.

"Arti, what the hell are you doing?"

"Greasing my rod."

Christine's eyes flew open in surprise. "What did he say?" she asked and started laughing.

Ojo smiled. "You know those steel rods inside his glass dome?"

"Uh, huh."

"Every now and then when he's in a cleaning mood he removes the dome and greases them."

"Oh."

Neither said anything for a moment. Then they both laughed loudly.

"Is that you, Christine?" Arti asked.

"It sure is, big guy," she replied.

"Anything going on over there?" Ojo asked him. "Anything unusual?"

"Nothing goin' on but the rent," Arti said then made a loud squeaking noise. A laugh of some sort.

"Arti, I'm talking to you!"

"Okay, okay. No. Nothing is going on. Nothing unusual," Arti responded.

"No problems?"

"No problems."

"Damn!" a frustrated impatient voice suddenly yelled. It came from the black disc on the dashboard. "Where the hell have you been?!" the voice demanded.

"What's going on there?" Arti asked.

"Unloading in Sector 7," answered a faceless voice.

"Quiet," Ojo said.

"When you're told to meet me at the Beta-1 Station, you meet me at the Beta-1 Station! Do you understand me?!"

"Ojo, are you there? Christine?"

"Shut up for a minute," Ojo told Arti.

"Yes, I understand you."

"You've kept me waiting fifteen minutes. I won't tolerate this again, Cecil," the man said in a stern tone.

"*Cecil?*" Arti asked. He could hear the transmission coming from the installation. "Who's *Cecil?*"

"*Arti!*" Ojo responded, trying to quiet him down.

"It won't happen again, sir. Now what is it you need?" Cecil asked.

"You can't talk to me like that! I've been slaving over a hot Thermalyzer. And for what?" Arti asked.

"Domino and Sara are to be transported to the Space-2 Heliport immediately," the voice instructed. "They'll be flown to the shuttle tonight."

"You still there, Arti?" Ojo asked.

"And what of it?"

"We're listening in on a bug we planted on the killer's shoe," Ojo told him.

"So. Who cares?" Arti responded sarcastically.

"What about the Thermalyzer?" Ojo asked.

"Did I say *Thermalyzer?*" Arti responded.

"Arti!"

"What?!"

"What about the Thermalyzer?"

"The *what?*"

"The Thermalyzer, Arti. The *Thermalyzer* for Chrissake! What about it?"

The sound of fading footsteps was heard. It was replaced by a high-pitched screeching noise.

"One of these days—" the deep voice quietly mumbled and a loud banging noise was suddenly heard. "Aw, fuck!"

It was immediately followed by the sorrowful cry of a monkey.

"Okay. I was working on—" Arti started.

"One sec, Arti."

"One of these days, I'm gonna kill that son-of-a-bitch!" the voice finished.

The screeching noise was heard again. Ojo envisioned the ugly killer struggling with the cage, dragging it from where it sat and moving it onto some carrier.

"So, there I am, working on the Thermalyzer—" Arti started.

"You were fixing it?" Ojo asked.

"No. Gathering up all the pieces."

"Oh."

"Anyway, so there I am, with the camera and thermal sensor in one hook and the viewer lens in the other. And suddenly it occurred to me. From outta nowhere, this great idea popped into my dome."

Nothing was said for a moment.

"Aaaand?" Christine asked.

"And what?" Arti replied.

"The idea, Arti. The *idea*," Ojo pushed him.

"Oh, yeah. So there I am. Wait, I mentioned that. The idea. Okay, okay. The idea. The Thermalyzer no longer exists. Not as it did before, anyway. You now have a viewer and an infrared camera."

"So? How does that help us?" Ojo asked impatiently.

"So, don't you see the point? When was the last time you greased *your* rod?"

Christine laughed loudly as Ojo lost his patience.

"Arti!" Ojo demanded.

"Okay, okay. Suppose you could modify the camera to *transmit* the thermal radiation it detects to a receiver somewhere else?"

"The viewer connectors are history," Ojo said.

"I mean without the viewer," Arti responded.

"Then the camera would only pick up the thermal radiation within a twenty-one-foot radius," Ojo said.

"Exactly. But the radius would be twenty-one feet, two and seven-eighths inches to be exact," Arti corrected him. He loved correcting Ojo.

Ojo looked at Christine with a raised brow and grinned.

"Now pipe the data into one of our Jennon LZ3 chip analyzers, convert it to transmitter frequency and send it to one of the microreceivers. And you've got—" Arti started to explain.

"A goddamn video bug!" Ojo said and started laughing.

"Exactly," Arti agreed.

"I love you, Arti," Ojo told him.

"What's not to love?"

"Well, what're you waitin' for? Get workin' on it," Ojo said.

"I'm glad you feel that way," Arti responded.

"Why's that?"

"'Cause I already have. It's done."

"Beautiful. Then send it to me. We're at the—" Ojo started.

"Valley Inn in Willow Valley. I know. FedEx already picked it up. You'll have it in the morning."

"Outstanding, Arti."

A proud squeak was heard.

"I just have one question," Christine said with a confused look on her face.

"What's that?" Ojo asked her.

"What the hell are you guys talking about?"

"A video bug. Like a hidden camera. Except we get pictures of today. *And* pictures of yesterday," Ojo explained as the palm-sized screen which rested against the stick shift lit up with color. A crystal clear picture of Selena's behind filled the small screen. The attaché case probably sat flat on Derek's lap with the microaperture facing her, Ojo thought.

Christine just watched with an entertained grin.

"Did you just get there?" Ojo asked.

A microchip in the body of the screen served as an audio transmitter and receiver. Derek wore a paired microtransceiver in his ear.

A moment later Selena's behind moved up and down on the screen as Derek shifted the case on his lap in response.

"Show time."

CHAPTER TWENTY-TWO

I'm interested in things that change the world or
that affect the future and wondrous new technology
where you see it, and you're like, 'Wow, how did
that even happen? How is that possible?'

Elon Musk

A complex and massive system of deck levels lay before
the floatron tunnels. A number of men, several in white
coats, others in military uniforms, stood at various points
on each of the thirteen levels of this system. Each deck
was constructed from interdigitated sheets of
lucitavoxium, a recently-engineered combination of
organic materials used in space shuttle design, and was
completely transparent. Twenty-two-foot cylindrical

lucitavoxium columns, one on top of the other, supported each deck.

As any of the levels could be seen from any other, so could the numerous floatrons which arrived and departed every few minutes within their transparent chutes. Upon arrival, the clear doors of the chamber would slide open a moment before those of the floatron did the same. Pressure within the chute would equalize with that of the deck during this brief time. Prior to floatron departure, a process of hyperpressurization to a level of three atmospheres would occur and the vehicle would take off on a frictionless cushion of air. The chutes guided the floatrons through hundreds of interconnected transparent tunnels, leading them to any facility, station, level or sector within this subterranean world which NEXUS had created.

A distinguished-looking middle-aged gentleman in a navy blue uniform, with two stars adorning each shoulder and a block of honorary pins decorating the breast pocket of his jacket, stood before the floatron chute on the seventh deck level, holding a silver cane as a floatron arrived and the chute's doors slid open.

After a moment's pause the platinum doors of the floatron parted. A tall thin man in a similar uniform, but with silver oak leaves on each shoulder and not quite as many pins decorating his jacket, stood at the vehicle's entrance.

"Good morning, General Parson," he greeted his superior officer as he stepped off the floatron onto the deck.

In a cold raspy voice the man with the cane responded as he boarded the vehicle. "Lieutenant."

The other man briskly walked across the wide deck, holding a large black envelope against his side, then stepped onto a hoverway which, in a matter of seconds, transported him from the floatron tunnels to the TSI Terminal Center.

He stood before the Center's entryway until a string of blue lights flashed within its chrome trim, then stepped into the large room, quickly passing between the numerous rows of terminals where several women in blue uniforms and a man in a white coat sat working, nodding at one of the women and removing his cap as he walked straight toward the control room at the rear of the Center.

The glass door swung open as an attractive young woman emerged from the room.

"Hello, Dayna," he said with a reserved smile as the small wrinkles at the corners of his eyes deepened.

"Morning, Benjamin," she replied with a pretty smile and walked past him.

"Rough night?" he called to her.

Dayna shook her head as she walked to the other side of the Center.

The officer stepped into the room. Two men sat behind the long control panel, one monitoring the life support systems within Sector 13, the other monitoring all computerized communications within the entire Facility.

"Monroe, Landers," he greeted them.

"Mornin', Hawkins," one of the men responded while the other adjusted several controls on the panel.

Hawkins took a seat in front of the terminal on the side of the room opposite the control panel. He struck several pads on the keyboard and the screen lit up with red and blue bars. He typed 'LASERgames' and the screen turned bright yellow. A number of Greek symbols appeared. They were interposed between several derivative and integration equations and a number of expressions defining the concentration of photon energy required to generate sufficient electromagnetic radiation within the microwave spectrum to produce a laser with the equivalent destructive capacity of twenty-two hydrogen bombs.

Hawkins looked away from the screen for a moment and scratched the rim of his ear a couple of times. He turned back toward the screen and carefully examined the equations as a chirping tone sounded from the pager clipped to his belt. His eyes remained fixed on the screen. He rested his chin on one hand as the other reached down and touched a button on the small black box. The chirping ceased.

With a rush of enthusiasm, he quickly punched a number of keypads and revised one of the equations. A pleased grin rounded the corners of his mouth as his pager went off again.

He pressed the button a second time and eyed the digital readout. 'SEC*GATE' flashed on the tiny screen.

"What is it?" he spoke into an intercom beside the terminal.

"Lieutenant Hawkins?" a dry whining voice asked.

"Yes, what is it?"

"Your daughter has arrived, sir."

"Very good, Harris. Send her through to the Atrium. I'll be there shortly."

"Will do, sir," the officer replied and smiled at Selena. "My apologies for keeping you waiting, ma'am," he politely told her and pressed a control switch on the wall of the stone booth in which he stood.

The large entrance gate rotated until it was perpendicular to the fencing on either side, then slowly descended into the ground.

"You can drive on through," the officer said. "Your father will meet you in the Atrium."

"Thanks much," Selena said and flashed a smile.

She drove along the only road that cut a path through the hot desert ground, approaching the black fortress as the formidable gate rose from the ground and swung into its protective position.

"So, uhh … come here often?" Derek asked her.

Selena giggled. "Actually, this is only the third or fourth time I've been here," she responded. "And I've gotten lost every time. The place gives a whole new meaning to the word '*maze*.'"

"Is that the only way in?" Derek asked, pointing over his shoulder.

"That and *that*," she answered, aiming a finger first at the entrance gate and then at a Percy helicopter that hovered above the roof of the structure.

"Looks pretty tight."

"Tighter than Fort Knox," Selena told him as she drove past a fork in the road and up to the building's main entrance.

Two smaller roads branched from the main one and led to a steel grating on each of the sides of the building adjacent to the entrance. A massive plate of black glass lifted straight up as Selena drove beneath it and into the building.

Arrows directed her along the perimeter of the octagonal structure and onto an elevator chute. A sheet of clear glass slid across the elevator's entryway.

"Destination?" a loud metallic voice asked.

"Atrium, please," Selena replied and the elevator quickly ascended eighty or ninety feet.

They watched as the elevator lifted them high above the ground and into direct view of a structure Derek had only seen pictures of.

"Unfuckinbelievable!" he said with childlike excitement.

Selena smiled. "What did you expect, Derek?" she asked as his eyes feasted upon an actual space. "This is NEXUS," she nonchalantly added.

Only the top half of the shuttle could be seen. The lower half extended below the ground level of the building into the bowels of the stone structure. Just below the cockpit and beside the emblem of the American flag was written one word. In large red letters. Just one word. ***CHALLENGER***.

Derek stared at that for a moment. Then a confused look shifted his eyebrows. "That doesn't make sense."

"Sure it does," Selena started to explain. "After the Challenger explosion, an identical shuttle was built by NEXUS as a memorial. And inspiration. And there it is," she said, pointing at the huge spacecraft as the elevator came to a smooth halt. "Don't even think NASA has one," she added with a proud grin.

"Atrium," the metallic voice squeaked. "You may leave your vehicle. It will be stored in the Parking Facility," the voice added as the entryway opened. "Request QR4466 when you wish to have it retrieved."

Selena took the parking ticket that emerged from a slot below the buttons as she and Derek stepped off the elevator and into the spacious Atrium. They stood on the wide landing beside the elevator for a moment, Derek's aluminum attaché case in hand, his eyes dancing around the octagonal Atrium.

Along its perimeter were sparsely placed the oddest assortment of chairs and tables, each piece sculpted from the most unusual stones and in the most unusual shapes imaginable. Were it not for the many people who occupied a good number of the seats and the countless books, papers and briefcases that lay across as many tables, their functions would leave much to speculation, as would the intent that they actually be used.

A number of large platforms, some of stone, others of metal, hung suspended at varying levels from the roof thirty feet above. They brilliantly reflected the morning sun's rays, which penetrated the roof's transparent central section and fell upon the nose of the Challenger.

The shuttle rose straight through the central portion of the installation and into the Atrium, falling about ten feet short of touching the glass ceiling. It was something to see, Derek thought as he stared at the large red, white and blue flag on its side and a rush of patriotic sentiment went through him. Something really spectacular. Something that made him proud that he was American. Something that made him prouder at that very moment than he had ever before been.

With a distant look in his eyes, he bent his neck back, glancing past the shuttle and through the roof of the Atrium. Beyond that section of the roof, which was transparent, Derek watched as a black helicopter with a NEXUS emblem on its tail wing fell from the sky and hovered about twenty feet above the roof's center for some time before gliding out of view. He suddenly remembered his reason for being there.

"Over there," Selena said and grabbed Derek's arm.

"Huh?"

"Daddy's over there," she repeated, pointing toward a small group of men who stood holding coffee mugs on the other side of the Atrium.

They walked along the landing, eyeing the splendor of the shuttle as they moved around it, until they came to a pretzel-shaped onyx table where three men stood speaking. One of the men wore a blue uniform and the others long white coats.

Selena walked up to the uniformed man and kissed him on the cheek. "Good morning, Daddy," she said with a glowing smile.

"Morning, angel," he replied with a sparkle in his eye.

The other men greeted her with warm smiles.

"I'd like you all to meet Mr. Cannon. Derek Cannon," she told them. "Derek, this is my father, Lieutenant Hawkins," she said and teasingly deepened her voice.

"It's a pleasure," Derek told the man as they shook hands.

"This is Dr. Erikson," Selena said, pointing to a short stocky man wearing bifocal eyeglasses, "and this is Dr. Taka … Dr. Taka …?"

"Taka*gawa*," the small Japanese woman helped her and laughed.

"Right, Dr. Takagawa," Selena said and blushed.

Derek exchanged handshakes with each of them.

"Welcome to the world of NEXUS," Dr. Erikson offered.

"I'm honored to be here," Derek responded.

"I understand you have some real interest in lasers," Hawkins remarked.

"That's right."

"Don't get carried away now," Ojo's voice flowed from the microtransceiver in Derek's ear. "Just keep it light."

"I've done some space navigational simulation programming over the last few years," Derek said.

"Great," Ojo sarcastically said, "that's keepin' it real light."

"You mean war games?" Hawkins asked him.

"Absolutely. War games," Derek replied.

"Better," Ojo whispered.

Hawkins smiled. "If you'll excuse me gentlemen," he told the others, "I'd like to take this young fellow on a quick tour. I think I've got one or two things that might interest him."

Derek and Selena followed the lanky officer as he walked toward a ramp several feet behind the onyx table.

"Sector 3 at 1800 hours, right?" he called back to the group.

"That's right," Dr. Erikson replied.

"Good," Hawkins commented as he led Derek and Selena out of the Atrium and onto a hoverway just beyond the ramp.

"Please identify," a computerized voice spoke.

Derek watched closely as the officer placed his palm on the glowing blue sensor pad. The pad beeped several times and the hoverway slowly began to move.

"Destination?" the voice asked.

When Hawkins turned his back Derek quickly pulled the metal rod from his shirt pocket and pressed the button on its end. With a single smooth stroke he let the rod glide over the surface of the sensor pad just before it was out of reach.

"Floatron tunnels," Hawkins answered as the handles rose. "I'd hold on if I were you," he told Derek.

Derek held the handle tightly with one hand and the attaché case with the other as the hoverway soared through a number of twisting corridors and along several wide landings. He watched as a section of the hoverway just ahead snapped off and shot through a tunnel before the section on which they stood came to a sudden, crisp stop.

"C'mon," Hawkins said as he briskly stepped from the hoverway and quickly walked toward the waiting floatron.

Derek and Selena followed right behind him.

"So what do you think so far, Eric?"

"Derek. Not too shabby."

Hawkins laughed as he and Selena boarded the floatron. Derek stepped back for a moment to observe the unique vehicle. It looked like the twenty-second century's version of the hovercraft, he thought as he tipped the attaché at an angle.

"Good boy," he heard Ojo's voice in his ear.

"C'mon, son," Hawkins called to him.

Derek stepped onto the floatron and seated himself beside Selena. In his mind, and as discretely as possible with his microcam, he meticulously recorded every detail of the trip. And every move Hawkins made.

"*Higher*," Ojo directed.

Derek tipped the attaché on his lap so it faced the transparent compartment at the helm of the floatron where Hawkins inserted his hand before taking a seat. He made a careful note of the officer's exchange with the computerized voice.

"Destination?"

"TSI Facility, Sector 9."

The floatron filled with a purplish mist as it made a humming sound and shot into the tunnel system. If ever Derek felt like a kid in a candy store, it was now. He marveled as the floatron effortlessly soared through the installation. It rapidly descended several levels as Derek caught a brief view of the lower portion of the Challenger before the floatron passed beneath it and into the heart of the transparent maze.

"So this is NEXUS' answer to the Lamborghini Countach, huh?" Derek asked as he held his hand out.

Selena smiled. "Certainly looks like it."

Within several minutes, the floatron emerged on the other side of the installation and came to a dramatic halt within a pressurized chute.

"TSI Facility," the computerized voice announced. "Transporting to Sector 9."

The floatron was lifted fifty or sixty feet before it glided into another tunnel. After a few moments, it came to another stop. The purplish mist cleared and the doors slid open.

"Sector 9. Atmosphere controlled."

Derek hung several steps behind the Lieutenant and his daughter as they exited the vehicle. He opened his palm where there sat a red quarter-sized disc with a yellow dot in its center. He covered the dot with a finger and placed it in the transparent compartment where Hawkins had inserted his hand. The disc beeped and Derek promptly removed it from the compartment. The dot was now white and the rest of the disc blue. He smiled and tossed it back in his pocket.

"Derek?" Selena called to him.

"Yeah," he replied as he caught up to her. "Just tyin' my shoe."

"Well, let's get a movin'," she told him as her eyes fell upon his feet.

He was wearing black monk strap shoes. No laces. Their eyes met in silence.

They stepped onto another hoverway that took them within a few feet of the entryway to Sector 9.

"See them?" Derek whispered in Selena's ear, motioning with his chin toward the man and woman who remained on the hoverway as it departed. The man was about thirty-five, the woman a few years younger. Each wore a blue uniform and carried an attaché case in one hand and a large manilla envelope in the other.

"Uh, huh," she answered.

"G-man and G-woman," Derek said. "Bet they have a dog 'G-spot'."

Selena turned toward him and laughed. "You are definitely weird."

Derek laughed quietly. He watched as Hawkins held his hand up and a burst of bright blue light shot from a small orifice above the triangular entryway, striking his hand before it faded.

"Entry permitted," a computerized voice with a distinctly effeminate tone announced.

"Your design," Derek questioned the Lieutenant.

"Who else's?" he modestly replied.

Selena was proud of her father. As proud as any girl

could possibly be of her father. You could see it in her eyes, Derek thought. He wondered about something as they passed through the entryway and around the triangular slab of granite that stood several feet behind it. He wondered if she would still be proud of him when it was all over. Maybe. Maybe not. If it could ever be all over. Maybe. Maybe not. And would he be the one to take that away from her? Maybe. Maybe not ... maybe.

"*This*, young man, is the Hawkins LASERgame Simulator," the Lieutenant proudly told Derek with a hand extended toward the series of control panels and monitors which sat on a long white bench. "Only one of its kind in the world."

"What can it do?" Derek asked him.

"The question is, 'what *can't* it do?'" Hawkins told him and dimmed the room's lights. "Have a seat and I'll show you."

Derek placed the attaché case on the bench opposite the one on which the Lieutenant's Simulator apparatus lay, then took a seat beside him.

Hawkins adjusted several of the panel's numerous controls and then activated each of the monitors. There were three of them. Each screen was completely covered with a different color. One blue. Another red. And the third yellow. He struck several pads on the keyboard in front of the monitor on the right side. The color on each screen quickly changed. Yellow triangles appeared on the blue screen, blue diamonds on the red screen, and red squares on the yellow screen. Then it got interesting.

All of a sudden the small shapes on each screen began to rotate and immediately they were no longer two-dimensional. Every triangle, every diamond and every square was now a three-dimensional form with depth and shadow. And without limitation of mobility. Hawkins pressed several buttons on one of the panels and the forms jumped from each screen to each of the others. Then back again. It was as if all three screens were part of one larger screen. But they weren't. Each was separate and this was no illusion.

"I must say," Derek began, "that's quite an effect without using holographic techniques."

"Don't need to," Hawkins told him. "Only the principles of the laser come into play here."

"I can think of a hundred applications of graphics like these," Derek said. "But *war games?*"

"Not just war games," Hawkins corrected him. "*Laser* war games. Watch," he said and typed the word 'LASERgames' on the center screen then leaned back in his seat and rested the keyboard on his lap.

The colorful shapes quickly dispersed from that screen and appeared on the others. They were replaced by an aerial map of a fictitious country, as Hawkins explained. A number of targeted cities each displayed a red star. He struck the keyboard several times and the forms that danced wildly on the right screen vanished and reappeared on the left screen. An aerial map of the United States replaced those forms. Blue stars highlighted those cities in which laser warheads had been deployed.

Hawkins pressed a switch on one of the control panels and the colorful shapes on the left screen became organized in rows and columns. Each yellow triangle represented a laser warhead with the destructive capacity of six hydrogen bombs, each blue diamond a warhead with the capacity of fourteen hydrogen bombs, and each red square a warhead with the capacity of twenty-two hydrogen bombs. Suddenly the shapes took meaning in Derek's mind. They were no longer pretty. No longer colorful. They represented death and destruction.

With a light-sensitive pen Hawkins touched one of the yellow triangles. Then he touched one of the fictitious cities and one of the American cities. In an instant, a small yellow triangle soared from the blue star of the American city. It flew from the left monitor and appeared on the center screen. A moment later, it struck the red star which represented the targeted city. In another instant, the red star and the city were both gone. That brief instant represented the actual estimated time required for the laser warhead to annihilate that city.

A table appeared on that screen. In its numerous columns were listed the quantity of photon energy distributed at ground zero and for every mile beyond that. It also listed all anticipated collateral damage, including the population that had been assigned to that city and the expected numbers of dead and wounded at ground zero and at each of the levels beyond it. A number of additional equations and statistics were listed below the table.

Hawkins proceeded to explain the significance of each when his pager sounded. He pulled it from the clip on his belt and eyed the flashing display. 'TERM*CTR'.

"Would you excuse me for a second?" he asked Derek as he placed his pager beside the terminal and walked to the phone a few feet away.

"Absolutely."

Derek studied the complex equations for a moment. Then his eyes fell upon the pager.

"Hawkins," the Lieutenant spoke into the phone.

"Something's wrong," Ojo's voice echoed in Derek's ear. "Get out of there," he told him. "All hell's about to break loose!" he yelled as quietly as he could.

"What kind of problem?" Hawkins asked as his brow became tense. "*Again?*"

Derek picked the pager up and turned it over.

"Well, you *find* the source," Hawkins said as the level of his voice began to rise.

Selena watched as Derek stared at the frequency number that had been etched on the side of the pager. Derek turned and caught her eye as he returned it to the table.

"Get out of there, Derek. Get out of there now!"

"Do you understand me?! You find the damn source! I'm on my way!" Hawkins yelled and slammed the phone down.

"Daddy, what is it?"

"I'm gonna have to cut this short. You'll excuse me

Eric," Hawkins mumbled as he briskly escorted Derek and Selena out of the lab. Then he turned toward his daughter. "See to it that your friend leaves the Facility," he told her, handing her a clear plastic card with several small rectangular holes in its center as he quickly stepped onto the hoverway.

He placed his hand on the sensor pad and the hoverway sped off.

"*Now*, Derek! Get your ass out of there *now*!" Ojo yelled in his ear. But there was no turning back now. Not for Derek.

CHAPTER TWENTY-THREE

F. Scott Fitzgerald

"... some son-of-a-bitch is transmitting from *within* the TSI Facility!" a husky voice yelled.

Derek and Selena stepped onto the hoverway.

"Oh, one sec," she said. "I think Daddy may've left his pager in the lab. I'd better check."

Selena walked back toward the entryway to Sector 9. She inserted the plastic card into a slot on the side of the triangular entrance. When the laser field deactivated itself, she stepped into the room.

Derek secured the attaché case under his arm. He quickly took the small metal rod from his pocket and pressed the button on its end.

"Please identify," the computerized voice spoke.

When the dull light flowed through the string of tiny holes on the surface of the rod, he passed it over the blue sensor pad with a slow steady stroke and the hoverway began to move.

"*This* is how we *do* it," Derek sang in a whispery voice.

"Well played," Ojo told him. "Now get your ass out of there!"

"Non-NEXUS frequency?" a deep vaguely familiar voice questioned.

"Of course, *non*-NEXUS frequency!" another voice responded. "That's the point, Cecil! Someone has penetrated the goddamn Facility!"

Ojo and Christine listened closely to the voices that flowed from the receiver which sat behind the stick shift on the console. They could hear the cold callous sound of the killer's voice. *Cecil,* he was called. And the angry voices of those with whom he spoke. They could also hear all that Derek said and all that was said to him.

"Destination?" the computerized voice asked Derek as he grabbed onto a handle.

"Sector 13," he responded.

"And you're gonna find him!" the first voice stammered. "Start with Sector 4."

The hoverway sped off through the corridors as Derek pressed the rod to his lips and then returned it to his pocket.

"Did you just hear that?" Ojo asked Derek.

"'Course, I heard it," he replied.

"Then where the fuck are you goin'?!"

"Sector 13."

Christine was terribly worried. She nervously chewed on her lip while Ojo made several adjustments on the receiver.

"Are you cra—" she started.

Ojo quickly held a finger up to quiet her as he desensitized the voice-activated transmitter to the frequency of her voice. It was essential that Christine's voice not be heard by Derek. Not now, anyway. Definitely, not now.

"Forget about Sector 13, Derek! Don't be a hero. Just get the fuck outta there! Do you hear me?!"

There was no response.

"Damn!" Ojo yelled. "I'm gonna kill him!"

Derek grinned as the small section of the hoverway on which he was standing snapped off and soared into a narrow corridor. "Trust me," he said quietly.

The corridor spiraled as it rose past the fifth level. It gained velocity and continued on its incline as he held the handle tightly. Past the sixth level. The seventh. The eighth.

"What the hell is going on?!" Derek heard Hawkins' loud angry voice through the microtransceiver. The bug on Cecil's shoe worked like a charm.

"We have an intruder in the Facility," the husky-voiced man told him.

"I know that, Landers, for God's sake!" Hawkins yelled. "But how? *How?!*"

"We don't know," the other man answered.

Past the ninth level. The tenth. The eleventh.

Selena entered the Terminal Center. She hastily walked past the rows of terminals and into the backroom where her father stood.

Hawkins turned as she walked into the room. "What is it?" he asked her.

"Your pager," Selena said. "You left it in your lab. I thought you might need it," she told him.

"Unfuckinbelievable," Ojo said as Selena's conversation with her father loudly blared into the car. "You tagged his pager, didn't you?"

"Who *me?*" Derek said sarcastically. "Would I do that?"

Hawkins took the pager from his daughter's hand. "You'd best be on your way now," he told her with a trace of an appreciative smile.

"Say," Hawkins called to her, "what happened to your friend?"

"One minute he was waiting on the hoverway while I ran back to get your pager…"

"*And?*" he asked her in a stern voice.

"And the next, he was gone."

"*Gone?*"

"Yeah. Someone must've instructed the hoverway before he had a chance to get off. That's happened to me before."

"Well, you find your friend. And get him off the premises. This isn't a good time for him to be running around the Facility."

"Don't worry, Daddy. He's probably waiting for me in the Atrium right now. I'll check there," she said and walked out of the room.

"Monroe, have you localized the transmission?" Hawkins asked the other man.

"It's coming from somewhere in the TSI Facility," Monroe replied.

"Somewhere in the TSI Facility? *Somewhere in the TSI Facility?!* Jesus *Christ,* you're gonna have to do better than that!" Hawkins told him.

"Cecil's already in Sector 4," Landers said.

Past the twelfth level. And onto the thirteenth.

"You mean *imbecile*, don't you?" Hawkins asked him.

"Sector 6," Monroe cut in. "He's moved onto Sector 6," he said, eyeing a computerized schematic of the Facility on the screen before him.

"Forget Sector 6," Hawkins told Monroe. "Send him to Sector 9."

"What's so special about Sector 9?" Monroe asked.

"Just do it!" Hawkins yelled. "My daughter's little friend may just be behind this."

"Okay, okay," Monroe replied, hitting several keys on the panel.

The hoverway flew from the spiraling corridor and raced through a number of winding passages before coming to a halt several feet from the entryway to Sector 13.

Cecil moved through Sector 6 as quickly as he could, limping and dragging, when his pager sounded. He pulled it from his belt and eyed the display. 'GoTo*SECTR*9'.

Derek jumped from the hoverway and ran behind a curved section of wall adjacent to Sector 13 as he heard the footsteps of several men approaching.

"Derek, where are you?" he heard Ojo's voice in his ear.

He didn't respond. He couldn't. Holding his breath, he stood behind that wall. And did not move. With his back flat to the wall and his attaché case clutched to his chest, he stood there. Silently.

Suddenly, the sound of footsteps stopped. Only the beating sound of his heart throbbed in his head. All at once its quickening pace became deafening. He tried to listen. He tried hard to listen as the footsteps came to a dead stop not more than three feet from where he stood. Just three feet away on the other side of the wall.

"Can you hear me? Are you alright?!" Ojo called to him.

Derek put a hand over his ear. He shut his eyes tightly for an instant and prayed Ojo would shut the fuck up. Then he heard a quick rustling sound. A moment later, he heard the sound a second time. A match. He was sure that's what it was. A match.

A moment after that he heard the footsteps again. From behind the wall Derek watched as two men in blue uniforms, each with occupied gun holsters resting on their hips, came into view. He watched as one puffed on a cigar while the other pulled the pistol from its holster and spun its cylinder a number of times. He watched as the two men walked past him and were soon out of view. He could hear their footsteps as they faded in the distance.

"Yes," Derek sighed with some relief. "I can hear you. I'm right outside Sector 13 and I'm not leaving till I see what's in there."

"Fine," Ojo said with a tone of concession. "I'm not gonna talk you out of this, am I?"

"Could *I* talk *you* out of it?" Derek asked him as he carefully opened the attaché case and removed a black and turquoise disc. It was the Delta Ray Viewer.

"I guess not," Ojo replied. "But you just watch yourself and listen to what I say."

Derek held the disc up and pressed a button on its side. A conical beam of blue light shot from a thin slot and collided with the wall. But nothing happened. He pressed another button on the disc's small control panel. The beam spun faster. And faster.

"Cecil's leaving Sector 11," Landers told Hawkins.

"You hear that?" Ojo asked. "Our friendly neighborhood killer's on your tail, Derek. But I don't want to worry you. Just get your ass out of there! Do you hear me?!"

Derek didn't answer. He watched the blue light cut through the wall and into Sector 13. The stream of blue light raced through a long corridor before colliding with another wall. A wall adjacent to the operating facility. After another moment, the laser penetrated the second wall and Derek could see into the very room where Erikson had implanted a human embryo into a monkey the night before.

At this moment, another patient lay upon the operating table. Derek's eyes darted around the large room in which a number of men stood in scrubs, several around the table, others beside a vast array of equipment.

His eyes then fell upon the patient's hand which peaked out from beneath a green sheet where it was loosely secured to an arm board. The skin was dark in color but there was no fur. Its fingers were long and thin but there were no claws. Just painted fingernails. It was the hand of a woman.

Derek returned the Viewer to a small compartment in the attaché and then closed the case. He took two quarter-sized discs from the pocket of his jacket. One silver. The other blue with a white dot in its center.

Carefully he listened for any sign of someone approaching. There was none. Derek stepped out from behind the wall and sauntered past the entryway to Sector 13. He stepped onto the hoverway as he held his hand high in the air. The blue and white disc nestled his palm.

"He's moving to Sector 13," Landers' voice echoed.

"*Derek!*" Ojo yelled as a burst of blue light shot from an unseen orifice above the entryway.

"Please identify," the hoverway's computerized voice instructed.

The light struck Derek's hand and the laser field deactivated as a clicking sound and dragging noise were suddenly heard. They grew louder and louder as Cecil approached.

Derek grabbed the silver disc from between his lips where he had been holding it. With a whipping motion, he cocked his wrist and the disc flew from between his fingers. It soared through the entryway and across the long corridor before striking a wall adjacent to the operating facility. The disc stuck to that wall.

The footsteps grew louder still. Derek took the small metal rod from his pocket another time and activated it. He waited for the tiny holes to light up.

"Please identify," the voice repeated as Derek's stalker turned the corner.

Finally, he passed the rod over the blue sensor pad and the hoverway departed from Sector 13.

"A little close there, guy," Ojo said. "But smooth. *Very* smooth."

Derek grinned. He was pleased with himself. But the ride wasn't over yet. Not even close.

"Destination?" the metallic voice asked.

"Floating tunnels."

"Destination?"

"Floating tunnels."

"Floa*tron* tunnels, asshole," Ojo corrected him.

"Destination?"

"Floatron tunnels."

The hoverway sped along a winding corridor that branched off in several directions. After moving through a number of passages, the hoverway suddenly came to a halt. Derek nervously watched as the two armed guards he had seen outside Sector 13 stepped onto the hoverway about thirty feet ahead of him. One of the guards placed his hand on the sensor pad as the hoverway departed.

"Floatron tunnels," Derek could hear the guard respond to the computerized voice.

"The Image Displacer," Ojo coached him. No response. 'The fucking *Image Displacer!*" he repeated. "Did you hear me? Derek, did you *hear me?*"

Derek finally moved the attaché up and down slightly in response but the hoverway was moving too rapidly for him to open it. When it came to a stop, Derek about-faced and walked as briskly as he could to the nearest platform. The floatron had not yet arrived.

He stood against one of the lucitavoxium columns and undid the case's latches. He pulled a small grey titanium box from it. It resembled one of those Brownie cameras that everyone's grandmother has safely tucked away for some rainy day. But it wasn't. It did have a tiny lens on one side and two shutters on the opposite side. But it was definitely not a Brownie camera.

When he was sure no one was watching, Derek activated the device by placing a finger over its lens and clicking one of its shutters.

Nothing happened. Or rather, nothing colorful. No burst of light, no unusual humming sound, no impressive laser. Nothing. But in an instant, a very quick instant, Derek was gone. Sort of.

He could no longer be seen leaning against the transparent column. His image had been projected some sixty feet away on the other end of the platform. There, and only there, did he appear to lean against one of the columns.

"I coulda sworn he was here a second ago," one of the guards told the other as the floatron arrived.

"Wait, there he is!" the other responded and they both ran across the platform toward the image on the other end while Derek boarded the vehicle.

The blue and white disc was still in his hand when he inserted it into the compartment at the helm of the floatron.

"Clearance granted," the voice of the floatron announced as the doors slid shut. "Atmosphere controlled."

Derek watched through one of the vehicle's small portholes as the guards came upon the fading image on the platform.

"Destination?"

One of the men quickly turned and caught his eye. He threw a pointing finger toward him as he and his partner ran toward the floatron. Derek responded to the guard's gesture with a finger of his own.

"The Atrium," Derek nervously responded as one of the guards reached for his gun.

The heavyset guard pulled it from his holster and held it at eye level just as the floatron shot into the tunnel.

Derek leaned back in the large cushioned seat and sighed heavily.

"I hear that, guy," Ojo told him.

"Oh, yeah?" Derek replied. "Did you also hear me shit my pants?"

"No," Ojo answered. "But I could smell it."

A long silent moment passed. Then he could hear Ojo's loud laugh. He also laughed. Nervously.

"Nothin' like first class, huh?" Ojo asked him as the floatron soared through the transparent maze. One tunnel after another. One chute after another. One passageway after another.

"No," he replied, "nothin' like it."

A few moments passed as the floatron entered a pressurized chute and rapidly ascended from the depths of the installation. The Challenger could once again be seen. For some reason that Derek himself wasn't sure of, a relieved smile rounded his lips.

"Atrium," the voice announced. "Atmosphere controlled."

Derek jumped off the floatron as soon as its doors opened. He stepped behind a young woman in a yellow sundress as she walked onto a hoverway. He followed her. She activated the hoverway and it rapidly passed over several wide landings and through a number of twisting corridors before coming to a halt.

The woman followed a small group of people as they all walked toward a ramp. Derek followed the woman. The ramp led right into the Atrium.

"Fine. Ignore me," Derek playfully whispered in the woman's ear.

When she turned around, he smiled. It was Selena.

"Hey, small world," Derek teased her.

She laughed. "Where on earth have you been all this time?"

"Looking for you. Where else?"

"Never mind," Selena said and laughed again. "Let's get outta here."

They walked toward the elevator which led to the Parking Facility. A small intercom was fixed into the wall beside it.

"QR4466," Selena spoke into the intercom, reading the number from the ticket in her hand.

Several seconds passed and the large glass door lifted. Selena's glistening 911 greeted them. They stepped into the car and the glass door slid shut again.

"Destination?" a loud metallic voice asked.

"Entry Level, please," Selena answered.

The elevator gently lowered them onto the ground level. When the glass door lifted another time, Selena drove beneath it, down the adjacent ramp and through the main entrance of the octagonal structure.

Derek breathed a sigh of relief as she drove along the path which led to the large entrance gate. Selena glanced at him and smiled as she came to a stop beside the guard who stood waiting outside the stone booth.

"Good afternoon, ma'am," the guard said.

"Afternoon, officer," she replied. "We'd like to go on through, if that's alright with you," she added and flashed a friendly smile.

"I'd love for you to, ma'am," he said as he pulled the gun from his holster and held it to Derek's head, "but I'm afraid that's just not going to be possible."

CHAPTER TWENTY-FOUR

Everyone is a genius at least once a year. The real
geniuses simply have their bright ideas closer
together.

Georg Christoph Lichtenberg

Cecil stared at the writing on the ivory tiles above the urinal. A number of sloppily written limericks amused him and brought a crooked smile to his badly scarred face. With a quick shake, he was finished. He zipped his trousers up as he turned and clumsily walked toward the sink on the other side of the brightly lit bathroom.

He mumbled several indiscernible slurs as he stumbled and fell against the door of a stall. The door flew open, revealing a curious-looking Dr. Erikson seated on the toilet with a neatly folded copy of the *New York Times* spread across his lap.

Cecil grabbed onto the corner of the door to stop himself from landing on the doctor's lap as their eyes met. The men stared at each other for a brief moment but nothing was said. Neither excusing himself nor offering a word of apology, Cecil quickly pulled the stall door shut. He turned again as his eyes fell upon the untied shoelace that was at fault.

He lifted his long leg with some difficulty and placed his dirty orthopedic shoe on the porcelain surface of the sink. As he tied the lace, he noticed the unusual reflection of one of the ceiling's lights on a small silver disc on the back of the shoe's thick metal sole.

Cecil pulled the small disc from the sole of his shoe, then carefully lifted his foot from the sink with both hands and lowered it onto the floor.

"What the …" he said with some confusion as he held the disc up in the light and examined it. The confused look on his face gradually faded. "Oooooh, *shit!*"

* * *

"*Damn!*" Ojo yelled, barely parting his lips as the scratchy sound of static filled the car while Cecil handled the transmitter. "He found it," he said, lowering the volume on the multiple receiver equalizers and squelching the annoying noise.

"Found what?" Christine asked him.

"The transmitter."

"Who did?"

"The killer. *Cecil.* He found the transmitter we planted on the sole of his shoe."

* * *

"Good work," Monroe spoke into the phone. "Now get your ass over here and bring it with you," he added, returning the receiver to its hook.

Hawkins looked up from the terminal with questioning eyes.

"That was Cecil," Monroe told him. "He just found a transmitter in Sector 13—"

"Good," Hawkins said before Monroe finished.

"On his fucking *shoe!*"

"Are you kidding?"

"No. I'm not. He's on his way over. But I'm still picking up some foreign transmissions within the Facility. And I think I know where they're being received," Landers commented, adjusting his headset with a couple of fingers. "Right here," he said, tapping a small flashing signal on the radar analyzer unit of the control panel.

Hawkins jumped from his seat. He stood behind Landers, eyeing the round radar screen from above his shoulder. "Jesus *Christ!*" he flared. "That's less than a thousand meters from the installation!"

Landers struck a switch on the panel and several columns of data appeared on the screen. "Seven hundred and ninety-one meters southwest of the main landing, to be exact."

"Send Renker and Smythe to the Space-1 Heliport and get that goddamn chopper over there!" Hawkins stammered. "*Now!*"

* * *

"What the hell do you think you're doing?!" Selena angrily asked the young officer.

"Sorry ma'am, but I have my orders," he replied in a calm voice. "Now get out of the car," he told Derek, pressing the pistol's barrel to his temple, "or I'll blow your fuckin' brains out."

"Do you know who I am?!" Selena asked. "I'm Lieutenant Hawkins' daughter," she told him without waiting for a reply.

Derek sat as still as he could, listening to the conversations in his ear while his fingers carefully reached into the side pocket of his jacket.

"That's funny, ma'am."

"Oh, really?! Why is *that*?!"

"My orders are *from* Lieutenant Hawkins."

"Then *surely* there has been some mistake."

"There's been *no* mistake," the officer told her. "Now out!" he said, losing his patience as he pulled the handle of the door.

"If you insist," Derek said, forcefully ramming the door into the officer's groin.

"Fuck!" the officer moaned as he doubled over in pain.

Derek jumped out from behind the door and slammed the back of his fist into the man's side as hard as he could, knocking him to the ground and the gun out of his hand. He stepped over the officer, pressing the control switch on the wall of the stone booth as the entrance began to rotate.

The officer unsteadily rose to his feet. He wavered for a moment, then grabbed the sleeve of Derek's jacket and plowed into his gut with a hard fist. Derek closed his eyes tightly for an instant, then sent his fist flying across the man's jaw, knocking him to the ground a second time.

"Go!" he yelled to Selena as the gate swung open enough for her car to pass through. "*Go!*"

"But what about—"

"Just *go!*" he told her as the officer reached for his gun with an extended arm.

Derek pulled a triangular prism from his pocket and gripped it in his palm. In an instant, a fiery red beam as thin as a needle shot from the weapon like a bullet, striking the officer's chest.

The gun dropped from his hand as he fell back onto the ground. He would've awakened several hours later if his head hadn't struck the stone base of the gate when he fell.

Selena had already driven through the gate and was turning onto the road it crossed. Derek ran after her. She brought the car to a sudden stop as he whipped the door open and jumped into the passenger seat. The triangular prism was accidentally knocked from his hand and thrown onto the ground as he pulled the door shut.

The thunderous roar of a helicopter taking off filled the sky while Derek watched the prism roll several feet from the car.

"Fuck it," he said. "*Just go!*"

Selena turned onto the main road which led away from the installation. She stepped hard on the accelerator and the car sped two or three hundred feet along the open road that soon forked. She followed the only branch leading to the unpaved road that cut an obscure path through the dense forest.

The car slowed considerably as it passed over the gravel and dirt that formed the winding road between the rows of tall oaks. The road turned several times as it weaved a path that led to a still narrower road that passed alongside Banner Creek.

"Who *are* you?" Selena asked with an unfamiliar look in her eyes.

"Someone who cares," Derek told her with a serious expression.

"Cares about *what?*" she asked him as they drove past the creek.

Its clear fresh water glistened as serenely now as it had a couple of hours earlier, racing over the shallow bed of the creek, smacking into the algae-covered rocks that jutted through its surface and gliding over the innumerable pebbles, branches and trout that lay beneath it.

There was but one difference now. The gentle soothing sounds of the creek had become obscured by the loud clattering noise of the helicopter's propellers.

"Cares about doing the right thing," Derek responded. "You're gonna have to trust me."

Selena brought the car to a screeching stop. She looked him hard in the face. "*Trust* you?! I don't *know* you! And I don't know what the hell's going on!" she yelled. "I don't even have a clue! One minute I'm introducing you to my father and the next—"

"Look," Derek said, grabbing her chin in his hand, "you're gonna *have* to trust me 'cause the lives of innocent women and children are at stake." He looked into her eyes for the compassion he knew was there. "Please. Trust me."

The car slid to the side for a moment, racing over the loose ground as Selena stepped on the accelerator.

"Which way?" she asked.

"Straight ahead," Derek told her, pointing to a clearing where the trees thinned considerably. "On the other side of the clearing there's a cliff."

"Where are you?" Ojo's concerned voice shot across the microtransceiver in Derek's ear.

"'Bout five hundred feet away. Around the bank. Get movin'!" he told Ojo. "We've got trouble!"

"Who're you talkin' to?" Selena asked.

Derek ignored her question.

"Tell me about it! The fuckin' thing's comin' right at us!" Ojo yelled.

Derek was clearly preoccupied or he would have picked up on Ojo's inadvertent reference. Another slip. He surely would have asked him whom he meant by 'us' but this slip went unnoticed as they both raced from harm's way. The black helicopter overhead was coming in fast.

The late morning sun cast a long southern shadow on Ojo's car as it sped along the edge of the cliff.

Selena followed the road as it sloped upward and around a large mass of bushes. As she turned and drove to the other side of the sandy bank, she and Derek could spot the tip of the shadow peeking out from beneath a huge cloud of dust while the helicopter swooped down upon it.

There was nothing they could do, Selena thought. Except turn back. She stepped on the brakes and the car slid to a stop about two feet from the edge of the cliff.

"What the hell are you doing?!" Derek yelled.

She looked at him with frightened eyes.

"Just keep going, Selena," he told her as calmly as he could. "Just keep going."

She continued along the narrow path which followed the shape of the cliff's edge.

Derek watched with both anger and fear in his eyes as the helicopter attempted to force Ojo over that edge. With the curved tip of its skid, the chopper struck the side of his car. The car swerved but remained on the road.

"*Motherfucker!*" Ojo yelled.

The helicopter rushed several hundred feet ahead of his car and then turned to attack. It dove in front of the car and lifted away just moments before colliding. Ojo hit the brakes and the car swerved again. It spun a hundred and eighty degrees as one of the rear wheels slid over the edge of the cliff. He floored the accelerator but it was hopeless. There was no way that rear wheel was lifting.

"*Noooooo!*" Derek screamed.

The chopper turned another time before lunging toward the helpless car. With a quick motion, the side of its skid struck the rear of Ojo's car just beside the wheel that lay frivolously spinning over the cliff's edge. The force of the impact lifted that wheel and the rest of the car. It rolled over onto its roof before sliding off the sloped side of the mountainous road and rolling over a second time. And a third time. The car finally came to rest on its roof.

"Hurry! *Hurry!*" Derek yelled at Selena as they raced along the road to the site of the crash.

She came to a stop about thirty feet from the overturned vehicle. Derek pushed the door open and ran toward the car. He could hear a rumbling noise as he approached it.

"Ojo! *Ojo!*" he called to his friend as the car exploded with a deafeningly thunderous noise. Red and orange flames and a black cloud of thick smoke shot a hundred feet into the air.

Derek was thrown back ten or fifteen feet by the force of the explosion. He righted himself after a moment and raced back to Selena's car as the helicopter circled overhead.

He reached over the door and grabbed the attaché case. The helicopter descended rapidly and flew right toward the car. Derek threw the attaché open on the car seat and pulled a brass case from it.

He furiously worked the combination lock on the side of the L-shaped case as the helicopter soared just a few feet above the car, taunting its prey before it turned and rose to a considerable height.

Finally the case sprung open. Derek pulled the lucite rod from it and jumped onto the hood of the car. The helicopter approached another time.

"C'mon, you goddamn sons of bitches!" Derek furiously yelled at the chopper. "Make my *year!*"

When the helicopter came within thirty or forty feet of the car, Derek held the device above his head with both hands. A thin jet of turquoise light shot from the long end of the transparent rod. It struck the large propeller which sat on the chopper's roof. Suddenly its blades froze. It spun no longer. The tail propeller threw the helicopter into a counterclockwise spin, carrying it over the edge of the cliff as it plummeted to the ground below.

Derek jumped from the car's hood and ran toward the burning car. "Call an ambulance!" he yelled back to Selena.

The sounds of glass smashing and metal ripping apart were heard as the helicopter crashed against the hot desert ground with a fiery explosion.

"Where are we?" Selena called to Derek, pulling the phone from its seat on the dashboard as flames shot into the sky from the helicopter wreckage below.

"Just tell 'em Route 41 and Banner Creek," he shouted back.

"And then?"

"Then look for the fuckin' clouds of black smoke!"

CHAPTER TWENTY-FIVE

No great genius has ever been without some
madness.

Aristotle

Derek stood seven or eight feet from the burning car. The heat and glare of the hostile flames prevented him from moving any closer. He watched with mournful eyes as the car lay turned over on its roof, its wheels still aimlessly spinning while the flames consumed it.

He removed his jacket quickly and covered his head with it as he ran to the side of the car. "Ojo!" he screamed, kneeling a foot or two from the flames that filled the front seat and danced across the dashboard and the dark smoke that poured from the space where the windshield had been. "*Ojo!*"

There was no response.

Nothing could be seen through the dense smoke and flames. Derek turned away from the car and began to cough violently. He stood up and moved several feet back as he struggled to catch his breath.

It was only then that he thought he heard a voice through the crackling sounds of the flames and the rumbling of the car's smashed radiator. He was sure of it. It was definitely a voice. A man's voice. But it was not coming from within the car.

"… the ecurity … the rojec … must be maintai … and it … obligat … absolut … respons … traitor …" a faceless voice mumbled.

The words were barely discernible over the other noises. But Derek heard them. He grabbed the jacket from over his head and ran around to the other side of the car, which had come to rest against a number of short dry bushes. The bushes were also aflame.

Two large green bushes rose at an angle fifteen or twenty feet from the sloping mountainous ridge on which the overturned car lay. It was from behind those bushes that Derek thought the garbled words were coming.

He raced toward them, stumbling over a thick branch that jutted out from the slanted ground but maintaining his balance. When he came to the bushes, he immediately found the source of those words.

The LX-3 modulator, which received intercepted signals from the microtransmitters that had been planted in the installation, lay on the ground between the bushes.

"… if he too has betrayed me," the German-accented words were now somewhat more audible, "then he will be dealt with the way his colluding associate, our dear Dr. Barnes, was!"

Derek stared at the receiver. A rush of excitement filled his eyes. A hand lay over it. Grasping it as it lay on the ground. Ojo's hand.

Derek anxiously separated the bushes. Within them, he found a groggy Ojo. A large welt covered most of his bruised forehead. His clothes were badly torn and a few minor scrapes and cuts showed through the ripped material but there was no sign of any serious bleeding.

"Ojo," Derek called to him, "can you hear me?"

Ojo gazed at him with a confused look in his eyes as he ran a couple of fingers over the lump on his forehead. He nodded.

Derek smiled with relief.

"Where's Christine?" Ojo asked him as his head began to clear.

"Christine? What d'ya mean, '*where's* Christine'?!"

"She was with me."

"Oh, my *fucking* God!" Derek nervously yelled.

He quickly jumped to his feet. His eyes frantically

raced among the bushes and branches and tree stumps.

"Christine!" he yelled as his voice cracked. "*Christine!*"

Derek ran to a cluster of bushes about fifteen feet away. "Christine!"

But she was not there. He raced toward another large bush a few feet away when he heard Ojo call to him.

"Over here, Derek!" he yelled. "Over here!"

Derek turned and ran toward him. He found Ojo behind a fallen tree, kneeling over Christine's body. The blood drained from his face and his heart pounded as he looked at her.

A drop of blood flowed from the corner of her mouth. It ran onto her chin. Her angelic face was ghastly pale and her eyes closed.

"Please, please," Derek whispered, "*not* Christine."

"She's alive," Ojo told him, taking his fingers from the side of her neck where he felt her carotid pulse.

"Thank God," Derek said, bending to his knees as he quickly took his jacket and placed it over her. "Where's that fuckin' ambulance?!" Derek called to Selena.

"Chrissy, are you alright?" Derek gently asked her, taking her hand in his and rubbing it.

Christine didn't respond. She lay there quietly. Silently.

"Can you hear me, Chrissy?" Derek asked her, gently brushing the hair away from her face. "Can you hear me?"

She began to stir. Her head moved around just a bit as her eyes struggled to open.

"Where's the ambulance?!" Derek called out to Selena another time.

"It'll be here in a minute," she finally responded as she appeared over Ojo's shoulder. "Is there anything I can do?"

"Just watch for the ambulance and let 'em know where we are when they get here," Ojo told her.

Selena turned and ran back to the road as Christine's eyes opened. She caught Derek's worried stare and a soft smile rounded her lips. "I love you," she whispered.

A tear fell from Derek's eye and rolled down his cheek. He squeezed Christine's hand and then put it to his lips.

"Does it hurt anywhere?" he asked her.

"Only over here," she told him, putting her hand over the ribs on her left side. "I think I'm gonna be fine."

"Of course, you are," Derek told her, wiping the streak of blood from her chin as the sound of an ambulance siren was heard. "You're gonna be just fine," he said and winked at her. "Isn't she, Ojo?"

"Absolutely," Ojo answered with a confident smile as two paramedics arrived.

He and Derek stepped out of the men's way. One of them wrapped a blood pressure cuff around her arm and put a stethoscope to his ears as she passed out.

"Sixty over forty," he said. Her blood pressure was dangerously low.

The other paramedic quickly fastened a pair of mast trousers around her legs and then inflated them while his partner inserted an intravenous line in her arm.

"Give me the neck brace," one of the paramedics said.

The other one handed it to him and he carefully placed it around Christine's neck. His partner positioned a backboard alongside her and together they rolled her on her side, then slid the backboard underneath and tightened its straps.

"One, two, three," one of the men counted as he and his partner lifted Christine off the ground.

They carried her to the ambulance, which sat waiting on the road beside the cliff's edge. Together they climbed into it and placed her on the waiting stretcher. Derek and Ojo climbed in after them and the ambulance's doors slammed shut.

A cloud of dust was all Selena could see of the ambulance as it took off in a hurry and sped along the winding road that led away from the cliff. She could hear its loud siren fade in the distance.

* * *

With each passing minute Derek grew more worried. He checked his watch now as he had every five or ten minutes for the past three hours while he nervously paced back and forth between the wide window on one end of the surgical waiting area and the door on the other.

"What's taking so damn long?!" he anxiously asked himself aloud. "How long can it take to remove a ruptured spleen?"

Ojo sat quietly in a seat beside the window. He stared through it at a number of youngsters playing soccer on the field behind the hospital, nervously chewing on the corner of his lip while a couple fingers gently rubbed a sore spot on his temple. Every now and then he looked away from the window and toward Derek. Two or three times he was accosted with a livid glance from his friend.

Derek looked at him now.

"I don't know what to say," Ojo told him with a sorrowful expression as he stood and leaned against the window.

Derek looked away for a moment. Then he turned and caught Ojo's eye another time.

"You don't know what to say?" Derek asked him.

His eyes raced over Ojo's shoulder and through the window toward the grey sky. In a quick moment they returned and locked onto the pathetic expression on Ojo's face.

Derek grabbed Ojo by the collar of his shirt with both hands and looked him square in the eye. "You don't know what to say?! You *son-of-a-bitch*!" Derek yelled and threw him up hard against the window.

Ojo stared defenselessly into Derek's irate eyes as several others in the waiting area watched with charged stares.

"Christine was supposed to be on that goddamn plane back to New York! What the fuck happened?!" he yelled.

Ojo hesitated for a moment. "I told her she could stay."

"You did *what*?!"

Ojo didn't respond.

"*You* told her she could stay?!"

Ojo nodded slightly while Derek held onto his collar.

"*You* told her she could stay!" Derek repeated as he threw Ojo against the window another time. "Jesus *Christ*! What d'you mean *you* told her she could stay? Huh? What the fuck do you mean?!"

Ojo didn't answer. He knew this would happen. He expected it. And the best thing he could do was just let Derek unload on him.

"What the fuck do you mean?! I'm talkin' to you, you son-of-a-bitch! What the fuck do you mean you told her she could stay?! You knew I wanted her out of here! Why the fuck would you let her stay?! Why?! Tell me, dammit! *Why*?!"

Again, Ojo didn't respond. There was nothing he could say. Derek was beside himself. Ojo had never seen him like this before. But nothing like this had ever happened before.

A young resident in scrubs ran into the room and grabbed Derek's arm as he tried to pull him from Ojo.

Derek looked the resident in the eye. "Get your fuckin' hand off me or I'll put you through that wall!" he told him with clenched teeth.

The resident looked at Ojo. Ojo nodded, assuring the resident he would be fine and he let go of Derek's arm.

"Do you know what it feels like to know the woman you love might be dying on the goddamn operating table and there isn't anything you can do to help her?! You can't do one fuckin' thing to help her! Do you know what that feels like?! *Do you*?!" Derek furiously yelled at Ojo.

Ojo shook his head slightly.

"And all for nothing! For nothing! There isn't one goddamn reason why she's on that operating table instead of me! Do you know that?! Not one goddamn reason! Not one! Or is there?!"

Ojo's eyes fell to the floor.

"Look at me, you son-of-a-bitch! *You're* the reason she's on that table! Do you know that?! You're the goddamn reason she's on that table! If you did what I asked you to do, she wouldn't be in there! Do you know that?!"

Ojo looked him dead in the eye but didn't respond.

"And the worst part—do you know what the worst part is?" he asked Ojo as his eyes welled and a tear raced down the side of his cheek. He paused for a moment. "I didn't even tell her I loved her before she was taken into surgery! I had a chance to but I didn't say it. I don't know why. I just didn't. And I may never have another chance.

Do you know how that feels?!"

There was no response. Then Ojo looked at the floor and shook his head slightly acknowledging that he didn't.

A tall grey-haired man wearing bloodstained scrubs beneath a long white coat stepped into the room. He walked over to the resident, who stood several feet from where Derek held Ojo against the window.

"Have you told him?" the surgeon asked the resident.

"I chose not to be put through the wall, Dr. Higgins," the resident replied.

Dr. Higgins looked at the resident with a curious expression on his face, then turned toward Derek.

Derek noticed the surgeon beside him and let go of Ojo. He looked into the man's eyes with apprehensive curiosity.

"Christine pulled through," Dr. Higgins told him with a hint of a tired smile as he placed a hand on Derek's shoulder. "She's going to be fine."

"I don't know how to thank you," Derek told him, grabbing the man's extended hand.

"You just did," the surgeon replied.

"But why did it take so long?" Derek asked him. "I've been goin' out of my mind," he said with a relieved smile.

"In addition to the ruptured spleen we knew about preoperatively, she also had a serious laceration of the left lobe of her liver. We couldn't see it on her CAT scan before surgery.

"How is she now?"

"She's fine," Dr. Higgins told him in a confident tone of voice. "She's lost quite a bit of blood. But she's fine. Of course, we transfused her."

"When can I see her? How long will Christine be in recovery?" Derek asked the surgeon.

"She'll be there for just a short while before being taken to the ICU."

Derek was anxious to see her. Excited but anxious. It was obvious.

"But I think I may just be able to sneak you in there for a minute or two," the surgeon told Derek. "C'mon."

A boyish grin of excitement lit up Derek's face as he followed Dr. Higgins out of the waiting area. Ojo stood by the window and watched as they walked away.

* * *

Fourteen occupied beds managed to keep the seven surgical nurses, three anesthesiologists, and numerous respiratory therapists, X-ray technicians, phlebotomists and other workers within the Recovery Room sufficiently busy while a number of surgical residents and attendings moved among the patients as they made their post-op rounds.

Derek and Dr. Higgins were among them.

"Over there," Dr. Higgins said, pointing to a bed on

the far side of the Recovery Room as he and Derek stood just inside its entrance. "Slot 10."

Derek looked at the surgeon and smiled appreciatively.

"Just two minutes, now," Dr. Higgins told him. "I want to get her to the ICU."

"Two minutes," Derek replied. "I promise."

Several nurses and one of the residents brushed against him as he walked past several beds on the right side of the Recovery Room. In one lay an elderly woman who breathed with the assistance of a ventilator. In another lay a young boy with one leg elevated in traction and the other bearing the shiny ends of the fixation rods, which held the bones of that leg in the proper position. A number of other patients, several young, several old, several male, several female, lay in the beds that followed along that section of the wall against which slot 10 lay.

Derek squeezed between the bed in slot 11, where a middle-aged black man lay watching the cardiac monitor of a patient on the opposite side of the room while his casted arm rested on a couple of pillows, and Christine's bed.

Derek stared at her as she lay peacefully sleeping. He reached over the bed's rail and gently took Christine's hand in his. It was warm. And soft. It was so soft, he thought. His eyes ran over her pink fingernails while his fingers traced their curves.

He stared at her face for some time. He stared at her long eyelashes and noticed the way they curved away from her eyelids. He stared at her cute pug nose. The one he always teased her about. He stared at her beautiful lips and noticed the way their corners bent upward ever so slightly, even when she slept.

With a gentle touch, Derek ran a finger over the side of her cheek. He leaned over the rail and softly kissed her on the forehead, then leaned back and looked at her again. Her eyes slowly opened.

"Derek," she called to him with a sleepy voice. "Is that you, Derek?"

"Yes," he whispered to her. "It's me."

"Am I okay?"

"Yes, you're okay."

"I told you I'd be okay."

"Yes, you did," he said and laughed.

"Are you laughing at me?"

"Oh, I would never laugh at you, Chrissy," he told her and held her hand to his lips. "I love you."

"I know you love me," she said. "And I love you, too. But I still laugh at you," she said and started to giggle quietly. "Oh, it hurts when I laugh."

Derek started to laugh again. He was so relieved. "You'd better save your energy now," he told her and bent over to kiss her. "Get some rest. I'll see you a little later," he said and turned to leave.

"Oh, Derek?" Christine called to him.

"Yes, Chrissy."

"Don't be upset with Ojo."

"Yeah," Derek mumbled.

"Please don't," she pleaded with him. "It's not his fault. It's really not." She paused for a moment to catch her breath. "I begged him to let me stay. He hated the idea but didn't know how to get rid of me. He loves you, Derek. He really does. He loves both of us."

There was another pause.

"I know he does," Derek told her then turned to leave.

Derek slowly passed between a number of nurses and carefully around a large Jamaican woman who stood bent over a patient while she drew his blood. He stepped out of the way of a technician as he pushed a portable X-ray machine into position beside slot 2, then walked through the glass doors that led out of the Recovery Room.

Immediately to the right of the doors stood Ojo. He had walked there from the surgical waiting area and stood leaning against the wall while Derek checked on Christine.

Derek turned and faced him. Their eyes met. But neither said a word. They just stared at each other for a long silent moment. Derek could see the sorrow in Ojo's eyes. Ojo could see the compassion in Derek's.

A peaceful smile rounded the corners of Derek's lips.

The hint of an uncertain smile appeared on Ojo's face. Derek threw his arms around him and they embraced.

CHAPTER TWENTY-SIX

The difference between Talent and Genius is that
Talent says things which he has never heard but
once, and Genius things which he has never heard.

Emerson

A dull hazy light flowed through the narrow spaces
between the vertical blinds and carefully crept into the
hospital room where Ojo lay sleeping on a small flattened
cot that was pressed up against a wall on one side, Derek
lay sleeping awkwardly twisted into a wooden armchair on
the other, and Christine lay with several pillows
supporting her back, and another gently cushioning the
dressing on her abdomen, as her eyes bounced among the
numerous piles of papers scattered across her bed, each

with its own chapter heading, to the stack of pages attached to the clipboard on her lap, reviewing each in turn while the rising sun announced the dawn of a new morning.

Christine looked away from the clipboard for a moment. Her eyes fell upon Derek. A warm smile rounded her lips. She watched while he lay sleeping. A pillow cushioned his back as he lay against one arm of the large wooden chair while his legs dangled over the other. As uncomfortable as the position appeared, a tranquil expression covered Derek's face. Christine knew that Derek was content because she was okay. She also knew that he loved her. And that made her very content.

Christine turned toward the other side of the room and looked at Ojo. He, too, was still asleep. His face lay buried beneath a pillow while his feet dangled off one end of the small cot and his outstretched arms off the other. She stared at him for a moment and thought about the deep friendship they shared. He was more than a friend. He was family, she thought. Family. That brought another smile to her face as her eyes returned to the page on the clipboard.

Christine read the lines that she had scribbled on that page fifteen or twenty minutes earlier. She looked away for a moment, stared aimlessly at the blue sky through the room's corner window, then looked back at the page. She read it again. Then, with a quick snapping motion of her wrist, she pulled it from under the clip and crumpled it in her hand. She tossed it onto the tall pile of crumpled papers that now overflowed from the wastebasket beside her bed.

She tapped the point of her pen several times against the clean sheet of paper which now sat directly under the clip, then quickly began writing as if all at once the solution to some convoluted scene had occurred to her.

It was now the eighth day of deliberation. The jury had still not reached a verdict. The townsfolk grew weary of waiting. How much more of this could poor Miss Betsy stand? How much? The trial had been torment enough for her. And now the waiting. Would there be no end to the madness?

That poor Miss Betsy could even have been accused of such a crime was an outrage. That one would even think her capable of stabbing her adulterous husband forty-seven times with a butcher's knife before dismembering and decapitating him was preposterous.

Christine quickly read the two paragraphs another time. She liked them. She smiled and continued writing.

Surely Miss Betsy could not have committed such a heinous crime. Not one of the townsfolk believed she had. Not one other than little Billy Bradford. The sheriff's six-year-old son. The prosecution's only eyewitness to the cold-blooded murder. Not another soul in the town thought Miss Betsy capable of the crime. Not another soul. Only little Billy Bradford. Of course, there were initially other suspects. Three of the dead man's mistresses had been extensively interrogated. But there was only one eyewitness. Only one. Little Billy Bradford. And little Billy swore he had seen Miss Betsy kill her husband. Yet not another of the town's two hundred and fourteen residents thought Miss Betsy capable of the crime. Not one.

But someone had brutally murdered Jesse Cummings. As the county prosecutor had so eloquently demonstrated during one of his most outrageously facetious outbursts, Mr. Cummings could not have committed suicide. For even if he could have stabbed himself forty-seven times in the face, chest and back, then chopped off both legs and one arm before cutting off his nuts, shoving them down his throat and chopping his head off, he would still have been left with one arm. But, as the decaying corpse that was dug up from behind Miss Betsy's house was missing both arms, there was absolutely no way Mr. Cummings' death could be dismissed as a suicide. Absolutely none. The county prosecutor was sure of it. And he was no fool.

Clarification of little Billy's testimony had several times been requested by the jury during these eight endless days of deliberation. Each day began at eight in the morning and continued until five in the afternoon. A thirty-minute break was allotted in the middle of each day and another toward the end of each before the jury's twelve members were escorted to the town's one and only motel where they were sequestered each night. At the Shady Tavern Inn. For sixty-three hours and fifteen minutes the twelve men and women of the jury reviewed the testimony, reconstructed the murder with charts and diagrams and, more than anything else, argued amongst themselves as they held the life of poor Miss Betsy in their hands.

Whether she was hanged from the town's gallows or absolved of the murder and released from her shackles a free woman would depend upon their decision. And only theirs. Could the life of this twenty-two-year-old daughter of the town's only judge really depend upon the testimony of a six-year-old boy with a vivid imagination? Actually, it could. Actually, it did.

The jury believed that little Billy had been playing ball in the grass field behind Miss Betsy's house the day of her husband's murder. They also believed that his ball had bounced through a small hole in the tiny window that led into the basement of Miss Betsy's house and that he had gone after it to retrieve it. But Miss Betsy's life depended upon whether they believed the events little Billy claimed to have seen through the small hole in that tiny window on that warm spring afternoon.

A hush ran through the noisy courtroom as the door to the deliberation chambers opened slightly. It creaked on its loose hinges as the foreman of the jury pulled it open.

With bated breath every man, woman and child of Sleepy Waters, New Hampshire, watched on the edge of their seats as the twelve men and women of the jury seated themselves in the jury box.

"Has the jury reached a verdict?" questioned the heavyset Judge Farrow.

"We have, Your Honor," the foreman responded and handed a folded slip of paper to the court bailiff. He quickly delivered the paper to the Judge's open hand.

Judge Farrow unfolded the paper and stared at it for quite some time. He looked up into the nervous eyes of Miss Betsy who sat behind a long oak table at the front of the courtroom.

"Will the defendant, Miss Betsy Farrow, please stand and face the jury," the judge told his daughter.

"What say you, Mr. Foreman?"

Miss Betsy's eyes desperately raced across each of the jury member's faces as she stood before them. She searched in the brief instant before the foreman announced whether she would live or die for some last hope. Any last hope. But why, she asked herself. Why should there be any? And did she need any? What difference would it make? That old bastard was finally dead. Dead and buried. And nothing would change that. Nothing.

"We, the Jury, find the defendant, Miss Betsy Farrow," the foreman began then paused for a brief moment, "guilty of murder in the first degree."

As each of the jury's eleven other members repeated the verdict in turn, Miss Betsy bowed her head and looked to the ground. She looked up again as the condemning words echoed throughout the courtroom. She turned around and faced the townsfolk. A contented grin slowly rounded the corners of her parched lips. That old bastard was finally dead. Dead and buried. And nothing would change that. Nothing.

"It's done," Christine quietly said aloud with a sweet sigh of relief as she gently dropped her pen on the clipboard. "It's finally done."

Derek stirred in the chair and his eyes opened. He looked at Christine as he rolled off the chair and walked toward her on his knees. "Did you say something, hon?" he asked her as she started to laugh.

"*Deadlock!*" she blurted with excitement in her voice. "It's finished!"

"That's great, Chrissy," Derek told her, "but I'm gonna kill you," he said. "You're supposed to be resting, not working on your book. Did you forget you had major surgery yesterday?"

"No, I didn't forget. But gimme a break, would you?" she snapped at him in her usual adorable way. "You're supposed to congratulate me, not scold me."

"What's goin' on?" Ojo asked as he wiped the night from his eyes with the back of his hand.

"I finished *Deadlock*!" Christine excitedly told him.

"Alright! Congratulations!" Ojo said and kissed her on the cheek.

Christine looked at Derek with a sarcastic smirk on her face. "See that?" she asked him, pointing to Ojo. "You can learn a thing or two from him."

"Come here, you knucklehead," Derek said, throwing his arms around Christine and pressing her cheek to his. "You know how proud I am of you, don't you?" he whispered in her ear.

"Of course, I do," she said and kissed him on the lips with a soft smack. "I'm just giving you a hard time."

Derek looked at her and raised his brow.

"Don't say it," Christine warned him and they both laughed.

She grabbed her side after a moment. "Ooh, it hurts when I laugh," she said and laughed some more.

Derek searched the room for a clock then looked at his wrist. "Oh, there it is. Shit. It's almost 10:30. They're gonna be here any minute."

"Who's gonna be here any minute?" Christine curiously asked.

"How long have you been up writing?" Ojo asked her.

"Since the crack of dawn," she replied. "Who's gonna be here any minute?"

Ojo and Derek exchanged a smile.

"Should we tell her?" Derek teased.

"C'mon, who's coming? Tell me, dammit," Christine pouted curiously.

"Hmm. I think we can wait a little longer," Ojo suggested.

"I agree."

"C'mon, tell me. C'mon. Who?"

"Okay, okay, control yourself," Derek told her. "Do the names George Hansen and William Kruthers ring a bell?"

A blank look covered Christine's face. She thought and thought. But neither of the names seemed familiar to her.

"Think Chrissy," Ojo told her. "Think back about two years."

"Hmm. Two years, you say?"

She thought for another moment. The blank look quickly faded and a wide grin replaced it.

"Well?" Derek asked her.

"You don't mean Goose and Tucker, do you?"

Derek and Ojo smiled.

"Bingo," Derek said.

"But what are they doing in Houston? And how do they know we're here?" she asked him.

"Mind if I answer that for you, Capt'n Kirk?" a tall red-headed man in a navy blue windbreaker asked as he walked through the door.

Beside him stood a slightly shorter man, also in a navy blue windbreaker, with only a hint of hair along the sides of his head.

A brilliant smile brightened Christine's already-beaming face. She quickly gathered up the piles of papers on her bed and placed them in the manuscript box that sat on the night stand.

"Be my guest, Tucker," Derek told him as he shook hands with each of the men.

"Well, you see it's like this, ma'am," Tucker started. "There we are, Goose and me, that is, sittin' in our car chompin' on donuts when this body from hell just plunks down on our roof. I look at Goose. Goose looks at me."

"And the first thing that comes to mind is," Goose cuts in, "does this son-of-a-bitch know we're on break, or what?"

"Okay, okay," Christine said when she stopped laughing. "I get the picture. The boys have filled you in on every last detail. So just shut up. Both of you. And come here and gimme a big hug."

Ojo and Derek watched with wide smiles as the three of them hugged.

"You still haven't told me what the two of you are doin' in Houston."

Goose glanced at his watch. It was almost 10:30 a.m.

"Don't tell me you two have been kicked off the force."

They didn't respond.

"That thing works?" Goose asked, pointing to the televison which sat high on a shelf on the wall opposite the bed.

"Yeah, sure," Christine told him, holding out the remote control.

Goose took it from her and turned the TV on.

"Well, is that what happened?" she curiously asked them.

"Something like that," Tucker responded.

"But not exactly," Goose added as he flipped through the channels.

"We've been promoted, sort of," Tucker said.

"Promoted? But weren't you already detectives?" Christine asked.

Goose and Tucker looked at each other and smiled. Then they turned around so Christine could see the backs of their jackets. Three large white letters boldly stood out on the navy blue material.

"Pretty impressive," Christine said. "FBI. Agents, huh? I like that. Congratulations."

"Thanks. It's something we've always wanted," Tucker told her. "So when they offered us the positions, we jumped at the chance. It happened 'bout six months ago."

"Your boys, here, tracked us down in D.C. last night. Pretty fine detectives themselves," Goose commented as his eyes bounced between Christine and the television.

"What are you looking for?" she asked him.

"The NEXUS space shuttle. The Genesis. It's lifting off today," Goose replied. "Don't you guys read the papers?"

"Only the funnies," Derek answered.

"So when Derek told us about the situation out here, the first thing I thought was, 'Hey, this could mean another story for Christine,'" Tucker teased her.

"Watch it, Red," Christine jokingly snapped at him.

Tucker laughed loudly. "Okay, seriously, we thought we could lend them a hand. They're gonna need some outside backup when they're back inside."

"*Back inside*?!" Christine nervously asked.

"Watch," Goose said as the astronauts prepared for liftoff.

A raspy commentator's voice was heard while a picture of the Genesis Shuttle strapped to its two rocket boosters filled the small television screen.

"... our crew of seven astronauts will rotate every

three months while the Genesis remains in orbit and Project SpaceBirth comes to term!" the man said with excitement in his voice.

"So *that's* what they're calling it," Ojo sarcastically commented as he exchanged a suspicious glance with Derek.

"10 … 9 …" the countdown began as a voice from Ground Control overlapped with the commentator's.

"Don't they mean Project *New State*?" Derek said.

"C'mon, fellas," Goose quieted them, "I'm really into this shit."

"… 7 … 6 …"

"… this is a historic day, indeed!" the news commentator continued. "For the very first time since the space program was established, we will experience the miracle of birth in space! One hundred and sixty-four days from today," the commentator went on as two huge balls of flame shot from the shuttle's boosters, "scientists are anticipating the birth of a healthy rhesus monkey aboard the Genesis! Exactly one hundred and sixty-four days from this very day!"

"… 3 … 2 …1!"

The excited sound of the Ground Controller's voice was heard. "We have ignition and liftoff!" he said.

"Confirm for us, Genesis," another voice instructed.

"Roger, Ground Control," one of the astronauts responded, "we have ignition and liftoff."

A monstrous cloud of greyish-white smoke poured from the boosters and filled the launch pad as a thunderous roar sounded and the Genesis Shuttle lifted free of the ground. Everyone in the room remained silent as the shuttle soared into the heavens. It was a beautiful liftoff. It was flawless. When the Genesis could still just barely be seen, its rocket boosters gently broke free and coasted back to the ocean on paths of their own while the shuttle continued beyond the clouds and into the stratosphere as it traveled onward to its predetermined orbit hundreds of miles above the Earth. It was soon out of view as it journeyed along its history-making course.

Ojo and Derek looked at each other for a long silent moment with fearful concern in their eyes.

"It's happening," Derek finally said flatly.

A disgusted expression distorted Ojo's face. He slowly nodded in agreement.

CHAPTER TWENTY-SEVEN

If I had asked the public what they wanted, they
would have told me a faster horse.

Henry Ford

Christine's eyes were filled with apprehension. She stood
leaning against one side of the room's corner window
which overlooked the hospital's small parking lot. A
number of people were either crossing the lot on their way
to the hospital or leaving the hospital and returning to
their cars on this sunny morning. She watched as an
elderly white-haired man gingerly pushed his wife's
wheelchair along the carpeting beneath the awning that
hung over the side entrance. The man wheeled his wife
toward the taxi that waited at the curb. The driver helped

the couple into the cab then quickly folded the wheelchair and tossed it in the trunk.

The taxi pulled away from the curb in a hurry and rushed past the stop sign that stood right below Christine's window just as Goose and Tucker turned the corner. She watched as they stepped from the narrow strip of pavement adjacent to one of the hospital's marble column supports to the asphalt ground of the lot and gasped as the taxi came to a screeching stop only inches from their knees.

"Asshole!" Goose yelled at the driver as he brought his fist down hard on the hood of the taxi.

A small Indian man jumped out of the car. Goose and Tucker continued walking. Goosed looked back at the man over his shoulder and made a loud snarling noise with his throat. The man jumped back into the car and pulled the door shut without saying a word.

Derek and Ojo were several steps behind them, laughing loudly as they stepped from the curb. They followed as Goose and Tucker quickly walked past several cars and toward an unmarked black sedan. The silver attaché case swung back and forth slightly as it hung from Derek's hand. Fortunately, Selena had brought it by the hospital the night before. He had left it in her car when he and Ojo joined Christine in the ambulance just the day prior.

Goose turned and tossed a set of keys in the air. "This one's yours," he said, pointing toward the car as Ojo caught the keys.

"That'll work," Derek said with an appreciative grin.

"Thought we'd be better off with two cars," Tucker said over his shoulder as he and Goose walked toward another black sedan several cars over.

"Always thinking," Derek told him.

"That's why they pay me the big bucks," Tucker said with a chuckle.

"Why don't you follow us back to the Valley Inn," Ojo suggested. "We'll set up camp there."

"Sounds like a plan," Goose replied as he and Tucker pulled the car doors open.

"Just a sec," Derek said before they got in.

He opened the attaché case and removed two microtransceivers from a small compartment.

"What've ya got there?" Tucker asked.

"Walkie-talkies, sort of," Derek answered as he held them out with an open hand. "So we can start working on some strategy while we head back to Willow Valley."

"The cars have radios," Goose commented.

"Not like these," Ojo confidently told him.

"G'head," Derek told them, "take one."

Goose and Tucker each took one of the microtransceivers from his hand.

"What now?" Goose asked.

"What d'ya mean, 'What now?'" Tucker sarcastically

snapped at him. "Ain't it obvious?" he asked, pretending to stick the microtransceiver in his nose.

Ojo and Derek laughed. Goose turned beet red.

"FBI, huh, Goose," Derek asked him.

"Just shut the fuck up, Capt'n Kirk," Goose told him. "Knowing you, I thought maybe it's supposed to go up my ass! Like some transmitter suppository, or somethin'."

When Derek stopped laughing, he explained the proper way to position the device right up against the ear drum.

"This isn't gonna fuck with my hearing now, is it?" Goose asked.

Ojo gazed at him with a blank look on his face. "What was that now?" he innocently asked. "Didn't quite hear you."

"Asshole!" Goose replied with a chuckle.

"Just follow us, alright?" Derek said.

"You got it," Tucker replied.

The sharp clicking sounds of four doors were heard. Christine still leaned against the window, watching as the two black sedans briskly exited the lot and followed a narrow path that led away from the hospital and toward the main road. In a moment both cars were out of view.

Christine remained by the window. Long after the cars had gone, she stood leaning with her cheek against the cold glass as her eyes remained filled with apprehension.

She stared at the parking lot a moment longer, then walked to the bed and sat on the side near the night stand.

Her eyes focused on the manuscript box. On its cover was affixed a sheet of paper bearing just one word. *Deadlock*. The novel's title. Christine took the box from the night stand and set it on her lap. She thought about the hundreds and hundreds of hours of hard work she had devoted to this project while she stared at that title page. Then she heard Derek's words. They echoed in her mind. She could hear him telling her how proud he was of her. That brought a warm smile to her worried face. That made it all worthwhile, she thought.

A soft tapping noise startled Christine. She turned quickly and found Dr. Higgins in a tailor-fitted Italian suit and an exhausted resident in stained scrubs, a wrinkled white coat, and two days' growth on his face, standing by the door.

"How are you this morning, doctors?" she asked them.

"Ms. Stratton," the resident started with a caring smile, "the sixty-four dollar question is how are *you* this morning?"

"I could be better," Christine replied as she laid back in the bed.

"Really?" Dr. Higgins asked. "What's the matter?"

"Oh, nothing until he starts pulling on that tape," she told him, lifting her gown a bit and pointing to the dressing on her abdomen. It started on one side and extended across her belly.

"Fear not," the resident said. "I've done this as least once or twice before," he teased her.

Dr. Higgins smiled while the resident carefully removed the bulky dressing. Christine covered her eyes with her hand.

"Well?" she asked a moment later.

"Well, what?" the resident responded.

"Well, when are you gonna take it off?"

"I already have," he told her. "Have a look."

"Must I?"

"Yes. You must," he told her and started laughing.

Christine slowly peeled back the fingers over her eyes and looked at the incision. It was a long midline incision. But neatly covered with Steri-Strips. A relieved smile parted her lips.

"What now?" she asked.

"Now you rest," Dr. Higgins told her. "We've got to get you healed up. You just underwent major surgery, young lady."

"Can't go home today, huh?"

"Uh … no," Dr. Higgins told her flatly.

"When then?"

Dr. Higgins exchanged a smile with the resident.

"You know something," he told her, "you're almost as impatient as that Derek fellow," he finished with a teasing grin.

The look on her face indicated she was waiting for an answer. "By the weekend then?" she eagerly asked.

"Assuming you behave, I think that would be a right good plan," Dr. Higgins told her. "You know," he continued, "that Derek fellow really is something else."

"He really is," Christine agreed and grinned. "He really is."

* * *

A small piece of folded paper was taped to the door of the motel room. Ojo pulled it free. He unfolded the paper and smiled. Derek and the others looked on curiously.

"Be right back," he told them as he walked toward the office.

Herman Tate sat on an ancient-looking wooden chair behind the long reception desk with his legs propped up against the middle shelf of a contiguous bookcase. A bowl of spaghetti and sauce rested on his lap while he leisurely watched the dusty television that sat on the edge of the desk.

"Buy a vowel, you idiot!" he yelled at the television as Ojo stepped into the office. "Buy a vowel!"

"Sorry to interrupt," Ojo told him. The man slowly lifted the bowl from his lap as Ojo walked toward the desk. "But it seems you've got a package for me," he added, holding up the notice.

"Let me see now," Tate mumbled, grabbing the paper from Ojo's hand. "Oh, yeah. Small package from Tennessee," he said, bending to look for it behind the desk. "I know it's here someplace."

"What about that over there?" Ojo suggested, pointing a finger at a package near the telephone on the other side of the room.

"Huh?" Tate asked, banging his head on the edge of the desk as he stood up. "Damn! What's that now, boy?"

"Over there," Ojo pointed again.

"Oh, yeah," Tate said. "Now I remember puttin' it there." He grabbed the package and manipulated it in his hands as if he were inspecting it. "There y'are," he said and handed it to Ojo. "Straight from New York. Ain't that right like I said?"

"Sure is." Ojo thanked the man and left the office with the package under his arm. Derek and the others had already gone into the room. The door was left ajar. Ojo could hear Tucker's loud voice as he entered the room.

"… so this, *men*, and I use the term loosely," Tucker said in a kidding tone as he pulled what looked like an Etch-a-Sketch from the large shoulder bag he had dragged into the room and thrown onto one of the beds, "is how we're gonna nail these bastards."

He propped the grey board up against the side of the television on the bureau. With the tip of a clear plastic rod he began drawing as Ojo quietly closed the door and took a seat on the edge of the bed where Goose sat.

Derek glanced at the package under Ojo's arm and smiled.

"*This*," Tucker went on, pointing to the octagon he had drawn in the center of the board, "is the installation. And *this*," he said, drawing a box around it and pointing to several other shapes he had scribbled along the perimeter of the sloppy picture, "is the electrified fence, the guard's booth, and the only path leading in." He continued to draw as he spoke. "Two of us are over here by the booth and the other two are behind this group of trees on the diamond-shaped cliff about eight hundred meters due south of the main entrance."

"How do you know so much about the layout of the facility?" Derek cut in.

"Where do you think Goose and I were this morning? Wackin' off? Uh, uh. We were scoping the place out. If we're gonna do this, we're gonna do it right," Tucker replied.

Ojo and Derek exchanged a smile.

"We hear you," Ojo said. "Loud and clear."

"So which of us are goin' in?" Goose asked.

"One of us and one of them," Tucker told him.

"I don't think so," Derek said.

"How's that now?" Tucker asked.

"I don't think so," Derek repeated. "I *have* to go in since I'm the only one who's already been inside. I already have a sense of the layout and how to get around. I've already been to Sector 13. I even planted a goddamn transmitter there."

"Fine," Goose said. "So it'll be you and one of us."

"Let's think about this for a second," Ojo said. "The two of you may have more experience than—"

"A fuck of a lot more experience," Tucker interrupted.

"Granted," Ojo agreed. "But the two of you are a team. A solid team. And the two of us are a team. Do you think now's the time to start experimenting with new combos?"

Nothing was said for a moment. Ojo had a good point there.

"He's right," Goose said after a long pause.

Tucker nodded. "Then that puts the two of you over here," he said, drawing an 'x' beside the guard's booth, "and the two of us right here," he added, tapping the plastic rod against the board where he had drawn a diamond to represent the cliff. "Agreed?"

"Agreed," Ojo and Derek replied.

Tucker turned toward Goose. "Agreed?"

He nodded. "Agreed."

"Good," Tucker said and then shook the board a couple of times. The picture disappeared.

"Pretty sophisticated apparatus you've got there," Ojo teased him.

"If I shake you like that will your ass turn white?" Tucker snapped and the four of them laughed loudly.

He propped the board against the television again and quickly drew another picture.

"This is the roof," Tucker said. He drew a triangle on two diagonal corners of the board. "Each of these is a chopper," he said, "and this over here," he went on, pointing to a square in another corner, "is a goddamn missile launch pad."

"*Two* choppers?" Ojo asked. "What about the one that crashed?"

"Forget about the one that crashed," Goose told him. "There were two up there this morning."

"This is fuckin' NEXUS we're dealing with. C'mon," Tucker told him. "Did you think you blew away half of their arsenal by downing that chopper?"

Ojo didn't answer.

"Anyway," Tucker said, "let's just keep these toys up here in the back of our minds. It can get dangerous if we forget they're there. As you already discovered."

"Okay, now how are the two of you gonna get back in there? Do you have a plan?" Goose asked.

"That's all taken care of," Ojo replied.

Derek opened his attaché case and withdrew the

receiver panel that Ojo had managed to hold onto when he was thrown from the car. He pressed a button on the side of the receiver.

"*Send Renker and Smythe to the Space-1 Heliport and get that goddamn chopper over there!*" an angry voice shot into the room.

"What the hell is that?" Goose yelled.

"*That* is Hawkins," Derek coolly replied. "I bugged that bastard's pager. What you just heard is a recording of his voice from yesterday."

"What of it?" Tucker asked. "How does that help us?"

"I've also got his pager frequency," Derek explained, "and can intercept his pages whenever I want."

"Like when that brain-dead guard checks where you're goin'?" Tucker asked, catching on quickly.

Derek grinned. "You got it."

"As they say back home," Ojo commented, "we is *in!*"

"Okay," Tucker said. "From there we play it by ear. You watch your asses but at the first sign of trouble we're comin' in. No heroes, you got that?"

Ojo and Derek nodded in agreement.

"How will the two of you be getting in?" Ojo asked.

"Special invitation," Tucker said and grinned.

"How's that now?" Derek asked.

"Between *this*," Goose replied, pulling a thin leather

wallet from his pocket and unfolding it to reveal a gold badge and FBI identification, "and *this*," he added, pulling an Uzi submachine gun from inside his jacket, "Tucker and I are invited just about everywhere." They laughed loudly. "Wouldn't you agree?" Goose asked his partner.

"No, actually, I'd say we *are* invited *everywhere*."

Ojo and Derek exchanged a curious glance.

"Since when do FBI agents carry Uzis?" Derek questioned with a shade of skepticism in his voice.

Silence suddenly filled the small room.

"We don't work for the FBI," Tucker quietly said.

A nervous look filled Ojo's eyes.

"We work for another Agency," Tucker said with a mischievous grin. "But it's gotten some bad press recently so we use the FBI as a cover."

Derek stared at him with questioning eyes.

"I don't know why but people get real uptight when the Central Intelligence Agency starts investigating things. Their sphincters tighten right up," he said as he held a closed fist in the air and laughed.

"The CIA?" Ojo asked with relief in his voice. "You fuckers work for the *CIA?*"

"Yeah," Goose replied. "You didn't start thinkin' we worked for, say, *NEXUS*, did you?"

"Oh, uh, no, no, of course not," Ojo replied. But it did cross his mind.

The image of Elmer van Husted flashed in Derek's mind. And the conversation he had with Tomkin. Did Goose and Tucker *know* him? Did they *work* with him?

"Really?" Tucker asked him. "Then why'd the two of you just shit your pants?"

The four of them shared another loud laugh.

Of course, Derek had reason to be concerned. He told them about van Husted. And the role he played in his father's crash. He told them all of it. They had never heard of van Husted.

"It's a *big* organization," Tucker told him. "'Elmer van Husted' could just be his own cover. For all practical purposes, high-level operatives are *invisible. Untraceable.* That's what keeps them—*us*—alive."

"Send us that thermalyzed image and we'll look into it," Goose offered.

"Will do," Derek told him.

"But it will almost certainly be a dead end," Goose added. "So what's in the box?" he asked Ojo.

"Yeah," Tucker joined in. "You gonna show us or trade it for what's behind the fuckin' curtain?"

Ojo looked at Derek and grinned. He unzipped the duffel bag beside the bed and from it removed a small monitor.

"C'mon," he said. "I'll show you."

Ojo held the monitor with one hand and steadied the box under his arm as he opened the door and stepped out of the motel room. The others followed him.

He walked past several of the rooms and stopped in front of one particular door. A plaque marked 'SEVEN' hung loosely on that door. Derek smiled. He knew what Ojo was up to.

Ojo handed the monitor to Derek and lifted the cover off the box. A piece of paper lay on top. 'KICK SOME ASS, PARDNERS!' it read. It was signed, 'ARTI'.

A small titanium case sat beneath the paper. The *Thermalyzer*. Sort of. It was Arti's *new and improved* salvaged version of the Thermalyzer. There was no viewer arm. In its place was a short platinum rod. An antenna. A small metal panel with several controls was also in the box. Ojo put his ear to the door. He heard nothing. He tapped on the thin wood. There was no response. He turned the knob and the door opened.

"What the hell are—" Tucker started.

"Just watch," Ojo told him.

He took the Thermalyzer from the box, held it just inside the door and pointed it toward the bed. He pressed a key on the panel that activated the device. He pressed another key that captured the area and sent a thermalyzed image to the monitor. Derek turned the monitor on and they watched the screen from outside the room as Ojo closed the door and placed the Thermalyzer back in the box.

"What d'ya think?" Ojo asked as a red hue coated the screen and multitudes of tiny black and grey dots organized and formed an unmistakable image.

"I thought no one was in there!" Goose jumped with excitement as his eyes remained fixed on the screen.

There, in shades of grey beneath a red hue, was the image of a young man, the same one Ojo and Derek had seen rushing out of the motel office with his girlfriend a couple of nights ago, stretched across the bed. The face of the young woman was completely buried between his legs.

"No one is."

CHAPTER TWENTY-EIGHT

The people who are crazy enough to think they can
change the world are the ones who do.

Steve Jobs

"Kinda like old times, huh, fellas?" Goose's sarcastic voice flowed through the microtransceivers. The loud sound of laughter followed.

Ojo turned off the main road and onto the path that led to the massive entrance gate and the guard's booth beside it. With one hand on the wheel and the other adjusting the small transmitter in his ear, he glanced at Derek. A wide smile covered his face as Derek twirled a few strands of the long blonde wig he was wearing with an unsure finger and nervously stared at his reflection in the mirror on the overhead visor.

Rich black mascara highlighted his eyelashes while a soft shade of emerald coated his eyelids. A delicate rose-colored powder brought definition to his cheekbones while a deep red tone glistened on his lips. Small pearls dangled from his lobes, gently obscured by the strawberry curls that flowed freely in front of one shoulder and behind the other and down the back of his peach sundress. God, he was beautiful.

"Not exactly!" Derek snapped, angrily flipping the visor up against the roof with a quick shake of his wrist. "I don't do pumps."

"Okay, okay," Ojo said, checking the contents in the pocket of the long white lab coat he was wearing as his laughter subsided, "ready aaaand action."

Derek held what looked like a plastic cassette box in his palm as Ojo drove up to the booth. Within that box sat the Jennon TZ-3 Signal Relay.

"Good morning," a young officer greeted them.

"Morning, officer," Ojo replied. "I'm Dr. Logan. I'm with Dr. Constance Lingus. We're here to see Lieutenant Hawkins," he told the officer as Derek casually opened the small box.

The officer bent down to look in the car. "Morning, ma'am."

Derek waved politely and smiled in a lame kind of way.

The officer stepped back into the booth and ran a finger along a list of some sort. "Sorry," he said, "he's not in the Facility."

"There must be a mistake," Ojo said. "We're supposed to meet with him at 1500 hours," he added, glancing at his watch, "which is ten minutes from now."

"Sorry, but he's still logged out."

"Then would you please page him?"

"Sure, but you'll see it's useless," the officer insisted. "He's not on the premises."

Derek lifted the lid of the box and glanced at the small piece of paper he taped to it. Several letters and numbers were scribbled on it. *FX-8796537637-bz.* It was the frequency of Hawkins' pager. He quickly struck a number of buttons on the tiny keyboard in the box and entered the code. A blue light flashed.

The officer lifted the receiver of the phone on the wall inside the booth and punched in a paging code.

In a moment, the blue light on the Signal Relay stopped flashing. It glowed steadily while 'SEC*GATE' appeared on its tiny screen as it intercepted the officer's page. Derek pressed the SEND button and the blue light flashed again.

The officer's phone rang. He lifted the receiver while Derek expertly fingered the keyboard.

"Yes, what is it?" Hawkins' voice flowed through the receiver.

The officer responded, surprised by the quick call back. "Good morning, Lieutenant," he said. "This is Officer Robinson. Were you expecting anyone this morning, sir?"

Derek worked at the keyboard, quickly punching groups of keys to produce sentences, which were then transmitted by the Signal Relay to the officer's phone—*in Hawkins' voice.* "Yes, I'm expecting Dr. Logan and Dr. Lingus."

"Well, they're here, sir."

"Very good," Hawkins' voice shot into the officer's ear. "Have them meet me in the Atrium."

"Will do, sir," the officer said. "Oh, sir?" he asked before hanging up.

"What is it?"

"Is there a reason why you're not logged in?"

Derek paused for a moment. He pensively glanced at Ojo.

"Sir, are you still there?"

Ojo spun a finger in small circles and Derek understood. He quickly struck several keys and the officer heard Hawkins' voice another time.

"My mistake, Robinson. I came in by chopper at 0900 hours. I forgot to log in."

"No problem, sir. Sorry to question you."

"Keep up the good work, Robinson."

Derek pressed the SEND button another time and the line disconnected.

"Thank you, sir," Robinson spoke into the dead receiver with a proud grin on his face. He activated the gate and it slowly swung open. "You were right, Dr. Logan," he told Ojo. "Sorry for the confusion. Lieutenant Hawkins will meet you in the Atrium."

In a moment the gate disappeared into the ground.

"You have a good one now," Ojo told the officer and drove past the booth and along the path that led to the Facility's main entrance.

"Not bad," Tucker said. "Not bad at all."

"Like I said before," Ojo remarked loudly with a contrived southern accent, "we is *in*!"

* * *

"Sector 13," Derek told the computerized conductor on the floatron, then removed his disc from the transparent compartment and took a seat beside Ojo. He led Ojo from the Atrium to the floatron tunnels as if he worked there. They passed a few men in Air Force uniforms and a few others in white coats along the way but no one stopped them. The trick, as Derek would often say, is to look like you belong. Look like you know where you're going. And no one will question it. And no one did.

The floatron hummed for a brief moment as the cabin filled with the purplish mist. Then it shot into the maze of interconnecting tunnels. Ojo watched with sheer amazement through a porthole as the vehicle soared across the installation. He steadied the silver attaché case on the floor between his feet while Derek held a large white purse on his lap.

They exchanged a silent smile. Derek held his hand out. Ojo grabbed it.

"This one's for Chrissy," Ojo said.

Derek nodded. Ojo's comment brought a warm smile to his face.

"Yeah," Derek replied.

A disturbingly loud crashing noise suddenly shot through their microtransceivers.

"What the fuck was that?" Ojo asked.

"You imbecile!" a husky voice yelled. "You incompetent imbecile!"

"Dynamic duo, you still there?" Derek called to his undercover team on the cliff.

"Still here," Goose responded.

"Do you realize what you have done?!" the berating voice continued.

There was no reply.

"How many more embryos will you let die, Okami?! How many more?!"

"I am terribly sorry, Dr. Erikson. It was not Okami's error," a quiet voice with a Japanese accent spoke up.

"Then whose, Koshi?! *Whose?!*" another voice angrily questioned.

"Mine, Dr. Flint," Dr. Takagawa responded. "It was mine."

"This is inexcusable, Koshi!" the husky voice insisted. "I'm sick and tired of you constantly covering for your incompetent assistant! Now just get out of my operating room! Both of you! And take that damn life support system with you!" he continued yelling. "Whatever's left of it. Just pick up the pieces and get it out of here! It's worthless now!"

Ojo and Derek looked at each other for a moment as they listened to the uproar.

"They're in Sector 13," Derek said.

"How d'ya know?" Goose asked.

"Where the hell is Hawkins?! Schmit, would you bring us another staged embryo from the Epsilon storage chamber?"

"Certainly, Dr. Flint."

"*Now!*" Dr. Erikson screamed. "Our patient is waiting. Move it!"

"The Delta Ray images I showed you," Derek told them.

"What about 'em?" Tucker asked.

"I was standing right outside Sector 13 when I took them," Derek said. "That's where the OR is."

"Hans, if this project is to succeed this cannot happen again with Okami," Dr. Erikson remarked. "Please see to it that it does not."

"Cecil will see to it," Hans responded.

After a few moments all became silent while the men awaited Schmit's return before proceeding with the implantation.

"Talk about perfect timing," Ojo commented.

"Yeah, but I'm not sure if that's good or bad," Derek replied as the floatron entered a pressurized chute.

"TSI Facility," the computerized voice announced. "Transporting to Sector 13."

Derek looked Ojo in the eye. "In case we separate and you get into trouble," he told him, placing a blue and white disc in Ojo's palm, "use it just as I did. And don't look back."

The floatron glided into another tunnel beside a large landing then came to a stop. The purplish mist cleared and the doors slid open.

"Sector 13," the sharp metallic voice announced. "Atmosphere controlled."

"We're not gonna get into any trouble," Ojo said with a stern voice, "but we're sure as hell gonna cause some."

After a silent moment they heard Goose's voice through the microtransceivers. "Remember, fellas," he reminded them, "no heros."

Ojo placed the disc in his pocket and lifted the attaché case from the floor while Derek smoothed the folds of his dress with the side of his hand. Together they stepped off the floatron, the white purse gripped tightly under Derek's arm as he made a quick adjustment to reposition his bra.

"There's another thing I may not have told you recently," Ojo said.

"What's that?"

"*You* look *mah*-velous."

* * *

"I still don't know what the hell happened yesterday," a voice familiar to Derek commented. "But three men died."

There was a brief pause.

"It's Hawkins," Derek whispered.

He and Ojo stood several feet behind a group of men as they held onto the black handles while the hoverway sped past several stations on the octagonal level. Two of the men wore long white coats. Another two wore blue Air Force uniforms.

"Right now?" the scratchy voice asked. "I'm on Route 41."

There was another pause.

"I can't. I'm already late for an important conference."

A few moments lapsed before the voice continued.

"You really try my patience, Selena. Why do you insist on defending this friend of yours when you don't know him from Adam?!"

She had no response. After another pause, the loud clicking sound of Hawkins' receiver slamming against its base to disconnect the line was heard.

"Damn," Ojo said. "That was intense. I feel bad for Selena."

"What'd I tell you?" Derek remarked.

"Good ear," he heard Tucker respond. "Now just keep 'em on the sides of your head, you hear me?"

"I definitely hear you," Derek replied as the section of hoverway on which the group of men were standing broke off at a sharp angle and shot into a narrow passageway.

After another moment, the section on which Ojo and Derek stood broke off from the rest of the hoverway and followed a course that bent around a number of angling walls and flowed past several research stations before coming to a stop.

"Sector 13," a robotic voice announced.

Ojo and Derek stepped off the hoverway and briskly walked past the entrance to the operating facility as they heard the sound of clicking footsteps against the hard floor.

"C'mon," Derek said and grabbed the sleeve of Ojo's shirt. "Over there."

They jogged toward a curved section of wall adjacent to Sector 13. It was the cove where Derek had spent several breathless moments during his last trip to the installation.

"Oh, fuck," he mumbled under his breath as the footsteps grew louder and his anxious eyes fell upon the huge liquid nitrogen chamber that now sat within the concave section of the wall.

"There," Ojo said and threw a finger toward a triangular entrance about thirty feet away. An illuminated sign hung on the wall beside it.

'TSI CRYOGENIC STORAGE', it read.

Derek noisily scuffled across the tile floor as he followed Ojo through the angling corridor. He reached into one of the dress's pockets for a disc, but Ojo already stood holding his in the air.

As the footsteps approached that final turn in the corridor where they were standing, a burst of bright blue light shot from a small port above the triangular entryway, striking Ojo's hand before fading and deactivating the laser field. They hurried through the entryway only instants before two guards and a small Japanese woman in a long white lab coat strode past it.

The room was cold and dark. In an instant its heat-sensitive lighting system was automatically activated. The pentagonally-shaped room was filled with a soft kind of light that flowed from countless filaments that ran the length of the chrome ceiling.

In fact, except for the floor, which was covered with onyx tiles, the entire room was chrome. Huge freezers lined two of the room's walls, large chrome cabinets stood fixed against two others, and a massive liquid nitrogen chamber, similar to the one in the corridor, covered the fifth. In the center of the room sat a long narrow workbench.

A small object rested atop that workbench. It was a specimen jar. Derek walked over to the bench and picked the jar up. He held it up and turned it in his hand, examining it as Ojo looked on.

"No question about what's going on here," Derek commented.

Ojo took the jar from his hand and, with a disgusted look on his face, returned it and the tiny fetus it contained to the surface of the workbench.

"Check those cabinets," he told Derek. "I'll work on the freezers."

Combination locks secured the doors of the cabinets. From his purse Derek removed two silver discs. He placed one directly above one of the locks and one to the left of it. As he turned the large combination dial the tumblers could be heard as they fell in place. 14-25-26-31 click, 30-26-21-17 click, 20-24-29-31 click, 29-27-26-21 click. As the final tumbler fell into place, the sound of a shifting bolt was heard as the lock opened. Derek pulled the handle beside the dial but nothing happened.

"Fuck this," he said and reached into his purse another time.

He withdrew the triangular laser device and aimed it at the lock. A crisp red beam of light flew from the contraption in his hand and struck the disc above the dial. A moment later, the entire mechanism of the lock, including its dial and handle, fell right out of the cabinet's door, landing hard on the floor before Derek could catch it.

"God, *no!*" Ojo yelled with disgust in his voice, pulling one of the large freezer doors open as a rush of frigid air drenched with the stinging odor of formaldehyde struck his face.

* * *

A silver Mercedes hastily drove up the pathway that led to the guard's booth beside the formidable electrified gate. Lieutenant Hawkins anxiously glanced at his watch when the young officer standing in the booth with a clipboard in his hand turned and faced him with a look of utter surprise on his face.

"What's the matter, Robinson?" Hawkins asked the guard. "You look like you've just seen a ghost."

"Not exactly, Lieutenant, but we may have a problem," Robinson replied with a nervous rattle in his voice.

"What sort of problem?"

"Sir, did I speak with you on the phone maybe thirty or forty minutes ago?"

"No," Hawkins flatly answered. "Why do you ask?"

"Are you sure, sir?"

"Of course, I'm sure, you idiot!" Hawkins snapped. "Why do you ask?!"

"Then you didn't fly in by chopper this morning?"

"What the hell's goin' on here, Robinson?! I haven't been on the grounds since last night!"

"Five, four, three, two, one," Goose said, pointing a finger at the receiver on the dashboard as he and Tucker listened to Hawkins' conversation with the guard, courtesy of the transmitter Derek had planted on his pager. "The shit's gonna hit the fan right about now."

"Then we've got a problem, sir," Robinson said. "A real problem."

"What is it, Robinson?! What kind of problem?!" Hawkins yelled again.

"We've had a breach, sir. Two intruders have penetrated the Facility," Robinson nervously told him.

"*What?!*"

"What should we do, sir?"

A loud click echoed as Tucker slammed a cartridge into the load shaft of the .357 Magnum in his hand. He held the heavy gun up in the air, his hand tightly gripping its handle, his fingers snugging against its grooves while he eyed its long barrel.

Goose stared at the Uzi which lay on his lap. It was the most powerful handheld submachine gun in the world. He ran a finger over its wide nozzle, then along its automatic chamber and onto the safety latch that hung arched over the weapon's slightly curved trigger. With the slightest shift of his finger, he unlocked the protective latch and removed the disarming pin.

Together Tucker and Goose listened while Robinson explained the interesting conversation he had had with 'Drs. Logan and Lingus'. And, of course, with the 'Lieutenant' himself.

"You *idiot!*" Hawkins yelled at the guard as the gate disappeared into the ground. "*Now* you're asking me what you should do?! *Now* you're asking me?!"

"Uh, yes sir, I am," Robinson timidly replied with a pathetic tone to his voice.

"Just page Flint and Erikson, for God's sake! And tell them what the fuck's goin' on, would you?!" Hawkins angrily yelled at the officer. "Whoever the intruders are, I want them! Dead or alive!"

A loud screeching noise and a small cloud of grey smoke filled the air as the Mercedes' wheels spun in place for an instant before the car was propelled along the road that led to the Facility's glass entrance.

"What d'ya think?" Tucker asked, returning the .357 Magnum to its holster under his jacket.

Goose placed the Uzi in the small space between the driver's seat and the gear shift console and then started the car. He looked Tucker in the face. "I think that's our cue."

* * *

Derek stood beside Ojo. Together they stood in front of the massive freezer. The pile of papers in Derek's hands, one of the many stacks of documents and protocols stored within the large metal cabinet he had unlocked, fell to the floor. He paid no attention.

The freezer's doors lay wide open. Twelve or thirteen steel plate shelves lined the ten-foot freezer. Each of them was four or five feet deep.

Ojo and Derek stared with horror at the freezer's contents. Dozens and dozens of specimen jars stood in neat rows on each of its shelves. Ojo carefully lifted a jar from one of the shelves and removed it from the freezer.

Sorrow filled their eyes as they stared at the small twisted specimen within the jar. It was a fetus. Its skull, despite severe distortion, remained distinct in shape. Its facial features, marred in their development, remained characteristic. Each of its hands and feet, despite crippling bony deformities, still presented evidence of five small webbed digits. Thin membranous structures barely veiled its small functionless heart. And the formaldehyde in which it bathed added a leathery grey appearance to its outermost layers. Yet there could still be no mistaking it. It was a *human* fetus.

Derek looked at Ojo, then took the jar from his hand as his eyes fell upon a label that had been fixed to its lid. The label contained several lines of data:

DATE:	**3 November 1991**
SOURCE:	**Samantha Gibbons**
CLONE CODE:	**RX-3yir-xx5022**
GENE CODE:	**Kryptonic**
GESTATIONAL AGE:	**22 weeks**
INVESTIGATOR:	**Dr. Hans Flint**
HARVEST/IMPLANT:	**Dr. Avery Atkin**

"1991!" Ojo muttered.

"How long have they been doing this?!" Derek questioned.

He replaced the jar on the shelf and reached between several others on one of the higher shelves to retrieve another. The jar was covered with a thick layer of frost. Ojo rubbed several fingers over the cold glass until the specimen within it could be seen.

"Oh, God," Derek mumbled.

He looked away and closed his eyes tightly for a moment. Then he looked back at the grotesque specimen within the jar. He and Ojo stared at it in silence. In disbelief.

A small eye stared back at them through the glass. A sharpened fragment of tooth lay embedded within its pupil. Thick folds of skin surrounded the eye and small clumps of thin hair sprung from its edges. Several narrow pieces of bone connected that skin to a fleshy mass of tissue, which in some ways resembled a shrunken brain.

From that mass of tissue arose a number of structures reminiscent of intestinal loops and internal organs encaged by a cluster of small metatarsal bones. One additional structure seemed adherent to a group of stringy blood vessels. It was a penis.

On the verge of being nauseated, Ojo and Derek exchanged a glance. They were sure it was another fetus. Certainly mammalian. Probably a monkey, they thought. But there was no way to tell.

Derek's eyes fell upon the lid of the jar. He brushed away the heavy layer of frost with an anxious finger. Beneath it was another label. He stared at it with disgust and anger.

DATE:	**28 June 1989**
SOURCE:	**Pamela James**
CLONE CODE:	**WRZ-173646-sap**
GENE CODE:	**Osteonic**
GESTATIONAL AGE:	**14 weeks**
INVESTIGATOR:	**Dr. Hans Flint**
HARVEST/IMPLANT:	**Dr. Chris Erikson**

Their eyes were fixed on the date. 1989. *1989.* Then the source. Pamela James. *Pamela James.* The fetus was *human!*

"I don't believe it," Ojo said. "These fuckers have been experimenting with human fetuses for more than ten years!" He looked at Derek with despair in his eyes. *"Ten years!* How could no one have known about this?!"

Derek returned the specimen to the shelf. His eyes darted among the countless jars within that one freezer. He quickly rubbed his fingers over as many of the lids as he could, brushing away the frost that had collected on each of them as he eyed the label beneath it.

"They're human," he said in a quiet sorrowful voice. "*All* of them are human."

"Enough!" Ojo said and slammed the freezer doors shut. "We've seen enough!"

Derek's eyes fell upon the floor and the papers that had spread across it. He thought about the pain and agony they must have caused. All those innocent women. All those innocent babies. All the pain. All the agony.

"You hear that?" Ojo whispered.

Derek shook his head.

A moment later, he too heard a faint clicking sound. It was followed by a scratchy dragging noise. The sounds grew louder. They approached the storage room. First the clicking sound. Then the dragging sound. They knew the sounds. It was Cecil. The sounds grew still louder. The clicking sound. And the dragging noise. Until they stopped. But only for a moment. They resumed as the killer stepped into the room.

For a few moments he stood behind the triangular slab of stone several feet from the entryway. He stood there silently. He stood there motionlessly. Not a sound could be heard. Not a thing moved. Cecil's heart beat rapidly as he steadied his gun at eye level with both hands.

Suddenly, he stepped away from behind the triangular stone. His eyes trapped Ojo and Derek as they stood in front of the freezer. With surprisingly remarkable agility, the killer held his cocked gun with extended arms and fired one deafening shot after another until he emptied its chambers into his victims.

CHAPTER TWENTY-NINE

But it does move!

Galileo Galilei

As the massive plate of black glass quickly lowered, sealing the installation's entrance behind the silver Mercedes, an unmarked black sedan drove up to the guard's booth.

Robinson stood within it, the phone's receiver to his ear, while he nervously jotted several notes on the paper attached to his clipboard.

"Okay, sir, okay," he spoke into the receiver, "I'll take care of it."

There was a brief pause.

"You can count on me, sir," Robinson nervously said before returning the receiver to its hook.

He scribbled a few more notes and then looked up from his clipboard.

"We've got an appointment with Dr. Flint," Goose told the officer.

"Dr. Flint isn't seeing anyone this afternoon," Robinson replied.

"How can that be?" Tucker leaned forward and mumbled.

Robinson stepped out of the booth and walked over to the car. He rested a hand on its roof as he bent down to look inside. "One more time," he told Tucker. "I didn't get you."

"That may very well be," Goose told the officer, lifting the Uzi from its nest between the seat and console as he grabbed the man's collar with a tight fist and pulled him toward the gun's nozzle. "But I've got you."

"What the hell are you doing?!" Robinson asked, far more nervous now than he had been a moment earlier. "What do you want?!"

"I told you," Goose calmly said as Tucker jumped out of the car and raced to the booth on the other side, "we've got an appointment with Dr. Flint."

"But he's not available," Robinson said as Goose pressed the mouth of the Uzi into his neck.

Tucker pulled the revolver from the officer's holster and then ran into the booth. He turned a small lever on the wall inside it and the entrance gate began to pivot.

"That bastard is gonna see us," Goose told him. "I assure you. 'Cause you're gonna see to that."

"I'm telling you," Robinson pleaded, "there's no way. I can't."

"You can," Goose told him as his voice took on a firmer tone. "And you can bet your ass you will. As our personal escort."

"But I can't! You, you don't understand! He's, he's—"

"In *surgery?*" Goose sarcastically asked him.

Robinson nodded with terrified eyes.

Tucker grabbed his collar from behind and put the tip of the Magnum's barrel in his ear as Goose pushed the car door open.

"Let me put it another way," Goose suggested, jabbing Robinson's neck another time with the submachine gun's nozzle as Tucker forced him into the car. "Ever wonder what it feels like to have two hundred bullets rip through layer after layer of flesh until your neck is torn into shreds of dead meat and your head finally tips forward and falls right off your shoulders and into your lap?"

Tucker slammed the car door as the large gate disappeared into the ground. He took off in an instant, racing toward the glass entrance at the path's end.

"Oooh," he said, empathetically rubbing a hand over his throat. A sick smile distorted his face as he turned toward Robinson. "I hate when that happens."

* * *

A puzzled look distorted Cecil's ugly face. The loud deafening echo of the gunfire bounced off the room's chrome walls with an eerie and frightfully high-pitched sound. There was no blood splattered across the freezer's doors. No guts in a pile on the floor.

Ojo and Derek remained standing in front of the freezer. Neither appeared hurt. Or even touched.

The killer held his gun at eye level another time and pulled as hard as he could on its trigger. He pulled and pulled and pulled. The gun clicked several times but it did not fire. Its chambers had already been emptied.

He stared long and hard at Ojo and Derek. Then their images suddenly began to fade … and fade … and fade. In a moment, they were gone.

"Over here, you son-of-a-bitch!"

Cecil turned quickly and found Ojo standing right behind him.

"Remember me?!" Ojo yelled, pulling back on his arm as he let his fist fly fast across the killer's face.

Cecil clumsily stumbled and fell back against one of the walls. A loud ping rang out as his head hit the chrome. Ojo grabbed his shirt and pulled him off the wall. He stared hard into the killer's eyes. A thick red streak oozed from his nose. His mouth was all bloodied.

"And that night in the park?!" Ojo questioned him through clenched teeth as his grip tightened on Cecil's collar and he slammed his head hard into the wall.

Derek stood beside Ojo, disgusted at the sight of the killer's badly scarred face. Ojo pulled him from the wall another time. Streaks of blood painted the wall where Cecil's head had hit it.

"When *you* killed Barnes!" Ojo screamed in his face. "Then set *me* up! You *son-of-a-bitch!*"

"And don't forget about Arti," Derek cut in.

Ojo lost control. He threw Cecil against the side of the freezer and struck him square in the face again and again until his fist was covered with the killer's blood. Cecil limply sank to the floor. Ojo stared at him as he lay there, his face covered with blood, his lips cut up and swollen, and his nose bent to the side. Ojo bent down and grabbed Cecil's collar again. He was about to connect with his face another time when Derek pulled him back.

"Save your energy," he told Ojo. "He's already out."

"Maybe," Ojo responded, "but I'm gonna trash him for the Vette also."

"C'mon. He's not worth it."

Ojo let go of Cecil's shirt and pushed him back onto the floor. His head clunked loudly against the side of the freezer.

"Fine," Ojo said, rinsing his hands in the sink that was built into the workbench in the center of the room.

Derek walked to the other side of the room and lifted the Image Displacer from its position atop the attaché case that had been carefully set on a ledge above the nitrogen chamber. He kneeled on the floor as he rearranged several of the objects within the case, then returned the device to its compartment as his eyes darted beneath the sink where Ojo stood and across the room.

"Look out!" Derek suddenly screamed as the killer held out a small gun.

A beam of fiery red light shot from the small triangular weapon in Derek's hand, gliding under that sink and between Ojo's legs before striking Cecil's chest. He slumped back against the wall as his limp finger unconsciously pulled back on the gun's trigger. A loud noise echoed as the weapon fired. A shrill ping rang out as the bullet struck the lid of the small specimen jar, which sat atop the workbench eight or ten inches from where Ojo stood, barely missing him. Before he could catch the jar, it flipped on its side and rolled off the edge of the table, crashing against the hard floor as fragments of glass raced in all directions while the tiny human fetus it contained lay pathetically abandoned in a puddle of formaldehyde.

Ojo and Derek stared at the fetus. Ojo shook his head with repulsion. Derek closed his eyes and rubbed them hard. But it would still be there when he opened them. He knew that. But he rubbed them anyway.

* * *

Within kicking distance of the hoverway's path, behind a cluster of small steel drums and inactive missile shells that sat in a cove adjacent to the WATER Facility, there lay the form of a man with his mouth sufficiently gagged and hands and feet all tightly bound together. That man was Robinson.

The handkerchief that had been stuffed in his mouth pressed tightly against its corners, permitting only garbled utterances that were just about inaudible. He tried to stand but could not. He would roll from his back onto his side, fall over onto the tips of his hands and feet, then drop backward again. And when he rolled onto his lower back, as he did with each attempt, knifelike tearing pain raced through him. It was there that he had made hard contact with the tip of one of the missile shells when Goose and Tucker had tossed him off the moving hoverway.

* * *

A loud beeping sound flowed from the microtransceivers. Goose and Tucker exchanged a silent glance, gripping the handles tightly while the hoverway soared through a number of winding passages.

"We're ready to proceed," a husky voice remarked.

"Very well, Dr. Erikson," a young woman responded.

"Give me a minute, would you?" commented a voice with a heavy German accent.

Nothing was said for a moment.

"You guys still alive?" Tucker asked.

"Still alive," they heard Derek reply.

"What is it now?" the accented voice questioned.

A long pause followed.

"If I must, I must! I'll be right there!"

"What is it, Hans?" Dr. Erikson asked.

"Another problem at Space-3!" Dr. Flint replied.

"What's going on here lately? It's one foul up after another," Dr. Erikson commented.

"Plus one of the guards has been abducted!" Dr. Flint told him.

"*Abducted?!*"

"Abducted! Am I not speaking English?!" Dr. Flint yelled. "Hawkins can fill in for me while I see what this is about. There's too much to be done today. We must keep going."

"You're right about that," Dr. Erikson agreed. "After we're done with McMurphy, we've still gotta do Stevenson and Westcott."

"Those bastards!" Derek's furious voice shot through the microtransceivers.

"Those names mean somethin' to you?" Tucker asked.

"Yes, they mean something!" Derek angrily replied.

"Those are the three women in the protocol we weren't able to get hold of," Ojo said.

"The only three that haven't been '*done*' yet!" Derek hammered. "Those motherfuckers!"

"Where are you?" Ojo asked.

"Who the fuck knows?" Goose replied. "We just passed a row of nitrogen tanks."

"Then you're right around the corner," Ojo told them.

In another moment the hoverway came to a halt just outside Sector 13. A tall man in scrubs angrily brushed past Goose and Tucker as they stepped off. They walked toward the triangular entryway several feet away as the man stepped onto the hoverway.

"Wait a second," Goose whispered and quickly turned to look over his shoulder. "Flintstone!" he called to the man as a section of the hoverway began to move.

Dr. Flint turned and grinned.

"That's him!" Ojo yelled as he and Derek jumped through the storage room's entrance when the hoverway sped by. "That's the *Nazi* motherfucker!"

"C'mon," Derek called to Tucker. "I think I know where he's heading."

"Fine," Goose said, pointing toward Ojo. "Then it's you and me, Buckwheat."

Derek activated the glowing sensor pad as Tucker stepped onto the hoverway behind him.

"Destination?" the computerized voice questioned.

"Space-3 Heliport."

* * *

"The patient's moving, dammit!" Dr. Erikson angrily yelled, throwing a sterile towel over the operative field. "Would you do something behind that drape, already?!" he told the anesthesiologist.

"Sorry," a young woman with a scratchy voice responded. "It'll be another minute," she added, quickly injecting half of a syringe of propofol into the patient's IV then adjusting the isoflurane and nitrous oxide valves on the anesthesia machine to titrate the gases.

A long pause followed. Derek and Tucker listened to the conversation as it flowed through the microtransceivers while the hoverway carried them through a busy concourse where a number of workers loaded steel cylinders onto triangular dollies.

"She's still light, for God's sake!" Dr. Erikson's impatient voice echoed in their ears.

There was another pause.

"How about now, Dr. Erikson?" the anesthesiologist nervously asked him a moment later.

"Fine," he replied. "That's better. Why don't you activate the life support system, Hawkins? Schmit can assist me over here."

"You boys gonna make an entrance soon, or what?" Tucker asked.

"Still workin' on it," Goose whispered in response. "We're in the outer portion of the operating facility. Puttin' on scrubs."

"*Scrubs?*" Tucker asked. "What the hell for?"

"Look," Goose told him, "you take care of Flintstone your way. Our boys in here," he went on, "their asses are all ours."

The hoverway slowed down slightly as it turned onto a curving path that spiraled quite a number of times before reaching the top and coming to a halt.

"Space-3 Heliport," the computerized voice announced.

Tucker and Derek quickly stepped from the hoverway and passed through a set of sliding glass doors that led to the roof of the installation.

"There he is!" Derek yelled, pointing a finger at the figure of a man running toward the black helicopter on the other side of the roof.

"Ready for a little action?" Tucker asked him with a fiendish grin on his face as he pulled the .357 Magnum from the holster under his jacket and affectionately raised the side of the barrel to his lips.

Derek removed the shiny triangular weapon from his pocket and displayed it in his palm for a moment before his hand closed tightly around it. "Let's nail that son-of-a-bitch!" he said with fire in his eyes.

"C'mon," Tucker said as they ran from the doors toward a large turbine near the roof's center.

Flint was about two hundred feet ahead of them. A pilot sat in the helicopter on the roof's far corner as he ran toward it. The copter's skids hovered about three feet above the landing pad as its propellers made a loud howling noise.

"Flintstone, you son-of-a-bitch!" Tucker called to him.

Flint turned for a quick second to look over his shoulder. He fired off several poorly-aimed rounds from the pistol in his hand and kept running.

Derek and Tucker threw themselves on the ground and rolled across the glass portion of the roof that covered the Atrium. They stared down at the nose of the Challenger as they rolled past it and the curious viewers within the Atrium.

Flint made it to the helicopter. He stepped up onto one of its skids and grabbed the handle alongside its doorless entry. He turned to look over his shoulder another time and discharged the gun's remaining bullets in the direction of his pursuants.

One of the bullets struck Derek's arm right below his shoulder. The triangular weapon fell from his hand as the impact of the shot knocked him to the ground.

"You alright?!" Tucker looked back and yelled to him over the noise of the chopper's propellers.

Derek nodded. "I'm fine!" he yelled. "Keep goin'! Just nail him!"

Tucker stood about fifty feet from the landing pad as the helicopter lifted straight up and then soared past them.

"Now we've got his ass," Tucker said with a hint of satisfaction in his voice as he held the Magnum high over his head with both hands and carefully aimed. "And now it's personal!"

Derek watched him and grinned. He definitely liked the way this man thought.

The helicopter rose about seventy feet, then made a wide turn and doubled back in an attempt to fly due West.

Tucker steadied his weapon and then smoothly pulled back on its tight trigger just once as the gun made a thunderous sound.

Derek watched in amazement as the bullet struck Flint's head. A burst of flesh and blood shot onto the chopper's windshield as his head exploded. Pieces of the dead surgeon's brain and skull flew out of the open chopper and glided back to the surface of the roof. In an attempt to guide the chopper in the opposite direction and lift it out of range, the pilot pulled back hard on the throttle. With one smooth move, the helicopter spun around as Flint's dead body rolled from its seat and fell toward the center of the roof. With a loud crash, the body shattered the glass that shielded the Atrium, falling through it and landing on the nose of the shuttle.

Tucker looked Derek in the eye as he rose to his feet, cradling his injured arm. A satisfied grin distorted his face as he mumbled several words in a quiet triumphant voice. "Yabba dabba doo."

* * *

A number of men in scrubs stood around the operating table, watching as Dr. Erikson prepared Karynne McMurphy for embryonic implantation. One of the men adjusted an overhead light while another held onto the curved handle of a retractor for Dr. Erikson.

Hawkins carefully removed a shiny black canister from the barrel-sized drum of liquid nitrogen that had been placed beside the anesthesiologist. Tiny fingers of frigid air bounced off the cylindrical life support system as he positioned it atop a small stand into which it fit snugly.

Two rows of yellow lights orbited around the top of the canister as a single red light flashed with a beeping tone in the center of the cylinder. Hawkins operated a control panel on the back of the canister and the yellow lights stopped revolving then faded. The red light, however, continued to flash.

With gentle and delicate movements, Hawkins unscrewed the top of the life support system as a rush of bluish mist flowed from the hollow container. The scrub nurse immediately double-gloved him at this point, then handed him a long curved clamp. He retrieved a metal disc from deep within the canister with it and carefully handed it to the nurse.

"Is the laser ready?" Dr. Erikson asked as two of the men in scrubs stepped closer to the table, one of them holding a stack of sterile blue towels in his hands.

The scrub nurse held out the thin silver instrument to which a coiled cord was attached and ran to the two monitors that sat atop a shelf suspended from the ceiling. She struck a small switch on the side of the instrument and a blue light pulsed up and down its length. "It's ready, doctor," she replied.

"Lambda setting," he said.

"Lambda setting," the scrub nurse repeated, handing the instrument to Dr. Erikson.

A hand suddenly jumped between the surgeon and the nurse, grabbing the laser and pulling it free of the cord. It was Ojo's hand.

"What the hell are you doing?!" Erikson screamed furiously.

Ojo threw the instrument across the room, shattering one of the cabinets' glass doors as he brought his fist hard across Erikson's jaw. The surgeon fell back against the wall beside the operating table.

"What the hell is going on here?!" Hawkins yelled loudly as he approached Ojo.

"I'm afraid this case has been canceled," Ojo calmly replied as Goose pulled his badge from the pocket of his green scrub shirt and pushed it in Hawkins' face.

"In fact, all of your cases have been canceled," Goose announced as Erikson eyed the scalpel that sat between a couple of instruments on the Mayo stand.

"Go ahead," Goose tempted him, dropping the towels in his hand to reveal the Uzi in his grip. "I've been waiting all day to use this."

No one moved for some time. Everyone just stood in silence. Erikson stared coldly at Goose with beaded eyes. Goose returned the affection as his fingers caressed the weapon's trigger. Suddenly, Erikson snatched the instrument from the stand and lunged toward him. The loud crackling sound of submachine gunfire echoed through the operating room as the scalpel fell from Erikson's dead hand.

CHAPTER THIRTY

They always say time changes things, but you
actually have to change them yourself.

Andy Warhol

APPROXIMATELY 6 MONTHS LATER

Strings of lights clung to the snow-covered branches of
the oaks that lined Columbus Circle, shining magically as
the setting sun's glow stretched across the darkening sky
on this crisp December afternoon. The snow continued
to fall, blanketing the chains of cars that lay parked up and
down both sides of the busy street. It also added a slippery
frost to the crowded sidewalks and caused a light glaze
over the numerous storefronts as throngs of pedestrians

cautiously stepped across them, many window-shopping.

Neither the coming of nightfall, the brutally frigid air, nor the impending blizzard could deter the expanding group of browsers and passersby that stood on Columbus and 59th, between the MoMa Design Store and Les Belles Femmes. The new Contraptions store had finally opened. The viewers enthusiastically gazed through the tinted storefront at the futuristic miniaturized toboggan course that occupied the window display. The twisting and turning transparent course with interconnecting chutes and tunnels passed over, around and through a number of geometrically-carved turquoise stones. The maze of NEXUS floatrons had definitely inspired the elaborate display.

The crowd stared with delight as several unusually-shaped red and black lucite objects soared within the chutes and tunnels. One of the objects was pyramidal. Another rhomboidal. A third tetrahedral. And a fourth octahedral. The objects spun on different axes as cushions of air lifted and rapidly propelled them through the interconnecting passages, their narrowing pin-like points and sleek razor-sharp edges gliding effortlessly as they rotated.

Most of the spectators desired entry to the popular store but the 'CLOSED TILL NEW YEAR'S DAY' sign that hung from the locked door prohibited it. Yet there were probably twice as many people already in the shop at that very moment. And with good reason.

A large area of the main floor had been cleared. Many

of the displays had been pushed against the surrounding walls, while others had been moved to the workshop upstairs or the basement below. A number of large spotlights had been set up along the perimeter of the store. One cameraman steadied his equipment against the railing of the spiral staircase. Another had attached his camera to a tripod that had been positioned directly in front of the cleared area where Arti and a middle-aged balding man stood, both in business suits.

An attractive woman with waist-length jet-black hair and a creamy olive complexion stood with a blowhorn dangling from her hand. The woman was Sasha. She raised the blowhorn to her lips with a sudden gesture. "Aaaaand *cut!*" her voice echoed through the room. "Let's do it again."

Ojo came up to her from behind. He brushed her hair aside and whispered in her ear. "I'm up for another round if you are."

"C'mon, darling," Sasha turned toward him and started laughing. "We need to wrap this shoot," she told him, eyeing her watch. It was almost 6 p.m.

"Okay, what d'ya want?" he asked her.

"Let's take it from Arti's first line," she said as a number of grips scurried across the main area of the display floor, which had been converted to a set.

"We have speed," one of the cameramen announced.

"HoloFax commercial. Take 14," one of the production assistants called out as he struck the clapper board in his hand.

Sasha held up three fingers. Then two. "Aaaand *action!*"

"Wait a second!" Arti yelled. "Can we get some makeup over here?"

"Cut!" Sasha responded. "Arti, you don't need any makeup," she told him.

"But my dome feels shiny," he insisted as several blue and pink sparks flew from the revolving rods within his glass top.

Sasha shook her head in disbelief. She turned toward the makeup woman and nodded.

The woman stepped onto the set and brushed Arti's dome with a soft pad.

Arti turned toward Derek, who stood on the other side of the set.

Derek pointed a threatening finger at him. "Don't even think of saying it," he warned him.

"Okay, let's roll," Sasha said.

"We have speed," the other cameraman said.

"HoloFax commercial. Take 15," the production assistant announced and struck the clapper board another time.

Sasha signaled with her fingers. "Aaaand *action!*"

"I'm looking for a companion," Arti told the nerdy salesman. "Someone for my, uhh, my *son.* Yeah, that's it.

Someone for my son," he said.

"I think I know what you mean," the salesman courteously replied with a nebbishy smile as he adjusted his thick-rimmed eyeglasses. "If you'll roll this way, please."

Arti followed him to the fax machine. The man pressed a switch and the machine hummed. Within an instant, a colorful print of an all-glass robot slid onto the adjacent tray. He presented it to Arti.

"Just in from Paris. Newest design by Lassalle."

"Hmm," Arti muttered with an unexcited tone.

"Well, this Swedish number is sure to spin your rods," the salesman said, presenting Arti with another print as it slid out of the machine. "An original Haagen Klahmer!" he said with excitement.

"Hmm," Arti replied with a bored voice.

"Okay," the salesman told him as the fax machine hummed another time and produced a third print. "This is the one. Design by Ninovelli. Body by Lamborghini!"

"Hmm."

"Is that all you can say about these unbelievable prints?!"

"Can you inflate them?" Arti asked.

"Uhh … no."

"Can they do the sea monkey dance if you add water?"

"Uhh … no."

"Good day," Arti said flatly and began to roll toward the door.

"Wait a second," Ojo called to him as he stepped onto the set.

"Over here," Derek said.

Arti rolled to the other side of the set, where Ojo and Derek stood beside a hexagonally-shaped glass machine. Two large words were etched on its surface. JENNON HOLOFAX. On the floor beside the machine stood three cylindrical platforms. A turquoise glow covered the surface of each.

"Was it the Lassalle model you were interested in?" Derek asked him as he pressed a button on the side of the machine.

Arti's dome quickly lifted on a thin silver rod as the three-dimensional holographic image of the Lassalle robot suddenly appeared floating on the first platform. She was all glass, from the tip of her delicately carved top cylinder to the bottom of her smoothly-designed rollers. Sparks of red and orange light burst between Arti's rods as they spun around wildly.

"Or perhaps the Swedish version?" Ojo nonchalantly suggested as the image of a tall curvaceous robot materialized on the second platform.

Arti's dome bounced back and forth between the images as they rotated in front of him. It moved up and down on the silver rod as blue and green flashes of light mixed with the sparks in his dome.

"No?" Derek said, turning toward Ojo and smiling, "Then it's got to be the Body by Lamborghini," as the third three-dimensional hologram appeared on the remaining platform.

The robot had a large glass dome similar to Arti's but with several smaller domes revolving around it. The central dome attached to a narrow platinum body that ended in three sleek rotary balls.

Arti's side cylinders pumped up and down as a bluish mist flowed from beneath his dome. Small colorful explosions of light crackled within his dome as his rods spun in every imaginable direction.

With a gasping sigh, Arti fell backward. The shot zoomed in on him as he lay on the floor and the echo of a loud overhead voice was then heard.

"When it absolutely has to be there now, but doesn't fit in a fax machine, there's HOLO*FAX*," the overhead voice announced as the room filled with bluish mist. "The next best thing to *beaming* there. *Only* at Contraptions."

"Aaaand *cut*! It's a wrap!" Applause filled the room.

* * *

A loud popping noise was heard over the music and laughter as the cork flew from the mouth of the champagne bottle in Derek's hand. It soared across the crowded living room, where nine or ten couples danced in the area beneath the rows of twisted streamers and balls of crepe paper that hung from the ceiling. The cork continued to travel in the air between the curved white sofa and the glass tables pushed to the side and flew beyond the large screen television covered with a shot of Dick Clark standing in the heart of Times Square in his parker and ear muffs blowing icy breath into cupped hands.

It continued above the dancing couples' heads, past a glass showcase displaying Christine's newest novel, *Deadlock*, sitting on a lucite stand on the top shelf, its cover featuring a wooden gavel entrapped within a chain net. The framed cover of the September issue of *TIME* sat on the shelf below it. A photo of the Genesis Space Shuttle emerging from a huge grey cloud upon liftoff filled the cover. '**SPACE COLONIES: THE TRAGIC RACE,**' the caption read. Derek was especially proud of Christine with *Deadlock* on its way to the bestseller list and her exposé of NEXUS earning a Pulitzer nomination.

The cork finally struck the pendulum of the grandfather clock on the opposite wall. A high-pitched metallic ping rang out as the cork bounced from the pendulum and landed with a small splash in the glass in Ojo's hand just as he lifted the drink to his lips.

Ojo exchanged an embarrassed glance with Christine and Sasha who sat on the loveseat in front of him, giggling and sipping from the wine glasses in their hands. He eyed the clock as the soft metallic echo faded. The new year was but five minutes away. He eyed the cork with a raised brow as it floated in his glass, then turned and caught his partner's eye on the other side of the room.

The champagne foam poured over Derek's hand as he

slowly made his way through the crowd, the overflowing bottle in one hand, several glasses in the other, while he laughed loudly, receiving several pecks on the cheek and slaps on the back as he squeezed between his friends, handing out drinks.

"How's that for service?" Derek casually asked Ojo, eyeing his wet face as he reached into his glass with a couple of fingers and removed the cork.

"Not bad," Ojo replied as he lifted the glass and poured the remainder of his drink over Derek's head. "Not bad at all. How 'bout another?" he asked with a playful grin, holding his empty glass out.

"Sure thing," Derek said with an accommodating smile as he lifted the bottle and emptied half of it over Ojo's head.

The four of them broke out in loud laughter. Then Ojo and Derek exchanged a mischievous grin and stared at the girls for a silent moment.

"Be good now you—" Christine started to warn as Derek lifted the bottle another time and emptied the rest of it over her and Sasha.

With pouts that soon faded, they looked up and giggled as the Dom Perignon dripped from their hair.

The music suddenly stopped and the group gathered in front of the large screen that was suspended from the ceiling as the countdown to the new year began. The huge ball on Times Square started its slow traditional descent down the side of the Macy's building.

"… 50 … 49 … 48 …" a loud chant began in Derek's living room.

Derek pulled Christine from the seat and held her against him as the countdown continued.

"But I'm all wet," she told him.

"Just the way I like you," he whispered in her ear and kissed the back of her neck.

She looked into his eyes and grinned.

Sasha stood and wrapped her arms around Ojo as they joined the countdown.

Ojo turned toward Derek with an extended hand. "It's been some year, huh?"

"It definitely has," Derek replied, grabbing his hand as they embraced.

Everyone stared at the fiery red ball as it made its way down the side of the building. Everyone except Derek. He suddenly noticed a silver-haired man with bifocals standing on the other side of the crowded room. *Elmer van Husted.* Their eyes met and locked for a moment.

"And there's my '*dead end*,'" Derek muttered under his breath. He was shocked to see van Husted standing in his living room. Right there. *In the flesh.* Just standing there.

There was a calmness about van Husted's worn face that somehow put Derek at ease. He took his eyes off the old man to glance at the screen for a second as the chanting grew louder and louder.

"… 10 … 9 … 8 …"

When he turned back, van Husted was gone. Then the screen suddenly went black.

"What the *fuck!*" someone yelled out.

"We interrupt this program with a Special Bulletin from Eyewitness News," a commentator's voice was heard a moment later as the word NEWSBREAK covered the screen.

Groans of disappointment raced through the room.

"Reporting live from the NEXUS Space Center is Peter Jennings," the faceless voice added as a shot of the Ground Control terminal center outside Houston filled the large screen.

Derek's eyes darted around the room but there was no sign of van Husted. He had no idea how he just showed up. Or *why*. Of all nights why on this one? But he knew he would come face to face with him sooner or later. There was no avoiding it.

Dozens of NEXUS officials, space engineers and computer specialists filled the Center. Each of them stared at the huge screen that hung suspended from the Center's high ceiling.

"On the eve of a new year," Peter Jennings' excited voice was heard as footage of the orbiting Genesis Shuttle was seen, "and for the first time since Neil Armstrong first set foot on the moon more than a quarter of a century ago, we are about to witness the miracle of birth two hundred and forty-eight miles above the Earth! The

Genesis has been orbiting the Earth in that part of the atmosphere, where the International Space Station lives, called the 'thermosphere'!"

A dead silence filled the room. Everyone stared at the screen. A picture of Sarah, the pregnant rhesus monkey that was sent into orbit on that warm summer morning one hundred and sixty-four days ago, appeared. She lay positioned on a cushioned table, throwing herself from side to side as her loud grunting howls and painful sounds of laboring breaths echoed throughout the shuttle as the crew of astronauts attempted the world's first space delivery.

Several sharp banging sounds were heard and the picture wavered. The noises became louder and the picture oscillated rapidly for a few moments. Then it disappeared.

"We've lost visual. Genesis, do you read?" the concerned voice of a Ground Controller was heard over the black screen.

No response. Black screen. And lingering silence.

"Genesis, *do you read?!*"

"Roger, Ground Control," one of the astronauts finally responded over the grunting moans in the background, "we've entered a meteorite storm."

A shot of the mission control center filled the screen while visual contact with the Genesis was lost.

"Just a little more, hon," the soft, comforting voice of Lieutenant Samantha Stone, the crew's veterinarian, was heard as she spoke to Sarah. "Just a little more."

With a final deafening howl, the newborn entered the world.

Lieutenant Stone gasped as the newborn took his first breath and let out a healthy cry. The mission control center and the living room both filled with a loud cheer.

"You're not going to believe this," she said after a long pause.

The screen flickered for a second as an image struggled to appear but remained black.

"Is there a problem, Lieutenant Stone?" asked one of the Ground Controllers.

"You are *not* going to believe this."

Ojo and Derek exchanged a long silent glance while the newborn cried loudly and forcefully. At that moment, they understood that the depraved genetics research in Sector 13 had finally come to fruition. The newborn cried out again. But it was not the cry of a rhesus monkey. It was definitely *not* the cry of a rhesus monkey. Or *any* monkey. *They* knew that.

And when the meteorite storm subsided and visual transmission resumed, so would everyone else.

ABOUT THE AUTHOR

JEFFREY WEINZWEIG, MD, is an American author, surgeon and founder of a nonprofit foundation that provides pro bono surgery for children with congenital craniofacial anomalies in developing countries who would otherwise receive no treatment. He is an emeritus chairman of plastic surgery and the author of six surgical textbooks, which have been translated into numerous languages worldwide, and over 200 publications and book chapters related to his specialty. He holds more than twenty patents for surgical innovations in his field. *Contraptions* is his first novel.